I0663054

FORT COLLINS

DENVER CEREAL, VOLUME THIRTEEN

Claudia Hall Christian

Cook Street Publishing
Denver, CO

THE DENVER CEREAL

The Denver Cereal
Celia's Puppies
Cascade
Cimarron
Black Forest
Fairplay
Gold Hill
Silt
Larkspur
Firestone
Grand Junction (Denver Cereal V1-10)
Fort Lupton
Fort Morgan
Fort Collins

ALEX THE FEY THRILLERS

The Fey
Learning to Stand
Who I am
Lean on Me
In the Grey
Finding North

THE QUEEN OF COOL

The Queen of Cool

SETH AND AVA MYSTERIES

Tax Assassin
Carving Knife
Friendly Fire (Spring 2016)

SUFFER A WITCH

Suffer a Witch

Photo credit: Kevin Torres in his Colorado Highways series.

First edition © March 2016
Cook Street Publishing
ISNI: 0000 0004 1443 6403
PO Box 18217
Denver, CO 80218

For love.

WHAT'S HAPPENED SO FAR

Denver Cereal is an addicting, fun, sweet and crunchy serial fiction filled with the tension, drama, and love of urban life.

The best way to catch up is to read *Grand Junction*, *Denver Cereal* Volume 1- 10 It's very affordable and available wherever eBooks are sold or online at StoriesbyClaudia.com.

We used to write a section here that gave a synopsis of all of the previous books. Frankly, the synopsis' wasn't very good. More than anything, they deprived you of the chance to hang out in Denver Cereal for a while. We were only be spoiling your fun

You deserve a chance to read all the crazy twists and turns, mischief, and wild adventures of Denver Cereal. These aren't books to be accomplished or checked off a list. They are stories to be savored and enjoys.

Get to it.

We'll be here when you get back.

CHAPTER THREE HUNDRED AND SIXTY-ONE
ONE STEP FORWARD

Saturday morning — 5:45 a.m.
New York City, New York

Standing next to the thick white door, Jill slipped a shiny brass key into the first deadbolt and clicked it open. The lock moved with ease. Taking the next key on the ring, she clicked the lock open. The third lock was older and more ornate. It reminded her of some of the old locks at the Castle. Jill found the key and slipped the key into the lock. The lock clicked open.

She pressed open the door. Like the locks, the apartment was clean, beautiful, and easy to use. For the briefest moment, Jill wondered how wealthy Seth O'Malley was. The thought disappeared almost the moment it appeared. Jill went into the small galley kitchen. Like everything else, the kitchen was immaculate. She opened the refrigerator and found it full of everything she needed — water bottles, trays of cold cuts, cut fruit, and bottles of white and sparkling wine. A case of red wine sat on the counter next to the refrigerator.

She closed the refrigerator and tried to remember what she'd said to Seth.

"I wonder if I can borrow your apartment," she'd said. "I want to talk to everyone to see if we can find a way to protect our children from this trickster that wants to steal Katy's soul."

He'd smiled, nodded, and said, "Of course."

That was it.

"Of course," he'd said.

Jill went into the living room. Everything was perfect. The

furniture was expensive but very comfortable. She recognized an African rug that had to have been Jeraine's when he owned the apartment for a brief time. A large vase of cut flowers was sitting on the coffee table.

Just to be thorough, Jill checked the bathrooms — clean, with plenty of toilet paper and clean towels — and the two bedrooms — clean, with fresh linen. She was in the second bedroom when she heard the apartment door open and close. She went out into the main room to find a matronly woman standing in the kitchen.

"Hello?" Jill asked.

"You must be Jillian," the woman said.

"Jill Roper-Marlowe." Jill held her hand out. The woman gave her a hug.

"It's such a pleasure to finally meet you," the woman said. "Sorry if I seem informal. I feel like I've known you your entire life. You're our Sandy's best friend, isn't that so?"

Overwhelmed, Jill swallowed fast and nodded.

"Poor love," the woman said. "Sissy's better, though?"

"She is," Jill said. "They're not out of the woods, but it looks like they'll both make a full recovery."

"That handsome Ivan," the woman said. "I've seen him dance."

The woman nodded with just enough wiggle of the eyebrow to indicate that Ivan was sexy. Jill blushed.

"You're probably wondering who I am," the woman said with a wink.

"I..."

"I'm Seth's next-door neighbor," she said with a smile. "I've lived in this building my entire life. Seth bought this place when he was ten years old or some such nonsense."

The woman laughed. She started moving around the kitchen with a comfortable ease. She turned on an espresso machine.

"He was ten and in college," she said. "I was fifteen and in high school. We've been friends since the moment we laid eyes on each other."

The woman nodded and started taking out the ingredients for brownies. Jill could do no more than gawk at her.

"Latte?" the woman asked.

"Uh," Jill said.

"It's all right, Jill," the woman said. "I take care of this apartment. I even did it for that rascal Jeraine."

"But. . ." Jill started.

"My husband died while I was pregnant with my third," she said. "Seth hired me on the spot. He's helped me raise my girls and send them to college. My baby has just graduated from medical school — Columbia, no less."

The woman went through the easy motions of making Jill the coffee. She placed the hot liquid in a travel mug.

"I'm sure you're heading back to the hospital," the woman said.

Jill took the mug from the woman. She felt a question formulate in the back of her mind.

"You're not. . . interested," Jill said, "in Seth, I mean."

"Not in the least." The woman laughed. "He's like a brother to me. Plus, have you ever noticed that the man can barely care for himself?"

"Um," Jill shook her head.

"He has Maresol in Denver," the woman said. "Jammy when he's on the road. Me in New York. I'm Claire, by the way."

The woman nodded and started making brownies.

"I love him, of course," the woman said. "But a man like Seth is better suited for a woman like Ava. I really love that girl, don't you?"

Jill gave a slight nod.

"My big brother died in Vietnam." The woman looked up at Jill and gave her a soft smile. "Seth brought him home to my mother. She was able to die in peace. You just can't repay that kind of thing."

Jill took a drink of the latte.

"Are the fairies coming?" the woman asked. "They can't have certain spices, makes them sick."

"Uh," Jill said.

"How about your father, Lord Perses?" the woman asked. "Your mother?"

Jill's mouth fell open, and she gave a kind of cough. The woman laughed.

"I'll take that as a 'Yes,'" the woman said. "Now go on. I'm sure you have plenty to do."

The woman picked up Jill's handbag and the key ring.

"You're sure?" Jill asked as she took her belongings from Claire.

The woman smiled and waved Jill to the door. A few minutes later, Jill was standing on the sidewalk below Seth's Greenwich apartment and wondering about Seth O'Malley's wealth. She glanced up at the apartment one last time before waving down a cab and heading back to the hospital.

~~~~~~~~~

Saturday morning — 5:45 a.m.
New York City, New York

Sissy felt consciousness come in waves. One moment, she felt like she was asleep, and the next she felt like she was waking up. Like being on the swings in Olympia, she swung back and forth between being awake and being unconscious. She felt someone grab her hand and opened her eyes.

"Hedone," Sissy whispered.

"Here I am Heather," she said.

"I remember," Sissy said. "'Our little game,' you used to say."

Heather smiled.

"Where's the baby?" Sissy asked.

"Maresol grabbed him the moment I got here and won't give him back," Heather said. "I think she needed someone to care for."

Sissy attempted a smile, but it came out as a kind of grimace.

"How are you feeling?" Heather asked.

"Sick," Sissy said.

They sat in silence for a few minutes.

"Ivan?" Sissy asked.

"He's in the bed next to you," Heather said. "Asleep. They expect to move him out of here by the end of the day."

"Where's here?" Sissy asked.

"Private ICU," Heather said.

"Seth?"

"Otis," Heather said. "He didn't want his star ballerina to have to mix with common people."

Sissy's eyes took in the statement while her eyebrows worked out the logic.

"He and Jill have been here quite a bit," Heather said with a pointed nod.

"Nice of them," Sissy grunted.

"Is the pain horrible?" Heather whispered.

Sissy nodded. Her eyes slipped closed. Heather fell silent. Sissy's eyes popped open.

"Swings?" Sissy said with effort.

"In Olympia," Heather said. "Children can slip in and out of Olympia when they are in a dream. You had been there before, so it was easy to get you there when you had. . . let go of being here."

"It's beautiful," Sissy said. "Who?"

"My father, Eros?" Heather asked. "You asked him in Olympia, too."

Sissy shook her head.

"Woman," Sissy said. "Goddess."

"Oh," Heather smiled. "Aphrodite. She's my grandmother. Eros's mother. She was quite cruel to my mother. Awful, really."

Heather shrugged.

"I try to stay out of it," Heather nodded and leaned in. "They are all a little crazy."

Sissy felt a giggle develop inside but wasn't sure she expressed it.

"She likes me," Heather shrugged. "I'm not sure why. And, for the record, I always feel quite guilty about her liking me and not my mother. You know what that's like."

Sissy nodded.

"Anyway, I asked her for help," Heather said. "She was very interested in fixing this problem that her son had created."

"Why?" Sissy asked. "Isn't it more fun for them if we suffer?"

"Right," Heather snorted a laugh.

"So?"

"Oh," Heather said. "She takes love very seriously. She feels like her son went crazy because of my mother, Psyche. She's been helping me fix these dark arrows. That's what we call them — 'dark arrows' — because they cause people to fall in love with someone they'll never meet. We've been working on it for a long, long time."

Heather sighed. Sissy nodded.

"I mean, it's easier now with the Internet and everything," Heather said. "Someone in Romania can meet their beloved in Idaho on Facebook or whatever. In the last ten years or so, a lot of people shot with his dark arrows have met each other and lived happily ever after. My dad has no idea. He'd be so pissed."

Heather chuckled.

"Won't tell," Sissy said. "Can I ask?"

"Anything."

"You and Blane?" Sissy asked.

"We're one," Heather smiled.

"Sandy and Aden?" Sissy asked.

"Delphie fixed their dark arrow," Heather nodded. "Just like she fixed you and Ivan. She just didn't know she was doing it. If she had, she would have never gone up against Olympia. It's part of her code. But you know how practical Delphie is — see a problem, fix a problem. I certainly am not going to tell her. You?"

Sissy shook her head.

"Charlie and Tink?" Sissy whispered.

"Not them." Heather shook her head.

"Who else?" Sissy asked.

"Jeraine and Tanesha," Heather said.

Sissy looked shocked.

"That's a recent development," Heather said. "He let them fall in love and then shot them with the dark arrow. They could know love but never be together. It's something he did because I dared to confront him."

"When I was little," Sissy said.

Heather nodded.

"Delphie, Celia, and Sam," Heather nodded. She looked off into the distance as if she were thinking. "I'm trying to figure out who you know. You are so focused on ballet that you don't know that many people."

"Wanda?"

"Yes, Wade and his boyfriend."

"Wanda," Sissy said firmly.

"Right," Heather said. "That's the point. If Wade stays Wade, he can't really be with his heterosexual beloved."

Heather nodded.

"Your father's an asshole," Sissy said.

Heather chuckled.

"MJ and Honey," Heather said. "Rodney and Yvonne — you know Tanesha's parents."

Sissy gave a slight shake of her head to indicate that she thought it was incredible.

"You're probably wondering why there are so many around me," Heather said. Sissy gave a slight nod. "My father was trying to get me to tell him where and when my mother was living."

Sissy made a sour face.

"If I'd told him, my mother would have freaked out," Heather said. "When I didn't tell him, he tortured the people around me."

"He has your mom now," Sissy whispered. "Why didn't he want to fix this?"

"Punishing me for not telling him," Heather said. "He wanted me to feel incompetent so that he would be forced to return to Olympia."

"Because he doesn't want to be with your mom?" Sissy asked.

"No," Heather said. "By all accounts, they're really happy together. It's just that his ego won't let him acknowledge that the world doesn't need him as much anymore."

"It doesn't?" Sissy asked.

"There's less violence and wars," Heather said. "Love is a value now. Children are loved by parents instead of used as property. People get together in love relationships. Just a hundred years ago, love was some weird phenomenon that happened sometimes when family honor and duty to your parents were fulfilled. Eros was needed then to remind people that there was something more, something beautiful. Now, the idea of the glory of love is ubiquitous."

"How did you fix it with me and Ivan?" Sissy asked.

"That's a long story for another time," Heather said. "You should be resting."

"Just glad it worked out," Sissy said.

"Me, too," Heather said.

"Hedone?" Sissy asked.

Heather looked at the girl, and she was sound asleep. Heather kissed Sissy's forehead and leaned back to sit in a chair. She hoped Sissy would never find out how it all worked. Some things were better left to the mystery and romance of life. Heather smiled. She was just glad it had worked out.

~~~~~~~~~

Saturday morning — 7:55 a.m.

New York City, New York

Seth's apartment was a buzz of activity and happy voices. This group of people not only knew each other, they were old friends. Tanesha had taken over the espresso machine the moment she'd walked in. The screeching sound of the espresso maker created a back beat for the story telling and resulting laughter. Ava and Valerie had gone shopping, while Maresol hung out with the teenagers.

Otis had sought Delphie out immediately. Worried that her intense grandfather would overwhelm Delphie, Jill had hovered around them long enough to learn that they played chess once a week when Otis was in town. Delphie set up a chess set, and they started a game before anyone else had settled in their seats.

The fairies took the couch. Fin on one side and Mari on the other, with Abi in the middle. Although Jill had worried that the siblings wouldn't get along, she soon learned that Fin and his first wife had raised Mari. They bickered like siblings, but, with Abi as referee, the love between them was obvious. Right now, they were arguing what to name the two babies — Abi's and Mari's. Bestat weighed in on the debate from an armchair next to the couch.

Heather and Jill's father, Perses, were deep in soft conversation near the back of the living area. Jill wasn't sure what was going on, but she felt like it was better to stay out of it. Sandy was sitting in a dining-room chair while Sam Lipson rubbed her shoulders. Mike and her mother, Anjelika, were talking and laughing with Seth O'Malley at the other end of the table. Katy was taking everything in from her vantage point on Anjelika's lap.

Every cup was filled with coffee or wine or the ridiculously expensive Scotch Otis had brought. The first round of snacks had been eaten. They were loose and laughing.

Jill cleared her throat and walked to the edge of the living area. Tanesha scooted from the kitchen into the living area. The people at the table turned their chairs to face Jill. Otis and Delphie put the chess game away. All eyes were on Jill. She swallowed hard.

"As you know, I wanted to get everyone together to talk about. . ."

And everyone spoke at once.

~~~~~~~~~

Saturday morning — 7:55 a.m.
New York City, New York

"Hi."

Ivan's voice woke Sissy. She opened her eyes. Puzzled, she tried to get up but found that she couldn't.

"You're tied down. I'd come to you, but I find myself unable."

His hand came onto the bed, where he felt around for the buttons to move the bed. As the bed lowered down, Ivan came into view. He was sitting in a wheelchair.

"Hello," he said.

He gave her a bright smile, which Sissy returned. She was surprised at how delighted she was to see him. She felt her face redden, and her hand instinctively went to straighten her hair. She rolled her eyes.

"What?" Ivan asked.

"Oh, I look like I've been hit by a bus," Sissy said. "I smell, and. . . here you are."

"I'm in much better condition," Ivan said with a laugh.

Sissy's eyes took him in. His hair was clean but a mess. He had a few days stubble on his cheeks, and his glasses were missing. He was wearing the same stylish blue hospital gown that she was wearing. To Sissy, he looked really good.

"You look good to me," Sissy said and blushed.

"You are beautiful, as always," Ivan said.

Sissy moved her hand, and he took it. He kissed the backs of her fingers. Rolling his wheelchair closer to the bed, he held her hand to his heart.

"How are you?" Sissy asked.

"I'm. . ." Ivan sighed and nodded. "Angry. I have much regret. This entire thing is my fault. If I. . ."

"It's not your fault," Sissy said. "It's just something that happened."

"No," Ivan said. "You don't understand. If I hadn't argued with Katia, she. . ."

"She was crazy," Sissy said. "One way or another, she would have made trouble for you and for us."

Ivan shook his head.

"Awful woman," Sissy said. "It's me she didn't like. She only stabbed you so that I wouldn'y have you."

"No, Sissy," Ivan said.

"Yes," Sissy said. "Sandy talked to her husband. He came by to offer to pay the hospital bill and support us financially until we get on our feet."

"He did?" Ivan asked.

"He said that he knew that Katia hated me," Sissy said. "She talked all the time about getting back at me. She even talked about it after the board meeting last night. I mean, I think Schmidty, Seth's lawyer, encouraged Katia's husband to do it, but he's paying for everything. He says he could have stopped this and didn't."

"But, how. . .?" Ivan asked. "You were a child when she was in Denver. She had this whole big life and. . ."

"Some things just don't make sense," Sissy said. "Heather says. . ."

"Heather?" Ivan asked. "The woman who was here this morning? I saw her when she was leaving."

"She's one of Sandy's friends," Sissy said. "One of the

girlfriends."

"Ah, the girlfriends," Ivan said with a knowing nod. "I had the strangest dream about her."

"Oh?" Sissy asked.

"I was on a swing set in this gorgeous playground," Ivan said. "You can't imagine how beautiful it was — better than at the royal palace."

Ivan glanced at Sissy, and she smiled at him.

"You were there," Ivan said. "Swinging. Your sister's friend Heather was there, too."

"She was my babysitter when I was young," Sissy said.

"I remember," Ivan said with a nod. He opened his mouth to say something and closed it.

"What were you going to say?" Sissy asked.

"Oh, nothing," Ivan said.

"I want to know," Sissy said.

Ivan sighed and looked at her for a moment. She nodded.

"When I was a child, I loved the swings," Ivan said. "It sounds ridiculous, but I used to spend many hours swinging and dreaming of my future love. She would cherish me, and I would make my whole world around her. It was very real to me on the swings, but in real life. . ."

Ivan shrugged.

"It sounds silly," Ivan said. "But that time of the swings was the only time I wasn't dancing or studying or doing chores. It was my time to dream of. . . love, life, dancing. I felt a terrible longing and loneliness. I never thought my dreams of love could possibly be real until I met you. And then you were four years old."

Ivan's face flushed with emotion.

"I almost lost you to that woman," he said.

"Shh," Sissy said. "I'm here. You're here. She didn't take anything from us."

Ivan kissed her hand again.

"I love the swings," Sissy said.

"Then we shall go when we are better," Ivan said.

Sissy smiled, and he returned her smile.

"I am here until your sister comes back or we pass out," Ivan said. "Would you like to watch television or play cards or. . ."

"Can we just talk?" Sissy asked.

"Perfect," Ivan said. "What would you. . .?"

"You could teach me Russian," Sissy said. "Sandy got me one of those courses on tape."

Sissy held up an mp3 player. Ivan's face lit up with delight.

"I thought I'd practice, but you could help," Sissy said.

"Where shall we start?" Ivan asked.

"Numbers," Sissy said. "One is. . ."

"A-deen," Ivan said.

"A-deen," Sissy said with a smile. "And two?"

Ivan paused for a moment just to look at her.

"What is it?" Sissy asked.

"You are barely alive, and you give me the gift of wanting to learn my language," Ivan said. "It is more than any woman has ever given me. Ever. And you do it from your hospital bed."

"I have all this time lying around!" Sissy said with a smile. "So, 'two'?"

Grinning at her, Ivan set about teaching her one through ten in Russian.

Saturday morning — 8:11 a.m.
Denver, Colorado

Ivy kicked her legs against the wooden picnic table post and sighed. With her elbow on the table, she leaned her head on her hand. The workbook on the table had gone from fun and challenging to boring in the last ten minutes.

"What's wrong?" Edie asked.

Edie was wearing what Jill called her "twin sandwich" with one twin on her front and the other on her back. The twins were sound asleep. Maggie was sleeping in the front compartment of a double stroller. Mack was running with the dogs in the Castle backyard. James Kelly gave the boy the string end of a kite, and Mack ran around the backyard, trying to make it fly.

"I wish. . ." Ivy shrugged.

"What is it, sweet pea?" Edie asked.

Ivy looked up at the fairy. Edie looked like she hadn't slept in a week. Her usually tidy braid was frayed, and small, fly-away hairs had escaped. Edie's shirt had spots of spit-up from the boy,s and her makeup was smudged. Ivy shook her head and looked down.

"It's hard to be left behind," Edie said.

"I just. . ." Ivy looked up at the sky before looking at Edie again. "Why didn't I get to go?"

"You have a reading class all afternoon today and tomorrow," Edie said.

"Oh, yeah, reading," Ivy said with an exaggerated roll of her eyes. "Like that matters over Sissy's life!"

"Sissy is going to be fine," Edie said.

"Why did the other kids get to go, and I have to stay here with the babies?" Ivy's voice rose with indignation. She glanced at Edie. She'd expected Edie to look more tired, but Edie just grinned.

"Why indeed!" Edie said.

"You don't know?" Ivy asked.

"I know that you have a reading seminar," Edie said.

"Oh," Ivy said. "Why do I have to go?"

Her voice had such a whining pitch that Edie had to grin. Ivy saw Edie's grin and smiled herself.

"I guess that's pretty whiney," Ivy said.

"What's happening on Monday?" Edie asked. When Ivy didn't respond, Edie added, "Anything important?"

Ivy shook her head.

"Could it be that those who love you wanted you to stay home and practice your reading, so that you are safe and rested for Monday?" Edie asked.

Ivy looked down at her hand.

"Maybe?" Edie asked.

"Maybe," Ivy said grudgingly. "But. . ."

"I know," Edie said, cutting Ivy off. "That doesn't make up for being left behind."

"Like a baby," Ivy nodded. "With the babies."

"Indeed," Edie said.

"I wish. . ." Ivy looked up at Edie and stopped talking.

"What do you wish?" Edie asked.

"I wish I were a fairy," Ivy said. "Then I could do my reading class *and* be in New York. I'd get to be a good reader *and* be with everyone."

"Being a fairy's not all it's cracked up to be," Edie said.

"You're immortal!" Ivy said.

"We have a very long life," Edie said. "That is true."

"That's awesome!" Ivy said.

"I had to learn to read, just like you," Edie said. "But I had to learn to read in Latin, Greek, and a bunch of languages you wouldn't recognize now."

"Oh."

"We were at war for almost three thousand years," Edie said.

"But you didn't die!" Ivy said.

"War is war," Edie said. "It was awful, just horrible."

Ivy gave her an unconvinced look.

"We can have children only every thousand years or so," Edie said. "My younger sister is Mari, and my mom is just now going to have another daughter."

"I heard it was a son," Ivy said.

"From whom?" Edie asked.

"I don't know," Ivy said. "Charlie, probably."

"They never tell me anything," Edie said.

Edie scowled so hard that the twins work up. The twin facing her put his hand on her face, and she smiled. He nodded. He grinned to his twin before dropping off to sleep again.

"Don't quote me," Ivy said.

Edie cleared her head with a vigorous shake.

"Well, you can see being a fairy isn't all it's cracked up to be," Edie said.

"Hmm," Ivy said.

James cheered, and they looked up to see the little kite take flight. Edie cheered, and Mack screamed with laughter. Ivy looked up. Ivy couldn't help but smile at the little boy's glee. Ivy clapped.

"Oh, good — you're clapping," a woman's voice came from the side of the house.

Terrified of someone else trying to kill her, Ivy ducked under the picnic table. Edie jumped up and put her arms around Ivy.

"I'm so sorry," the woman said. "I was... oh, gosh — is everything ruined?"

"We're just a little nervous," James said.

Ivy heard James pick up Mack and the boy giggle. She felt James move toward them.

"James Kelly," he said.

"It's all right, love," Edie whispered. She kissed Ivy's cheek and whispered, "This is why you didn't go to New York."

Ivy froze.

"Come on," Edie said. "We'll take a look together."

With her hands on Ivy's shoulders, Edie forced Ivy to look to see who had arrived.

"Auntie Gracie!" Ivy exclaimed. She jumped up to hug her aunt. "What are you doing here?"

"I promised I would be here when you testify," Grace said. "Delphie suggested I come a bit early so we could spend some time together. Is that okay, Ivy?"

"That's more than okay!" Ivy said. She looked at Edie. "You kept a secret from me."

"I did," Edie said with a smile. In that instant, Edie's braid straightened, as did her clothing. The exhausted look on her face evaporated.

"You tricked me!" Ivy said with pure delight.

"I did," Edie said.

Ivy clapped and laughed.

"Her bag is packed and. . ." Edie said.

She turned toward the door to show where the bag was.

"I'll get it," James said. He set Mack down and jogged to the kitchen with Mack on his heels.

"Are we going somewhere?" Ivy asked.

"Sam Lipson is letting me borrow their cabin," Grace said. "I thought it would be nice to get some fresh air and rest before the drama of next week. Does that work?"

Ivy answered her with a broad grin.

"What about my reading class?" Ivy asked.

"Fairy," Edie pointed to herself.

"You mean there isn't a reading class?" Ivy looked both delighted and surprised.

"Not this weekend," Edie said.

Ivy clapped the tips of her hands together in a kind of mocking applause. Laughing, Edie curtsied.

"Is the cabin. . ." Ivy scowled. "Safe?"

"I checked it out myself," James said. "You'll be safe and have a wonderful time. The only risky time is getting there, and you have an escort."

James pointed toward the side of the house. Colin Hargreaves waved to them.

"They have a cabin nearby," James said. "His family is waiting in the car. He's going to take you up and bring you back."

"Hi, Mr. Colin," Ivy said.

Ivy looked happier than she had since Delphie had left for New York. Ivy hugged Edie. Leaving Maggie in the stroller, Edie walked Ivy to Colin's SUV. James swung Mack onto his back and followed them. They helped Ivy and Gracie get in the SUV and waved them on their way.

"Well?" James asked.

He leaned over and kissed Edie. She smiled at him.

"Let's go home," Edie said. "We have the whole weekend to ourselves, and. . ."

"As you wish," James said.

He leaned over to kiss her again. When he leaned back, he was standing in the open field that served as her backyard on the Isle of Man. Her goats bleated in hello. Mack squirmed his way to the ground and began chasing after the goats. Scooter, Sarah, and Buster, the Castle dogs, ran around the little boy. Maggie and the stroller were sitting on the deck next to the back door.

"It's nice to be home," James said. "Come on, Mack!"

The little boy led the dogs into the house. James grabbed the stroller. They made it inside just as it started to rain.

"It is nice to be home," Edie said.

~~~~~~~~

Saturday morning — 10:30 a.m.
New York City, New York

They had argued for about an hour before Jill decided to split them up into groups. The outcome of the groups was disappointing. No one believed there was anything Jill could do to protect Katy from the Trickster. In fact, the overall opinion was that Katy needed the opportunity to defend her soul.

"This is why my mother wanted to keep Katy," Mari said, summing up what the fairies thought.

Jill scowled at her. She sent a dark look to the rest of the room and went into the kitchen. Sandy, Tanesha, and Heather sheepishly followed.

"I know you're frustrated. . ." Sandy whispered.

"The trial starts on Monday!" Jill said. "If I don't find out today. . ."

Jill glared at Sandy, who grinned at Jill's gloom.

"If you ask me. . ." Heather said.

When Jill scowled at her, Heather immediately shut up. She shrugged as if she didn't care.

"I think she's already asked you," Tanesha said in a low voice.

"Oh, sorry," Heather said with a smile. "You're asking a question that's never been asked before."

Jill looked up at Heather and scowled.

"It seems like everyone is going on tradition," Heather said. "And the tradition is that when a child reaches the age of five, his or her soul is open for collection by the Trickster. It's up to the child to set herself free."

"That's such BS," Jill said. "There's got to be another way."

"You have to teach a child to walk," Sandy said in her most helpful voice. "I wonder if we could figure out what everyone learned from the Trickster — you know, what Katy needs to learn. Maybe we could teach her what she needs to know."

The girlfriends turned to look at Sandy. She blushed.

"It was just an idea," Sandy said.

"A great idea," Tanesha said. "We've learned from, well, everyone, that Katy needs to learn some skills. These skills are usually taught by this creature they're calling the Trickster."

"If you keep her away from the Trickster, she won't learn the skills and will be attacked by him later in life," Heather said. "Boy, there are tons of stories like that."

"There are?" Sandy asked.

"Sure," Heather said. She opened her mouth to tell them what they were when she noticed Jill's scowl. She hugged Jill instead. "Why don't you let me lead this part?"

"You would do that?" Jill asked.

"Of course," Heather said. "I'm happy to help."

"Me, too," Sandy said.

Tanesha nodded.

"That settles it," Heather said. "We'll split them up into three groups. . ."

"I can do one," Jill said with a nod.

"Four groups, and we'll get them to figure out what they learned from the trickster," Heather said.

"Then we'll figure out how to teach it to Katy," Tanesha said with a nod. "Good plan."

Sandy nodded in agreement.

"Jill?" Heather asked.

"Let's do it!" Jill said.

They went out into the living area. Standing together, they were such a formidable group that everyone in the room fell silent. All eyes fell on them.

"Here's what we're going to do," Heather said.

~~~~~~~~
Saturday — 10:30 a.m.

New York City, New York

Sissy awoke to the sound of Nadia laughing. She tried to look to her left, where Ivan's bed had been, but didn't see anything. Then she remembered that Ivan had been moved out of this ICU earlier this morning. Sissy was supposed to sleep all day today so that she, too, could get out of this private ICU, and getting out of the ICU was the first step toward getting out of this horrible hospital. Feeling a wave of frustration, Sissy sighed.

"I know that frustrated sigh," Ivan said. "She is awake."

Sissy saw his hand grope around on her bed again. Before he found the controller, Nadia appeared. She kissed Sissy's cheek, lowered the bed, and sat on the edge.

"I thought I had to sleep today," Sissy said. Her voice filled with frustration and sorrow. "If I'm awake, I have to stay here."

"That would suck," Nadia said with a smile.

"What is wrong?" Ivan asked.

Nadia replied in fluent Russian. Sissy had the overwhelming feeling that Nadia was really Ivan's soul mate and that she was just a stupid, little girl. Her dreams were vanishing before her. She looked away from where she now knew Ivan was sitting.

"No," Nadia said, as if she could hear Sissy's thoughts. She leaned over Sissy. "Don't go there."

"But. . ." Sissy's bottom lip vibrated with sorrow.

"It's the anesthesia," Nadia said.

"And the trauma," Ivan said.

Sissy refused to look at him. Nadia leaned over that so her face was inches from Sissy's. She gave Sissy a soft smile.

"We have been here waiting for you to wake up," Nadia said.

"But I'm supposed to sleep today!" Sissy's voice rose with frustration. "Or I'll never get out of this *fucking* place."

At her swearing, Ivan's eyebrows rose, and his mouth clamped closed to keep from laughing. Nadia owed Sissy none of that kindness.

"Did you curse?" Nadia laughed.

Sissy scowled at her. Nadia kissed her cheek again.

"Take a deep breath, Sissy," Nadia said in a low, intimate voice. "Can you feel it?"

"What?" Sissy glared at her.

"You can breathe," Nadia said.

Nadia's face disappeared from in front of her. Sissy took a breath and felt nothing. No pain. No stiffness. No immovable phlegm. No constriction. She took another breath. She'd never felt so happy to be able to do something so incredibly simple. Sissy's eyes welled with tears. She felt Ivan's big hand grab hers. As always, she was steadied in his tight grip. She looked at him for the first time. He smiled.

"There you are," he said in a low voice. She smiled. Nadia lowered her bed so that Sissy could see them out of the corner of her eye.

"The doctors are taking credit for it," Nadia said. "But, of course, it was Otis and Jill."

Nadia nodded at Sissy.

"Miraculous," Nadia said. "I grew up hearing about the miraculous Russian healers. Frankly. . ."

Nadia's face appeared over Sissy again.

"I thought it was complete bullshit," Nadia said. "My mother, God rest her soul, and I fought over this very thing. 'The only healing is science!' I'd say. 'You know nothing!' she would say. And guess what?"

"She was right," Sissy said.

"She was right," Nadia said with a snort. "Who knew?"

Nadia looked down to see Ivan holding Sissy's hand. She smiled.

"We should get down to business before the doctors come to brag about their awesomeness," Nadia said.

"Business?" Sissy asked.

"Nadia has a proposal for us," Ivan said. "Well, for you, mostly."

"For me?" Sissy asked.

"You're all set to return to Denver," Nadia said. "And Ivan will go where you go, so it's really up to you."

"You have family," Ivan said with a nod. "I have you and Nadia."

"What are we talking about?" Sissy asked.

"I'd like it if you'd consider staying in New York," Nadia said. "We can easily remodel Ivan's place to accommodate your hospital bed, if you still need one."

"If you are here, you are close to the ballet," Ivan said. "We can go to watch ballet every single night while we heal."

"Now that sounds like fun," Nadia said with a roll of her eyes.

Ivan chuckled and shook his head at her.

"Eet vill git you reedy for dance," Nadia said in an imitation of Ivan's accent. Sissy couldn't help but giggle. Ivan laughed.

"I don't know if I'm ready to... um..." Sissy blushed. "You know, to live with Ivan and... I'm still sick, and..."

"You would have your own rooms," Ivan said. "We agreed to go slow. This will not change our agreement."

Nadia nodded.

"How big is your place?" Sissy asked.

"I have a whole floor," Ivan said.

"How?" Sissy squinted her eyes at him.

"I bought floor when I moved to US," Ivan said.

"The building was falling down around him," Nadia said.

"It was fine for me," Ivan said.

"You were in Denver," Nadia said. She smiled at him and looked at Sissy. "It's how we met. My father's company, which means my mother, wanted to rehab the building. She'd been able to buy all of it but had this 'Russian bastard on the tenth floor' who wouldn't budge. My mom pressured me to talk to Ivan because I was young."

"She was too embarrassed at her situation," Ivan said. "She knew of me from the Bolshoi and thought I would Judge."

Ivan snorted a laugh, and Nadia gave him a grateful smile.

"I didn't sell," Ivan said.

"The company rehabbed the building around him," Nadia said. "It's very nice now."

Ivan shrugged.

"So we have space," Nadia said with a nod. "You could have as much or as little room as you'd like. You can get well, and, when you're ready, you can train right there."

"She is right, Sissy," Ivan said. "This is a better plan to get you on your feet again."

"If you go to Denver, you'll still have a chance to heal and a chance to train," Nadia said. "The actual difference is very small. It's just that if you stay here, you'll be here — in New York City, with us."

"Can I think about it?" Sissy asked. "Sandy would be so upset if. . ."

"This isn't a secret," Ivan said.

"We've spoken with Sandy," Nadia said.

"She said it was okay?" Sissy asked.

"She said she would wait to talk to you before saying anything," Nadia said with a shrug. "We have another option."

"Okay," Sissy said.

"Ms. Behur has offered to have you continue to stay with her," Ivan said. "She said you were welcome there as long as you want to stay."

"Seth O'Malley said you're welcome to stay in his apartment," Nadia said. "He said that was the original plan."

"Before we knew someone was trying to kill us," Sissy said with a nod.

"The question is. . ." Nadia started and then looked at Ivan.

"Would you like to stay in New York City?" Ivan asked. "Or

go back to Denver?"

"Gosh, I. . ." Sissy said. She blushed.

"Why don't you think about it?" Nadia asked.

"But. . ." Ivan said.

Nadia gave him a hard look.

"No, we have to decide. . ." Ivan said.

"Sorry, Sissy," Nadia said. "Ivan needs a moment."

Nadia winked at Sissy, and Sissy smiled.

"Mostly, I wanted you to know that you're welcome here," Nadia said. "In our family, I mean. As Ivan's love, I mean."

Nadia's face flushed.

"Nadia needs a moment," Ivan said with a wink.

Sissy smiled.

"Thanks," Sissy said. "It's all just been. . . a lot."

"Miss Delgado?" Sissy recognized her doctor's voice. "Are your sister and aunt here?"

"We are," Nadia said brightly.

"Dr. Kerminoff," Sissy's doctor said. "Ivan."

"You can talk in front of them," Sissy said.

She suddenly felt overwhelmed and exhausted. She waved her hand for the doctor to continue. He started talking about the wonderful things he and his team had done to save Sissy's life. The more he talked, the more Sissy checked out.

Ivan wanted her to live with him. Nadia was going to be her friend and family. She could stay in New York! Sissy's heart fluttered as the glimmer of her original dream of being a real ballerina with a real company appeared in front of her. She glanced at Ivan, and he smiled at her. She felt such a well of strong emotions that she had to break her eyes away from him.

The doctor kept talking. Sissy glanced at the clock and hoped Sandy would be back soon. Sissy took a clear breath. Her life was starting again. Grinning, she tried to listen to the doctor. Her eyes flicked to Ivan. He'd been watching her. When he saw her eyes on him, he flushed. Sissy realized that she'd seen him do this before. In that moment, she realized that Ivan had always loved her — not in some creepy way, he just loved her. The thought made her smile.

"I'm glad you're smiling, Miss. Delgado," the doctor said. "You have a lot to smile about."

Ivan squeezed her hand.

"Yes, sir, I do," Sissy said.

CHAPTER THREE HUNDRED AND SIXTY-THREE
SKILLS

Saturday afternoon — 3:48 p.m.
New York City, New York

When Bestat, Fin, Abi, Mari, and Tanesha laughed, Jill looked up from where she had been coloring with Katy. She glanced to the back to see that Anjelika and Otis had their heads pressed together like they were plotting how to get back at Putin. Heather and Jill's father, Perses, looked immensely civilized as they drank tea near the edge of the room. From where she sat, she could tell that Sandy, Sam, and Mike were engrossed in an out-and-out battle to the death in a game of hangman. A burst of laughter came from the kitchen, where Seth and Delphie were supposedly putting together snacks.

"You think it's time?" Jill asked in a low voice to Katy. The girl gave her mother a sincere nod. Jill smiled. "You want to stay here?"

With her eyes wide and luminous, Katy shook her head. Jill held out her hand, and Katy took it with a smile. They walked to the front of the room. Katy leaned against Jill so firmly that Jill put her arm around the child's shoulders.

"It looks like you're done," Jill said.

The room fell into a deep silence. Jill cleared her throat. Seth came out with a tray of mixed drinks, which he started passing around the room. Delphie set out a tray of sliced meats and cheese.

"I'm wondering if you might have..." Jill swallowed hard. "Um..."

"We came up with one thing the fairies and Bestat learned from the Trickster," Tanesha said.

"We have, too," Sandy said. "Just one, though."

"We have one," Delphie said. She scurried over to sit back down in her spot. Seth sat next to her.

Otis raised his hand, partially stood, and nodded.

"If it's not the same thing, then one is good, I guess," Jill said. She looked from face to face. "Is it the same thing?"

"No," Delphie said. "We are willing to teach Katy. . ."

". . .all of the children," Seth said with a nod.

"Right," Delphie said. "We're willing to teach all of the children our skill."

"Yes, we will, too," Fin said.

"Same," Otis said.

Sandy nodded. Jill glanced at her father, and he gave her a sincere nod so similar to Katy's that Jill looked down at her daughter. Katy smiled.

"We'll go first," Fin said at the same time that Mari said, "Fairies first!"

Otis groaned and rolled his eyes. Delphie gave a little giggle.

"Does anyone mind?" Jill asked. She glared at her grandfather. "Otis?"

"It is fine," Otis said. "I am getting used to fairy impatience."

Fin grinned at the sound of his voice.

"Let them talk," Otis said. "It's not like they don't have an eternity to live while we have just a few years."

Fin mouthed his words. Abi nudged him with her elbow. Tanesha looked embarrassed, and Bestat glanced at Otis.

"Go ahead," Jill said to Fin.

"When the Trickster had me. . ." Fin said. "I. . . Well, it was a very long time ago."

"No longer ago than when he had me," Perses said.

"Touché," Fin said. He turned and nodded to Perses. "And you're right. You're *a lot* older than I am!"

Everyone laughed at the way he said the words.

"Please, little one," Perses said. "Go ahead."

Everyone laughed, and Fin cleared his throat.

"When my soul was taken by the Trickster, there were no guns or ammunition or planes or... toilets, for that matter," Fin said. "We had swords. And not great swords. We had big, heavy, dull swords. I went around and around and around with him until I learned to..."

"Stand your ground," Katy burst out saying. She jumped up and down. "Stand your ground. Stand your ground."

"What?" Jill looked down at Katy.

"He's teaching Paddy to use his shiny sword," Katy said with a giggle.

"Plant your feet," Abi said in her distinctive Isle of Man accent. "It is: 'plant your feet.'"

Katy danced around for a moment because she'd gotten it right. Jill looked up at Fin and saw the fairies grinning at them.

"The key is to make certain you are grounded," Bestat said. "It's not always where your feet are. Often it's your mind and soul that are in the clouds. We must learn to ground to the earth. Without grounding, we have no traction."

"We are unable to move with our feet on the ground," Mari added.

"Our minds, hearts, and souls must be planted firmly on the ground," Fin said. "This is what I learned when I was with the Trickster."

Mari, Abi, and Bestat nodded in agreement.

"What do we think?" Jill asked.

Everyone applauded.

"So we have one thing to teach Katy," Jill said. "Will you...?"

She looked at the fairies, and they nodded.

"It would be my honor, as well," Bestat said.

Jill beamed at them. She put her arm around Katy's shoulder

to stop her from dancing around.

"Grandfather?" Jill asked. "Will you honor us with your learned opinion?"

Hearing the sarcasm in Jill's voice, Otis laughed.

"It was not such a long time for me," Otis said. "So I have better memory. My angel is much younger than either of you old geezers."

Perses and Fin laughed. Mari turned around on the couch to watch him. He grinned at her, and she smiled.

"This will not be a surprise to you, Jillian," Otis said. "It is the rules of our work as healers."

Jill tipped her head to the side.

"You gain more if you use your gifts for worthy causes," Otis said. "That is what I learned. My daughter, knowing my learning, was able to slip away from the Trickster. Her children weren't disturbed by him at all."

"How do you determine what is a worthy cause?" Mike asked.

"This is the question, no?" Otis asked. "You may give to someone with cancer but only drive the cancer to grow faster."

"And it's not always about what you gain," Anjelika said. "You can give a lot to a worthy cause and gain nothing. That doesn't make it not a worthy cause."

"Mmm," Otis said. "Maybe it's better to say, 'When you give to a worthy cause, it grows exponentially.'"

"That's it," Seth said in encouragement.

"Make more sense?" Otis asked.

"If you want to heal an entire family, cure the parents," Otis said. "It will grow to the children."

"Same for sick children," Anjelika said. "Heal the doctor, the nurses, and the most sick child. The whole hospital will feel it."

Anjelika and Otis nodded as if what they were saying made perfect sense. Everyone in the room looked at them in a kind of confused silence.

"What are you talking about?" Jill asked finally.

"I think we can help," Seth said. He nodded to Delphie, who sat up a little straighter.

"The Trickster taught me that I didn't have to give away my gifts to just anyone," Delphie said.

Seth nodded.

"I can see anyone's destiny," Delphie said. "Anyone's."

"I don't have to play for anyone who asks me," Seth said. "My music is a gift, and I choose who gets to hear it."

"First step," Otis said with a nod. "You decide who gets your gifts. Your choice. Next step, pick those who are worthy, and cause your gift to grow like compound interest."

"I guess I was trying to match what they said, with my own experience of the Trickster," Abi said. "And I have to say. . ."

She glanced at Fin, who was watching her face. She gave him a soft smile.

"This kind of knowledge — who to use your magic with, who to pick — it's taught in Fairy 101," Abi said.

"I learned to ground before using the piano," Seth said with a nod. "It was the first lesson my mother gave me."

"Me, too," Delphie said with a shrug. "It's something that must happen if you're going to reach out to the ether."

"This is really good," Sandy said with a bright nod. "Everyone will be able to help."

"Mom? Otis?" Jill asked. "Delphie? Seth? Will you teach Katy what she needs to know?"

"Of course," Seth said at the same time Anjelika said, "Absolutely" and Otis nodded.

"Delphie?" Jill asked.

"Oh," Delphie looked embarrassed. "I'm already doing that with Katy."

Jill looked down at Katy, who nodded.

"You don't give your precious brownies to just anyone!" Katy said with a grin.

Jill smiled at Katy's oft-repeated statement and realized that Delphie was already teaching Katy valuable lessons.

"Will you continue?" Jill asked.

"Of course," Delphie said. "Seth, me, Anjelika, and Otis — we'll do it."

"You can trust us, Jill," Otis said.

Jill nodded her thanks and turned to Sandy, Sam, and Mike. They looked at each other until Mike pointed to Sandy. She nodded.

"We, um." Sandy stopped talking as soon as she noticed that everyone was looking at her. She tucked a loose piece of hair behind her ear and swallowed. "We believe that the reason humans don't have as much trouble with this Trickster is that we — humans I mean — know that love is everything."

Sandy cleared her throat.

"Love is the most powerful force on this Earth," Sandy said.

"If Katy is able to keep loving, she'll be able to vanquish her Trickster like that," Mike said, snapping his fingers.

Sam nodded. The room was silent for a moment. Tanesha started to applaud and soon everyone was clapping.

"Brilliant!" Otis said, and everyone nodded.

"Dad?" Jill asked. "What do you Olympians know?"

"There is no Trickster," Perses said. "That is the trick."

Every head turned to gawk at him.

"But. . . Katy and. . ." Jill started.

"It was one thing for me to be tortured, but when my daughter, Hecate, was tortured by the creature..." Perses scowled.

Jill's eyes flicked to Anjelika. There was not even a glimmer of jealousy on Anjelika's face. Instead, she was listening to him intently. Jill turned back to look at her father.

"I looked the world over for a millennium," Perses said. "I was intent on destroying this creature that dared to torture my beautiful daughter. I followed every lead, listened to every wise man, shaman, and even the infernal Plato. I promise you, there is no Trickster."

Heather nodded.

"Then, what is this thing?" Fin stood up and turned to face Perses. "I *still* have nightmares about my time with. . ."

Every head moved up and down in agreement.

"I still wake screaming," Delphie said. She shivered.

"The Trickster is the dark side of our gifts," Heather said. "This dark side must be resolved in order for us to use our gifts for good."

"Are you saying Katy has some really dark side?" Jill asked. For her own comfort, she picked up Katy. Understanding her mother's fear, Katy pressed her face into the crook of Jill's neck. "My Katy?"

"That makes a hell of a lot of sense," said Seth, ignoring Jill's fear. He put his hand on Delphie's shoulder. "You are so powerful that you would have a depth of shadow. . ."

"Like Jung's shadow?" Sam said. "Celia and I went to a Jungian therapist to have our dreams analyzed. Delphie, you remember."

"That's actually the first time I got a handle on the entire business," Delphie said with a nod.

"But Katy. . ." Jill said.

"We need to help Katy become whole without tearing herself apart," Perses said. "These suggestions are useful."

"But you'll help?" Jill asked.

"Of course," Perses said.

"I will do as I pledged," Fin said. "Will you help our child?"

"I will," Perses said.

Fin's head went from person to person and saw that they all agreed.

"Then we are in agreement," Perses said. "You will help, Katherine, as I will help your children."

Some said "yes," while others simply nodded.

"Good," Jill said. "Thank you."

Caught up in their own thoughts, everyone stared straight ahead. The warm companionship of the afternoon slipped away, and they were merely powerful individuals who happened to be in the same place. The gathering was clearly over. Jill thanked each person individually as they left.

"How do you think it went?" Sandy asked as she left.

"I know what we need to teach Katy," Jill said.

"Seems like something we should teach all of our kids," Tanesha said. "Jabari could use it. Hell, I need to learn to plant my feet."

"She's right," Heather said. "Tink could really benefit from knowing this stuff."

The girlfriends nodded.

"Are you back to the hospital?" Heather asked Sandy.

"I need to find out what Sissy wants to do," Sandy said.

"Any ideas?" Tanesha asked.

"She'll stay here in New York," Sandy said. She gave her friends a sad smile. "She's on her way to her dreams. We are already in her rearview mirror."

"Not until we teach her this stuff," Tanesha said. She held out an arm, and Sandy let Tanesha hug her.

"Sissy will need to know it," Heather said with a smile.

Sandy gave them a sad smile.

"I should go," Sandy said. "You want to share a cab?"

"Sure," Jill said.

The solemn mood stayed with them long after they'd left the apartment. The girlfriends knew that they would each have to confront their inner demons someday soon.

At least, they would be able to do it together.

~~~~~~~~

Saturday evening — 6:07 p.m.
New York City, New York

"It sounds pretty weird," Sissy said to Sandy as they shared a contraband pint of butter pecan ice cream.

"It was weird," Sandy said with a nod.

"And the final outcome was some Carl Jung stuff about the shadow?" Sissy asked.

"Exactly," Sandy said. She looked into the ice cream container before setting it down. "All gone. Sorry."

"It was delicious," Sissy said with a smile.

Sandy smiled.

"I'm amazed at how well you're doing, Sis," Sandy said. "I really thought I'd lost you this last time."

"I thought I was done, too," Sissy said. "Jill and her grandfather have saved my life."

"Oh? Huh," Sandy said.

"What?"

"I think you saved yourself. They just helped the process along," Sandy said.

"Why do you say that?" Sissy asked.

"I was reminded today that love is the most powerful force in the world," Sandy said. She gave Sissy a soft smile. "You have Ivan now. There isn't much you two can't do."

"But. . ." Sissy sighed and lay back on the bed.

"What's going on?" Sandy asked.

"They asked me to move here," Sissy said. "I guess you know that."

"Ivan told me," Sandy said.

"What do you think?" Sissy asked.

"It doesn't matter what I think, Sissy," Sandy said. "It only really matters what you think."

"Oh," Sissy said. She didn't say anything for a few minutes.

"You love Ivan, right?" Sandy asked.

"I think so," Sissy said.

Sandy grinned at her sister.

"What?" Sissy asked.

"You used to talk a lot more freely about loving Ivan when you were four years old," Sandy said. "Do you remember?"

Sissy nodded.

"So...?" Sandy asked.

"That was before I knew about..." Sissy lowered her voice, "... sex."

"Ah," Sandy said. "You're worried about sex."

Sissy winced, and Sandy smiled.

"He's so..."

"Sexy," Sandy said with a nod.

"And has been with lots of people," Sissy said. "And I... He wants me to live with him. I've been really sick and I don't feel ready to... you know, I mean I want to, but... maybe not for a while... I mean, I just had my first grown-up kiss. Well, second, if you count that time under the mistletoe with Charlie's friend, Carlos."

"Carlos," Sandy said. "That's right. I'd forgotten all about him."

"I haven't," Sissy said with a firm nod.

"Is Ivan pressuring you?" Sandy asked.

"Not at all," Sissy said. "We agreed to go really slow. He says he doesn't want to blow it now."

"That sounds good," Sandy said.

"I know," Sissy said. She smiled.

"But if you live with him?" Sandy asked.

"I don't know," Sissy said. "Don't you think I should date a little bit?"

"Well, dating is really about trying to find the right match," Sandy said.

"What about random sex?" Sissy asked. "You used to really like that."

"I..." Sandy shook her head. "I had a problem of committing to someone because I'd been hurt so badly by Mom and my father."

"Oh," Sissy said.

"When I was ready, I dated to find the right person," Sandy said. "That's what most people do. Do you feel like you need to find the right person?"

"No," Sissy said. "Ivan *is* the right person for me."

"I thought you'd say that," Sandy said.

"So you're okay with me, at fifteen years old, shacking up with some old guy?" Sissy asked.

"I'm okay with you staying in New York with your beloved," Sandy said. "If staying in the same place is too much, let's set up for you to stay at Ms. Bestat's home. When you're well again, you can move into Seth's."

"But. . ." Sissy's hand moved to her heart.

"You want to live with Ivan," Sandy said.

"I'd miss him," Sissy said. "Plus, I'm going to be with him all the time anyway. Training, stretching, rehab. . . But. . ."

"You're not ready for sex," Sandy said.

"Maybe I am," Sissy said. "I don't know. How do you know?"

Sandy shook her head. One of the disadvantages of having been molested as a child was that you never have the chance to choose when to start having sex.

"Oh, Sandy, I'm sorry," Sissy said.

"Don't be," Sandy said. "I'm so happy for you."

"I'm happy for me, too," Sissy smiled.

"Aden wants to talk to Ivan," Sandy said. "They're supposed to talk tonight at. . ." Sandy gestured to the clock. "They're probably talking now."

"They are?" Sissy looked nervous.

Sandy looked up at Sissy's heart rate monitor. She put her hand over Sissy's.

"It's going to be all right," Sandy said.

"How can you say that?" Sissy's eyes welled with tears. "Aden's going to. . ."

"Aden and Ivan have spent a lot of time together in the last year, actually," Sandy said.

"What?"

"You forget that you've been living with us for more than a year," Sandy said. "Ivan and Aden met when you moved in and he returned. They're about the same age and get along well. Ivan goes fishing with Jacob and Aden."

"Oh," Sissy said. "So it's not really new?"

"None of this is unexpected," Sandy said.

"But you'll tell me what they said?" Sissy asked.

"I will," Sandy said. "Do you want to watch a movie? I have Seth's phone, so we can watch anything."

"Will you stay with me?" Sissy asked.

"Of course," Sandy said.

Sandy laced her fingers through Sissy's. She held up Seth's phone. They picked a romantic comedy to watch. Before long, Sissy was sound asleep. Sandy let go of Sissy's hand and turned the phone off.

"I don't want to lose you, Sandy," Sissy whispered. Tears squeezed out of Sissy's guarded eyes. "If I live here and get better and dance and. . . I'll never see you. You'll be way back in my past and not my future, and I can't stand that."

"You can't lose me," Sandy said. "I'll always be here for you — past, present, and future. Becoming who you are, growing up, doesn't change that, Sis."

"You are my home, Sandy," Sissy said.

"I will always be your home," Sandy said. She kissed Sissy's cheek. "Would you like to watch or sleep?"

Sissy didn't answer because she was asleep. Sandy smiled and settled in to watch the movie.

CHAPTER THREE HUNDRED AND SIXTY-FOUR
CAUGHT

Saturday evening — 7:47 p.m.
New York City, New York

Nash looked up at the numbers above the hospital elevator's door. He had been given the responsibility of coming to the hospital to pick up her father and Sandy. Nash winced. No matter how much he loved Sandy, he never managed to think of her as his mother. It wasn't that Sandy wasn't his mother. She was truly the only mother he'd ever known. And she was really good at mothering.

Noelle told him he was a moron. "Sandy loves us," Noelle always said. "She is our real mother."

Truth be told, Nash knew he was an idiot about this.

He just felt like he didn't deserve a mother like Sandy. The elevator reached the floor Ivan was staying on, and he got off. He went down the hallway and asked at the nurses' station for Ivan. Nash liked Ivan. Nash had spent a lot of time with Ivan when he was hanging out with his father. He just wasn't sure how he felt about Ivan dating Sissy. Then again, Nash didn't think Sissy should date anyone.

He smiled at himself. He felt very protective over Sissy and Noelle. They were family.

"But not Sandy?" an irritating voice in his head asked.

Nash gave a quick shake of his head to clear the voice. Standing in front of Ivan's door, he heard his father laugh. Ivan and Aden had become fast friends in the last year. Nash scowled. If his father wasn't going to take this Sissy thing seriously, he would definitely make sure Ivan explained himself.

Nash pushed open the door. From where he stood, the door blocked his view of the bed and his father. In front of him sat a woman with steel blue eyes. Her long black hair was in a tight bun at the back of her head. She wore a dark blue turtleneck and jeans with a white doctor's coat over it. The doctor's white coat she was wearing was stuffed full of pens and what looked like pieces of paper. Her lower pocket held a stethoscope. At the moment he opened the door, she was laughing at something that was happening near the bed.

Nash stopped moving. He had never seen a more beautiful sight. He felt as if all time stood still. The air seemed clearer and his sight sharper. He stopped in the doorway. Since turning thirteen, he felt things in places in his body that he'd never felt before. This woman brought his entire being to attention. He didn't want to even blink.

Feeling his eyes, the woman turned to look at him. Pink appeared on her cheekbones, and her jaw slackened. She looked like she had been hit by the same shock wave that had gone through him. Ivan said something in Russian and her eyes flicked to where she'd been looking before. She couldn't seem to tear her eyes away from Nash.

And Nash couldn't make himself go anywhere. He stared at the woman, and she stared at him.

"Who is it?" Ivan asked in English.

Nash felt more than saw his father walk to the door. The door moved from Nash's extended hand, and his father appeared.

"Nash?" Aden asked.

Aden looked at Nash and then at the woman. He stepped in front of Nash for a moment, and the spell was broken. Nash went to move, but Aden held him in place. His father's eyes flicked to Nash's belt in a way Nash had seen him do with Charlie. Nash adjusted himself. When Aden stepped away, the woman's face was bright red. From his hospital bed, Ivan was laughing at her. They were speaking to each other in fast Russian.

Nash felt like an idiot. What was he doing gawking at this woman? She was an adult! A doctor! The diamonds in her ears and her watch told him she was rich, too! He never felt more stupid or more like a little kid. Seeing Nash's shame, Aden put his arm over his shoulder. In the last month or so, Nash had sprouted up so that his head was almost at Aden's shoulders. The Irish bakers had said it was their loving care after getting beaten up. But Aden was tall, so Nash was likely to be tall, too.

"Nadia?" Aden asked.

The beautiful woman turned to look at Nash again. Nash felt the same shock and saw it register on the woman's face. Nash looked down at the ground.

"Have you met my son, Nash?" Aden asked. Nadia gave a quick shake of her head. "Nash, this is Dr. Kerminoff. She is a friend of Ivan's."

Nadia stood up and held her hand out. Nash looked at her hand for a moment.

"Have we met before?" Nash asked.

"I don't think. . ." Nadia's voice seemed to catch in her throat. Her perfect American English surprised him. "Uh, no. Ivan has told me about Aden's son, but I've never. . . um. . ."

Ivan laughed at Nadia.

"Byt' po-prezhnemu." Nadia shot at Ivan, which made him laugh even harder. She glanced at Nash. "It's my pleasure to meet you."

When Ivan started to cough, Nadia went to the bed.

"Look what you've done," she said as she examined Ivan's bandages. "You are bleeding."

She scowled at Ivan. Keeping her eyes on the ground, she left the room to get a nurse. Aden leaned into Nash.

"You okay?" Aden asked.

"I. . ." Nash said. "No, not really."

Aden smiled at him. Nadia and a nurse came in. They rolled Ivan onto his stomach and changed his bandages. Nash followed the entire procedure in disgusted fascination.

"Heather warned me about you and Nadia," Aden said in his ear.

"What does that mean?" Nash asked.

"You remember us talking about the 'dark arrows'?" Aden asked.

"Eros-the-dick shot people who could never possibly meet each other with his soulmate love arrows?" Nash asked.

Aden nodded.

"I thought it was a lame excuse for Ivan-the-geezer to mack on Sissy," Nash said.

Aden grinned at Nash's language. He leaned into Nash's ear.

"You don't like Ivan and Sissy?" Aden asked in a low tone.

"Just seems... weird, I guess," Nash said in a terse whisper. "We need to make sure that Ivan isn't taking advantage of Sissy."

"We?" Aden said with a grin.

"You're not taking this seriously," Nash said. "It's child abuse!"

Aden pulled Nash's head to him and kissed the top of it. Aden pulled Nash in front of him in a hug while they watched the nurse and Nadia change Ivan's bandage. When Ivan was settled again, Aden led Nash toward the bed.

"Nash is concerned that you might be abusing Sissy," Aden said in an even tone.

"I am, as well," Ivan said.

Ivan glanced at Nadia. Nash refused to look directly at her, but he tracked her out of the corner of his eye. He noticed Nadia nod.

"We are all worried," Nadia said with a nod.

He glanced at her, and her face flushed. She stammered. Nash cleared his throat.

"What are you going to do about it?" He made an effort to keep his original indignation in his voice. The words came out flat. Surprised, Ivan looked up at him. His eyes searched Nash's face.

"That is the question, isn't it?" Ivan asked. "The Oracle. . ."

"Delphie?" Nash asked. Looking at Ivan, he regained some of his indignation. "What's she got to do with it?"

"She told Ivan. . ." Nadia's voice came from behind Nash. He didn't dare look.

"Both of us," Ivan said.

"Yes, she told Ivan he would meet me," Nadia continued. "She said we would love each other, but to be careful not to get too settled."

"We are family, not destiny," Ivan said.

"Our soulmates were too young for us," Nadia said. "She told Ivan to be very careful with Sissy, or he might destroy something perfect in every way. Ivan has lived with this for more than a decade."

"That is what we were joking about," Ivan said.

"I thought the whole soulmate thing was about Ivan and Sissy," Nadia cleared her throat. Her voice came out as a whisper, "Not me."

Nash saw Ivan give Nadia a kind look.

"What would you do, Nash?" Aden asked.

"Uh." Nash shifted from one foot to another.

"We talk about it — Sissy and I," Ivan said. "We talk and talk and move very slow. That's our plan. And we'll see. We may not be able to have it."

"But we're sure as hell going to try," Nadia said.

Nadia's voice held so much emotion that Ivan looked past Nash to Nadia. He smiled at her.

"Why don't you show Nash to Sissy's room?" Ivan said to Nadia.

Nash sucked in a breath.

"Sandy texted that Sissy is asleep," Aden said. "I'll meet you in the lobby in a minute."

Aden grabbed Nash's shoulder and turned him around. Nadia caught his eye before looking at the ground.

"Just breathe," Aden said in Nash's ear.

He gave Nash a shove in the direction of Nadia. Nash stumbled but caught his feet. Remembering his manners, Nash gestured for Nadia to procede him through the door. Outside the door, Nadia laced her hand in his elbow. They were standing on the elevator landing when Nadia cleared her throat.

"It's very nice to finally meet you, Nash Norsen," Nadia said.

"You, too," Nash managed.

"For the record," Nadia's voice dropped to a low tone, "they didn't tell me who, just that I would know when."

Nash grunted. Nadia looked up into his face.

"You, too?" Nadia asked.

"Delphie didn't tell me," Nash said in a low voice. "I just left her. She told me to take the limo and come get Dad and Sandy so they wouldn't have to take a cab. She told me to see Dad first because it would take him a while to wrap up with Ivan and that Sissy was asleep."

Nash swallowed hard and nodded. Nadia's eyes scanned his face. She took a breath that seemed to make her an inch taller and let it out.

"Well. . ." Nadia said.

The elevator door opened to an empty car.

"Wanna make out?" Nadia asked in a joking tone.

Nash laughed. As if they were doing some kind of synchronized dance, they shuffled to the back of the elevator and turned in unison to face the door.

"Maybe later," Nadia said with a nod. Nadia leaned forward to press the button for Sissy's floor. "Like in five years or so."

"I hope not that long," Nash said with a crack in his voice.

Nadia chuckled, and Nash smiled.

"First, tell me — why do you have these healing bruises?"

Nadia asked.

Nash glanced at Nadia.

"Oh God — you're not a part of that horrible trial are you?" Nadia's voice rose with concern and her hand went to her heart.

Nash chuckled and looked down.

"I guess we have a lot to catch up on," Nadia said.

The elevator door opened. They stood at the back of the elevator. Neither one dared to move.

"My shift starts again in a half-hour," Nadia said.

"Why don't I text Sandy?" Nash asked. "I'm sure she knows all about this."

"Probably," Nadia said.

"Can I buy you a cup of coffee?" Nash asked.

"Sure," Nadia said. "I love coffee. You?"

Nash shook his head.

"There's a quiet place down the street," Nadia said. "I have to go back to work in a half-hour."

The door opened to Sissy's floor. Sandy was standing on the landing. She looked at Nash and then at Nadia.

"If you hurt him, you will answer to me," Sandy said.

"If I hurt him, I will answer to me," Nadia said.

Sandy nodded.

"We're going for coffee," Nash said. "She has to work in a half hour. Is it okay?"

"Sure. We'll wait for you," Sandy said with a smile. "You know, your father loves this awful cafeteria food. We'll be there. You'll come to find us?"

Nash nodded. Sandy waved, and the elevator door closed. Nash let out a breath he didn't know he was holding.

"What is it?" Nadia asked.

"I have this feeling that my life has just begun," Nash said. "My dad told me that he felt that way when he met Sandy."

Nadia was silent until the elevator hit the ground floor.

"I feel the same way," Nadia said.

Grinning, Nash ushered her off the elevator.

~~~~~~~~~

Saturday night — 10:07 p.m.
New York City, New York

"Hey," Jill said into her computer screen.

Jacob smiled when he saw her face.

"Hey to you," Jacob said. "How was your meeting?"

"Amazing," Jill said. "Bizarre."

"I bet," Jacob said. "I want to hear all about it, but first. . ."

"Yeah?" Jill asked.

"Do you have any idea where our children are?" Jacob asked. "Or the dogs?"

"Edie took them to the Isle of Man," Jill said. "I told you she might. You weren't listening."

"I wasn't listening," Jacob said. "I was. . ."

"Worried about everything," Jill said with a nod. "How is it going at Lipson?"

"Good," Jacob said. "Easy. I have. . ."

He stopped talking and rubbed his face. He looked exhausted.

"You have?" Jill asked.

"I'm thinking of leaving the company," Jacob asked.

His eyes went wide, and his eyebrows went up and down. Jill nodded.

"It's probably time," Jill said.

Jacob let out a breath.

"I wasn't sure how you'd react," Jacob said.

"You've been working toward this day as long as I've known you," Jill said. "The employees own over half of the company. . ."

"More than forty percent," Jacob said.

Jill shrugged. Jacob looked off to the side.

"Did you tell me where the boys are?" Jacob asked.

"Isle of Man," Jill said. "Edie and Jimmy took the kids and

went home."

"And the. . ."

"The dogs, too," Jill said. "You must be tired."

"I don't sleep well when you're not here," Jacob said. "Too restless."

"Me too," Jill said.

"You mean, you'll leave the four chefs, private bedroom, masseuse, and everything to come home to this drafty old place?" Jacob asked.

"I'll be home tomorrow," Jill said with a smile. "The kids and dogs, too."

"Good," Jacob said.

He closed his eyes and leaned on his hand. Jill realized that he was asleep.

"Jacob?" Jill asked.

"Mmm," Jacob said.

"See you tomorrow," Jill said.

Jacob opened his eyes long enough to wave good-bye. Shaking her head at him, she shut off the computer and went to bed. A few hours later, her cell phone rang.

"The kids are on the Isle of Man," Jacob said, without saying hello. "Dogs, too."

Jill laughed.

"Good to know," Jacob said with a chuckle. "Love you."

"Love you!" Jill said.

~~~~~~~~~

Saturday mid-night — 12:07 a.m.
New York City, New York

"O'Malley," Seth said into his vibrating phone.

"What is it?" Ava whispered.

Seth shook his head and shrugged. He looked at the phone before holding it to his head.

"Bumpy here," a breathy male voice said.

"What can I do for you, doctor?" Seth asked in a wry tone.

"You're hilarious," Bumpy said. His voice dropped to speak to someone else, "Yes, sir, thank you."

"Give me the phone," Dionne said.

While Bumpy and Dionne argued over the phone, Seth got out of bed. He pulled on the pajama bottoms Sandy had given him for these family adventures. He had gone to the bathroom and had a drink of water by the time Dionne's voice was on the phone.

"Sorry about that," Dionne said.

Bumpy seemed to be talking non-stop in the background.

"What can I do for you, my dear?" Seth asked in false romantic tones.

Dionne laughed.

"What's so funny?" Bumpy's voice asked in the background.

"O'Malley's working his sexy tonight," Dionne said.

"You tell him to keep his dick where it belongs," Bumpy growled.

"And where *is* that?" Seth asked.

Dionne laughed again. Bumpy groaned in the background.

"Sounds like a self-help book," Seth said.

"You've got that right," Dionne said.

"What's going on?" Seth asked.

"You don't know?" Dionne asked.

"I was asleep when you called," Seth said.

"That's right," Dionne said. "It's only nine here on the West Coast. Sorry, Seth. I wasn't thinking. We're just go, go, go here."

"What's going on?" Seth repeated.

"One of the acts canceled," Dionne said.

"For what?" Seth asked.

"Grammys," Dionne said. "Remember old man — we were all going to the Grammys together?"

"I'm in New York," Seth said.

Dionne groaned. The sound of echoing footsteps on tile came through the phone.

"You're at LAX," Seth said.

"They want us to perform Jer's song live," Dionne said.

"Because one of the acts canceled," Seth said with dawning awareness. "I can't make it to LA, Dionne. Tanesha's here, too."

"We're coming there," Dionne said. "Jer's already in the air."

"What?" Seth sat down in an armchair. Ava turned on the bedside lamp and sat up in bed. He raised his eyebrows at her naked form.

"We're performing Sunday at sunset," Dionne said. "Some rooftop garden. They want us to perform the song live. Outside. On the rooftop. They'll broadcast it with the Grammys to fill in the place for the band that canceled."

Seth didn't say anything.

"You have a problem with that?" Dionne asked.

"Give me the phone," Bumpy said.

The phone jostled from Dionne to Bumpy.

"We are traveling across this great country to play with you," Bumpy said. "What's your problem?"

"I don't have a problem," Seth said. "I was just thinking through what we need."

"The producers are supposed to take care of everything," Bumpy said. "Schmidty worked all of this out. I thought he would have told you."

"We were sleeping," Seth said.

"Old man," Bumpy said. Seth laughed. In a quiet voice, Bumpy said, "I feel like I'm a hundred years old."

"You won't," Seth said. "We'll get up there and show the kids how it's done."

Bumpy chuckled.

"Schmidty's working overtime, but you know how that boy is," Bumpy said.

"I've got this," Seth said. "Don't worry. You flying here?"

"We're just about to get on the plane," Bumpy said. "You're at the apartment?"

"No, we're still supposedly on our honeymoon," Seth said.

"Ah," Bumpy said. "Well, enjoy it. We'll take the apartment."

"See you soon," Seth said.

"You'll call Claire?" Bumpy asked.

"My guess is that Claire already knows," Seth said. "But I'll take care of it."

"You'll get some. . ." Bumpy started.

"I've got this," Seth said. "Don't worry."

Chuckling, Bumpy hung up the phone. Seth was waiting only a moment before Schmidty called.

"Someone canceled, and we. . ."

"I've got this," Seth said.

The young man's relief was evident.

"I'll text you what I know," Schmidty said.

"Good," Seth said. "See you soon."

Seth hung up the phone.

"What is it?" Ava asked.

"Want to go to a concert?" Seth asked.

"Sure," Ava said. "Who's playing?"

Seth grinned.

"This is the best honeymoon ever," Ava said.

Seth laughed.

CHAPTER THREE HUNDRED AND SIXTY-FIVE
PREPARATION

Sunday morning — 8:05 a.m.
New York City, New York

"Well, I, for one, think we should stay for the concert," Nash said.

Noelle screamed with laughter. Teddy's big blue eyes followed Nash as he paced back and forth in the dining room. Sandy rolled her eyes and shook her head. They were sitting around the formal dining-room table, eating the last gourmet breakfast to be provided by their generous host, Bestat Behur. Sandy was sitting at the head of the table. Rachel was sitting on her lap, and Sandy was feeding her oatmeal.

"I'm just saying that Seth is our family and our friend!" Nash said with a chuckle in his voice.

"Ba!" Rachel said and raised her hand in agreement with Nash.

Tink pointed at Nash and laughed. Using his crutches, Charlie came into the room.

"What's going on?" Charlie asked.

"Jeraine is our good friend, Tanesha's husband, no less!" Nash continued. "Tanesha's staying. We should stay with Tanesha! She needs us!"

"Nash thinks we should stay for the concert," Tink said.

"So?" Charlie asked.

"Nadia gets off work at noon," Noelle said in the sing-song voice perfected by younger sisters everywhere.

Charlie grinned. When Nash walked by him, Charlie nodded.

"Thinking with your other head now, are we?" Charlie asked.

Nash blushed but kept pacing.

"I've taught him well," Charlie said.

"What's happening?" Aden asked as he entered the room. He leaned down to kiss Sandy and plucked Rachel from her lap. "Shouldn't you kids be packing?"

"Nash thinks we should stay here for the concert," Sandy said.

"And his girlfriend!" Noelle squealed with laughter. Teddy chuckled.

"Nice try, buddy," Aden said. He patted Nash's shoulder and sat next to Sandy.

"Next week is going to be really hard," Sandy said. "You guys have been up every night at plays and expensive dinners. You've had almost no sleep since we got here. We need to get home and get some rest."

"You're absolutely right, *Mom*," Nash said.

"Stop manipulating!" Noelle said.

"Next week is going to be hard. That's why we need to celebrate tonight," Nash said with a nod.

"Sandy and I will talk about it. We. . .," Aden pointed to Sandy and back to himself, "will decide and let you know."

"But. . ." Nash said. "They're going to win the Grammy — you know it. We'll totally miss out."

"Either way, you need to be packed," Aden said. "If you're done eating, go pack."

"But. . ." Nash tried one more time.

"We'll decide," Aden said and pointed out of the room.

Nash went to the other end of the table and plopped down in the chair.

"Nash!" Aden said.

"I haven't eaten," Nash said. "I'm starving."

A plate of food appeared in front of him. Ever the boy, Nash started shoveling food into his mouth.

"Nash! Slow down, or you'll choke!" Sandy said.

Nash looked up at her and made some effort to chew.

"If you're not eating go pack," Aden said.

Noelle and Teddy got up and left to get packed. Tink pointed to her full plate, and Aden nodded. Charlie sat down next to Tink. He was there only a moment before one of Bestat's helpers brought him a plate. Wanda sat down next to Charlie, and another breakfast plate appeared.

"What do you want to do?" Sandy asked.

She nudged Rachel's oatmeal toward Aden. Seeing the bowl, Rachel stuck her hand in the warm cereal and laughed. Sandy moved, and Aden shook his head. By the time he'd cleaned off Rachel's hand, a fresh bowl of oatmeal had appeared. Sandy watched his actions closely. He grinned at her and started feeding Rachel. Sandy grabbed her coffee cup, leaned back in her chair, and closed her eyes.

"I think we should stay," Charlie said.

"Stay?" Aden asked. He looked down at Rachel. "What part of 'we'll decide' is confusing?"

"Okay, okay, you don't have to be a dick," Charlie said.

Aden scowled at Charlie. He moved to get up, but Sandy put her hand over Aden's hand. Charlie raised his hands as if Aden was holding a gun.

"We're all exhausted," Sandy said. She gave him a partial smile. "Charlie doesn't mean anything."

"Sorry, man," Charlie said. "It's just nice to be here. You know?"

Aden blinked at Charlie a few times.

"This is my first time out. I've been in the hospital or Seth's house since. . . a long time. Anyone who gets in the way of that is bound to be a dick," Charlie said with a nod. "And next week, we are going to be in that stupid trial. I'm scheduled for Tuesday. Tink tomorrow. Wanda's up on Friday. And you know about Noelle and Nash. Sissy's on the stand next week with Ivy."

"That's why you need rest," Sandy said.

Charlie shrugged.

"Or stay," Aden said with a nod to Charlie. "Sorry, I'm just. . ."

"On edge," Charlie said with a nod.

"We're all exhausted," Sandy said. "Sissy getting shot and. . . everything. Noelle. . . Nash and Teddy getting beaten up. Your injuries, Charlie. Everything that's happened, and now we have to gear up for that *stupid* trial."

Aden looked at Sandy. For a moment, their eyes held. Aden's head went up and down in a slow nod. Sandy smiled. She raised her eyebrows to encourage him to make the decision. He tipped his head sideways to encourage her. She nodded.

"Here's what we're going to do," Sandy said.

Nash looked up from his second plate of food. Noelle and Teddy miraculously appeared in the doorway.

"Today, we rest," Sandy said. "And I mean rest. You get back in bed and sleep. The most you're going to do is watch a movie. You can hang out together in the entertainment room, but if it seems like you're not resting, you go back to your rooms."

"First they have to pack, so we're ready to go," Aden said, and Sandy nodded.

"And tonight?" Nash asked.

"We'll see the performance," Aden said.

"And fly home as soon as it's over," Sandy said. "I'll talk to Seth about using his plane."

Aden and Sandy nodded in unison. The kids didn't dare move or say anything. Rachel made a questioning sound.

"Yay!" Charlie said.

The rest of the children cheered.

"Wanda, call your parents," Sandy said. "I'll call Jill."

Tanesha and Heather appeared in the doorway.

"What are you going to wear tonight?" Heather asked Sandy. "Tanesha has some designer dress that she can't wear now and. . ."

"You mean you knew?" Tink asked.

"What else would they do?" Tanesha winked at Tink, who smiled.

"I've got this," Aden said, gesturing to Rachel. "Kids?"

"We're going," Noelle said.

Teddy followed her. Nash ran around the table and hugged Aden.

"Love you guys," Nash said as he hugged Sandy.

"To bed!" Sandy said.

"Yes, ma'am," Nash said and ran out to the room. In the hallway, he yelled, "Yes!"

Aden laughed. Laughing, Sandy got up from her seat. She nodded to her friends.

"I'm going to rest," Sandy said.

She set her coffee cup on the table and sauntered down the hall. She was asleep before her head hit the pillow.

~~~~~~~~~

Sunday mid-day — 12:37 p.m.
New York City, New York

"There you are!" Seth said to Sandy as she stepped off the elevator. Ignoring him, she looked around at the mass of activity on the rooftop of the building. "I was beginning to wonder if something had happened."

"I was asleep," Sandy said with a little more force than she'd wanted. "I have approximately a hundred teenagers to care for, and. . ."

Seth smiled. He held out his arms, and she let him hug her. Her eyes tracked all of the activity. People were running from place to place. A large stage was being set up near the street.

"How are you, my precious Sandy?" Seth asked in her ear.

"I'm fine, Golem," Sandy said.

Laughing, Seth kissed her cheek and let her go.

"Schmidty said you were going to play in Midtown," Sandy

said.

"I changed the venue," Seth said. He took her hand and led her into the fray.

"Why?" Sandy asked in a tone that made Seth stop walking. He turned to look at her. "Are you making things hard for no reason?"

Seth was a recovering drug addict and alcoholic. One of his triggers to use drugs was becoming overwhelmed in situations that he had made harder than they should be. He grinned at her.

"I am making things difficult," Seth said. "My specialty. But. . ."

"Seth," Sandy said.

"I have a reason," Seth said.

"Which is?" Sandy asked.

He pointed to the building behind them. Sandy turned around to see the hospital wing Sissy and Ivan were currently healing in.

"The hospital gave their okay," Seth said. "Sissy, Ivan, and the other patients can watch. We're also going to ask for a donation for the hospital from people to come see the show and down on the street. The NYPD are going to close off this block so people can watch."

"You realize that at least half of the people up here are family," Sandy said.

"Isn't that great?" Seth asked.

Sandy gave him an affirming nod. He laughed at her hesitance to approve.

"It looks like they'll be ready soon," Sandy said.

"Our time slot at the Grammys is around five," Seth said. "But we're going to start playing around three. I've asked a bunch of. . ."

"People to come play with you," Sandy said with a smile. "It's going to be a whole festival."

"Anyone who's in town," Seth said. "We'll use them for the performance."

"Do you need them?" Sandy asked.

"Bumpy and I can't carry the whole thing," Seth said.

Sandy scowled again. She'd seen Jeraine perform this song with only his guitar as accompaniment.

"I'm worried that you're on track for a relapse," Sandy said.

Seth turned his full attention to her.

"There are a lot of triggers here — performing, having all your old friends around, big-deal performance, television," Sandy said. Seth nodded. "That's not to mention that your life is going really well. You and Ava just got married. You're working on interesting mysteries. Your music has been outstanding."

"Time to tank it all?" Seth asked.

"That's what I was thinking," Sandy said.

Putting his hands on his hips, Seth nodded with his eyebrows. He looked away from her before looking down at the ground.

"Well. . ." he said and looked up at her. His head nodded. "I do feel that manic energy, and I can see how it could happen."

"Someone brings a joint," Sandy said with a nod. "One thing leads to another."

Seth nodded.

"What are you going to do to stop this?" Sandy asked.

"I'm going to leave the rest of the setup to the professionals," Seth said. "The show's producers are here. They can deal with the details. Would you like to go to lunch with me?"

"I can't," Sandy said. "I have to get something for everyone to wear tonight."

"Then I'll head back to the hotel for sleep," Seth said. "I'll get grounded and ready to play."

"In case you run into an old friend or whatever at the hotel, I already called Maresol and Ava," Sandy said.

"Nap it is!" Seth said with a smile. "I'm a lucky man to have you care so much."

"Yes, you are," Sandy said.

"It's going to be all right," Seth hugged her again.

"Why did you want me here?" Sandy asked.

"Oh, I need to guarantee the bill here," Seth said. "The show will reimburse me. They've already signed papers to that effect. But since it's all just unfolding, they need me to front the money."

Outside of a small stipend, Sandy had full control of Seth's finances as a way of slowing down his drug use should he happen to relapse.

"Is Schmidty here?" Sandy asked.

"There." Seth pointed toward the stage. "I'll head out, then. Will you tell him I've left?"

"I will," Sandy said.

She started across the rooftop garden toward where Schmidty was talking to someone. She'd just passed the small plot of grass when Seth called her.

"Sandy?" Seth asked.

Sandy turned around. Walking backward, she ran into one of the workmen. He grabbed her to keep her from falling. He set her on her feet and kept walking.

"Thanks," Seth said.

Sandy waved and made her way to Schmidty. The young lawyer was sitting at a table near the stage with an older man. They were bent over some papers. Schmidty looked up when she approached.

"Sandy!" Schmidty said. "Nice to see you."

His voice resonated with the understanding that the entire thing was ridiculous.

"Classic O'Malley," Sandy said with a grin.

"Do you think he's going to relapse?" Schmidty asked.

"I just talked to him about the same thing," Sandy said. "He's going back to the hotel for some rest."

"He's been up all night setting this up." Schmidty nodded. "You think he'll actually. . ."

"I told Ava and Maresol he was at risk for relapse," Sandy said. "And Delphie's staying with Maresol. He won't slip away from them."

Schmidty laughed. He introduced the man sitting next to him. The man dug through a briefcase for a stack of papers.

"You're sure we'll get reimbursed?" Sandy asked.

"How much is it?" Schmidty asked. He turned the papers around and said, "Cool million. Shit, Sandy, you could just write a check for this."

Sandy gave him a withering look.

"This will just about liquidate the cash fund," Sandy said. "We can't really afford to spend all of it on this event while O'Malley is on his honeymoon. You know how he is."

"Good point," Schmidty said.

"We will reimburse," the producer said. Schmidty nodded. "We have agreed to that. Also, we're covering the insurance."

"My next question," Sandy said. "Can I see that?"

The producer pulled out the event insurance policy.

"And the injury. . ."

"Here," the producer said. "Wow, you're up to snuff."

"Experience," Sandy said. She scanned through the insurance documents and nodded. "Did you take a look at these?"

Sandy held up the stack of papers.

"Read them," Schmidty said. "You'll see my initials on every page."

Sandy gave him a slight smile.

"I had to check everything three times when your father was in charge," Sandy said.

Schmidty smiled. She initialed and signed everything.

"Anything else?" Sandy asked.

"Nice to meet you, Miss O'Malley," the producer said. Sandy tried not to wince at the name. He shook her hand.

"Now if you'll excuse me, I need to find clothing for the kids and formal wear for Aden and myself that we can by some miracle *afford*," Sandy said.

"But. . ." Schmidty looked worried.

Putting the papers into his briefcase, the producer nodded his good-byes.

"Sorry, Jammy, I've got to go," Sandy said.

"Can I walk with you?" Schmidty asked.

"Sure," Sandy said.

Schmidty got up, and they walked through the crowd of people setting up the event.

"Know any second-hand places for formal wear here?" Sandy asked.

"I don't get it," Schmidty said.

"What don't you get?" Sandy bristled.

She was sure he was going to ask the "Why don't you just spend Seth's money?" question. She didn't spend it because it wasn't her money.

"You're a very wealthy woman," Schmidty said.

"How do you figure?" Sandy asked.

"Your mom's symphony," Schmidty said.

"What about it?" Sandy stopped walking and turned to him. He turned to look at her.

"I can't believe Seth didn't tell you," Schmidty said.

"Tell me what?" Sandy asked.

"Maybe I didn't tell him," Schmidty said with a nod. "You know, I bet I didn't tell him."

Like she did with Nash, Sandy grabbed the young man's arms and gave him a little shake.

"What are we talking about?" Sandy asked.

"Oh, I sold your mom's symphony," Schmidty said with a smile. "Surprise!"

"And what does that mean to me?" Sandy asked.

"You're a very wealthy woman," Schmidty said. "Let me just say that you've made me a very wealthy man."

"You mean you weren't rich before?" Sandy asked.

Schmidty blushed and chuckled. She smiled and shook her head at him. She started walking toward the elevator.

"None of this nonsense changes the fact that I need to find clothing for a bunch of teenagers and myself and Aden," Sandy said. "I haven't worked in almost a month. And. . ."

"That's right," Schmidty said. "I sent it to the Castle."

"Sent what?" Sandy asked.

"The check for the sale," Schmidty said and blushed.

"Whatever," Sandy said. "I haven't been at the Castle in what feels like forever."

"Here's what I'll do," Schmidty said.

"Coming through," a workman yelled.

Sandy stepped back so two workmen on either end of a large speaker could get between her and Schmidty. After they had passed, she stepped back. Schmidty was holding a credit card.

"Take this," Schmidty said. "Buy what you need."

"I can't take your money," Sandy said.

"I use these for clients," Schmidty said. "You can spend as much as you want on it."

"How will I repay you?" Sandy's voice edged with despair.

"When you get home," Schmidty continued, "and read the packet about the sale of your mom's work. Then, you can write me a check or you can just accept this as my gift. I appreciate all the business you and O'Malley give me. It's the least I can do."

"You're sure?" Sandy asked.

"Positive," Schmidty said. "And when I said, 'Spend what you want,' I meant it. Sky's the limit."

"I'll be shopping with Val," Sandy said. "Her sky is pretty high."

"Even better," Schmidty said. "Just call me when you get through the packet."

Because she was desperate, she took the card. She gave

Schmidty a vague nod and got on the elevator down. Jill, Tanesha, and Heather were waiting for her on the street.

"How'd it go?" Heather asked.

"Weird," Sandy said. "Hey, did Eros shoot Schmidty and Lizzie?"

Heather nodded.

"They *are* perfect together, though," Jill said.

"It would never occur to my father that a nice Catholic girl would convert to Judaism to marry the nice Jewish boy of her dreams," Heather said.

"There they are!" Tanesha said.

They jogged to the arriving limousine and got in the back, where Valerie was waiting for them.

"Guess what I have?" Sandy asked. She held up the credit card. "Unlimited spending from Schmidty. He said it was a 'thank you' for all the business O'Malley gives him."

"Go, Schmidty," Valerie said and grabbed the card.

"I know just where to go. Driver?" Valerie leaned forward to give the driver instructions.

"This is going to be fun," Valerie said when she turned around.

Smiling, Sandy leaned against the seat. She was asleep before the limousine left the curb. Jill pointed at Sandy.

"She's exhausted," Jill whispered.

"Let's take her back to Bestat's," Valerie said. "We can get everything. By the time we're done, she'll be ready for tonight."

The girlfriends nodded in agreement. The limousine headed to Bestat's where the driver carried Sandy inside. Moments later, they were on their way to their first destination.

~~~~~~~~

Sunday mid-day — 11:37 p.m.
Denver, Colorado

"Hey brother," Fin said to Jacob.

Jacob looked up from his bowl of Cap'n Cruch with

Crunchberries. He shook his head and looked down at his bowl.

"What was that?" Fin laughed.

"The last time you showed up unannounced, I spent a fair amount of time in the Sea of Amber," Jacob said.

"That wasn't me," Fin said.

"So you say," Jacob said. "The surprise arrival of a fairy usually heralds horrible things to come."

"Old wives' tale?" Fin asked.

"Fact," Jacob said.

Fin pulled out a chair and sat down at the table. He clapped his hands, and a bowl appeared in front of him. He poured himself a bowl of golden sugary squares with brightly colored balls. Jacob nudged the milk in his direction.

"You need this," Jacob said.

Fin looked at the milk. Jacob pantomimed putting the milk on the cereal. Fin poured some milk on the cereal.

"Now what?" Fin asked.

"And a spoon," Jacob said.

A spoon appeared in Fin's hand. He watched Jacob eat for a moment before digging his spoon into the cereal. He took a bite.

"Wow," Fin said before finishing the entire bowl. He was pouring another bowl of cereal when he said, "You will not tell Abi."

"I'm supposed to have one bowl," Jacob said, pointing his spoon at Fin before pouring another bowl for himself.

"What's that?" Fin asked.

"Five?" Jacob shrugged. "I kind of lost count."

"I can see why," Fin said.

They fell silent while they ate their cereal. When they'd finished their bowls of cereal, Jacob looked at Fin.

"Did you come here for a reason?" Jacob asked.

"Oh. Yeah," Fin said.

He reached across the table and touched Jacob's hand. The

next thing Jacob knew, he was standing in Jill's bedroom at Bestat's apartment. Katy was reading a book on the bed.

"Jill! Katy!" Jacob flushed with delight.

"Hi, Daddy," Katy said.

"Oh great, you're here," Jill said. She held up an informal tux. "Can you try this on?"

"What. . .?" Jacob asked.

"You said you wanted to see the concert," Jill said with a smile.

Katy laughed.

CHAPTER THREE HUNDRED AND SIXTY-SIX
ON THE ROOF

Sunday afternoon — 4:35 p.m.
New York City, New York

The knot in Sandy's stomach dissolved the moment she saw Seth. He was hopping to his feet to give the piano to world-class jazz pianist Muhal Richard Abrams. Muhal clapped Seth on the back and sat down in his place. They managed the swap without missing a beat. Seth said something to Muhal and they both laughed. When he looked up, he was clear, clean, and happy. Sandy sighed with relief.

"He looks good," Maresol said in her ear.

The music was loud and the crowd boisterous. Sandy shook her head to indicate that she'd missed what Maresol had said. Maresol pointed to Seth and smiled. Sandy nodded.

"What did you do?" Sandy asked loudly in Maresol's ear.

Maresol snorted a laugh and gestured to Delphie. Feeling their look, Delphie looked up. She smiled.

"Found him at the bottom of the elevators talking to Jeraine and some rapper," Maresol said. "She bullied Jeraine and Seth back to their rooms. Scared the *cojones* off the rapper. Tanesha was furious."

Maresol and Sandy laughed.

"You should have seen it," Maresol said. The elder woman's eyes scanned Sandy's face. She said in her ear, "I've been worried about you."

"*I've* been worried about me," Sandy said with a smile.

"It will be good to go home," Maresol said. "You know, when we get back, I can help. O'Malley's staying in New York for a while."

"Thanks," Sandy said. "I may take you up on it."

"Please do," Maresol said. "I love you and my grandchildren — Charlie, Nash, Noelle, Sissy, and my baby, Rachel."

Smiling, Sandy nodded. On stage, Jeraine's mother leaned in to harmonize with Alicia Keys. Right now, there were no cameras. Today was about music and friendship. Every single person Seth had asked to play had shown up. The first Tweet that went out from the rooftop drew every other musician in New York area. The crowd below was growing, and people lined the windows of the surrounding building. This rooftop was the place to be.

Sandy gestured toward Aden and began to move away. Maresol touched her arm. She nodded to where Nash and Nadia were standing. Maresol's eyes asked the obvious question.

"Eros," Sandy said when she leaned in.

Maresol rolled her eyes at information she already knew.

"What do you think?" Maresol asked and pointed to her head.

Sandy lifted a shoulder in a shrug and looked over at Nash and Nadia. Nash wore one of the informal tuxes Valerie, Heather, Jill, and Tanesha had purchased for everyone. While clearly a child, he looked fit and handsome. She'd done his hair in the faux hawk the male models wore. Nadia wore a deep-blue tux similar to his. Neither one seemed to dare touch the other, and yet, they were clearly together. Nadia was chatting with Abi and Fin.

The sound dropped as Henry Treadgill began a low flute solo. For the moment, they could talk freely.

"Nash has always had this. . . maturity about him," Sandy said.

"An old soul," Maresol said.

"I was going to say that was because of his mother," Sandy said.

Maresol pointed to Sandy, and she shook her head. She tried again.

"Nash knows what he wants in life," Sandy said with a nod.

"When he was a baby, his father was a drug addict. Aden's fought his way out of addiction and extreme poverty. I think it's changed both of the kids. They know that they are in charge of their lives."

Sandy nodded, and Maresol nodded. They both jumped when the horn players blasted a beat. Maresol shook her head in the direction of the stage. The music lowered again.

"I don't know this Nadia," Maresol said. "Do you like her?"

"I do," Sandy said. "She's super smart. You've seen her and Ava."

"Soul sisters in science," Maresol said with a nod.

Sandy nodded.

"She was fabulous when Sissy came in," Sandy said. "When I got there, I thought I'd have to bully the staff around so that Sissy got what she needed. Nadia had already taken care of it. Amazing. I keep thinking I should introduce her to John Drayson."

Maresol pointed to their right. John Drayson and Alex Hargreaves were laughing at something MJ had said. Sandy smiled.

"They are friends," Maresol said. "Nadia said Dr. John was one of the best surgeons she'd ever met."

"I guess it doesn't surprise me that they know each other," Sandy said.

"So you think it's okay?" Maresol asked.

Maresol gave Sandy a probing look. Sandy was good at relationships. She might not be Delphie, but she had an uncanny ability to know the good and bad of relationships. Even Seth trusted it.

"I think it's going to work," Sandy said.

"How?" Maresol asked.

"No idea," Sandy said.

The women laughed. Hearing her name, Sandy looked up to

see Seth gesturing her toward the stage.

"Time to meet another old friend," Maresol said.

"Wanna come?" Sandy asked.

"Claire!" Maresol yelled and waved.

Maresol saw Seth's apartment caretaker and ran over to her. Sandy gave the woman a wry look and went to meet another world-class musician who also happened to be a long-lost friend of Seth's. They went through the "Oh, my God, you look just like Andy" thing and the "Have you found her, Seth?" thing and the "Good Lord, that's terrible" thing in rapid succession. Sandy did her best to be polite. When they were done, she gave Seth a hug and went to find Aden.

On the way, Sandy ran into Jill, Jacob, and Katy. She picked up Katy, and they danced for a song. She left them only to find Tink and Charlie sitting on a bench a few feet away. She checked in and got a hug from Teddy's father, Zack. The handsome pilot let her go, and she said hello to Teddy and Noelle. She spotted Aden. He was standing away from the press of the crowd near the back. With Rachel on his hip, he was chatting with Sam. Jill and Jacob's twins were playing nearby with Bestat's daughter, Neuth.

"Rachel doesn't want to play with them?" Sandy asked.

"They keep making things fly," Aden said. "It makes Rachel mad."

"Those boys might be babies, but they're already rascals," Sandy said. She took Rachel from Aden and snuggled her close. "Sorry, sweetie."

"Neuth gives what she gets," Aden said.

"Really?" Sandy asked.

Aden nodded. Sandy held Rachel's head near hers and smelled her wonderful baby smell. The music played, and the crowd grew. Sandy cast a worried eye toward the entrance only to see Schmidty and Lizzie standing next to the fire inspector. She did not have to take care of this.

"Want to dance?" Aden asked.

Sandy nodded. Aden put his arms around her. With Rachel between them, they danced.

~~~~~~~~~

Sunday night — 5:35 p.m.
New York City, New York

Standing next to the hospital windows, Tanesha looked up at the clock and realized that it was after five. She jogged down the hospital hallway to where Jeraine was playing with the children on the children's ward. She slid to a stop on the edge of a small gathering. Jeraine looked up when she came into room.

She gestured to her watch. Still playing, he shook his head.

Tanesha nodded to say, "Yes, now is the time."

He shook his head. She held her hands palm up and shrugged.

He stopped playing. The children, who had been sitting around quietly listening to him play, now turned to look at her.

"O'Malley forgot, or pretended to forget, the time difference," Jeraine said. "We go on at five-forty in LA, not five here."

"Oh," Tanesha said. Jabari came up to her. She picked him up and nuzzled his neck.

"He figured no one would mind if we just played anyway," Jeraine said. "Do you kids mind?"

"No." The children shook their heads.

Tanesha had to smile. Most of the children had oxygen tanks sitting next to them. Their parents' faces were etched with a lot of worry while their children's heads' held very little hair. They watched with rapt attention as Jeraine sang and told stories. She was sure she'd never seen such a beautiful sight.

"So it's solved," Jeraine said. He grinned at Tanesha. "Do you think I should keep playing?"

"Please! Please! Please!" the children said at once.

He nodded to Tanesha and began playing again.

"Are you Miss T?" a woman asked in a low voice. Tanesha turned to look at her. "I just wanted to say 'Thanks.' My daughter is up there in front. She is a big fan. They don't think she has much longer. This will be the highlight of her entire life. She's five."

Tanesha hugged the child's mother. Jeraine raised an eyebrow at her in a reminder that she'd promised not to hover. She kissed Jabari and then set him down. Her son ran back to sit next to his father. Tanesha raised a hand in surrender and went down the hallway back to the windows.

This was certainly a concert to remember, and she wasn't going to miss any of it.

~~~~~~~~~

Sunday night — 6:45 p.m.
New York City, New York

"They're going on in a bit," Nadia said. "I'd like to use the restroom before they start."

Nadia cast a dim look toward the long line of women waiting for the bathroom.

"Come with me," Abi said. She touched Nadia's arm, and they disappeared.

"We should avail ourselves," Fin said.

"I don't want to go anywhere," Nash said. "Sandy told me that I have to stay on the roof. If I leave, I'll lose my privilege to stay with Nadia."

"I'm glad you say that," Fin said. He leaned into Nash to say, "I love the men's bathroom. They are so seedy, so human. I'd never been in one until I started medical school."

"Shall we make use of the pleasure?" Nash asked with a laugh. He gestured toward the public bathroom.

"As you wish," Fin said.

Fin patted Nash on his back, and they started toward the public bathroom near the back of the building. They stopped to say hello to Aden and Sandy, before heading into the bathroom. The room held three stalls and a line of urinals. The bathroom attendant gave them the once-over before gesturing for them to come inside.

Fin stood in the middle of the room with a goofy look on his face. Nash tapped him on the arm and pointed to the urinal.

"I haven't used these," Fin said with a grin.

Nash nodded. He went to a porcelain bowl and unzipped his pants. Fin started to laugh.

"What?" Nash mouthed.

"I had no idea what to do with that," Fin said brightly.

Nash laughed.

"Oh, brilliant," Fin said.

They were standing at the urinal when a man's voice came from the stalls.

"Did you see that kid she was with?" the man asked.

"Nadia?" the other man asked. "Yeah, I saw him. Nice-looking kid. You think he's her kid?"

"I hope not," the first man said.

"Why?" the second man said. "You know what one kid means?"

"She likes to fuck," the first man said with a laugh.

The stranger came out of the stall. Nash slumped his shoulders to hide his face, and Fin snapped his fingers. The man walked to the sink.

"He can't see us," Fin said to Nash.

"I don't want anyone to get in the way of my access to her fortune," the first man said from the sink.

"I'm planning to ask her to marry me," the second man said.

The first man laughed.

"She has everything I want," the second man said. "She's hot as hell. She has a job to keep her out of my hair. She'll be home only for me to fuck her."

"Plus, she's rich," the first man said with a laugh.

"Plus, she's Bratva connected," the second man said. "Perfect for my little enterprise."

"And she's loaded," the first man said.

"Indeed," the second man said.

"If you are done here, you should move along," the bathroom attendant said in a distinctive Egyptian accent.

The men sneered to the bathroom attendant.

"Your conquest is not here," the bathroom attendant said. "Perhaps she is just outside."

Nash could have sworn that he heard Nadia's voice outside the entrance to the restroom. The men looked out the door toward the sound. They gave the bathroom attendant one last sneer and left the room. Nash let out a breath, and Fin snapped his fingers again.

"Prince Finegal?" the bathroom attendant asked.

"Sir," Fin said.

"I have shut the entrance," the bathroom attendant said. "You may take your time, sir."

"Bless you," Fin said.

"Why thank you, sir!" the bathroom attendant brightened.

Fin gave the man a regal nod. He moved to the sinks. Nash followed him.

"What did you do?" Nash asked. His eyes flicked to the bathroom attendant.

"He gave me a general blessing, Mr. Norsen," the bathroom attendant said. "I will use it to keep my wife and daughters healthy and happy throughout their whole life."

"Good choice," Fin said.

"Can you think of anything better, Mr. Norsen?" the bathroom attendant asked.

"No, sir," Nash said. "I cannot."

As his father and Sandy had instructed, Nash tucked a five-dollar bill into the bathroom attendant's tip jar.

"Why, thank you, sir," the bathroom attendant said.

Nash nodded to the man and followed Fin from the restroom. Seeing that there was no one around, Nash touched Fin's arm, and he turned to look at Nash.

"What was that?" Nash asked.

"Ms. Behur provided the attendants," Fin said.

"But..." Nash said.

"They are from a family who has served her through many eras," Fin said. "In exchange, their children have every advantage, and they live long lives. Most of the children prefer to join Ms. Behur's service after they complete college."

"For the long lives?" Nash asked.

"That man is more than a thousand years old," Fin said. "His wife, as well."

Nash glanced back at the bathroom.

"He's in perfect health," Fin said. "His family, as well."

"What if they don't want to do it?" Nash asked.

"They would be released," Fin said. "Another family would gladly take their place. It's not slavery."

Nash nodded. Fin gave Nash a broad grin and turned to go.

"Can I ask you...?" Nash started.

Fin turned back to him. The fairy scanned Nash's face.

"What is on your mind?" Fin asked.

"Nadia," Nash said. He looked down at the ground. "I didn't know... I mean, I knew she was beautiful and smart and speaks, like, seven languages and..."

"You didn't know about the money," Fin said.

"I knew she had money, you know," Nash said. "She's a doctor and everything, but ..."

Nash shook his head.

"Does that change anything?" Fin asked.

"I feel... I mean, how can I..." Nash touched his chest. "I mean, me?"

Nash's eyes held his confusion, and his head drooped with sorrow.

"Ah," Fin said.

"Ah?" Nash asked.

Fin put his hand on Nash's shoulder and leaned forward to make a kind of huddle. Nash looked up at the fairy.

"You've met Abi?" Fin asked.

Nash nodded.

"Do you know anything about her?" Fin asked.

Nash shook his head.

"She is my mother's equal," Fin said. "Gilfand tells a story of how mother became queen. He said they had to choose between Abi, my mother, and her sister. Abi denies this is true, but she's just being polite."

Nash was pretty sure Fin was telling him something — he just wasn't sure what.

"What are you saying?" Nash asked. His eyes filled with tears.

"She is much bigger, more powerful, smarter, and more experienced than I," Fin said with a nod. "She's led the Fairy Corps since it was invented. I have no idea how she gets all those stubborn fairies to do what they're told. My sister, Mari, was supposed to take over from her, but there's no way Mari could replace Abi. She doesn't even bother to try."

Fin nodded. Nash gave a confused shake of his head.

"I met her when I came home from the first war," Fin said. "I was young, opinionated, and unformed. Not unlike you. More arrogant, of course. After all, I was a prince. That was enough for me to get any fairy to fall for me. Not Abi. She didn't want anything to do with me. She was not impressed with me at all."

"Really?" Nash asked.

"Really," Fin said. "She told me that if she couldn't hold a conversation with me, she had no use for me. Me! Prince Finegal!"

Looking incredulous, Fin's hand went to his chest.

"I am first in line for the entire land," Fin said. "I am handsome, strong, a legendary lover, and. . ."

Laughing, Fin shook his head.

"What did you do?" Nash asked.

"I became very angry," Fin said. "I left for the outer edges of the Queendom. There, I ruled my own province. I married and had children."

"And Abi?" Nash asked.

"I didn't see her again until my wife and children were killed," Fin said. "She is the one who beheaded the men who raped and murdered my wife. Personally. By herself. She brought me their heads."

"Wow," Nash said.

"'Wow,' is right," Fin said. "I was heartbroken, angry, and intimidated."

"What did you do?" Nash asked again.

Fin looked at Nash for a moment before grinning at him.

"I became better," Fin said. "I grew to match her."

"But. . ."

"If I were you, I'd start learning languages," Fin said. "Communicating to people seems a priority to your beloved."

"I can do that," Nash said.

"I'd ask Anjelika to help you," Fin said. "She is older than Nadia but has the same depth and interests. She grew up in a similar household, so she'll know what you need to learn. In fact, she's standing right there. Ask her today."

"Today?" Nash asked.

"Abi came around when she saw that I was making an effort to grow," Fin said. "She helped me learn. She continues to push me, even now. She wants our Queendom to be a modern society. We can only do that if I keep up with modern life. In fact, this medical-school thing was her idea. I am enjoying myself immensely."

Nash smiled at Fin.

"You can do this, Nash Norsen," Fin said. "You can become the man your beloved deserves. I just know it."

"Is that a blessing?" Nash asked.

"You don't need one," Fin said.

Fin looked back to where they had been standing.

"Those cretins from the bathroom are courting our loves," Fin said. "We must get back."

"I'm going to talk to Anjelika, first," Nash said.

"You do that," Fin said. "I will fight them off."

"Thanks," Nash said. "And. . ."

"Don't mention it," Fin said with a grin. "Just make it happen."

"I will," Nash said.

Fin nodded and walked away. Nash watched him shoo away the men they'd met in the bathroom. Nodding to himself, he went to talk to Anjelika.

CHAPTER THREE HUNDRED AND SIXTY-SEVEN
TOMORROW

Sunday night — 8:20 p.m. MT
Over the United States

Feeding her new baby boy, Heather looked up when Jill walked toward her. They were flying back to Denver after a long weekend of fun and adventure. The mood on the plane was markedly different than when they went to New York City. Just a few days ago, they'd hoped to get to Sissy before she died. Tonight, everyone was happy and relaxed from an afternoon and evening of music and food on the roof.

Heather glanced to where the teenagers were hanging out. Tink was fast asleep. Heather looked up when Jill neared. Jill pointed to the spot next to Heather, who nudged Sandy to move over. Sandy looked up from her magazine and nodded to Jill before moving over. Jill sat down next to Heather on the bench couch. Her head in a textbook, Tanesha sat in a chair facing them. Her long legs stretched across the space so that her feet pressed against the couch they were sitting on..

"How is he?" Jill whispered.

"Perfect," Heather said with a smile.

Jill leaned over to look in his face.

"I feel like I never see him," Jill said.

"You were really nice to breastfeed him after I was shot," Heather said. "And now."

Heather gestured to the bottle she was feeding her baby.

"I certainly have enough milk!" Jill said with a laugh.

"Thanks," Heather nodded.

Jill put her arm around Heather in an open hug.

"Mack was ready to go the moment he was born," Heather said. She gestured to the chair next to Tanesha, where her eldest son was sleeping. "I didn't get this kind of snuggling with him."

"Like Katy," Sandy said. "You have to catch her for a snuggle."

The friends nodded.

"This boy is a love," Heather said. She leaned over to kiss his cheek.

"He is," Jill said.

Jill stroked the baby's tiny head before leaning forward to touch Sandy's knee. Sandy looked up at Jill.

"How are you?" Jill asked Sandy.

Sandy shrugged and looked back at her magazine. The girlfriends waited for Sandy to respond. When she didn't say anything, Heather knocked her shoulder into Sandy.

"Oh, how am I?" Sandy asked with a sigh. "At this moment, I feel pretty good. The concert went well. Everyone had a great time. Jeraine won, and I got to see my gorgeous friend Tanesha celebrated on live television."

Tanesha looked up, and Sandy smiled.

"But give me a minute," Sandy continued. "I'll go right back to feeling bad for leaving Sissy in New York City all by herself."

"Like she asked for," Tanesha said.

"More like begged," Heather said.

"It feels crummy," Sandy said.

"You've just been there — night and day — since she got shot," Jill said. "It makes sense that you feel weird for not staying."

"What is she going to do?" Tanesha asked the question that she knew was soothing to Sandy.

"She should get out of the hospital tomorrow morning. Bestat is going to help her move in to her home, where Sissy will stay for a week or so — maybe a month." As she had a few times already, Sandy repeated Sissy's plans. "When she's able to move around on her own, she'll move in with Ivan and Nadia. That gives them time to make a space for her in their loft."

"What's the loft like?" Heather asked the other question that made Sandy feel more confident.

"Kind of barren, really," Sandy said. "Concrete floor, lots of open space and open windows. But also really nice. They are going to make a couple of rooms and a bathroom for Sissy. She'll move in when she's ready."

"Will she move in by herself?" Jill asked the last question that made Sandy feel better.

"No, Charlie's moving in with her," Sandy said with a smile and a nod. "He has to testify this week, but then he's going to move in with them. Ivan's going to help them rehabilitate from their injuries. Charlie'll just stay there until he's strong again. He'll be home by the fall, at the latest."

"Tink's going to visit him this summer," Heather added.

Sandy smiled and nodded.

"Thanks," Sandy said. "I was feeling a little guilty."

"What's happening with Nash?" Jill asked the question that would calm Sandy's next worry.

Sandy grinned at Jill.

"Well?" Tanesha asked.

"He talked to your mom, Jill," Sandy said. "She's going to take him under her wing to help him get cultured."

Sandy leaned forward so her ample chest pressed against her knee.

"Me, too," Sandy said. "I get to go to museums and stuff. Anjelika bought us a family pass."

"Me, too," Jill said.

"And me!" Heather said with a smile.

"I catch up when I can," Tanesha said. "It sounds really fun."

Sandy smiled and nodded.

"And tomorrow?" Jill asked.

"That horrible trial." Sandy's mood darkened. "The whole thing is so awful. I mean. . ."

"No — I meant in the evening," Jill said.

"Marriage classes with our priest," Sandy said with a smile. "We're getting married at the Cathedral in June."

Heather and Tanesha shared a look.

"What was that?" Jill asked.

"Better you than me," Tanesha said. "I cannot imagine what Jeraine would have to say about it."

She shot a look to where he and Jabari were fast asleep.

"Did you ever talk Jacob into going?" Heather asked.

"Oh, he's going," Jill said with a firm nod. "Why wouldn't he?"

Heather and Tanesha laughed. Jill smiled and Sandy chuckled.

"They're scared shitless," Sandy said.

"Jacob *and* Aden," Jill said with a nod.

"Did I tell you?" Heather asked.

"That Blane's coming home tomorrow?" Tanesha asked.

"Only about fifteen times," Sandy said.

The girlfriends laughed.

"What?" Heather asked. "I'm excited!"

They laughed again and then fell silent.

"Tomorrow," Sandy said with a sigh.

Heather, Jill, and Tanesha looked at her. Sandy nodded. Caught in their own thoughts, they fell silent.

~~~~~~~~~

Sunday night — 11:50 p.m.
Denver, Colorado

The buzzing sound woke Sandy with a start. She sat up in bed. The glowing red numbers of the clock told her that they had climbed into bed only ten minutes ago. She groaned and got up to get her cell phone.

"Hello?" Sandy answered without looking at the number.

"Sandy?" Samantha Hargreaves's voice was on the phone.

Sandy pulled the phone away from her ear to look at the number.

"Sami?" Sandy asked. "What number are you calling from?"

"I'm calling from Art's," Samantha said. "I didn't know if you'd pick up."

"111-222-3333 is Art's number?" Sandy asked.

"Sure," Samantha said in a dry tone.

"Oh," Sandy said. When Samantha didn't say anything else, Sandy said, "Well, we're home. See you in the morning."

She hung up the phone and set it down. Hoping it wouldn't ring again, she backed away from the phone with her hands up.

"What was that?" Aden asked.

"Samantha," Sandy said. Her eyes never left the phone.

"Ah, shit," Aden said. "What does that mean?"

"Nothing," Sandy said. "I hope."

They stared at the phone. When it didn't ring, Sandy went to use the bathroom. When she came out, Aden was holding her cellphone.

"It's Samantha," he said.

Sandy scrunched up her face and shook her head.

"Can I tell her what this is regarding?" Aden asked.

"Very funny." Samantha's voice was loud enough for Sandy to hear.

Sandy held out her hand, and Aden gave her the phone.

"I'm here," Sandy said.

"You know how I warned you. . ." Samantha said.

"The defendant's last chance to fuck with the kids is tonight," Sandy said.

"Did I say that?" Samantha said with a laugh.

"Not in those exact words," Sandy said.

"They want Charlie, Tink, and Nash, and a few of the families," Samantha said. "I was able to keep the younger kids out of it."

"Thanks," Sandy said.

"They have to come downtown," Samantha said.

"Tonight?" Sandy asked.

"Right now," Samantha said. "This is his last chance to accept the plea bargain. The victims need to approve the plea bargain, so they need to be here."

"Tink has to testify tomorrow!" Sandy said.

"She's scheduled," Samantha said. "But the schedule is shifting. If the plea goes through, they won't have to testify, and that's really what we want. If the plea doesn't go through, the DA wants to spend the first day on procedures like picking a jury. Did I tell you he's decided to try this himself?"

"So everything is up in the air," Sandy said.

"All we have to do right now is go," Samantha said. "We sit in a room with each other while the lawyers work. The DA will bring us a deal. If we accept it, no one has to testify. If we don't, they start jury selection in a few hours."

Sandy grunted with disgust.

"You don't sound confident that we'll reach a plea tonight," Samantha said.

"I *am* confident that this is another game to convince these children not to testify," Sandy said.

"You know I can't respond to that," Samantha said with a yawn. "Will you meet me? Please?"

Sandy looked across the room at Aden. He nodded.

"We'll be there," Sandy said.

"The Marshalls offered to send security," Samantha said. "But I've recruited my own security. Do not leave the Castle until someone comes for you."

"Someone?" Sandy asked.

"Someone you recognize," Samantha said.

"You won't tell me who?" Sandy asked.

"I'm not sure," Samantha said. "That's part of the security. See you downtown in a half hour."

"I don't know when we'll get there," Sandy said. "The kids just got in bed. Charlie's taking meds and Tink is. . ."

"Just do what you can," Samantha said. "I'll be in touch."

Sandy clicked off the phone.

"What can I do?" Aden asked.

"We have to get them up," Sandy said. "Just Tink, Charlie, and Nash."

Aden pulled on pajama bottoms and went out into their living room, where the kids were sleeping together for one last time. They were wide awake.

"There's no freakin' way we're not going," Noelle said to Aden when he came in the room.

"No way," Wanda said.

"If they have to go, I have to go," Ivy said.

"They only need the older kids," Aden said. "Charlie, Tink, and Nash."

"Too bad," Ivy said. "He did the crime to us. He's going to have to deal with all of us."

Aden looked at Sandy as she came into the room.

"It's not going to be any fun," Sandy said. "Most likely, it's just some stupid thing meant to intimidate you."

"I'm not intimidated," Noelle said with a stubborn tilt of her chin.

"I'm not either," Ivy said.

"I don't know, guys," Aden said.

"I do," Noelle said. "We're going — even if we have to walk there."

"Sounds like they're clear," Sandy said.

Aden looked at her. She gave him a grim smile.

"Looks like we're going to the courthouse," Sandy said.

The children's heads went up and down in a nod.

"Okay, we have two bathrooms," Sandy said. "Use them as fast as you can. We'll leave as soon as our ride gets here."

"Our ride?" Ivy asked.

As if on cue, there was a knock at their apartment door. Aden went to answer it. He paused for a minute before opening it. Bruno, Otis's long time bodyguard, was standing on the other side of the door.

"Aden!" Bruno said. "I heard you needed a ride downtown."

"We have to go to the courthouse," Aden said.

"Lucky for you, the wife and I are visiting Colorado this week," Bruno nodded. "We're staying at Ivan's apartment just around the corner. Nice place."

"Thank you so much." Sandy came to the door to take his hands. "We need help."

"I hope you don't mind, but I called a few good guys," Bruno said. "In exchange, they want to speak with the Oracle."

"Delphie?" Aden asked.

"She had agreed, so the deal is set," Bruno said with a nod. "Now, they will do anything we ask."

"What guys?" Sandy asked.

"Bratva," Bruno said. "I'll wait right here. We go in eight minutes."

The kids jumped up and started running around. Soon, Sandy, Aden, and Bruno were alone in the living room.

"Works every time," Bruno said.

"What does?" Aden asked.

"Get the children moving," Bruno said. "Bosses, too."

Bruno winked.

"I wait for you outside door," Bruno said.

Sandy nodded to the man.

"Shall we?" Aden asked.

Sandy nodded. They went into their bedroom to get ready.

~~~~~~~~

Sunday night — 7:47 p.m.
Denver, Colorado

Sandy sat in a chair in front of a paper bag that had been filled with her mail. A small stack of bills was sitting on a folding chair next to her. An overflowing paper bag stuffed with envelopes, flyers, catalogs, and other things for the recycling bin were to her right. While they waited to hear the next plea deal, she'd been going through the mail she'd missed while visiting New York.

She gave an angry snort at the idea that they'd heard *any* plea deals. They'd rushed down to the courthouse only to sit in this room. Once an hour, a representative from the DA's office came to tell them that they were still negotiating. About an hour before, they'd brought the deal the defendant wanted — the single count of rape for the assault caught on the ATM tape. He'd be sentenced to ten years in jail at the most. The defendant was likely to be out with the time he'd already served. Tink had jumped to her feet and started screaming at the associate DA. The other girls joined her. Intimidated by them, the associate DA scurried out of the room.

Shaking her head, Sandy reached into the bottom of the bag to grab the last letter. It was stuck under a flap under the paper bag. She had to tug on it to get it free. Without looking at it, she turned the envelope over and pulled the letter out. Just then, the door opened, and the DA appeared. Samantha Hargreaves got up to speak with him. Sandy's eyes followed the interaction while her hands opened the letter. Seeing Samantha shake her head, Sandy looked down at the letter.

She gasped and swallowed hard.

"Sandy?" Aden asked. He got up from where he was playing cards with Charlie, Nash, Teddy, and a couple of the other fathers. "Are you okay?"

Her eyes flicked up to look at him and then back to the letter.

"You're pale as a sheet," Aden said. "What is it?"

He grabbed the letter from her hands and read it. Sandy stared at the check.

"Oh," Aden said. "Wow."

"Okay, this is where we are. . ." Samantha said.

The room became instantly silent. The children and parents turned their full attention toward the door. Aden turned around to look at Samantha.

"His representation is confident they can beat this case," Samantha said. "They've been through the evidence. They are sure their client will be exonerated. In fact, they're filing a defamation case when the courts open in an hour."

"What?" Sandy asked into the chorus of questions and swear words.

Samantha held up her hands for them to be quiet. The room became silent again.

"The problem is that they could be right," Samantha said. "We can connect the financier and this man. We know that Aden and Jake saw him when Noelle was attacked. But the financier is dead and otherwise. . ."

Samantha shrugged.

"What about the guys?" Sandy asked. "Surely the other boys are testifying against him."

"No," Samantha said. "The boys are shockingly quiet. Most of them have refused to participate in this case or can't because of their plea deals. He could easily walk"

No one said anything.

"Why would the boys do that?" Charlie asked.

"If this jerk is found not guilty, they can appeal their cases," Samantha said.

"How?" asked the father of one of the girls who had killed herself.

"They can say that he was the leader. If he's not guilty, then they aren't." Samantha gave a small nod of her head. "It doesn't feel fair, I know, but it is legal."

"What do you recommend we do?" Sandy asked.

"We have to go to trial," Samantha said.

"To trial?" one of the father's asked. "You said that my daughter wouldn't have to testify."

"I was hoping she wouldn't have to," Samantha said. "I'm sorry. They are betting that you would rather have him go free than have the kids testify."

"You've got that right," another father said.

"We have a few minutes if you'd like to think about it," Samantha said.

The children looked at each other. The parents whispered among themselves.

"I say we go to trial," Tink said with a nod.

Sandy glanced at Heather, who was giving Tink a worried look.

"I think so, too," one of the other girls said.

"I don't know," Ivy's Aunt Grace said. "Testifying can be really awful."

"What we went through was really awful," Wanda said. "And this guy did this in other cities. Imagine what those girls will feel like if we just let him walk."

"Or the girls who killed themselves," Charlie said with a nod. "We owe it to them to go through with it."

"We have to stand up for those who can't stand up for themselves," Noelle said with a nod.

Sandy's eyes flicked down the row of her children and their friends. The other girls were also clear. The children were ready to fight. Glancing at the other parents, she saw that their faces held the dread she felt in her own heart.

"I don't know," Aden said.

"You know he'll do it again," Tink said.

Trying to find some wisdom, Sandy looked up at the ceiling.

"I have to bring them something," Samantha said.

"Tell them we're going to trial," one of the other mothers said. "My daughter died at their hands as surely as if they'd murdered her themselves. If these kids are willing to testify in her place, I'm certainly not going to say 'No'."

The other parents gave grudging nods.

"Sandy?" Samantha asked.

Sandy glanced at the check for a second and then looked up at Samantha.

"I think we go to trial," Sandy said with a nod.

"Then you agree?" Samantha asked. She looked around the room at the nodding heads. "I'll go tell them."

Samantha left the room.

"Let's go home," Aden said.

"Can we get breakfast?" Charlie asked. "Sam's is right here."

"Yes, in fact, it's my treat," Sandy said. "I still have Schmidty's credit card."

She glanced at Aden, who nodded. Standing up, she folded the check and tucked it in her back pocket.

"Please, do join us," Aden said to the other parents. "It's going to be a long haul. We may as well get to know each other."

A few of the parents nodded, while the others begged off. They waited until their bodyguards came to get them. Sandy followed Ivy and Wanda out of the building. They were almost to the glass doors when Ivy tugged on her arm. Sandy looked at the young girl.

"Is that the guy?" Ivy pointed to a young man making his way across the lobby. His arms were handcuffed together and his legs in shackles. He sported a Denver Sheriff's Officer on either arm. The young man whistled at Tink and made kissing lips at her. Aden stepped between Tink and the young man.

"That's him," Sandy said.

"Oh," Ivy said.

"Why do you ask, Ivy?" Samantha asked.

"That's the guy who, you know. . ." Ivy said.

Even at ten years old, Ivy was a tiny girl. Samantha had to kneel down to see her eye to eye.

"You remember him?" Samantha asked.

"He made the guys let him go first," Ivy said in a soft voice. "Said he liked young virgins."

Ivy nodded. Sandy put her arm around the child's shoulders for support.

"We'll make sure we tell them that in court," Samantha said with a nod. She got up. "I love breakfast. I almost never get to go. I'm so glad we're going."

"No," Ivy said. "You don't understand."

Samantha knelt down to Ivy again.

"What don't I understand?" Samantha asked.

"He marked me," Ivy said. "On the place between, you know."

"Me too," the other young girl said. "Burned his initials there."

"And his ring," a third girl said. She looked up at her mother, and her mother nodded.

"We looked into getting it removed, but. . ." her mother said with a shake of her head. "At least she doesn't have to look at it."

Samantha looked down the line at the three youngest victims. Sandy gave the mother a grim look, and the mother nodded.

"He said it was so any guy who came later would know he'd been there first," Ivy said.

"Did you girls tell the police this?" Samantha asked.

"No one asked," Ivy said. "It's in my medical file because it got infected."

"Mine, too," the girl with her parents said.

The girl's parents nodded.

"Can you excuse me for a minute?" Samantha asked.

"We'll see you at breakfast," Sandy said. "Come on, girls. There are pancakes waiting for us."

They went out the door. Sandy walked with her arm around Ivy. Bruno was driving, so Sandy stayed with Ivy. They slipped into the back of the SUV.

"Where did she go?" Ivy asked when they were in the SUV.

"I think she went to talk to the DA," Sandy said.

"Am I in trouble?" Ivy asked.

"No," Sandy said. "If anything, you've solved their problem."

"What do you mean?" Ivy asked.

"We can connect this jerk to you in a real physical way," Sandy said.

"Oh," Ivy said. "Am I going to have to show everybody in court?"

"Not a chance," Sandy said. "But you might have pictures shown. Would that be okay?"

"I guess so," Ivy said. She thought for a moment before nodding, "Yeah, that's okay."

Sandy nodded. They fell silent on the short drive to Sam's No. 3 on Fifteenth Street. They were getting out when Ivy tugged on Sandy's shirt. Sandy looked at her.

"Is it okay to wish he was dead?" Ivy asked.

"I do," Sandy said with a smile. "It's probably not very healthy for me. But, man. . . I wish he die in some horrible way."

"Acid bath," Ivy whispered. "Giant garbage disposal. Whrrrrr."

Sandy smiled, and Ivy laughed.

"You may need to hold onto that anger just to get through this," Sandy said.

"And then what?" Ivy asked.

"Then we'll send you to an ashram to learn forgiveness," Sandy said. "Ommmm. . ."

Ivy giggled and nodded. The girl ran forward so that she could sit next to Charlie. It was the first time Charlie had been in the restaurant since he'd been beaten up. The wait staff made sure they were welcome. They had just ordered when Samantha Hargreaves arrived. She tucked into the seat that Sandy had saved for her.

"What happened?" Sandy asked.

"Turns out that everyone missed this," Samantha said. "Probably because they had to replace the entire crime team, but no one knew what I was talking about when I told them. They did not know that the perp marked his youngest victims. Not with his initials anyway. And they have that ring — took it from him when they booked him. It's a school ring with his name on the inside. While I was standing there, the detectives matched Ivy's burn to that ring. They are subpoenaing the other girls' medical records right now."

"And?" Sandy asked.

"I think we've got him," Samantha said.

"They're not going to go down without a fight," Sandy said.

"Nope," Samantha said. "We need to buckle up. It's going to be a wild road."

Sandy nodded.

"Now, when are you going back to work?" Samantha asked.

"I'm going in today to see what's what," Sandy said. "I haven't been there in a long time."

"And you're willing to do your friend Samantha's hair today?" Samantha asked.

Sandy looked at Samantha. She picked up a piece of Samantha's lovely auburn hair and looked at the ends.

"I haven't had a cut since long before the blessed birth was born," Samantha said.

"'Blessed birth'?" Sandy asked with a laugh.

"Once a nickname gets started in my family, it sticks,"

Samantha said.

"How is she?" Sandy asked.

"Oh, let me tell you," Samantha said with a smile.

Samantha took out her cell phone to show Sandy the pictures. For the next hour, they ate breakfast, laughed, and looked at the "blessed birth." Fortified, Sandy looked around the table.

"What are you thinking?" Samantha asked.

"I think we'll get through this," Sandy said.

"Yes," Samantha said. "We will."

~~~~~~~~~

Monday mid-morning — 11 am
Denver, Colorado

Heather stood on the hospital elevator for what she hoped was, at the very least, one of the last times. She wore her infant son in a tight sling that Valerie had helped her tie. Tink was leaning against the corner of the elevator in a sullen silence. Stunned and amazed by the elevator itself, Mack held tightly to her hand. A stranger looked at her and smiled.

"They are adorable," he said.

"Thanks," Heather said. Tink cast her a dark look. Shaking her head, Heather said, "What?"

"English?" Tink asked in a surly way at the same time the stranger said, "Excuse me."

"Sorry," Tink said. "My mom makes up code languages for the CIA. When she's working on one, she randomly speaks it. It's insane."

"Thank you for your service to our great country," the stranger said.

Heather gave him a vague smile. The elevator stopped, and he stepped off. The elevator doors closed and the elevator started moving again.

"CIA?" Heather asked.

"What language was that?" Tink asked. "It sounded like

gibberish."

"I spoke another language," Heather asked. She looked at Tink, who nodded. She glanced at Mack, who also nodded. "Sorry, I had no idea."

"What language was it?" Tink's voice rose with irritation and exasperation.

"Probably Olympian," Heather said. "I've been trying to re-learn it. I have to attend a meeting soon."

"Olympians speak their own languages?" Tink asked.

"Unfortunately," Heather said. "To make things more exciting, Titans do as well."

"Elitist snobs," Tink said.

Heather nodded. The elevator stopped, and the doors opened. Tink sneered at the doors but didn't move.

"Come on," Heather said.

"He doesn't want to see me," Tink said. "He wants to see his baby, then you, then maybe Mack, before he gets to the reject."

"Tiffany!" Blane's voice came from the landing. "I can hear her voice, but I don't see her! Is that you?"

Unable to stop herself, Tink ran off the elevator and into Blane's arms. Over Tink's shoulder, Blane winked at Heather, as she stood on the elevator landing. While Tink cried, Blane talked in her ear.

"Daddy!" Mack said. "Daddy! Daddy! Daddy!"

Mack wrenched his hand from Heather's tight grip and ran to where Tink and Blane were hugging. He put his arms around their legs. Blane kissed Tink's cheek and picked up Mack in one arm. He kept his other arm firmly around Tink. Heather hung back for a moment to give him time to enjoy his family. When he looked up at her, she stepped forward.

"May I?" Blane asked.

Heather gave a slight nod. He tapped Tink's waist, and she kissed him on the cheek again. Her face wet with tears, Tink let go of Blane and latched onto Heather's shoulder.

"Mommy!" Mack said and squirmed.

The boy held out his arm to Heather. She took Mack from Blane. He gave her a soft smile before carefully lifting their new son from the sling.

"Hello, son," Blane said, as he looked upon his son for the first time.

Blane stared down at his son, and the baby opened his eyes.

"Oh, my God — I think my heart just broke open," Blane said.

He held his arm out. Moving as a unit, Tink, Mack, and Heather hugged him. He kissed Heather.

"We love you, Daddy!" Mack said the words he and Heather had practiced for days.

Blane started to cry.

"Let's go home," Heather said in a soft voice.

"I have to check out and. . ." Blane said.

He looked up to see his nurse waiting with a wheelchair. Still crying, Blane gave their son back to Heather before doing another round of thanking his nurses. He went from person to person finally ending with his doctor.

"He's doing very well," the doctor said. "We've started him on a strict vaccine schedule but, just like with your baby, until we're done, he won't be fully protected."

Heather smiled at the information the doctor had already given her when he called this morning. The doctor went over the same information again — watch his diet, we don't know about allergies, take it very slow, try to avoid crowds, don't be around sick people, and other good advice for Blane's brand-new immune system. Heather nodded and smiled.

After all the talk and thank-you's and goodbyes, Heather's little family was finally standing at the back of the elevator. Blane's nurse wheeled him into the elevator, turned him around, and then pushed the button for the Lobby.

"You know that most of Lipson construction is waiting in the

Lobby," Heather said.

"They are?" Blane asked. His voice was laced with genuine wonder.

"Of course, they are," Heather said with a smile.

"Mr. Lipson," the nurse said. "Why don't you put on this mask? That way you can see your friends and reduce your risk of getting sick."

"You knew?" Blane turned around to look at her nurse.

"Of course," the nurse said with a smile. She nodded toward Heather.

Blane leaned back and smiled at her. She winked at him. The elevator opened to the Lobby.

"Is that him?" Sam Lipson's voice came from the landing. "Blane? Son?"

The nurse wheeled him out of the elevator. Tink was about to follow when Heather put her hand on the girl's arm.

"Let's give him a minute," Heather said. "They haven't seen him this entire time."

Tink looked into Heather's eyes for a moment before nodding.

"Isn't this hard for you?" Tink asked. "Don't you want him for yourself?"

"I'm okay," Heather said. "We'll have time later."

"If it was Charlie, I'd be mad that he didn't say 'Hello' to me first," Tink said.

She glanced at Heather, who shrugged.

"I've learned a lot about love in the last month," Heather said. She smiled at Tink. "Okay, go ahead."

Tink got off the elevator, and Heather followed. They stood outside the elevator, watching Blane's friends, family, and coworkers welcome him back.

"Wow," Tink said.

Heather smiled and nodded.

"Let's find a quiet place to wait," Heather said.

She didn't get far before Lipson Construction's head of estimating grabbed Mack. Jacob got Tink to introduce her to some of office staff she would work with this summer. Heather and the baby went to the bench in the corner. She hadn't been there more than a minute before Jill joined her.

"This is amazing," Jill said.

"Yes, it is," Heather said.

The baby squirmed and gave a squawk.

"Ahh," Jill said.

"He's hungry." Heather reached into her baby bag. "Would you like to feed him?"

"Can I?" Jill asked.

"Sure," Heather said.

"I can. . ." Jill said. She gestured to her swollen breasts.

"If you'd like," Heather said. "I brought bottles, too."

"You don't mind?" Jill asked. "My boys barely have time for this before they want to cause mischief."

"I am grateful for all you do for us," Heather said. "This is such a loving gift."

Jill greedily took the baby. She unhooked her nursing bra. Heather dropped a blanket over Jill's shoulder, and the baby began to nurse.

"You've changed a lot," Jill said.

"I have?" Heather asked. Jill nodded. "I hope it's for the better."

"You're less insecure, less fragile, more loving," Jill said. "Between almost dying and becoming the living embodiment of love — it makes sense that you might be a little different."

Heather smiled. They settled in to watch the party while the baby nursed.

~~~~~~~~~

Monday afternoon — 3:17 p.m.
Denver, Colorado

"Hey!" Tanesha yelled as she ran into the house. "I forgot my lab shoes again!"

She jogged through the house and took the stairs two at a time. Grabbing her Dansko clogs, she stopped. Jeraine's car was outside. He was supposed to be here.

"Jer?" Tanesha asked. She listened for his response. Hearing nothing, she scowled. "Jeraine?"

She checked the upstairs bathroom. He wasn't there. Holding her lab shoes, she jogged downstairs and set the shoes on the bottom step.

"Jeraine?" she asked and listened.

Nothing. It had been months since Jeraine had zoned out. The last time was... She thought for a moment. The day they'd received the DNA analysis on Jabari. She'd found him... in his office. She trotted down the basement steps. The basement studio was dark and empty. The lights were on in Jeraine's office. Jeraine's chair was pushed back as if he'd left his office in a hurry. She shook her head.

Where was he?

She slowly went back up the stairs. *It's not that big of a house*, she reasoned.

"Jeraine?" she asked at the top of the stairs.

Still nothing. She went through the living room and dining room in front of her. He wasn't there. He wasn't in the kitchen, either, or in the downstairs half-bathroom.

"Jeraine?" she asked as she opened the small bedroom downstairs.

He wasn't there, either. She called his phone. It rang from the hall table, where it was hooked up to the charger. The back door was open to the storm door. She went out to the backyard. Jeraine was standing on their back deck. His eyes were vague. His right hand was rubbing his reading glasses with a cloth.

"Jer?" Tanesha touched his arm.

He looked up at her. His eyebrows dropped with concern.

"Miss T? What are you…" Jeraine looked around. His head tipped to the side. "Where am I?"

"On the back deck," Tanesha said.

"Of our house?" Jeraine asked.

Tanesha nodded.

"In Denver?" Jeraine asked.

Tanesha nodded.

"When did we get grass and trees and…" He waved his hand toward their backyard. "Stuff?"

"Jake and his team put everything in last Saturday," Tanesha said. "You told me about it when we were in New York."

"I did?" Jeraine asked. "Truly?"

He shook his head. Tanesha guided him into the house.

"Oh, yes — this is our house," Jeraine said. "I love it here. It's so beautiful. So safe. And it…"

He took a deep breath through his nose.

"It smells like you." He gave her a broad smile. "This is the best place in the whole world."

"Do you have a headache?" Tanesha asked.

"My head? Why yes, it's killing me," Jeraine smiled at her. "Why is that?"

Tanesha shook her head. She picked up her cell phone and called Fin to tell him that she wouldn't make it back to school. When she turned back, Jeraine's eyes were vague again.

"Jer?" Tanesha asked. "You're really scaring me."

"Oh?" Jeraine asked. He scowled. "Aren't you supposed to be in lab?"

"Yes, I am," Tanesha said.

"Well, off you go!" Jeraine gave her a broad smile. She scowled at him. He looked confused and said, "What?"

"You're acting very strange," Tanesha said. "Are you high?"

"High?" Jeraine asked. He looked very surprised. For the first time, he seemed more himself. "I don't think so."

"I'm worried that you had a stroke," Tanesha said.

"A stroke?" Jeraine asked.

She scowled at him. She checked his balance and eyesight. His speech seemed fine. She led him upstairs. He let her help him out of his clothing without even one comment about having sex. Clearly, his head was killing him. She gave him his pain pills and his migraine inhaler. She laid a wet washcloth on his head. He was asleep in a moment.

Shaking her head, she picked up his shirt, checked for stains, and dumped it into the laundry bag. She pulled his wallet out of the back pocket of his pants. His front pockets held his keys and a few Post-its. She set the contents of his pants on the desk. Turning to hang up his pants, she realized what the Post-it read. She scowled and hung up his pants. She went back to the desk and picked up the Post-it.

"10 gigs US. 3 nights LA. 3 nights Chicago. 3 nights NYC. 3 nights London. Leave next week."

Tanesha dropped down on the bed. Jeraine had been asked to go on tour with... She turned the Post-it over. The gorgeous woman whose album he'd just finished —the same gorgeous woman who was the last girlfriend he'd splashed all over the tabloids. She turned to look at him.

Shaking her head, she went back to the desk to put the Post-it back, and she picked up the second one. It was another offer to go on tour. The third Post-it held another offer. She looked at him.

No wonder he'd had a headache. He had three competing offers to go on tour. She crept downstairs to the kitchen and made herself a cup of tea.

What should she do? She hadn't thought of him going on tour again. But he'd just won another Grammy. It made sense that he'd go on tour again. She sat down on a bar stool at the kitchen counter and thought it through.

He must have taken down these offers without thinking about her or Jabari. He'd just tucked them into his pocket. He'd probably heard the sprinklers for the new grass turn on and had gone to see what was happening. Standing there, he'd probably remembered her and Jabari. Hence the debilitating headache.

She needed to decide what she wanted to do. She drank her tea and made another cup. She'd finished her third cup of tea when she made up her mind. She went upstairs to retrieve the Post-its. Downstairs, she took her cell phone out of her bag.

"Schmidty?" Tanesha asked.

"Hey! Tanesha!" Schmidty said. It sounded like he was having dinner. "I'm having lunch in New York with Lizzie. We're heading to Denver tonight."

"I wanted to talk to you about Jeraine," Tanesha asked.

"What can I do for you?" Schmidty asked.

"I'm wondering if you knew anything about offers for Jeraine to go on the road?" Tanesha asked.

"On vacation?" Schmidty asked. "I can recommend a great place to. . ."

"Tour," Tanesha said.

"First I'm hearing of it," Schmidty said. "Give me a minute."

She heard him get up from where he was sitting. The noise in the background dropped.

"I'm sure he forgot that you were. . ." Tanesha said.

"I'm sure of it," Schmidty said. "Don't worry. I'm not offended. He's used to having to take care of this crap himself. Do you think he agreed to anything?"

"No way," Tanesha said. "I think he wanted to talk to me about it but freaked out. He was checked out when I got home. I thought he'd had a stroke."

"A stroke?" Schmidty asked. "Is he all right?"

"He's okay," Tanesha said. "He had a bad headache. I'm sure it's this stuff. He's asleep now."

"Good," Schmidty said. "Okay, give me the details. I'll call around and make sure everyone goes through me in the future. They know they're supposed to. They just don't do it."

"Why?" Tanesha asked.

"Because I'm a hard ass," Schmidty said. "I get the best deals for my clients, and everyone knows it."

"Good," Tanesha said. She gave him the details she'd found on the Post-its.

"I'll take care of it, but. . ." Schmidty paused for a moment. "Are you certain you want him to go on the road?"

"I'm certain that I'm willing to look at his options," Tanesha said. "The man is a sensation. That's his life. He loves performing. I won't stand in the way of that. I want him to be the best person he can be and live the biggest life he possibly can live. But I will not stand by and let him be a pawn in someone else's game. We've come too far for him to be injured on the road again."

"Good to know," Schmidty said. "Don't worry, Tanesha. I've got this."

"Thanks," Tanesha said.

"Tell Jer when he wakes up that I've got this," Schmidty said.

"I will," Tanesha said. "Thanks."

He was gone. She looked at her phone again and set it down. She only hoped that she'd done the right thing.

CHAPTER THREE HUNDRED AND SIXTY-NINE
BEING AT HOME

Monday afternoon — 4:27 p.m.
Denver, Colorado

"Knock, knock, knock."

A distinctively feminine knuckle hit Tanesha's front door, and she scowled. Cursing under her breath, she left her stool in the kitchen and went to the door. She peered through the peep hole. The air around her crackled and popped before she remembered to control her temper. She opened the door.

"What?" Tanesha asked.

"Jeraine here?" asked the beautiful singer.

The women pushed one hip out. Her silicone breasts looked as if one deep breath and they would break free of the tiny band of fabric around them. The woman was wearing something that looked like it might be a skirt. However, if she hadn't been wearing a slip of light cloth in the same color as the band around her breasts, you could have seen the entire landscape of what might be called her "private parts." Her light-brown skin glistened with what smelled like cocoa butter.

"He's not feeling well," Tanesha said.

She moved to close the door. The singer put her hand on the door to keep Tanesha from closing her out.

"What'd you do to him?" the singer asked.

The air around Tanesha crackled again. Out of the corner of her eye, she saw the door to her grandmother's house open with a bang.

"He's simply not feeling well," Tanesha said.

Crazy Aunt Phy flew out of Gran's house. She ran across the street pulling a flowery shirt over her tank top as she ran.

"He was all right when he spoke to me," the singer said with a seductive pop of her enhanced full lips. "He going to go on tour with this."

The singer ran a hand up and down her body. Her hand had just reached her hip when a giant white spark flew from the singer's hand to her hip.

"What the. . .?" the singer looked down.

"Static electricity," Tanesha said. "It's the altitude."

As if she were running the hurdles, Crazy Aunt Phy jumped Tanesha's white picket fence.

"But. . ." the singer started.

"I'm so sorry," Aunt Phy said in her craziest voice.

Crazy Aunt Phy pushed past the singer and into the house. The door closed with a crack.

"Did you forget to drink your tea, Tanesha?" Aunt Phy asked a stunned Tanesha.

"Uh. . ." Tanesha said.

The singer pounded on the door.

"Just one minute," Aunt Phy said.

She opened the door to the singer.

"Princess Tanesha is not taking visitors. If I were you, I'd leave before she turns you into something. . ." Aunt Phy looked the woman up and down. "Unsavory. Or catches you on fire, which, at this moment, is highly likely."

She snapped the door closed. Tanesha listened to see if the singer would leave. Crazy Aunt Phy waved Tanesha over to watch through the sheer covering the window. The singer huffed at the door for a few minutes before deciding to leave. The gate to the white picket fence snapped the singer's behind as it closed. The singer turned around and tried to get back through. The gate wouldn't budge. When the singer tried to step over the low fence, it grew a few inches. With each try, the fence grew a few more inches until it looked like it was almost ten feet tall.

"What did you do?" Tanesha put her hands on her hips.

"I'm coming back," the singer yelled before getting into her limousine again.

Jeraine's phone rang. There was a great snap, and the phone started to smoke.

"Nothing you can prove," Aunt Phy said. She wiggled her nose, and the phone stopped smoking. "Why do you think it was me?"

"Because I surely didn't do that," Tanesha said.

"No, you just tried to burn down the entire town," Crazy Aunt Phy said. "Damn, Tanesha. Drink the tea!"

"I had three cups!" Tanesha said.

"You did not," Crazy Aunt Phy said.

Tanesha stomped to the kitchen sink where her cup was sitting. She shoved the cup at Aunt Phy. Her Aunt took the cup and ran her finger over the brim. She scowled. She stuck her finger inside the cup to taste the remnant of tea.

"Damn," Crazy Aunt Phy said.

"Well?" Tanesha raised her eyebrows and looked at the woman.

"Three cups and you're still popping?" Aunt Phy asked.

"And?"

"Looks like our little girl has grown into a strong fairy," Aunt Phy said. Her eyes welled with tears. She gave an exaggerated sniff. "I'm so proud."

Tanesha scowled. Seeing her scowl, Aunt Phy laughed.

"What are we going to do?" Tanesha asked.

"*We* aren't doing anything," Aunt Phy said. "*I'm* going to sit on your porch and keep guard. *You* are going to study your school work and take care of your man."

"I have to pick up Jabari in an hour," Tanesha said. "Jer is out for the night."

"Your mother can pick up the boy," Aunt Phy said. "In fact,

she's just about to call and ask if she can keep the child for the night."

Tanesha's phone rang. Shaking her head, Tanesha answered. Her mother had called to ask if Jabari could spend the night. Rodney was getting off work early. They wanted to take him and Mr. Chesterfield for a picnic in the park. Her mother was delighted when Tanesha agreed to the plan.

"How did you do that?" Tanesha asked Aunt Phy after she'd hung up.

"Do what?" Aunt Phy gave Tanesha a cockeyed blink of her eyes.

Tanesha smiled. She was just about to say something when they heard the slamming of a car door.

"Uh, oh," Aunt Phy said.

She gave Tanesha a little wave before jettisoning out the door. Tanesha watched the door for a moment. She heard Aunt Phy settle into a rocking chair on the porch. Shaking her head, Tanesha took out her text book. She was about to sit down when she heard Aunt Phy yell, "Have another cup of tea."

Tanesha went to make the tea.

~~~~~~~~~

Monday evening — 5:52 p.m.
Denver, Colorado

"How you doing there, Mikey?" Lieutenant Colonel Alexandra Hargreaves asked over the intercom. They were flying to Denver in a Blackhawk Helicopter.

"He threw up again," Sergeant Margaret Peaches said in reply.

"Jeez, Mike," Captain Andrew "Trece" Ramirez said. "I went through it. I survived. How bad can it be?"

"B-b-b-ad," Sergeant Michael Scully, Junior said.

"He's stuttering, again," Captain Zack "the Jakker" Jakkman said from the cockpit.

"Man up, Scully!" Chief Royce Tubman said.

"Col, can you give him something?" Alex asked.

"Not and be sure he can safely parachute," Captain Colin Hargreaves said.

"You can jump with me, MJ," Captain Chris "The White Boy" Blanco said. "We can strap you on my back. I don't mind."

Everyone laughed.

"F-f-f. . . shit," MJ said. "Kiss my ass, Blanco."

"See! He's better," Trece said.

"Magic," the White Boy said.

"Holy, holy, holy!" Zack sang over the intercom.

Colin, Alex, and Captain Vince Hutchins picked up the song.

"Ok, whoever is going better get in position," Zack said.

"Who's going?" Major Joseph Walter said.

"Colin, me, MJ, Trece," Alex said.

"I'm assisting, Scully," White Boy said.

He stood up and wrapped his arms around MJ's waist.

"Get off me," MJ said.

"He's really a lot better," Trece said. "Keep up the good work."

"Thanks, man," White Boy said.

"You'd better jump if you're going to," Zack yelled.

They stood up and grabbed their parachutes. Their partners — Raz for Alex, Margaret for MJ, White Boy for Trece, and Joseph for Colin — checked their parachutes and gear.

Colin jumped first, followed by Trece. MJ jumped after Trece. Alex watched them drop before following them from the helicopter. Late, they dropped fast only to slow just before the ground. They landed in the parking lot of the Cathedral Basilica of the Immaculate Conception on Colfax Boulevard in Denver. Alex grabbed MJ's parachute, and Colin unhooked him.

"Come on!" Colin yelled. "I'll show you the way."

Colin took MJ's arm, and they ran into the Cathedral.

"D-d-don't know," MJ said when they reached the priest's office.

"What's the problem?" Colin asked in a low tone. "You love your life. You love Honey. Why are you so freaked out?"

"Sinner," MJ said and pointed to his chest.

"Eh," Colin lifted a shoulder in a shrug. "Just go to confession. You'll be fine."

Colin walked MJ down the hall. The priest's door was open. Near the door, Colin pushed MJ into the room. Stumbling, he tripped over the threshold.

"Michael!" the priest said. "Welcome! I believe you know everyone."

MJ saw Jacob, Jill, Aden, and Sandy. Honey smiled at him. His mouth fell open with surprise.

"You're here, too?" MJ asked. "How?"

"We're getting married together," Honey said.

"Would you prefer it was just you and Honey?" the priest asked.

"No," MJ said quickly. "No. This is. . ."

He looked at the two other couples.

"This is great," MJ smiled. "You didn't tell me because. . ."

"We didn't know either," Aden said. "Jake didn't tell me, and I didn't tell him. We left the same work site. You can't imagine my surprise to pull in to the lot right after he did."

Jill, Sandy, and Honey beamed at each other.

"Surprise?" Honey smiled at him.

Chuckling to himself, MJ leaned over to kiss Honey.

"Shall we start?" the priest asked.

"Sure," MJ said. He pulled off his helmet. "Sorry I'm late. We were. . . oh, never mind."

He sat down and took Honey's hand.

"Let's begin. . ." the priest said.

~~~~~~~~~

Monday night — 8:45 p.m.
Denver, Colorado

Tanesha was just starting the dishwasher when there was a knock on the front door. The doorbell rang. Tanesha looked up the stairs to see if the noise had awakened Jeraine. There was no sound from upstairs. She wasn't surprised. He'd gotten up to eat some soup an hour or so ago and was back asleep. She slid across the hardwood floors in her socks. Very carefully, she opened the door and peeked out.

Her favorite rapper and record-company executive was standing on their front porch. She put her finger to her lip, and he nodded. She opened the door and stepped out. Crazy Aunt Phy was no longer sitting on her front porch. She looked across the street. Aunt Phy waved to her and went inside her gran's house.

"How did you get past the fence?" Tanesha whispered.

"I told it that I had made an agreement with Jammy," the rapper said.

"Hrmpt," Tanesha scowled at him. He might be her favorite, but that didn't mean he could be trusted. She had to ask, "And Aunt Phy?"

"Gave her a Cuban," the rapper said.

"A cigar?" Tanesha asked.

The rapper shrugged. Still scowling, Tanesha nodded.

"I did make an agreement with Jammy," the rapper said. "He said it was up to you. If you agreed, he'd draw up the contracts."

"If *I* agreed?" Tanesha asked. "What about Jeraine?"

The rapper chuckled.

"It's *his* career!" Tanesha said.

"That may be true, but Jer doesn't give a shit about anything in this world other than you," the rapper said. He nodded. "I did four years on tour with him and three others off and on. I will tell you that, no matter what that man says or does, he belongs to you."

Tanesha frowned. She nodded toward the door. The rapper

nodded. She opened the door, and he went inside. For a moment, he stood on the threshold.

"Wow," the man said.

"Wow?" Tanesha asked.

"I wish my wife could see this," he said. "It feels so. . ."

Fin appeared out of nowhere.

"Hey, I came as soon as. . ." Fin said to Tanesha.

The rapper dropped to his knees.

"Prince Finegal," the rapper said.

Tanesha and Fin were so surprised that they both gawked at him.

"What?" the rapper asked. "Did I do it wrong?"

"Do what?" Tanesha asked.

"Show respect," the rapper said. "Jammy said that if a big guy with brother dreads appeared out of thin air that I was in the presence of a fairy prince. Prince Finegal. He said that Prince Finegal looked like a nice guy but that he'd just as soon kill me as have a conversation with me."

The rapper gave Fin a vague smile.

"I'd rather not die tonight," the rapper said.

"Fair enough," Fin said.

Fin nodded to the rapper. He held his hand out and helped pull the rapper to his feet.

"Are you truly a prince?" the rapper asked.

Fin cocked his head to the side, and his clothing transformed to his court attire. Overwhelmed at the sight, the rapper fell to his knees again.

"She is a princess," Fin said.

Before she could stop him, Fin transformed Tanesha into her court attired complete with jewels. The rapper's mouth fell open.

"Enough!" Tanesha said.

They instantly transformed to their usual clothing.

"Excuse me," Fin said. "I need to check on Jeraine."

The rapper gave him an odd nod. He was gone a few minutes before the rapper got up off his knees.

"You're having a strange night," Tanesha said.

"Different," the rapper said. "Magnificent."

"Did you wish to speak with me?" Tanesha asked.

"Yes," the rapper said.

She guided him into the living room.

"Did I tell you how much I love this house?" the rapper asked.

"No," Tanesha shook her head.

"It feels so... warm," the rapper said. "It's as if the house were alive. We are safe, warm..."

The rapper nodded.

"We've been very happy here," Tanesha said.

"That's not surprising," the rapper said.

"Did you want to talk about Jeraine?" Tanesha asked.

"Yes," the rapper said. "I spoke with Schmidty, and we ironed out a schedule that might work."

"Okay," Tanesha said.

"I think he'd like to tour with my wife," the rapper said. "She travels with her mother and our daughter. If it works for you, Jer can bring his mother or father with him until you're out of school. He can bring Jabari, if that's not too much trouble."

There was a tap at the door, and Rodney came in the door.

"Miss T?" Rodney called from the door.

"Oh, my God — that's Rodney Smith," the rapper said.

"I'm in here," Tanesha said. She got up. "This is my father."

"Your father," the rapper said. "I... I... Oh Lord..."

Rodney hugged Tanesha in hello. He scowled at the rapper.

"You are a great inspiration to me, sir," the rapper said.

"Me?" Rodney asked.

"Your interviews from prison," the rapper said. "You forgave everyone. You got on with your life. You and your wife — are you...?"

"Yvie's waiting for me at home," Rodney said. "We just took

our grandson to the park for a picnic."

The rapper beamed at Rodney. Feeling movement in the house, Rodney looked up as Fin came down the stairs.

"Rodney," Fin said.

He held his arm out. Rodney grabbed Fin's forearm. Fin returned the gesture. With the other arm, they hugged.

"How is he?" Rodney asked.

"His head is. . ." Fin said. He noticed the rapper. "You are still here."

"Knock it off," Tanesha said. "He wants to tell me about a plan for Jer, and you're all 'I'm the Prince.'"

Fin laughed at her imitation of his voice. Fin patted Rodney on the back.

"Shall we listen to the plan?" Fin asked Rodney.

"I need to get clothes for Jabari. And Toto," Rodney said. He looked at Tanesha. "Jabari said that Toto doesn't like school, so he stayed home. But Toto can't sleep without him."

"Oh," Tanesha said. "I washed Toto. He's. . ."

She was about to get the stuffed elephant. She stopped short and pointed at Fin.

"Behave," Tanesha said to Fin.

"You have my word," Fin said.

She left with Rodney. When they returned, they found Fin and the rapper drinking beer and smoking cigars on the back porch.

"He says Jer can bring someone with him to help," Fin said. "I guess James Schmidt has already spoken with the gorgeous Dionne and Leroy. . ."

"Who's that?" the rapper asked.

"Bumpy," Tanesha said.

"Really?" the rapper asked.

"I'd be happy to let the man know you think that about his name," Rodney said.

"I meant no disrespect, certainly not to the best bassist in the world," the rapper said. "I've just never heard his name."

Rodney gave the man a firm nod. Tanesha smiled.

"Looks like it's all handled," Rodney said. "That's good."

"When you're done with school this summer, you can come along," the rapper said. "He'll be in Europe. Jabari can come with him or come with you. Either way, he's welcome."

Tanesha raised her eyebrows.

"You've never been?" the rapper asked.

Tanesha and Rodney shook their heads in unison.

"Well, you'll both have to come," the rapper said. "On me. We'll show you the sights. It will be fun."

"What if Jer gets sick?" Tanesha asked. "Or can't handle it? Or both?"

"That's the beauty of it," the rapper said. "He's not on the bill. He can do as much or as little as he wants. When we get an idea of how he's doing, then we'll let people know or maybe just let the Internet do its magic. Either way, the chance that he'll be there will help us to sell out the tour."

Tanesha nodded.

"If I come to the Isle of Man, will you show me around?" the rapper asked Fin. "To all the secret places and shit."

"It would be my pleasure," Fin said. "Especially to show you the shit."

The rapper laughed. Fin smiled.

"I need to get back," Rodney said. "Yvie's waiting on me."

Tanesha showed Rodney out. He kissed her cheek and left the house. When she returned to the back porch, Fin was grilling steaks, and the rapper was laughing. She settled in to have a beer. She was so relieved that all of this had worked out that she didn't mind the late night or the grilling. She just relaxed and let Fin do his thing.

~~~~~~~~

Tuesday early morning —1:55 a.m.

Denver, Colorado

"Mom?" Tink asked in a loud whisper from the stairwell.

She rounded the corner into the sitting area by the kitchen. Seeing Blane and the new infant, she stopped short. He was holding a bottle for the baby. She glanced up the stairs.

"Hi," Blane said.

"Sorry," Tink said. "I thought Mom was here."

"Just me," Blane said. "I figured she could use a break. She's been up every night with him."

"I know," Tink said. She looked up the stairs.

"What's going on?" Blane asked.

"Nothing," Tink said. She started up the stairs.

"Why don't you keep me company?" Blane asked.

"I don't... I mean... you want me to?" Tink asked.

"Sure!" Blane said. "I haven't seen you in a month."

"It seems like forever," Tink said. She stood in place for a moment before going toward the kitchen. "Mom usually makes me tea."

"I can," Blane said. He tried to get up. The bottle fell, and the baby cried.

"It's okay," Tink said. "How 'bout I turn on the pot and come right back?"

"Great," Blane smiled. He sat down and resituated himself with the baby and the bottle. "This takes some practice."

"It does," Tink said. "Just a sec."

When she came back, he smiled at her.

"I had it down with Mack," Blane said. "But that was like gassing up a moving vehicle."

"Yeah," Tink smiled. "Mack is a wild kid."

Blane nodded.

"This little guy was inside Mom, you know," Tink patted her belly, "when Mom took over her role in Olympus."

Blane thought for a moment and then nodded.

"Do you think that's why he's so mellow?" Tink asked.

"Probably," Blane said. "He's very sweet."

Tink nodded. The kettle whistled, and she got up to make tea. She returned with a cup of peppermint for Blane and some relaxing tea for herself.

"I like that you call Heather 'Mom' now," Blane said.

"She took a bullet for me," Tink said. "She made me go with Tanesha."

"She's a good mother," Blane said. "Do you think I'll ever be 'Dad'?"

"Do you want to be?" Tink asked.

"Yeah," Blane said. "It surprises me, but I do."

"Okay," Tink said. "We'll try it out. But if it doesn't fit. . ."

"Fair enough," Blane said.

They sat in silence for a few minutes.

"Are you anxious about tomorrow?" Blane asked.

Tink nodded. Knowing there was nothing he could say to help, Blane gave her an understanding nod. Tink drank her tea. After a while, she was falling asleep, and the baby had finished his bottle. Blane touched her leg. She got up and went up the stairs. He followed her up. At her room, she stopped.

"Good night, Dad," Tink said.

"Good night," Blane said. "How was that?"

"Really good," Tink said with a smile.

She waved and closed her door. Blane went into their bedroom. He dropped the baby in his bassinette and checked on Mack. Slipping into bed, he sighed.

"It's great to be home," he whispered.

CHAPTER THREE HUNDRED AND SEVENTY
WHAT YOU BELIEVE

Tuesday morning — 10:45 a.m.

"Um, okay," Tink said.

She'd been up on the stand for almost two hours. Since she'd been the last girl to be assaulted, they wanted to start the trial with her testimony. In answer to the District Attorney's questions, she'd gone through all of the horribleness. She'd broken down twice and started to shake violently about a half hour ago. She'd just finished talking about her head injury and how she almost died. She'd just talked about being in a coma for nearly a month.

"We ask the court if we might recall this witness if we need her," the District Attorney said.

"So ordered," the Judge said.

The District Attorney gave Tink a warm smile and a nod. Tink swallowed hard. The next thing that would happen was the cretin's defense attorney would ask her questions. Feeling movement, Tink watched Samantha Hargreaves move up to the District Attorney's table. Samantha was acting as Tink's attorney. Samantha had told Tink that she would be there in case the Defense Attorney was a real jerk. Samantha had said that the Defense Attorney wouldn't risk being too mean because he might risk alienating the jury. Samantha gave Tink a toothy grin. Tink smiled back at her.

"Ms. Lipson?" the Judge asked.

Tink turned to look at him.

"Sir," Tink said.

"Do you know what's going to happen next?" the Judge asked.

"The jerk's attorney is going to try to make it seem like it was my fault that they beat me up and gang-raped me," Tink said.

For the briefest moment, the Judge flashed her a smile before giving a solemn shaking his head.

"He's going to ask you questions about what happened," the Judge said. "All we want here is the truth."

The Judge looked at the Defense Attorney, who was moving toward Tink.

"I will not put up with any witness baiting, grandstanding, or storytelling," the Judge said. "I have no problem putting you in contempt of court."

"Me?" Tink asked in a horrified voice.

"Him," the Judge said.

"Oh," Tink said. "Sorry."

The Judge smiled at her.

"If you have any questions — any at all — don't hesitate to stop and ask me," the Judge said. "You remember how to do this?"

"I listen to the question," Tink said. "Think and then answer."

"Exactly," the Judge said. "Not too fast, not too slow. Don't let him bully you into saying something you haven't thought through."

Tink nodded. The Judge gestured to the Defense Attorney.

"You may begin," the Judge said.

"So, Tiffany, you're a prostitute," the Defense Attorney said.

"I am not," Tink said.

"Objection," Samantha jumped to her feet.

"Fine," the Defense Attorney gave her an evil smile. "Tink is a prostitute, and Tiffany is not."

"What?" Tink gave the Defense Attorney a baffled look. "My fairy name is 'Tink.' My father named me, 'Tiffany.' I have two names."

"Overruled," the Judge said. with a nod to Samantha. "It's

better for her to do this."

"So you're a prostitute," the Defense Attorney said.

"I am not," Tink said.

"Objection, your honor," Samantha jumped to her feet again. "The Defense Attorney is badgering my client!"

"Your pimp is Charlie Delgado," the Defense Attorney said. "This trick got out of hand, and you expect my client. . ."

"Are you insane?" Tink asked.

"Give her a moment," the Judge said to Samantha. To the defense attorney, he said, "Ask a question or sit down."

"Yes, your honor," the Defense Attorney said as he gave the Judge a sickening smile. "Are you a prostitute?"

"No," Tink said.

"Were you ever a prostitute?" the Defense Attorney asked.

"No," Tink said.

"You expect me to believe that?" the Defense Attorney asked.

"I don't care what you believe," Tink said.

"Admit it," the Defense Attorney said. "This was a trick that you were well paid for and then cried rape afterward."

Samantha jumped to her feet again.

"That is not what happened," Tink said. "And when is it that I 'cried rape'? Was it when I was having a seizure from the hole they made in my skull? Or when I was in a coma for a month?"

"I. . ." the Defense Attorney started to say.

"How about when your client broke out my front teeth to make it easier for him and his buddies to force their dicks in my mouth?" Tink asked. "Or maybe it's when he did this so I would stop screaming?"

Tink jumped to her feet and pulled her top up to show a jagged scar that ran down her right side. The jury gasped, and the Defense Attorney started to scream. The Judge banged his gavel, and Samantha Hargreaves was yelling at the Judge.

"Your client gave me this with the pointy toe of the silver-tipped boots he's wearing today. Look, they're a perfect match for the cut." Tink pointed to the defendant's boot. She looked the defendant straight in the eye and added, "Thought those boots would scare me. Not a chance. I'm not afraid of you."

Breathing hard, Tink stopped talking. She glanced at Samantha Hargreaves. Samantha's face was red, and she was yelling. She glanced at the Defense Attorney. His face was a mask of cruelty. He looked like, given the chance, he would have punched Tink. The District Attorney was on his feet, but he looked like he'd just swallowed a canary. The Judge was pounding his gavel and yelling for order.

Tink began to panic. The world darkened, and her breath tightened. She glanced at the jury, and they were looking at her, which made her panic more. Her eyes floated over the crowd in the courtroom. A few reporters were taking notes. A few supporters of the rapist were sitting just behind him. Somehow, over the din of voices, Tink heard Heather clear her throat. Tink's eyes flicked to the back.

Heather and Blane had been sitting near the door. Right now, her parents were on their feet. Jill was standing next to Heather, and Sandy was standing on Jill's other side. Sandy looked furious. Jill looked worried, but Heather looked. . .

"Isn't this ridiculous?" Tink heard Heather's voice in her head. "Stupid man thought he could make you look bad so this would just disappear."

Tink covered her mouth so no one could see her smile.

"How are you doing this?" Tink asked into her hand.

Heather's eyes flicked to the statue of justice on the Judge's desk. When Tink looked, the woman transformed into the Goddess Hera. Tink grinned when Hera waved at her.

"You're not alone," the little statue Hera said.

Tink nodded. She squared her shoulders and leaned back in her chair. When she did, the adults stopped screaming. The Judge turned to her.

"Are you all right, Ms. Lipson?" the Judge asked.

"Yes, sir," Tink said. "I was a little... rattled, scared, but... it's nice to see my parents. They're in the back there."

Tink pointed. The Judge, the District Attorney, and the Defense Attorney turned to look. Not one to miss an opportunity to be heard, Samantha Hargreaves voiced her objections again.

"Can you continue?" the Judge asked.

"Yes, sir," Tink said. Her eyes flicked to Heather and Blane, who both smiled at her, and then to Hera in the statue. "I can continue."

Heather and Blane sat down in their seats. Sandy stayed standing for a minute before Jill pulled her back down into her seat. Samantha Hargreaves and the District Attorney were still standing.

"You," the Judge pointed at the Defense Attorney. "This is your one and only warning. If you cannot contain yourself, you will see the inside of my jail. You've got that?"

"Yes, sir," the Defense Attorney pretended to be regretful.

"Ms. Hargreaves?" the Judge asked.

"Your Honor?" Samantha asked.

"Your client has said she can continue," the Judge said. "As you know, we have a lot to get through. Are you all right if she continues?"

Samantha looked at Tink before nodding.

"Yes, your honor," Samantha said.

"Here's how we're going to continue. You, sir." The Judge pointed at the Defense Attorney.

"Your honor?" the Defense Attorney asked.

"You will ask the witness questions," the Judge said. "You will not make statements or tell stories or accuse this child of one thing. Do you understand?"

"Yes, your honor," the Defense Attorney said.

"You may proceed," the Judge said.

"I'm just wondering why, after being paid to have sex with all comers, you decided that you were raped," the Defense Attorney said.

"Bailiff?" the Judge pointed to the Bailiff. "Please take the Defense Attorney into custody. Twenty-four hours should help you remember to respect the rules of this court."

The Defense Attorney started to protest, and the Judge just pointed to him with the gavel. The Bailiff took the Defense Attorney out of the court. The assistant Defense Attorney got up from the table.

"Do you remember my instructions?" the Judge asked.

"Yes, your honor," the woman said.

"A toe out of line, and you will join your colleague," the Judge said.

"Yes, your honor," the woman said.

"You may proceed," the Judge said.

"Are you a prostitute?" the woman asked Tink.

The Judge banged his gavel. The jury looked worried.

"This witness has answered that question," the Judge said. "Would you like me to have the question and answer read to you from the record?"

"No, your honor," the woman said.

"Do you have another question for this witness, or shall I dismiss her?" the Judge asked.

"I. . . uh. . ." the woman ran back to the table. She grabbed a legal pad.

"This looks like a good time for a break," the Judge said. "Jury, you have your instructions. I want to see all of the attorneys — every last one of you — in my chambers."

The Judge banged his gavel. In a flow of robes, he disappeared. Tink sat for only a moment on the witness stand before Samantha arrived. The assistant Defense Attorney tried to get to Tink, but Samantha blocked the way. A small woman, Samantha still managed to keep the assistant Defense Attorney away from Tink. The assistant Defense Attorney said something, but at that moment Hera started singing. Tink heard only the Goddess's lovely tune.

"Did the statue move?" Samantha asked under her breath.

"It's Hera," Tink said.

"Good to know," Samantha said. "I have to go with them. Are you all right?"

Tink nodded and smiled.

"Go to lunch with your parents," Samantha said. "I'll call you if anything happens."

Tink nodded. Samantha followed the District Attorney out of the courtroom. Tink went to where Heather and Blane were waiting for her. They were leaving the courtroom when a group of photographers started yelling at Tink. She felt panic closing in again.

Blane grabbed Tink's left elbow, and Heather grabbed her right. They marched her right past the photographers. Heather and Blane stayed at her side as they walked out of the courtroom and into Civic Center Park.

"Where are we going?" Tink asked.

Heather smiled. She nodded toward a bench where Charlie, Wanda, and Ivy were sitting. Delphie was opening a cooler filled with sandwiches and sodas. Charlie's friend Dale arrived with bags of chips.

"I thought you could use some air," Heather said.

Tink smiled and ran forward to say hello to her friends. For the first time since she woke up in the hospital, she was absolutely sure that she was going to get through this.

~~~~~~~~

Tuesday mid-day — 12:45 a.m.

"Hi," Sandy said as she walked into the Castle kitchen.

Delphie's head was in the refrigerator, so she didn't hear her. Sandy stood at the counter for a moment. Delphie turned around to get the rest of the left-over picnic. She squealed and jumped when she saw Sandy.

"Sorry," Sandy said. "I said something, but you didn't hear me."

Delphie gave a nervous laugh. She shook herself head to toe before scowling at Sandy.

"What's happened?" Delphie asked. "Is Tink. . .?"

"Nothing," Sandy said. "They are doing some court procedures. Samantha filed those documents to protect the kids who are testifying. The defense filed documents against the court. The Judge dismissed the jury for the afternoon. Everyone is due back at three or so."

"Just another game," Delphie said.

"That's what Samantha said," Sandy nodded. "She thinks the defense is trying to unnerve Tink so they're letting her linger today. She doesn't think the court will convene again until tomorrow morning."

"Another awful night for Tink," Delphie shook her head in empathy for the girl. "We should have them over. Make a party out of it."

Sandy grinned at Delphie, and Delphie nodded.

"I'll call Jacob," Delphie said. She moved toward the phone.

"First," Sandy said. Delphie turned to look at her. Sandy took a check out of her pocket. "I wanted to give you this for rent for the last two years."

"What?" Delphie asked. She put her hands on her heart to not receive the check. "You don't have to. . ."

"We'd like to," Sandy said. "You rescued me when Aden went to prison. Nash and Noelle. We were planning on leaving town. I would have died if I hadn't been right here in this magical home. When Sissy and Charlie came along, you just made space for them. You never asked for anything."

Delphie's eyes welled with tears.

"We have been so overwhelmed with medical bills and... everything," Sandy said with a nod. "We haven't been able to pay rent. We've missed food bills sometimes."

"You always catch up," Delphie said.

"I know," Sandy said. "But..."

Sandy sighed. She set the check on the counter and held her hands out. Delphie released her heart and took Sandy's hands.

"Schmidty sold my mother's creation for a few hundred million dollars," Sandy said.

"What?" Delphie looked confused and shook her head. "I knew it would sell but..."

"*Hundreds of millions* of dollars," Sandy said.

"How... what...?" Delphie asked.

"Her project is set up in six pieces," Sandy said. "They go together beautifully, like phases of life. Seth has been hired to split them up and make them into something... a movie series, I think. I don't know."

"Wow," Delphie said. "What are you going to do?"

"We wanted to make real college funds for the kids," Sandy said. "I mean, we had these anemic funds that would have paid for one pizza or..."

Sandy shrugged.

"I went to the bank to make real accounts, but it turns out that Seth has already done it," Sandy said. "Nash, Noelle, and Teddy too. A percentage of what he makes goes into these funds."

"And you didn't know?" Delphie asked.

"There's a percentage of his money that's controlled by an investment banker. I keep track that the money going in matches what he has, but, otherwise, it's all controlled by this guy in New York," Sandy said. "It's supposed to be a retirement, injury, long-term care, life insurance, that kind of thing. He added these funds to that set."

"The kids don't need your money," Delphie said.

"No," Sandy said.

"I don't need your money," Delphie said. She stood up straighter and stuck her chin out.

"You do," Sandy said. "We do. Since Lipson had trouble with the state, we've all been pinching pennies."

"Your kids had really taken up the slack!" Delphie said.

"Please," Sandy picked up the check and held it out to her. "It's important to me to repay your generosity and kindness."

"Why?" Delphie asked.

"Because we want to stay," Sandy said with a smile. "We talked about moving, buying a house, or whatever, but we really love living here. You've made a real home for us — the first that Sissy and Charlie have ever known. Nash and Noelle won't hear of us leaving."

"You want to stay?" Delphie's hands went back to her heart. She gave Sandy a watery smile.

"But we want to be full partners," Sandy said. "We have some money now, so we can help with the rehabilitation and pay for the niceties."

"Like new trees to replace the apricots that died?" Delphie asked. "Jacob said we'd have to replace them with saplings. I might not live long enough to eat my own apricots again!"

"Like new trees," Sandy said.

She shook the check at Delphie, who took the check.

"It's so much!" Delphie said.

"We took the average rate for rent by square footage and figured out what our place was," Sandy said. "It might seem like a lot, but it's fair."

"Are you sure?" Delphie asked.

"I'm absolutely sure," Sandy said. "We'll start paying every month, too."

"You'll have to talk to Jake about all of that," Delphie said. She waved the check. "New trees for me!"

Delphie smiled and set the check on the counter.

"If you'd like, I can take you to the bank," Sandy said.

"Oh," Delphie blushed. "I don't have a bank account. Jake will take care of it."

Sandy winced.

"You already tried to give him a check?" Delphie asked.

"Aden did," Sandy said. "He refused it."

Delphie smiled at her.

"Cash?" Sandy asked.

"Just leave it to me," Delphie said. "I'll talk to him. He knows we need the money. He mostly doesn't want you guys to leave. We all love having you here."

Sandy smiled.

"What else are you going to do with the money?" Delphie asked.

"Well, you know how Honey and MJ's apartment building for the disabled is on hold," Sandy said.

"Ran out of money," Delphie nodded.

"We're going to join them as investors," Sandy said. "We're going to buy more of Lipson Construction, too. I can pay off my bill to Jacob for my studio and look at expanding."

"That's right — the shop next to you is open," Delphie said.

Sandy nodded and smiled.

"Mostly, we want to invest in our town — our community and friends," Sandy said. "When I had nothing, my community reached out and helped me. Now that I can, I want to help — starting with my friends and family."

"You know Blane lost his treatment room," Delphie said in a sly voice. "It flooded in the last storm."

"That's why I thought I could expand," Sandy said. "We could make a nice treatment center next door, and then. . ."

"Tink's brother could move in with them," Delphie said.

Sandy nodded.

"They need more space," Sandy said. "Heather's going to let us help them either get another house or add on to theirs. I owe her... so much... that... I'm just glad she's letting me help."

"I like the way you think!" Delphie said.

Delphie hugged Sandy.

"I need to get to the studio," Sandy said as she moved away from Delphie. "I'm so behind that people want to come in when I'm available. I have a couple of hours, so I can see a couple of people."

"Good thinking," Delphie said.

Sandy smiled and turned to leave. She was halfway through the living room when Delphie ran up behind her.

"Thank you," Delphie said. "Really, this will help a lot."

Sandy smiled.

"You'd better hurry!" Delphie said.

"Oh," Sandy said and ran out of the house.

Laughing, Delphie returned to putting their picnic away.

~~~~~~~~~

Tuesday afternoon — 3:45 p.m.

Tink shifted uncomfortably in the chair. She'd been called up here right after they'd returned to the court at three. She'd been sitting here while the lawyers did this or that. No one had talked to her or asked her any questions or anything. She'd just been sitting here while everyone argued. Her butt had fallen asleep a half hour ago.

The Judge banged his gavel.

"It's getting late," the Judge said. "You need to wrap this up, or we'll adjourn."

"Judge, I..." a new defense attorney started to ramble.

Tink watched the clock. She remembered this story that Albert Einstein figured out his great theory of relativity when he was staring at a clock. The great Einstein realized that time seemed to drag when things were slow while time seemed to speed up when he was having fun. The long hand of the clock clicked over to four o'clock.

"Ms. Lipson?" the Judge asked.

Tink shook herself out of her bored meditation. Her eyes flicked to the Judge. He gave her a kind, understanding smile.

"We're at a point where we can adjourn for the day," the Judge said. "That would mean that you'd have to come back tomorrow morning."

Tink nodded.

"Do you feel fit enough to answer a few more questions?" the Judge asked. "The defense assures me they only have one or two more."

"I'd rather do it today, if that's okay," Tink said.

"Of course," the Judge said. "Defense?"

Tink sat up straight in her chair. Even though she willed it not to, her heart pounded in her chest. Samantha Hargreaves leaned forward to be ready in case something happened. The District Attorney set down his expensive pen on a blank page of a legal pad. He leaned back with practiced ease. The jury shifted in their chairs.

All of the defense attorneys stared at Tink. Feeling their malice, Tink licked her lips and swallowed hard. She glanced at the statue and saw Hera scowling at the defense attorneys. She looked back, and the defense was whispering among themselves.

"Defense?" the Judge asked again.

"Sorry, your honor," the assistant defense attorney said. "We need just a moment."

Tink looked at the clock and it said four-o-seven. The thought that she'd been sitting here for more than an hour only served to make Tink more anxious. Feeling movement, she glanced back at the defense table.

"We have no further questions for this witness."

CHAPTER THREE HUNDRED AND SEVENTY-ONE
OW

Tuesday evening — 5:12 p.m.
Denver, Colorado

"How are you, Sis?" Sandy asked.

Sissy gave Sandy a beautiful smile. Sandy wasn't sure if it was the video link or if her sister had aged in the two days since she'd seen Sissy last.

"You look. . . great," Sandy said.

"I gained weight in the hospital," Sissy said. "It makes me look more human, less skeletal. Ivan says I will have to lose it."

Sissy shrugged. Someone said something off the screen, and Sissy laughed.

"Bestat said that suffering is causing me to grow into the edges of myself," Sissy said.

She smiled at Sandy and waited a beat for something to happen off screen. Sissy leaned forward.

"Any idea what that means?" Sissy asked.

Shaking her head, Sandy laughed. Sissy smiled.

"How are you, Sis?" Sandy repeated.

"Okay, I guess," Sissy said with a shrug of her shoulder. "I've been able to get around a little. Walk, I mean. The last couple of days, Bestat's massage person, Yuia, has been working on me. Twice a day."

"That sounds nice," Sandy smiled.

"It's awful," Sissy said.

"Awful? How so?"

"Painful," Sissy said. "Hard. It's like he's rearranging my

muscles. But. . ."

Sissy shrugged.

"I can walk, now," Sissy said. "So it's kind of miraculous. I still have to wear this."

Sissy pointed to the nose cannula pumping oxygen into her.

"How are your lungs?" Sandy asked.

"They're healing," Sissy said. "That's the best they can tell me. It's hard to heal something that I use all the time and need to live."

"Your lungs?" Sandy smiled.

"I know," Sissy laughed. "I keep remembering what you said to me when I was in the last eating-disorder place."

"What did I say?" Sandy asked.

"You told me that sometimes the thing we need the most is the thing we're the most afraid of," Sissy said. "You meant 'food.' But. . ."

Sissy took a full breath.

"Now, it means breath," Sissy said. "Yuia, the massage guy, says that I am afraid to breathe, so my body holds my ribs tight."

She gestured to her side. With her movement, Sandy noticed her sister's fuller breasts. Sissy was becoming a woman. She gave Sissy a soft smile. Sissy blushed when she looked back at Sandy.

"You noticed how big I am?" Sissy asked. "It's like the hospital gown made them big!"

Sissy held her hands in front of her to gesture to her breasts.

"Do you still want to cut them off?" Sandy asked.

Sissy shook her head.

"I'm coming to accept my precious body as it is," Sissy said with a giggle. "That's the mantra Yuia gave me. Well, his is: 'I accept my precious and beautiful body as it is,' but that was too much for me. Bestat suggested the change. I think it works for me where I am now. Someday, I'll be able to do the other one. I'm supposed to say it all the time."

"He sounds pretty fantastic," Sandy said.

"You wouldn't say that if you had to spend an hour with him," Sissy said. She leaned forward. Her face contorted in pain. "Ow."

Surprised, Sandy jumped, but Sissy laughed. Sissy was only imitating her time with Yuia. Sandy smiled. It seemed like a hundred years since Sissy had been so joyous.

"How is Ivan?" Sandy asked.

Sissy's face flushed. Her eyes seemed brighter, and her lips turned up with a smile.

"Ivan is Ivan," Sissy said. "He can't walk yet, but he's got a lot to say about what I should be doing."

Sissy grinned.

"He's been coming to see Yuia," Sissy said. "I think Yuia is harder on him, but he doesn't complain or groan like I do. He thanks Yuia for his treatment and is very sincere. It's nice."

"What's his mantra?" Sandy asked.

"'I am not the king of everything,'" Sissy said with a laugh.

"They *are* good mantras!" Sandy said. "Next time I'm there, I'll have to see this healer of yours."

"When are you coming?" Sissy asked in a bright voice. She wrinkled her nose. "I miss you."

"Well, it's kind of why I'm calling," Sandy said.

"What's happened?" Sissy asked. "Did someone die? Did they kill someone else?"

"No," Sandy said with an assuring smile. "Everyone is ridiculously healthy."

"Give them a minute," Sissy said.

Sandy grinned. Sissy wrinkled her nose again.

"I have to testify?" Sissy asked.

"Tink had a rough time today," Sandy said. "You know I can't talk about it, but they thought if you could testify before Charlie, we'd move forward faster."

Sissy lifted her lip in a classic teenage sneer. Sandy smiled.

"You can testify from New York," Sandy said. "It's all set up, but. . ."

"I should come to Denver," Sissy said with a nod. "That would be a better show."

Sandy smiled. Ever since Sissy was a little girl, she'd talked about the importance of putting on a good show. Sissy nodded.

"How would I do it?" Sissy asked.

"Seth and Ava will escort you," Sandy said. "That way, there's room for Ivan and Nadia and whoever else you'd like to come."

Sissy gave a slow nod.

"I don't really want to leave here," Sissy said.

"I know," Sandy said. "But real ballerinas travel around the world. This is a good chance to practice traveling."

"I don't think I'll ever be a ballerina." Sissy's voice echoed her sorrow.

Sandy stopped short. From the moment Sissy could talk, she'd spoken of dancing. From the time she could walk, she'd talked about ballet. Ivan didn't bring ballet to Sissy. Her sister's confidence that she would be a great ballerina brought Ivan to her via Seth and her father, Mitch. Sandy had never heard Sissy ever doubt that this was her future.

"What's going on, Sis?" Sandy asked.

"Oh, nothing," Sissy said.

"Nothing?"

"I feel. . . blue, I guess," Sissy said.

"How come?" Sandy asked.

"It just seems like the meaner, richer guys always win."

"What's going on, Sis?" Sandy asked.

"You remember that ballerina?" Sissy asked. "The one who made so much trouble for Ivan and me?"

"Sabrina?" Sandy asked. "I remember her."

"She's dancing the lead in the spring," Sissy said. "*She's* advancing while I. . ."

Ever the teenager, Sissy's mood jumped from pure delight to

absolute sorrow in less than a second. Sissy sighed.

"Sissy Delgado!" Sandy said. "You know darn well that you're going to get better. You know that you'll be dancing again. It just takes time. In a few years, you'll wonder why you have these scars."

"Will I?" Sissy asked. She shrugged. "Maybe it's good that I'm going home."

"It feels like defeat," Sandy said.

Sissy nodded.

"Well," Sandy said. She tipped her head to the side to think for a moment. "What if we make our own plan? You can come home for a short trip, like you're a rock star. You'll take care of this court stuff and return to New York by the weekend. This way you get to see everyone. . ."

"I miss Buster," Sissy said of their ugly dog.

"And Buster," Sandy said. "You'll be back to the toil in no time."

"But. . ." Sissy started.

"Seth has to be back in New York by next Monday, at the latest," Sandy said. "You can go with him. He won't let you down."

Sissy gave Sandy a sad nod.

"Did you talk to Schmidty?" Sandy asked.

Sissy nodded.

"He told me that he got the company to hold your place for a year," Sandy said.

"What if I can't dance in a year?" Sissy asked.

Sandy smiled at Sissy, but the girl was looking down at the floor. When Sandy didn't say anything, Sissy looked up.

"Oh." Sissy read her sister's look. "I was in surgery on Friday."

"And Saturday," Sandy said.

"That means that I'm still in active detox from the meds," Sissy brightened. "*That's* why I'm acting all weird."

"Probably," Sandy said.

"You don't think it's crazy that I still want to. . ." Sissy sighed. ". . .dance?"

"No," Sandy said. "I think you're Mitch Delgado's daughter. If there's a will. . ."

"There's a Delgado to get it done," Sissy said with a laugh. "Can Ivan come?"

"Of course," Sandy said. "You can bring anyone you'd like."

Sissy smiled.

"Oh, Bestat got me something to wear," Sissy said. "That's funny, I wonder how she knew."

Sandy shrugged.

"When do I leave?" Sissy asked.

In the background, the doorbell rang.

"Now?" Sissy asked.

Sandy nodded.

"Great!" Sissy said. "I'll see you in a few hours. Make sure that Buster isn't sleeping with Noelle, so he can sleep with me!"

Sissy waved and was gone. Sandy stared at the blank screen for a moment.

"She's growing," Delphie said. Sandy turned to look at her. "Don't worry, Sandy. She's going to be fine."

Sandy nodded. Standing, she took a breath.

"What can I do for dinner?" Sandy asked.

"Well. . ." Delphie turned and left the room.

Sandy glanced at the computer one last time before following her to the kitchen.

~~~~~~~~~~

Tuesday evening — 7:02 p.m.
Denver, Colorado

Tanesha walked down the street toward the little yellow house. She'd had a long day of being terrified by all that she needed to learn before the end of the term. She had so much work to do that her work had work to do. She was glad that Fin was her lab partner. His arrogant confidence in her abilities was her only defense against her bone-crushing fatigue and its dance partner — terror of failing. Everyone's confidence that she'd do well this year in medical school only served to make her more certain that she would fail miserably.

She'd gotten off the bus a stop early so that she could walk off her nerves before seeing Jeraine and Jabari. Her little family needed her to be clear and calm. Especially since Jeraine was likely to leave on Friday for at least the rest of the spring and summer and. . . She didn't know how long. She sighed.

She hated to admit it, but she was going to miss him. Plus, he was taking Jabari with him.

Of course, Heather and her tribe were moving in the moment he left. They were going to add onto their tiny home. Plus, Heather had to leave for Olympia in a week or so. They needed a safe place to stay until all of the chaos was over. Tanesha had agreed to let them move in as long as Blane promised to feed her through the next few weeks of studying and finals. Blane wasn't able to work, so he agreed to be her house frau.

She was still going to miss Jeraine, which bugged her to no end.

Turning onto their street, she saw that the lights were on and music was filtering out into the street. Aunt Phy and her gran were sitting in the rockers on her porch. She squinted at them as she approached.

"Look!" Aunt Phy said brightly. "Our Tanesha is home!"

Tanesha's gran turned to look at her. For the first time, Tanesha saw how much her gran had aged. She made a mental note to ask Fin if Gran was sick. The thought was pushed out of her mind when her Gran smiled. Tanesha couldn't remember a time that her gran had smiled. As she moved through the white picket fence, she noticed that Gran and Aunt Phy were smoking from a pipe.

"Phy! Gran!" Tanesha said. "Marijuana? Really?"

The elderly women looked at Tanesha and giggled like little girls.

"It's legal here now," Aunt Phy said.

Tanesha scowled at the women, which made them giggle more. Shaking her head, she went to the door.

"Oh, Tanesha?" Gran asked.

Tanesha turned to look at her.

"Will you bring us some of those brownies?" Gran asked.

"And maybe some lemonade?" Aunt Phy asked. "My mouth is just filled with. . ."

Aunt Phy stuck her tongue in and out of her mouth a few times, which made Gran laugh. Shaking her head, Tanesha went inside. She stopped short.

A gorgeous woman with perfect, straightened hair was sitting on her couch. The woman was wearing designer clothes, and her makeup was as flawless as her hair. Jabari was standing on her lap. He had his arm around her neck. She was laughing and talking to the rapper who'd come by the house yesterday. The house smelled of delicious food, which meant that Jeraine had been cooking. The music was playing just loud enough so that no one heard her come in. She was invisible to the beautiful and extremely wealthy.

Tanesha's heart stopped. Her hand instinctively went to her own small sister dreads. She felt small and stupid. Suddenly, the place that had been her home, her sanctuary, belonged to this modern Goddess who dominated the airwaves. Tanesha felt the loss with all the shock and horror of removing a limb.

Tanesha looked up to see her mother standing in the door to the kitchen. Her mother was positively radiant tonight. She heard the low rumble of her father's voice coming from the kitchen. Rather than grounding her into her own life, the fact her parents were there only served to confirm that Tanesha had been supplanted by these superior people.

Tanesha put her hand on the doorknob to leave, only to remember that Aunt Phy and Gran were stoned and sitting on her porch. She felt like a fox in a trap. She couldn't leave, and she couldn't stay. Her anxiety rose.

Feeling someone near her, Tanesha turned to see Jeraine. He put his arms around her and held her tight.

"You okay?" he asked in her ear.

She shook her head.

"What can I do?" he asked.

She couldn't respond. Tears came to her eyes.

"Does this help?" he asked.

She nodded, and he held on. For a few minutes — or maybe an eternity — they stood in the entryway to their home holding each other tight. Tanesha took a breath, and then another.

"What happened?" Jeraine asked.

"Ow," Tanesha spoke the only word that came to her mind.

He chuckled. He kissed her neck and let her go. He took her book bag and set it down next to the table. Taking her hand, he led her into the living room.

"*Mommy!*" Jabari squealed. "You're finally home."

He climbed off the modern Goddess's lap and ran to Tanesha. She picked him up, and he hugged her tight. The modern Goddess got up from the couch, as did her rapper husband. As Tanesha entered the living room, she saw that their daughter was sitting on the kitchen bar while Rodney changed the bandage on her knee.

Tanesha blinked, and her life came into view. Jeraine brought the woman, her child, and her husband home so that Tanesha would have a chance to meet them before he signed onto the tour. Her mother and father were there to take a look at the couple. She blinked again.

Jeraine was actually doing what she'd asked him to do. She'd asked him to set up a time when she could meet them and Jabari could meet their daughter. She'd even suggested that Yvonne and

Rodney come to make sure Jabari was taken care of. She'd just not expected him to do it so soon.

"I'm so sorry," the modern Goddess said. "You look like we've disturbed you. We so wanted to get a chance to meet you that. . . well, we forced Jeraine to make us dinner tonight."

The woman gave Tanesha a big smile.

"I love this house, Princess," the modern Goddess said.

"Just 'Tanesha' please," Tanesha said.

The woman gave her a bright smile and said that Tanesha could call her by her own name. Tanesha smiled.

"If you'll excuse me for a moment," Tanesha said. "My gran and Aunt wanted some lemonade and brownies."

"I'll get it," Yvonne said.

"But Mom. . ." Tanesha started.

"Don't worry, Tannie," Yvonne said with a bright smile. "She's not as mean to me when she's stoned."

Tanesha grinned. Yvonne winked at Tanesha and went to get the lemonade and brownies.

"She's incredible," the modern Goddess said. "So beautiful, smart, kind. . . I don't think I would be able to. . ."

The woman nodded after Yvonne. Tanesha watched her mom for a moment and smiled.

"Some people are simply special," Tanesha said.

The woman smiled.

"Are you hungry?" Jeraine asked. "We waited dinner on you. Fin and Abi said they'd be here in. . ."

The door opened. Fin and a very pregnant Abi walked in. The modern Goddess and the rapper's attention was distracted by the fairies' giving Tanesha and Jeraine a quiet moment.

"Oh, great — everyone's here," Jeraine said. He kissed Tanesha's lips. On a quiet inhale, he said, "I love you."

Feeling more like herself, Tanesha watched him head into the kitchen. The visiting couple's daughter ran up and introduced herself. Jabari wiggled out of Tanesha's arms, and the children ran off to play with Toto. Yvonne came into the house from dropping off the snack to Gran and Aunt Phy. As she passed Tanesha, she muttered, "That woman is crazy."

Tanesha laughed and followed her mother into the kitchen.

~~~~~~~~~

Tuesday evening — 10:12 p.m.
Denver, Colorado

"Ready?" Aden asked.

"I think so," Sissy said.

Aden swooped Sissy off her feet. Sissy yelped with pain. He stood still for a moment to give her a chance to adjust. MJ set Sissy's oxygen tank on her lap.

"I'll come up to check on you after I get Ivan settled," MJ said.

"Thanks," Sissy said. She tried to grin, but it was clear that she was in pain.

"Fast or slow?" Aden asked the age-old question: Did Sissy want to get through the pain quickly or slowly?

"Um... fast," Sissy said. "But I might need a break."

"Say the word," Aden said. "Here we go."

Aden started up the stairs to the second floor. They made the landing.

"Break!" Sissy said.

Aden stopped on the landing. Sissy panted.

"I wanted to talk to you about something," Aden said. "I don't know if now is a good time."

"Sure," Sissy said. Her face was pal,e and she looked like she was going to throw up. "Is it anything distracting? I could really use something distracting."

"Maybe," Aden said.

"Go ahead," Sissy said.

"You know Sandy and I are doing these marriage classes, right?" Aden asked.

Sissy nodded.

"One of our assignments is to make agreements with you kids around being married," Aden said.

"That sounds kind of lame," Sissy said.

"I'm not saying it right," Aden said.

"Try again," Sissy said.

"When I marry Sandy in the church, I am marrying you and Charlie, too," Aden said. "Sandy is marrying Nash and Noelle."

"What about Rachel?" Sissy asked.

"Rachel is our biological child, so we're already married to her," Aden said.

"Oh," Sissy said. "Do you still have that bag?"

Aden nodded. He wiggled his right hand. Sissy looked down and took a grocery bag from his hand. She threw up all of the welcome-home cake she'd just consumed into the bag. She took a deep breath after throwing up and yelped with pain. Her color worsened.

"Maybe I should set you down," Aden said.

"Not on your life," Sissy said. "I made it half way there. I'm not losing the half."

Aden grinned.

"Why's that funny?" Sissy asked.

"It's something Sandy would say," Aden said.

Sissy smiled at the idea.

"Tie up the bag," Aden said.

"What if I need it again?" Sissy asked.

"I have another bag," Aden said.

"Ok," Sissy tied up the bag and rested it next to her oxygen tank. "What's it mean to be married to you?"

"Well," Aden said. "The first thing is that I commit to you to be your father."

Sissy's eyebrows dropped with concern.

"I don't want to take Mitch's place," Aden said. "I will just be your 'now father,' a kind of second father, here to help you through the challenges of your life."

"Don't you do that already?" Sissy asked.

Aden was so overcome by her question that he welled up with tears. She looked at his face.

"You've been the best... I don't know what you'd call it," Sissy said. "You helped Charlie stop being such a dick. You've stood by me through all of this stupid stuff. You even made friends with Ivan, which is no easy task."

"I like him," Aden said. "He has a good heart."

"So do you," Sissy said. "You're already my... whatever you want to call it."

"Legally, I'm your guardian," Aden said.

Sissy mouthed the word for a few minutes before shaking her head.

"Do I have to call you 'Dad'?" Sissy asked.

"Not if you don't want to," Aden said. They were silent for a moment while Sissy weighed her options. "Do you want to?"

"Not really," Sissy said. "But I want to be able to say to other people, 'That's my dad' or 'My dad's coming' or... stuff like that."

"I can be that guy," Aden said. "I want to be that guy."

"You already are," Sissy said with a smile. "I mean, look at you. You're up here trying to get me to the apartment so I can sleep in my own bed with Buster. And you're doing it just because I want to. I could stay down there with Honey and MJ, like Ivan is doing."

"You wanted to come home," Aden said.

"That's what a dad does," Sissy said. She leaned forward with a grunt to kiss his cheek. "Thanks Aden. I want to be married to you or... oh, that sounds gross... what do we say?"

"'I want to be a family,'" Aden said.

Sissy nodded.

"Ready for the next flight?" Aden asked.

"Onward," Sissy said.

Aden raced up the stairs. When they reached the top, tears were streaming down Sissy's face. Buster bounded down the hallway from the other way. Noelle and Nash weren't far behind.

"Say something," Aden said in a low voice.

"Ow," Sissy said.

CHAPTER THREE HUNDRED AND SEVENTY-TWO
SISSY TESTIFIES

Wednesday morning — 9:10 a.m.

"Yes, your honor," the Defense Attorney said. "We agreed to the scheduling change. We also agreed to allow Ms. Delgado assistance to the witness stand."

"I appreciate your change in attitude," the Judge said in a wry voice. The Defense Attorney opened his mouth but decided against it. Noting the Defense Attorney's restraint, the Judge said, "Good thinking."

He nodded to Samantha Hargreaves.

"Go ahead," the Judge said.

Samantha got up from the District Attorney's table and went to the door to the courtroom. The Judge had sealed the courtroom today. Sissy could have only one family member with her. They'd decided on Aden because he could help Sissy get in and out of there. Samantha held the door open. Leaning on Aden's arm, Sissy made her way into the courtroom. With each painful step, the mood in the courtroom shifted. The jury's eyes were riveted on her. Even the Defense Attorney gawked.

Sissy was, very simply, stunning. Her long hair was loose and lightly curled at the bottom. Her long neck and trim figure were accentuated by a simple ankle-length dress. Her beauty and her pain gave her the look of a fragile Ophelia on the verge of full womanhood with all the innocence and strength of a child.

While Aden helped Sissy onto the stand, the Defense team mumbled back and forth. Samantha stood in front of the witness stand to help Sissy into the seat. Aden set her small oxygen tank onto Sissy's lap. He kissed her cheek and went to sit in the back. When Sissy was situated, Samantha moved aside. The Defense team stopped talking.

For a moment, the courtroom was completely silent.

"I want to be clear," the Judge said. "I will not accept any harassment of this witness. None. If any member of your team even attempts it, the entire team will spend the night in my jail. Got it?"

He pointed to the defense team and then the prosecuting table. No one dared to blink.

"Ms. Delgado, if you have any questions, you just ask me," the Judge said. "Ms. Hargreaves will be here as well. But if you have any problems or trouble, you let me know. I'm good friends with your Uncle, Judge Howard Alberts. He'd never forgive me if anything happened to you on my watch."

"Yes, sir," Sissy said.

Samantha returned to the prosecution table while Sissy was sworn in. The District Attorney stood up.

"Please state your name," the Defense Attorney said.

"Mitzi Delgado," Sissy said. "But everyone calls me 'Sissy.'"

"We have agreed that Ms. Delgado can be identified by 'Sissy Delgado,'" said the Defense Attorney, standing.

"So noted," the Judge said.

"Ms. Delgado," the District Attorney said. "Have you ever seen the defendant before?"

"Which one is he?" Sissy asked.

"The defendant will rise," the Judge said.

A young man in an expensive suit and cowboy boots stood from the defense table.

"No, sir," Sissy said. "I've never seen him before."

"What if he was wearing a beard or his hair was longer or shorter?" the District Attorney asked.

"No, sir. I've never seen him before," Sissy said. "Plus, that stuff wouldn't matter."

"Why is that, Ms. Delgado?" the District Attorney asked.

"I study ballet," Sissy said. "I look at people by body type and how he moves. The other stuff doesn't matter."

"You study ballet?" the District Attorney asked.

"The defendant may be seated," the Judge said.

"My sister says that I came out wanting to be a ballerina," Sissy said. "I've been dancing ballet since I was four."

"You mean you took lessons at the recreation center?" the District Attorney asked. "Kiddy ballet?"

"Oh, no, sir," Sissy said. "I've had individual lessons every day after school. My teacher was the youngest soloist in the Bolshoi Ballet. He is on contract with the New York Ballet Federation and has taught here in Denver for the Denver Ballet."

"Sounds like an expensive indulgence," the District Attorney said.

"Probably," Sissy said. "My Godfather pays for everything."

"Your Godfather?" the District Attorney asked.

"He was my dad's partner at the Denver Police Department," Sissy said. "Seth O'Malley? He and my dad were the 'Magic team' — detectives who cleared more cases than anyone ever in the Denver Police Department."

"Your father is. . ."

"Was. He's dead," Sissy said.

"I'm sorry," the District Attorney said. "Who was your father?"

"Mitch Delgado," Sissy said. "He and Seth had been friends since they met at East High School."

"We acknowledge the tremendous accomplishments of Mitch Delgado." The Defense Attorney stood. "And everyone knows Seth O'Malley."

"So noted," the Judge said. "Get on with it."

"We were talking about ballet," the District Attorney said.

"What would you like to know?" Sissy asked. "Ballet is my

entire life. I've spent every moment that I wasn't in school dancing. All summer, every summer. I've been in many professional shows. At the beginning of this year, I moved to New York City to apprentice to a large ballet company in New York City. I live there now."

"I'd like to submit into evidence this article from the *New York Post* concerning Ms. Delgado's apprenticeship," the District Attorney said. "Attached is an article regarding the extraordinary talent of Ms. Delgado's teacher."

The Judge looked at the Defense table. When no objection came, he banged his gavel and the District Attorney gave the articles to the bailiff.

"So you didn't do so well in school," the District Attorney said.

"That's right, sir," Sissy said. "I had only a 3.8. I'm not great at math. But now that I'm getting tutored, I'm starting to get the hang of it. Maybe. It's not natural for me."

The District Attorney let the silence linger.

"Why are you here?" the District Attorney asked.

"Because you asked my sister Sandy if I could come," Sissy said.

The jury and audience chuckled. The Judge banged his gavel, and the courtroom became silent again.

"Rephrase the question," the Judge said.

"Ms. Delgado, this is a trial regarding the guilt or innocence of the defendant," the District Attorney said. "You've never seen him before. So I'm sure the court is wondering why you're here."

"Oh," Sissy said.

She stopped talking and looked down at her hands.

"Please answer the question, Ms. Delgado," the Judge said.

"What if I start crying?" Sissy whispered to the Judge.

The sound was picked up by the Judge's microphone, and everyone became very silent. The Judge put his hand over the microphone.

"Then you cry," the Judge said. "We can handle it."

Sissy nodded.

"Ms. Hargreaves?" the Judge asked into the microphone. "We need tissues."

Samantha hopped to her feet. She brought a box of tissues to Sissy. She squeezed Sissy's hand and went back to her seat.

"District Attorney?" the Judge asked. "Can you repeat the question?"

"It's okay," Sissy said. "I know what he's asking."

Sissy tried to take a breath. Her chest rattled, and she began to cough. Aden ran from the back of the court. He vaulted the wooden gate and was confronted by the bailiff. The Judge nodded, and Aden came to Sissy's side. He helped her slow her breathing.

"Sir, my client is simply too fragile for. . ." Samantha started.

"No," Sissy roared. "I can do it."

Aden returned to the audience.

"Sorry," Sissy said. "I just got out of the hospital. I'm not breathing very good."

She gestured to the oxygen tank.

"Please continue," the Judge said.

"I was shot," Sissy said. "The shooter came for my step-sister Noelle and me. We were just getting home from dinner, and he. . ."

Sissy looked up for the first time. All of the adults were standing at the tables. The District Attorney's mouth was open. The Defense Attorney seemed stunned. Unwilling to look at her, the defendant looked down.

"I was shot twice in the ribs," Sissy said. "I died on the sidewalk, but they got me going again. Then last Friday, a piece of bone got loose, and I hemorrhaged. My family came to New York because they thought I was going to die. I fooled them."

She gave a slight smile.

"I've been really sick," Sissy said.

"What does this incident have to do with this trial?" the

District Attorney asked.

"The shooter tried to kill us to keep Noelle from testifying in this trial," Sissy said. "He tried to kill me so my brother Charlie wouldn't testify in this trial."

"Objection," the Defense Attorney said. "Assumption on the part of the witness."

"No, sir," Sissy said. "That's what the shooter said. Ms. Behur's guards caught him right after he shot at us. He confessed right away."

"I'd like to enter into evidence the confession of the man who attempted to murder the two children — Ms. Sissy Delgado and Ms. Noelle Norsen," the District Attorney said.

The District Attorney gave a packet of papers to the bailiff. The bailiff gave the testimony to the Judge and another copy to the defense.

"We apologize for the delay in admitting this evidence," the District Attorney said. "We received this testimony only at seven this morning. It was faxed to us from the New York Police at their start of business."

The court was silent while the Judge and the Defense Attorney flipped through the testimony. When the Judge looked up at the District Attorney, he nodded.

"The New York Police were holding this testimony as part of a larger trial," the District Attorney said. "They agreed to release the testimony to us only when they were sure that the courtroom was closed and everyone was sworn to not to divulge what happens here."

The Judge nodded.

"Defense?" the Judge asked. "May we proceed?"

The Defense Attorney looked up. He looked at Sissy and then at the jury. He nodded.

"Why would anyone want to keep your brother from testifying?" the District Attorney asked.

"I don't know, sir," Sissy said. "The shooter is a paid assassin. It's only for the grace of God that I'm not dead, but. . ."

Tears fell down Sissy's cheeks.

"I. . ." Sissy said.

"Ms. Delgado?" the District Attorney asked.

"I'll probably never dance again," Sissy said. "I. . ."

She stared at the defendant until he lifted his head.

"You should have just killed me," Sissy said in a ragged voice. "You've done it just the same."

The Defense Attorney was on his feet. Samantha Hargreaves was yelling at him. The District Attorney gave Sissy an amused look and went back to his table to sit down. The Judge banged his gavel. The whole time Sissy stared down the defendant. After a few minutes, everyone stopped yelling.

"Do you have any more questions, for this witness?" the Judge asked the District Attorney.

"We'd like to be able to recall her if we need to," the District Attorney said.

"So ordered," the Judge said. "Defense?"

"We have a few questions," the Defense Attorney said.

"Ms. Delgado? Are you up to a few questions or should we take a break?" the Judge asked.

"I can do it," Sissy said.

The Defense Attorney stood from the table. He walked toward Sissy and stopped.

"Do you know of your own knowledge that my client was connected to your shooting?" the Defense Attorney said.

"That's just dumb," Sissy said. "He's the only one who would benefit from my brother Charlie not testifying."

The Defense Attorney glanced at the jury. He nodded as if he'd heard them say something to him.

"You're just being dramatic when you say you'll not dance again," the Defense Attorney said. "Aren't you?"

Sissy looked like she'd been slapped. Tears returned to her

cheeks. She opened her mouth to say something, but the only thing that came out was a sob. She closed her mouth and looked down.

"Ms. Delgado?" the Defense Attorney asked.

When Sissy kept looking down, Samantha jumped to her feet.

"Your honor," Samantha Hargreaves said. She gestured to Sissy. "The Defense Attorney is asking. . ."

"I just don't know what to say." Sissy looked up at Samantha. "You're a person who helps liars and rapists get out of being punished. This guy thought it was okay to *kill me* so he didn't have to take responsibility for his own actions. How could you possibly understand what's in front of me? I have a year to get dancing again or lose my apprenticeship. If I lose my apprenticeship, I will lose my chance at dancing, probably anywhere. That's how ballet works. Am I going to give it my all? Sure. Am I going to work my ass off? Sure. But how could you possibly understand that? You make money off of scumbags."

Sissy turned to the Judge.

"I think I need to go home now," Sissy said.

"Motion to strike," the Defense Attorney said.

"Jury, you will disregard Ms. Delgado's last statement," the Judge said. "Do you release this witness?"

"Yes, your honor," the Defense Attorney nodded.

"We're going to take a break," the Judge said. "In this time, I want you each to think about what the hell we're doing here."

As the jury filed out of court, Samantha helped Sissy down from the witness box. Aden arrived just as Sissy was stepping down. With Samantha on one side and Aden on the other, Sissy made her way out of court.

"How did I do?" Sissy asked.

"I thought you were brilliant," Samantha said. "I particularly liked your last statement."

"But it won't matter," Sissy said. "The Judge told the jury to disregard it."

"They still heard it," Samantha said. "You should have seen their faces. They looked at the Defense Attorney like he was scum."

"He is scum," Sissy said.

"You've got that right," Samantha said.

At the door of the courtroom, Samantha let go of Sissy.

"I'll see you tonight," Samantha said.

"What's happening tonight?" Sissy asked.

"Oh, they didn't tell you?" Samantha asked.

Sissy shook her head. Samantha looked at Aden.

"The Denver Ballet is running through their production," Aden said. "They've invited us to come to watch."

"How fun!" Sissy said. She visibly brightened.

"So go home and rest," Samantha said.

Sissy gave Samantha a sincere nod. With Aden's help, they made it to the car.

"Meds?" Aden asked.

"Please," Sissy said.

Aden gave her a pain med, her antibiotic, and a bottle of water.

"Are you up for seeing people, or should we go home?" Aden asked.

"Home, definitely home," Sissy said.

"As you wish," Aden said.

Sissy held on until they reached the Castle.

"Can I just. . .?" Sissy asked.

She gestured to the couch in the main Castle living room.

"Of course," Aden said.

He whistled for Buster, who came trotting down the stairs. Buster jumped up on the couch, and Sissy lay next to him. She was asleep in a moment.

"How did she do?" Delphie asked.

"She's amazing," Aden said. "Truly amazing."

~~~~~~~~~

Wednesday afternoon — 12:25 p.m.

Sandy was sitting in the den area of Seth's house, reading a magazine. Sitting on the couch next to her, Charlie was practicing his French with Anjelika. He stopped talking when Sandy's cell phone rang.

"Hello?" Sandy asked.

"Hi. It's Samantha."

"What's the word?" Sandy asked. "Should I bring Charlie or not?"

"The Defense is asking if they can make a deal," Samantha said.

"Sissy must have been really good," Sandy said.

"Sissy was fantastic," Samantha said. "She's set the tone for the entire trial."

"What do we need to do?" Sandy asked.

"We need to get the victims together to see if they will accept a deal," Samantha said.

"We spent all Sunday doing that bullshit," Sandy said.

"I know," Samantha said. "They claim to be serious this time."

"You tell them that I'll get everyone together when and if they have a deal," Sandy said.

Samantha didn't say anything.

"Can you make that happen?" Sandy asked.

Samantha chuckled.

"Why is that funny?" Sandy asked.

"Because I can most certainly make that happen," Samantha said.

"Thanks," Sandy said.

"As always, Sandy, I'm amazed with you," Samantha said.

"Well, let's just see if they're not just torturing us some more," Sandy said.

"I'll call when I know something," Samantha said.

"Thanks," Sandy said and hung up the phone.

"What's the word?" Charlie said.

"The word is 'bullshit,'" Sandy said.

"*La connerie*," Anjelika said.

"*La connerie*?" Charlie asked. "What does that mean?"

"'Bullshit,'" Anjelika said.

Sandy laughed. Charlie smiled.

"Make a sentence," Anjelika said.

"*C'est la connerie*," Charlie said.

"*Ce sont des conneries*," Anjelika said.

Charlie repeated the sentence, and Sandy looked back at her magazine. They settled into wait.

~~~~~~~~~

Wednesday afternoon — 1:20 p.m.

"Anyone home?"

They heard Samantha's voice from the front door.

"In here," Sandy called from the den area of Seth's house.

"Sorry," Samantha said. "I rang, but no one came. I knew you were here, so I just let myself in."

"The bell's broken," Sandy said.

"And the foxy workman didn't fix it?" Samantha asked.

"The foxy workman has been taking care of Sir Charles here," Dale said as he walked into the room with a bowl of hot buttered popcorn. "Plus, Seth doesn't want it fixed. He'd rather people didn't come here. How did you get in?"

"Maresol gave me a key when Charlie first got here from the hospital," Samantha said.

"We were just about to watch a movie," Sandy said.

"Sorry, we need to get to court," Samantha said. "That's why I'm here."

"Why?" Charlie asked. "I thought they were getting a plea bargain."

"The District Attorney turned down their offer," Samantha said. "He feels confident that we'll win."

"Oh," Charlie said.

"Is that okay, Charlie?" Samantha asked. "If it's not, I'll call him and tell him we want this to be done with."

"Oh, no," Charlie said. "I'm just nervous, you know?"

"You can do this, Charlie," Anjelika said.

He glanced at her and nodded to her smile.

"Well, help me up," Charlie said.

Dale got Charlie to his feet. He gave Charlie his crutches. They all took a bathroom break before heading to court. Charlie was likely to testify for a couple of days.

"You okay, Charlie?" Sandy asked.

"I'm ready," Charlie said.

He gave Sandy a broken-toothed grin, and they set off toward the car.

Wednesday afternoon — 2:10 p.m.

"State your name," the District Attorney said.

"Charles Delgado," Charlie said.

He raised his hand in a kind of wave. He was wearing an expensive suit that Maresol had bought for him. His hair was long but styled. Even with his still broken teeth and healing bones, he was model handsome. Dale had helped Charlie up to the stand this afternoon.

When the Denver Police learned that Sissy and Charlie were testifying, they decided to make their presence known. They cleared the court of everyone except those involved in the trial and Dale. Two friends of Charlie's father, Mitch, were guarding the door.

"Charlie," he said before the District Attorney could ask a question. "I'm Mitch's son — Charlie."

The Judge put his hand on the edge of his desk, and Charlie looked up.

"Let him ask you, Charlie," the Judge said.

"Oh, sorry. You said that," Charlie nodded. He leaned over. "I'm nervous."

The Judge nodded, and Charlie sat back in his chair.

"Charlie, we notice that your legs are broken," the District Attorney said. "Your right arm and left hand are still in casts."

"Yeah," Charlie said. "That and my teeth are all that's left. My dad used to say that we Delgados heal fast. I don't know if that's true, but it's what he said."

"Two broken legs, a broken hand, and a broken arm seem like a lot to me," the District Attorney said.

"Oh, it was a lot worse," Charlie said. "Like I said, I heal fast. Sissy, too."

"How did this happen?" the District Attorney asked.

"Um, my dad got really sick after Vietnam. . ." Charlie started. "Uh, Agent Orange. . ."

"Your legs and arms," the District Attorney said.

"Oh, sorry." Charlie flashed a smile. "I haven't really been out of the house for a while so all of this is. . ."

Charlie nodded.

"Take your time, Charlie," the Judge said.

"I had to work late and. . . well, I didn't *have* to work late," Charlie said. "I was trying to help my co-worker clean up. We'd had this crazy night, and she was on clean up. I stayed to help."

"Stayed where?" the Judge asked.

"At Sam's No. 3, on Fifteenth," Charlie said. "I used to work there as a busboy. I mean, I didn't get fired or anything. I just. . . uh. . . They said I could come back if I'm better — *when* I get better, I mean. I don't want to be negative and stuff."

Charlie nodded.

"What happened?" the District Attorney asked.

"I was walking to the bus," Charlie said. "I used to take the Colfax bus — you know, the 15 — because it runs all the time. I. . ."

Charlie glanced at the Judge and then back at the District Attorney, who nodded.

"Go ahead, Charlie," the Judge said.

"Well, I don't remember very good," Charlie said. "I mean, well. I don't remember very well. Because. . . I just don't. I. . . um. . . remember walking up Fifteenth Street. Um. . ."

"What happened, Charlie?" the District Attorney asked.

"Oh, I got beaten up," Charlie said. "Some guys with baseball bats and stuff jumped me. I thought they were going to kill me. They almost did."

Charlie glanced at the Judge.

"I saw my dad," Charlie said. "When I was in the hospital, you know."

The District Attorney didn't move, and the court was silent for a moment.

"They were trying to make sure I didn't testify," Charlie said. "They got the idea that I was lying about all the stuff I saw — with the rapes, I mean. They were told that I was lying to get their brothers in trouble because they were Black — I mean, African-American."

Charlie nodded.

"Objection," the Defense Attorney said. "Assumption."

"How do you know what they thought, Charlie?" the Judge asked.

"Oh, they told me," Charlie said with a nod. "Dr. Bumpy set up this thing called 'Restorative Justice.'"

"Overruled," the Judge said to the Defense Attorney.

"Can you explain that to the court, Charlie?" the District Attorney asked in an attempt to regain control.

"Oh, I don't know a lot about it," Charlie said.

"What did you do?" the District Attorney asked.

"Um, Dr. Bumpy. . ." Charlie started.

"Let the record show that Dr. Bumpy is Dr. Bumpy Wilson," the District Attorney said.

"So noted," the Judge said. "Go ahead, Charlie."

"Dr. Bumpy set up a meeting for me and the guys who beat me up," Charlie said. "It was pretty cool. We sat at a table and talked. They told me what they knew. I told them what I knew. My friend, Dale, and my Godfather, Seth O'Malley, were with me. Sandy came, too, but having a woman there made it different. So she left. Um, Sandy's kind of my sister and my mother."

Charlie looked at the jury and swallowed hard.

"We were there for like three days. But. . . Uh. It was nice, felt really good," he added.

"And did you go to trial?" the District Attorney asked.

"No," Charlie said. "We agreed to a sentence and then presented it to you. You agreed to what we decided if I agreed, which I already had."

"And what was their sentence?" the District Attorney asked.

"The guys have to help me pay for the medical bills and something called 'restitution.' I don't know what that is. They have to pay a bunch of fines and stuff. I don't know how much. They also agreed to volunteer to help homeless kids and other disadvantaged boys. They have to do a whole bunch of hours, but they've already started. They're not bad guys. They just got mad. And if they don't beat anyone up for. . . I don't remember how long. . ."

"Five years," the District Attorney said.

"Then it all goes away," Charlie said.

"And that's okay for you?" the District Attorney asked.

"Sure," Charlie said. "Jeez, I've made mistakes and done stupid stuff before. They were really revved up on the idea that I was going to hurt their little brothers. If someone was going to destroy Nash's life, um, my step-brother, I don't know what I'd do. Of course, if I'd died, I probably wouldn't feel that way, you know."

The District Attorney shot Charlie a grin.

"Do you have any idea who might have told these men that you were going after the boys because they were African-Americans?" the District Attorney asked.

"Sure," Charlie pointed to the third attorney at the far end of the defense table. "That guy. David Wodes."

The Defense Attorney was on his feet. Before he could say anything, the District Attorney asked a fast question.

"And you know this because. . ." the District Attorney asked.

"Oh, the guys who beat me up told me," Charlie said. "It's kind of a big deal. Something called the 'Bar' — but not like a drinking bar, you know, something else — is holding a trial, and there's a criminal case against that guy. I have to testify in both of those."

The court was silent for a moment.

"I was surprised when I saw him just sitting there," Charlie said.

"We'd like to submit into evidence the record of the Restorative Justice session between Charlie and his attackers," the District Attorney said.

The Judge looked at the document before looking up.

"We need time to look through this document," the Judge said. "I'm going to dismiss us for the day. Charlie, you know what you have to do, right?"

"I can't talk to anyone," Charlie said. "That's okay because this is a big deal for all of my friends. We take it really serious — I mean, seriously."

"Good," the Judge said. "Court is adjourned. We'll reconvene tomorrow morning."

~~~~~~~~~

Wednesday night — 8:40 p.m.

"So how was it?" Sandy asked from behind Sissy's wheelchair as they left the Ellie Caulkins Opera House.

They left the Opera House and started down the glass-covered open walkway toward 14th Street, where Jill was going to pick them up with her big SUV. Aden pushed Ivan's wheelchair behind them. Sandy whizzed far enough ahead so that Sissy could speak without the men hearing.

"Did you see all of those girls?" Sissy said in a sad voice.

"I did," Sandy said.

"His ex-girlfriends," Sissy said.

"Glad they didn't have knives," Sandy said.

"Right," Sissy said. "What did Janine say to you?"

"She said that it was hard to believe that Ivan wasn't using the wheelchair as a joke," Sandy said.

"Oh," Sissy said. "Yeah, it is weird."

"Does it bother you?" Sandy asked. "The girls."

"Um. . ." Sissy said.

Sandy put her hand on Sissy's shoulder for support.

"They are so beautiful," Sissy said. "And. . . they can. . ."

"Dance," Sandy said.

"Yeah," Sissy said. "I felt. . ."

Sandy leaned over so she could see Sissy's face. She kissed her sister's cheek.

"You'll be dancing soon enough," Sandy said.

"It was so beautiful," Sissy said. "Have you ever seen anything more beautiful than ballet?"

Sandy grinned as Sissy sighed. Sandy waited for Sissy to say what she always said.

"Someday, I'm going to. . ." Sissy started.

She stopped talking. Sandy pushed Sissy to the side of the building. She went around to the front of the wheelchair. Sissy's eyes were vague. When she saw Sandy, her eyebrows furrowed.

"I. . ." Sissy said. Sandy watched Sissy's face. "I think that Defense Attorney was right. I was never good enough to do ballet. I mean, what was I thinking? Those women are so. . . and I'm. . . I mean look at me!"

Sissy gestured to her injured body. Sandy hugged Sissy. As she had when Sissy was a child, Sandy said, "Shh, shh, it's going to be okay. Shh."

"Everything okay?" Aden asked as they approached.

Sandy let go of Sissy. She gave Sissy a hard look.

"Everything's good," Sissy said after catching Sandy's look. She made an effort to smile. "I just feel. . . emotional, you know?"

"Was someone cruel?" Ivan asked.

"Who do we need to beat up?" Aden asked.

"Men," Sandy said.

She gave them an exaggerated roll of her eyes. Sissy giggled at Sandy's pretense.

"Huuh, huuh, huh," Aden said as if he were a caveman.

Ivan turned his head to look up at Aden. Grinning, Ivan joined in. Sissy began to laugh. Sandy kept her hand on Sissy's shoulder so Sissy wouldn't laugh so much that she'd lose her breath.

"Let's return to our mythical Castle," Ivan said. "I feel the desperate need to have ice cream."

"And cake!" Sissy said with a grin.

"But who would create such a delicacy for us?" Ivan asked.

"Sandy made another one for us!" Sissy said.

"Sandra," Ivan said. "Our heroine, again."

Ivan's mouth smiled at Sissy, while his eyes took in her wet cheeks and red eyes. He held out his hand for Sissy, and Aden rolled him nearer to her. Sissy took his hand. Reading his kind smile, Sissy nodded.

"Oh, look — there's Jill!" Sandy said as Jill pulled up in her huge SUV.

Sandy rolled Sissy to the sidewalk and left to get the SUV ready for them. Aden rolled Ivan next to Sissy and went to help Sandy.

At great cost to himself, Ivan leaned toward Sissy. She turned to look at him. He kissed her lips.

"I love you," Ivan said. Even though he was in pain, he held his face inches from hers. "Always."

Sissy kissed him. Ivan leaned back into his chair. He closed his eyes to absorb the pain that was shooting through him. Sissy squeezed his hand in support.

"Shall we?" Jill asked.

She touched Ivan's shoulders and then went to Sissy. Aden helped Ivan into the SUV. Jill helped Sissy to her feet, and Sandy got the wheelchairs.

"Did you help him?" Sissy whispered to Jill.

"Guy shouldn't have to suffer for kissing his beloved," Jill said.

She winked at Sissy and helped her into the SUV. Aden got in the driver's seat.

"What are you doing?" Jill asked in a pretend huffy voice.

"Huuh, huuh, huuh," Aden grunted like a caveman.

While Jill looked confused, Sandy, Sissy, and Ivan laughed. He kept it up until Jill laughed too. She got in next to Sissy, and Sandy sat next to Ivan.

"Driver?" Jill said in an exaggerated "rich" voice. "Take us home."

"As you wish," Aden said.

He took off toward the Castle.

~~~~~~~~~

Wednesday night — 8:40 p.m.

Tanesha pushed open her front door and stopped short. Her breath caught in her throat.

Jeraine's bags were sitting at the front door.

She swallowed hard. She forced herself to breathe. In. Out. In. Out.

Images of his bags sitting by a variety of front doors flooded past the walls she'd set around them.

"Breathe," she commanded herself. "Focus on in. Focus on out. In. Out."

Her mind flashed. She was her knees, begging him not to go.

"Breathe," she commanded herself. In. Out. In. Out.

Her mind jumped again. Jeraine was standing there, laying out his lies! *His lies! His fucking lies!* Rage flooded over her despair.

"Breathe," she commanded herself. She closed her eyes and felt the breath move in, and then out. In. Out.

She blinked. Her eyelids were like shutters on dramatic seems of desperate love. She'd thrown her wedding ring at him. She'd screamed and cried. She'd been indifferent. She'd been angry. She'd begged. She'd thrown things at him. She'd been loving.

And he'd lied.

"Aw, baby, 's all gonna be okay." "You know I always come home." "You is my one and only, baby." "Ah, honey, I'd never lie to you."

"Just breathe," she commanded herself. In. Out. In. Out. "You just have to breathe."

Feeling him approach, she looked up. His eyes on her face, he crept toward her as if he were a lion tamer approaching an unpredictable lion.

"Hi?" he asked.

"I thought you weren't leaving until Friday," Tanesha managed. In her head, she demanded herself to focus. *Breathe.*

"No," Jeraine said. "I have to leave in the morning."

"So that was just a lie?!" Tanesha's voice rose with a mixture of panic and rage.

"No," Jeraine said.

He looked like he wanted to say something else. Thinking better of it, he shook his head.

"No, what?" Tanesha asked.

"Uh," he started but stopped talking.

He looked at her. Her mind went completely blank. She felt like a bubble had formed where her thoughts should be.

She raised an index finger. She set her book bag next to the table. She picked up her running shoes from the pile of shoes next to the door and left the house. Sitting in a rocking chair on their porch, she forced her mind to focus on changing her shoes. She didn't bother to put her boots away. Once her running shoes were on, she took off running.

She ran as fast and hard as she was capable of running. After a few minutes, she settled into a steady and rapid pace. She'd just completed a mile when she realized someone was running behind her. She stopped running and turned around.

Jeraine ran up to her. She raised her hands in a "What?" gesture.

"Where are we going?" he asked.

For a long moment, they stared at each other.

"Nowhere." Tanesha's grief-stricken voice came out. "We're going nowhere."

"Nah," Jeraine said with a grin. "We're going somewhere."

They stared at each other again.

"Come on," Jeraine said. "Let's run City Park. If you're going to yell at me — and I certainly deserve it — you can yell while we run."

"Why City Park?" Tanesha asked. "It's a long way."

"We're supposed to get cake and ice cream with Sissy and Ivan. Charlie started testifying today," Jeraine said. He gave her a cocky grin. Imitating her voice, he said, "Remember? Our life? You can remember *our life*, for once, can't you?"

Tanesha gasped a sob. He caught her before she collapsed. Hot and sweaty from running, she sobbed into his shoulder. After a few moments, she spun in place and took off running.

"Catch me if you can!" she threw back to him.

"Oh, it's on!" he said.

Jeraine took off after her.

~~~~~~~~~
Wednesday night — 9:15 p.m.

"It's very late," Jabari said. He was holding onto Yvonne's neck as she and Rodney walked toward the Castle from the parking lot. "That's just the life of a rock star."

Yvonne pulled back to look at the little boy.

"Are you a rock star?" Yvonne asked.

"No," he giggled.

He buried his face in her neck.

"What is it?" Yvonne asked.

Rodney glanced at them. She nodded, and he knocked on the front door.

"I don't really want to go," Jabari said.

Yvonne held him close.

"Can't we just go to your house?" Jabari asked. "I can sleep in my big, grown-up bed? I can play with Mr. Chesterfield all day? Then I could go home, and Mommy would put me to sleep? And I could play with her in the morning and then. . ."

The Castle door opened. Delphie welcomed Rodney with a hug.

"I thought you wanted to go with your Daddy," Yvonne said.

"I do," Jabari said. "I just. . . um. . ."

Jabari watched Rodney and Delphie talk. Rodney turned his body sideways and reached out to them.

"Can you come with me?" Jabari asked. "And Mr. Chesterfield? And Mommy, too? And Mr. Rodney? And. . ."

Jabari sighed.

"What is this?" Yvonne asked in a low voice.

She gestured for Rodney to go in. He shook his head and walked toward them.

"I just. . ." Jabari's eyes welled with tears. Imitating Rodney, the child shook his head.

Rodney picked the small child up out of Yvonne's arms. He hugged him tight.

"This is the best my life has ever been," Jabari said into Rodney's neck.

"Me, too," Rodney said.

"Certainly, that's true for me," Yvonne said.

"I don' want anything to change," Jabari said.

"What if it just keeps getting better?" Rodney asked.

The little boy was so surprised that he leaned back from Rodney. He turned to Yvonne.

"Is it possible?" Jabari asked.

His eyes became so big and so full that they almost filled up his whole face. His mouth fell open in a tiny "o."

"Of course," Yvonne said with a smile.

"Really?" Jabari asked. "You wouldn't just want me to go so. . ."

"Stop," Rodney said. "You know none of that is true."

"I do?" Jabari looked at him.

"You know it here," Rodney said. Rodney put his hand over Jabari's heart. Jabari scowled. He put his own tiny hand over Rodney's big one. After a moment, Jabari nodded.

"You're right," Jabari said. "I *do* know."

Jabari smiled and held out his arm. Yvonne walked forward so Jabari could hug her, too. Rodney put an arm around Yvonne. The small child sat cocooned by two adults who loved him completely.

"I still don't want to go," Jabari said.

"We'll try it for a day or so," Yvonne said. "If you don't like it, we'll come right home."

"I forgot!" Jabari brightened. "You're going with me!"

"We're going to try it out together," Yvonne said. "If we don't like it — even for a moment — we come straight home."

Jabari nodded. Rodney kissed his cheek.

"Think of me," Rodney said. "I will miss you horribly."

"Poor Mr. Rodney," Jabari said.

He threw his arms around Rodney's neck in a tight hug.

"Ready to go in?" Rodney asked.

The gate to the Castle parking lot. Aden navigated the large SUV into the parking lot.

"Can you wave?" Yvonne asked.

Jabari waved to the SUV.

"Let's get out of the way," Rodney said.

Yvonne followed Rodney and Jabari inside.

CHAPTER THREE HUNDRED AND SEVENTY-FOUR
RELEASE

Thursday morning — 6:15 a.m.

"Gentlemen," Jacob said. This was his first meeting with them, so he made sure to look directly into each of their eyes. "We are about to engage in a long-held Lipson Construction tradition."

He scowled a bit and gave a solemn nod.

"Breakfast," Jacob said. Seeing that he had their attention, he continued, "This is a time when we set aside any conflict or difficulty and focus on eating pancakes and enjoying each other's company."

When he looked up, he saw that the person across from him was about to complain.

"No," Jacob said. He raised a finger. "This is a sacred time. We must dedicate ourselves to the task at hand — eating pancakes, eggs, and quite possibly a pork product. Your questions should be limited to which type of pancake — banana, blueberry, or plain old fashioned — you would like to have, which type of pork product — bacon, sausage links, or quite possibly ham — and, of course, how you would like to have your eggs made — scrambled, sunny side up, poached, or perhaps some other concoction.

"I see the confusion in your eyes," Jacob said. "You're wondering why we would waste our time in this ritual when there is so much to do. Well, frankly, I understand your confusion. I once asked my father this very same question. You know what he said?"

Jacob fell silent as the waitress brought menus and filled their water glasses. He opened his mouth to continue, but the waitress came right back to fill his coffee cup with the hot Nectar of the Gods. He waited until everyone had doctored their beverages before continuing.

"I asked my father why we spent our time in this ritual," Jacob said, to remind them what they were talking about. "He told me that, to get along with people, you must create stress-free situations in which to build shared experiences. What could be better at doing that than sitting down for breakfast? Especially at a fine dining establishment like Pete's Kitchen."

Jacob nodded.

"Truer words were never spoken," Jacob said.

"Jacob? Son?" Sam asked as he neared the table. "Are you feeling all right?"

"Here is my father right now," Jacob said. "Will you tell everyone why breakfast is important?"

"Uh," Sam looked across the table at Jacob's twins — Bladen and Tanner. "Uh. . ."

"Go ahead," Jacob said. "We're listening."

Sam leaned over so he was speaking into Jacob's ears.

"You realize they are babies, right?" Sam asked.

Jacob grinned, and Sam laughed. He pulled out a chair and sat down.

"Your father is right," Sam said. "Breakfast can be the difference between a happy company and everything falling apart. At Lipson Construction, we get together for breakfast almost every day. We encourage all of the teams to follow suit. Most of them follow our lead. It helps people understand each other, especially with the teams of mixed types of people. Nothing is more important than getting along with others."

Sam looked up to see the boys watching his face. He glanced at Jacob.

"That's very. . ." Sam said.

"Unnerving," Jacob said. "Yes."

"They're really listening," Sam said.

"I know," Jacob said.

Sam shuddered, and Jacob smiled. The waitress came to get their order. The manager came by to ask about Jill and introduce himself to the twins. One of Jill's waitress friends picked up Tanner to introduce him to everyone. Bladen watched the interaction with intent interest. She came right back to swap Tanner for Bladen. When Bladen returned, Tanner gave him a wide-eyed look. Jacob and Sam ordered.

Tanner pointed to Jacob and scowled.

"Bah," Tanner said.

Bladen nodded.

"You're absolutely right," Jacob said. "I do want bacon and not sausages."

"Bah," Bladen said.

"Good idea," Jacob said. "I will order you a pancake."

Bladen looked at Tanner, and they looked back at Jacob. They gave him a grin.

"You know what they're saying?" Sam whispered to Jacob.

"No idea," Jacob said.

Sam laughed. He put his hand on Jacob's shoulder.

"Thanks for inviting me to help you with your marriage-class homework," Sam said.

"This is their first Pete's experience," Jacob said. "You belong here."

Sam laughed. When the waitress returned, he placed everyone's breakfast order.

~~~~~~~~~
Thursday morning — 6:15 a.m.

"Katy-baby?" Jill opened the door to Katy's room. "I thought you wanted to have a special 'girls-only' breakfast."

Still under the covers, Katy lay on her side with her back toward the door.

"Katy?" Jill asked.

Katy rolled her shoulder and head toward the door. Her dark eyes blinked at Jill.

"What is it?" Jill fell to her knees next to Katy.

"Scooter isn't feeling very well," Katy said.

Jill noticed for the first time that Katy was wrapped around Scooter.

"Scooter?" Jill asked.

"Mommy." Katy rolled back to look at her mother. "Scooter thinks it might be time to say 'good-bye,' but he's too sad to tell you himself. I was just telling him that you wouldn't want him to hurt, but he. . ."

Katy sniffed back her tears. Her voice dropped to a whisper.

"He's never really healed from the. . ."

"Serpent," Jill said at the same time Katy said, "bad man."

Jill nodded.

"He doesn't want me to tell you," Katy said. She rolled over so that she was facing Scooter. "He doesn't want to say good-bye."

Jill went around Katy's bed to the opposite side to see Scooter's face.

"He's scared, Mommy," Katy said. "Really scared."

Jill put her hands on Scooter's face. In his kind face, she saw the puppy that was her bright light during a dark time in her life. She saw the friend who had been her playmate, running partner, and constant companion. Trevor, her abusive first husband, kept his own schedule. Scooter was Jill's responsibility and her joy.

Scooter's dark eyes looked into Jill's. For a moment, they simply looked at each other. When Scooter looked away, Jill knew that he'd been holding on long past what was good for him. He'd held on to spend time with her and Katy.

Jill knew that his passing was to be expected. She knew that this was one of those moments when she should be an adult. But her heart spasmed with pain. She began to cry.

"He doesn't want to leave us, Mommy," Katy said. Jill looked up to see her daughter's eyes peeking out over Scooter's head. "He wants to stay here with us."

"But he can't do it anymore," Jill said in a low voice.

She rubbed his ears, and he licked her hand.

"He says you can send him on," Katy said. "But. . ."

Her face wet with tears, Katy sniffed back her sorrow.

"I'm going to miss him so much," Katy said.

"Me, too," Jill said.

"Besides Paddie, he's been my best friend," Katy said. "What am I going to do without him?"

Heartbroken, Jill looked down. She pressed the back of her hand to her forehead so that her arm covered her weeping eyes. Scooter nudged her hand with the tip of his nose until her hand flopped on his head. She rubbed his ears again.

"I don't know, Katy," Jill said. "I don't know what we're going to do without him. He's been our dog friend for a very long time."

"Uh, huh," Katy said.

"Sometimes. . ." Jill sighed and looked up. Katy lifted her head from behind Scooter. "Sometimes, when we love someone, we have to do what's best for them, even if it doesn't feel best for us."

"But it's not *best* for Scooter!" Katy said. "He's going to miss us horribly. He's so scared."

"What does Daddy do when you're scared?" Jill asked.

"He tells me that he's big and strong and that he'll take care of me no matter what," Katy said with a nod.

"We have to be strong for Scooter," Jill said.

Katy nodded.

"Can you be strong for Scooter?" Jill asked.

"I can be strong for Scooter," Katy said.

"Then we must release him," Jill said.

"What does that mean?" Katy asked.

"We must release Scooter from our bond to him," Jill said.

"We must let him go so that he can be at rest. He loves you and me the very most out of anyone in the entire world."

"What about Delphie?" Katy asked. "She saved Scooter so that I could meet him and he could be my friend."

"You're right," Jill said. "I'll go get. . ."

"Jill?" Delphie's voice called from the entrance to their loft.

"We're in here," Jill said.

"She knew. . ." Katy said.

The child put her nose into the scruff of Scooter's neck and hugged him close. Delphie came into the doorway.

"Scooter isn't feeling well," Jill said.

"He's been hanging on for a while," Delphie said. Tears began to fall down the kindly woman's face. "Oh, Scooter."

Delphie went around the bed to see the dog's face.

"I was just telling Katy that we need to release him," Jill said.

"It's so hard to do when all we want to do is hold on tight," Delphie said.

In an attempt to get herself together, Jill wiped her eyes. One glance at Katy's crying face, and Jill's tears began to fall again.

"Should I call our vet?" Delphie asked.

"Mommy can do it," Katy said. "Scooter wants her to."

Delphie looked up at Jill, and Jill gave her a slight nod.

"We have to release him first," Jill said.

Nodding to herself, Delphie focused on Scooter. The Oracle put her hands on either side of Scooter's face.

"My dear, beloved friend," Delphie whispered. "Thank you for all you've been and all you've done. You will live in my heart for the rest of my life. I release you."

"Katy?" Jill asked.

Katy looked up at her mother again. Her eyes blinked, and she put her head back down.

"Katy?"

"I don't want to," Katy said.

"I didn't want to, either," Delphie said. "But it's what Scooter needs."

"We have to love Scooter more than we love ourselves," Jill said.

"Why?" Katy asked.

"Because we want him to stay with us, to be our friend no matter what," Jill said. "But Scooter is. . ."

"In lots of pain," Katy said. "Oh, Scooter."

Jill sat down on the bed so that she could pet Scooter and soothe Katy. The little girl's shoulders shook with sobs.

"But he's so afraid to be away from us," Katy said through her tears.

"It's so painful for him to be here," Delphie said.

"He doesn't like to be alone," Katy said.

"Can you imagine that our Scooter will be alone for long?" Jill said with a snort. "People and dogs will come from all over just to welcome him home."

"Everybody loves Scooter," Katy said in a soft, sad voice.

"He will be at peace," Jill said. "I will not let him suffer in fear and loneliness. He will be free from all of that suffering when we release him."

Katy gave a loud, moist sigh. She wrapped her arms around Scooter's neck.

"I love you, Scooter," Katy said.

"Thank him for being your friend," Jill said.

"Thank you for being my good friend," Katy said. "Especially when we moved to this house and met Daddy and all that scary stuff with our old-Daddy."

Katy pressed her face into Scooter's scruff and gave him a loud kiss.

"I release you from being my dog," Katy said. "But you'll always be my friend."

Jill gave Katy a soft smile.

"Are you ready, Katy?" Jill asked. "When I do this, Scooter will leave us really fast."

"I'm ready, Mommy," Katy said. "You sure he won't be scared and it won't hurt?"

"He won't be in pain," Jill said.

She slipped off the bed and knelt down. Scooter lifted his head. He made a small sound, a kind of whimper, and Jill let out a soft sob.

Jill thought of all the times this little scruffy mutt had cheered her up and given her hope. She thought of the moment she saw him again — her old friend risen from the dead. She remembered the moment Katy met him and how they'd loved each other on the spot. She remembered how Scooter had attacked the serpent with no concern for himself. He'd only wanted to make certain Katy and Jill were safe.

She'd known he was in pain. She'd tried to save him. She knew now that the only real way to save him was to let him go. Sighing, she put her hands around his face.

His eyes locked on Jill's.

"Precious Scooter," Jill whispered. "I release you. You may go."

Scooter seemed to smile. He took a slow breath, and then another. Her ears expected her friend to take another breath. When the breath didn't come, Jill's heart broke open.

"Scooter?" Jill said through her tears.

Scooter's warmth was gone. Her friend had been released from his pain, suffering, and joy of this life. She looked at Katy. Her daughter was crying her heart out. Jill looked up at Delphie. The Oracle was leaning against the wall. She held her hand in front of her eyes while she cried.

Jill went to the bed and scooped up Katy. Delphie sat down next to them and leaned into Jill. Wrapped in their grief, they held onto each other.

Jill knew that her resilient daughter would get over losing Scooter. She knew that Delphie would pray for him every day for the rest of her life. It was going to take them a long time to get over losing Scooter.

Jill knew for herself that this very moment would mark her life. Everything else would be considered "After Scooter." She'd never be the same.

~~~~~~~~~
Thursday afternoon — 2:15 p.m.

"Hi!" Blane said to Aden and Ivan from the white picket fence around Tanesha's house. "Sorry about the mess."

He held open the fence, and Aden carefully pushed Ivan in his wheelchair down the brick path.

"We're moving in," Blane said. "Or moved in this morning. Jeraine left this morning for tour, and we're living here until he gets back in the fall."

They got to the edge of the porch. Blane pointed to the right. The brick path continued around the house. Blane opened the gate to the backyard. Aden wheeled Ivan around the house to the back porch.

"Sandy was here this morning. Helping us move." Blane kept talking to ease the tension. "Tanesha's moved into the basement. Heather and I are taking the upstairs. Tink's staying in the living room so I can treat people in this bedroom."

Aden wheeled Ivan around the house to the back porch. A new ramp connected the path to the back porch, and another ramp connected the back porch to the house.

"Sam built these this morning," Blane said.

"Why are you moving?" Ivan asked.

"We're adding space onto our house," Blane said. "We've been planning to do it for a while — years really. But since I was sick and in the hospital, it was too much for us to do. When Jeraine decided to go on tour. . ."

Tink opened the back door and helped them get Ivan inside.

". . . everything worked out," Blane said. "Tanesha needs to study for finals so I'm taking care of the house and her while Jeraine's gone. By the time he's back, our house should be done."

Blane turned right.

"The room is right here," Blane said.

Aden rolled Ivan into what had been the spare bedroom.

"Thank you for letting me treat you," Blane said. "You're the first person I've seen since getting out of the hospital."

Clearly in pain, Ivan gave Blane a curt nod.

"What do I. . .?" Ivan asked.

"Why don't you stay there?" Blane asked. "Aden, you can wait either here or outside."

"I can help unpack," Aden said.

"You don't have to," Blane said. "We just brought the bare minimum — clothing, mostly."

He gave Aden an odd smile.

"Oh," Aden said and nodded.

"Oh?" Ivan looked up at Aden and then at Blane.

"The fairies will be here before Tanesha gets home from school," Aden said. "If anything's not done, they will fix it to Tanesha's perfection."

"Nice," Ivan grinned.

"Tanesha hates it, so they have to do it when she's not here," Blane said with a shrug. "I'm certainly not going to turn down their help. And, as I said, we're mostly done anyway."

He took one of Ivan's wrists and began taking Ivan's Chinese medicine pulse.

"Do you mind if Aden stays?" Blane asked.

"No," Ivan said. "I may need help getting up there."

"On the table?" Blane asked. "Let's see if we get that far."

He went around and took the pulse of Ivan's other hand.

"How long are you staying?" Blane asked.

"Until Sunday," Ivan said. "I've been receiving treatments from. . ."

"Yes, we spoke last night," Blane said. "He gave me some suggestions about how I can facilitate your healing. Sissy's, too."

Blane stepped back and looked Ivan up and down. He scowled for a moment and then nodded.

"Have you had acupuncture before?" Blane asked.

"Yes," Ivan said. "I never found it to be very helpful."

"Yes," Blane said. He continued to look at Ivan.

"Why is that?" Aden asked.

"Oh, sorry," Blane said. "I'm trying to decide what to do first."

"First?" Ivan asked.

"I'd like to see you, at the very minimum, once a day," Blane said with a nod. "Will that work?"

"Of course," Ivan said. "If it helps."

Blane nodded. He turned away and went to a shelf where boxes of his needles were sitting. He picked up a pack of needles and a sharps container. He set the sharps container on the treatment table and unpacked the needles.

"You have... um...." Blane looked up at the wall. "Sorry, I'm trying to find the right words for it. You have an energetic wall around a whole bunch of... garbage."

Blane gave a nod and started putting in needles.

"Garbage?" Ivan asked.

"Experiences, pains," Blane said. He was silent for a moment. "How did you hurt your leg?"

"Gulag," Ivan said.

Blane nodded. He stuck a needle just under Ivan's knee and one near his ankle.

"I have wound on back," Ivan said.

"Your biggest wound is in your heart," Blane said.

"What?" Ivan asked.

"This is taking a long time to heal, isn't it?" Blane asked.

"I was stabbed a week ago," Ivan said.

"Not a long time for normal people, but a long time for you," Blane said.

"*Da*," Ivan said.

"We will have to open this energy vault of yours," Blane said. "We can do it a little bit at a time so you don't get overwhelmed. Kind of siphon off the energy. Is that all right with you?"

"Will it make me better?" Ivan asked. "Healthy?"

"It will recharge your body's ability to heal," Blane said. "Can I take off your glasses?"

Ivan glanced at the overhead light. Blane pointed to Aden. He went to shut off the lights. Ivan took off his glasses.

"Take a breath," Blane said. Ivan took a breath, and Blane put a needle into the bridge of his nose. "Let it go."

Ivan let out the breath.

"Another," Blane said. Ivan took a breath, and Blane put a needle above the first. "Let it go."

Ivan's face flushed red.

"Are you ready?" Blane asked.

Ivan nodded. Without warning, Blane put in two needles in quick succession. Ivan gasped a breath. Blane looked at Aden.

"Take his hand," Blane said.

Aden grabbed Ivan's hand. Ivan looked up at Blane.

"You are safe here," Blane said. "Let it go."

Ivan crumpled forward and began to sob. Blane went to the shelf and picked up a box of tissues. He set them on the bed.

"Just remind him to let it go," Blane said to Aden. "He needs to release this."

Aden nodded.

"I'll be back in a half hour with some tea," Blane said.

Aden nodded in agreement. Blane put a firm hand on Ivan's shoulder for support before leaving the room.

CHAPTER THREE HUNDRED AND SEVENTY-FIVE
LAND OF PAIN

Thursday afternoon — 2:25 p.m.

Charlie stifled a yawn. He'd been up on the witness stand for most of the day. The afternoon session started at two, but no one had asked him a question yet. They were busy arguing over whether or not his high school transcripts could be used as evidence. Charlie wasn't sure why this was a big deal, but, according to the Defense team, it was vital.

Charlie's biggest problem was that his arm itched under the cast. It had started to itch that morning, but Tink and everybody came to have lunch with him and he'd forgotten all about it. Now his itchy arm was all he could think about. He had spied the Judge's ruler when he was sitting there that morning. It was the perfect size for scratching under his cast. In this boring moment, it took all of his will not to grab the ruler.

Plus, the Judge seemed particularly annoyed this afternoon. As if the Judge could hear his thoughts, the elderly man turned to look at Charlie. He glanced at his ruler and then back at Charlie. Grabbing the ruler, the Judge tossed the metal object at him. Charlie caught it.

"Excuse me," Charlie said.

The lawyers were so busy with their own words and voices that they didn't notice. Charlie took the ruler and scratched under the cast on his right arm. The Judge put his hand over the microphone.

"Better?" the Judge asked in a low voice.

"Yes, sir," Charlie said.

"Keep it," the Judge said with a nod.

In a world that had been incredibly cruel, in a trial about some of the most brutal crime anyone in the city had ever seen, this Judge's simple gift of this metal ruler overwhelmed Charlie. His eyes welled with tears. He could only nod at the Judge.

"Soldier on, son," the Judge said with a nod. He took his hand off the microphone and gave the lawyers all of his attention. "While it is lovely to hear your voices, I'm wondering if there's a point to all of this."

"We wish to determine that Charles Delgado is not. . . shall we say, an honor student," the Defense Attorney said.

"If that's an issue, I can tell you myself," Charlie said with a nod. "When I was at Westy, I never went to school."

The courtroom fell silent. Charlie glanced at the Defense team and saw them lean forward in the hopes that he would give them their point. He glanced at the District Attorney. He was nervously licking his lips.

"I. . . uh. . ." Charlie said. Intimidated, Charlie swallowed hard.

He heard the Judge's words in his mind: "Soldier on, son."

"I don't think it's too weird," Charlie said. "My dad was the center of my world, and he died. No, he didn't just die. My mom kicked him and us out of her house. We lived on the streets and in this horrible, smelly hotel. And then he died at Uncle Seth's house. I was in school. I wasn't even. . ."

To Charlie's surprise, his eyes welled with tears.

"I wasn't even there," Charlie said. He felt tears roll down his face. "I. . . did drugs and. . . and. . . anything, everything that would make the pain go away. It drove my mother crazy — or made her crazier. She kicked me out so she could get my dad's pension and not have to spend it on me. My little sister started to starve herself, and I was cold, hungry, sleeping on the streets, and. . . and. . . Pain. Pain. Pain."

Charlie looked around at the stunned faces of the lawyers.

"All I felt all the time was pain," Charlie said. "People say they don't have any idea why I would help the girls who... you know... who this jerk hurt... but to me..."

Charlie swiped at his tears and took a breath.

"I *know* the contours of pain," Charlie said. "I know what it tastes like, what it smells like, and what it feels like. I found those girls when they needed me the most because they entered my land."

Charlie hit his chest.

"Horror and pain were all I knew for a very long time," Charlie said. "My friends and I, we were like... like..."

Charlie's mind searched for the best way to describe what he was thinking. When it clicked in, he nodded.

"We were like Charon, the ferryman, on the river Styx," Charlie said. "We ferried these poor girls' broken bodies and souls from the land of pain to the land of the living, where they belonged."

Charlie felt like his entire body was on fire. He spoke his truth clearly and with authority.

"That's why this jerk is so angry with me," Charlie said. He locked eyes with the young man who was on trial. "He thought he could toss the beautiful girls of the world into the land of the tragically broken. And maybe he would have, but we were there to send them right back where they belonged — the land of the living."

Charlie nodded.

"Why did you do it, Charlie?" the District Attorney asked.

"Because we had to hope that, someday, we, too, could leave the pain and horror we lived with every day, the land of pain," Charlie said. "These girls were just visiting our horrible life, our horrible world. Every time they returned to the world, they proved that maybe, just maybe, someday, we might be able to join them."

Charlie raised an eyebrow and nodded.

"And you know what?" Charlie asked. "We don't live there anymore. Not any of us. And the girls he tried to destroy don't live there, either. We're on the other side of that river."

Charlie nodded his head and crossed his arms. Oddly out of breath, he tried to cover his panting. Out of the corner of his eyes, he saw the Judge shoot him a nod.

"I think you're going to have to explain to them who Charon is," the Judge said. "And the river Styx."

"No way." Charlie shook his head and leaned forward. "You don't know?"

He looked at the tables of lawyers. Samantha Hargreaves looked amused. She nodded for him to go on, and he grinned. He heard Anjelika's voice telling him that nothing looked worse than a bragging young man. Charlie checked his smugness and just told the court what he knew.

"The river Styx separates the land of the living from Hades," Charlie said. "Charon is her ferryman. He takes souls across the river. The only way to get into Hades and return alive is on Charon's ferry. That's Greek, um, mythology. You know, like Hercules? Sartre's Sisyphus? The Beautiful Psyche?"

Shaking his head in amazement, Charlie leaned back in his chair and attempted to stifle his inner braggart.

"Thank you for the lesson, Charlie," the Judge said. "Shall we?"

"Charlie, we want to start with general parameters," the District Attorney said. "When did you find your first rape victim?"

Nodding, Charlie settled in to give his testimony.

~~~~~~~~
Thursday afternoon — 4:45 p.m.

"Ivan?" Sissy asked. She poked her head into MJ and Honey's guest bedroom, where Ivan was staying. "Are you there?"

The room was dark. As Sissy's eyes adjusted, she saw his body, covered by a thin sheet, in bed. Normally, she would feel embarrassed at waking a boy or a man— or really anyone of the male persuasion. She'd never awaken Aden, for example, or even Nash, especially if they were naked. Charlie was, well, Charlie, her stupid older brother. She didn't mind waking him, and he mostly slept naked.

This was Ivan! She'd seen Ivan in every state of dress. She'd found him in bed with a variety of beauties. She'd seen him in various stages of undress. They'd spent so much time together that she shouldn't be embarrassed. She wasn't, really. It was just that everything was different now.

"Ivan?" Sissy asked again.

"I'm here," he said. His voice was low and thick with sleep.

"You asked me to come get you when I got back," Sissy said. She was surprised at her own defensive tone. "I can come back."

"Sissy?" Ivan asked.

When he called her, her body automatically moved into the room and sat on the bed. Her heart fluttered. He reached to turn on the bedside lamp.

"I have slept in so many places in the last few weeks," Ivan said. He voice was very formal. "Remind me, my love, where are we?"

"Denver," Sissy said.

She pursed her eyebrows with concern. Ivan spoke in this rigid, formal tone when he was upset.

"Yes," Ivan said. "MJ and Honey are hosting me in their guest bedroom. I spent this morning playing with their magnificent daughter, Maggie. She is delightfully funny. I've never laughed so much with a toddler."

"She likes to make people laugh," Sissy said.

"Yes," Ivan said. He sat up in bed and scooted back to lean against the headboard. "Do you remember why we're not at my apartment?"

"Bruno and his wife are staying there," Sissy said.

"That's right," Ivan said with a nod. "She wants to have her baby here."

"Best hospital in the country," Sissy said.

"That's my friend Bruno," Ivan chuckled. "He wants the best for his wife, no matter what the cost."

Sissy smiled.

"How was shopping with your sister?"

"Good," Sissy said. "We got some clothes and some basic stuff — you know."

"'Basic stuff'?" Ivan asked.

He opened his eyes wide in an attempt to wake up. He started stretching by moving his right arm across his body.

"Underwear, bras," Sissy said. Blushing, she shrugged, "Stuff Sandy buys for me."

"That's kind of her," Ivan said with a smile.

"She's always bought that stuff for me," Sissy said. "Even when I was a little kid living with mom. I like it because I feel like she's close to me."

"You didn't wear yourself out?" Ivan asked.

"No," Sissy said with a suppressed cough. "I mostly sat in one place while Sandy brought me stuff to try on."

"Good." Ivan smiled, and Sissy returned his smile.

"How was Blane's?" Sissy asked. "Sandy and I got there right after you left."

"I apologize," Ivan said. "I didn't realize we were meeting there."

"We didn't agree to meet there," Sissy said. "Blane called when we were out and arranged for us to come."

Sissy gave a curt nod. She'd expected him to become less formal as he awoke, but his formality remained. She responded by being proper.

"How was it?" Sissy asked again.

"Exhausting." Ivan looked past her toward the door. She'd left the door open a crack as she'd agreed with Aden to do when she was alone with Ivan. Noting the door, he turned back to her and said, "I feel like I could sleep for a week."

Sissy scowled.

"What's going on?" Sissy asked.

"What do you mean?" Ivan asked.

Sissy opened her mouth to respond. Instead, she shook her head and stayed still. Ivan watched her face.

"Okay," he said. "You are correct. Give me a moment."

When he got out of bed, Sissy was oddly relieved that he was wearing his boxer briefs. Sissy's eyes followed him into the small bathroom off the guest bedroom. The moment the door closed, Sissy collapsed against her knees.

She grunted against the pain the movement caused. She coughed from the bottom of her lungs.

"What am I doing here?" Sissy whispered under her breath. "I can't do this."

Her arms went around her knees. She instinctively rocked back and forth. Her panic told her to flee this room immediately. Yet, her entire being was rooted in place.

"What is it?" Ivan asked from the doorway of the bathroom.

She jerked to look up at him. Her side spasmed with pain, and she sucked in a breath. He read her face and gave her a slight nod.

"You're walking," she said.

"*Da*," Ivan said. "A gift from Blane. You don't have your oxygen tank."

"Blane," Sissy said. "I'll probably get it, though."

Nodding, he went to the other side of the bed and climbed in. He held out his hand, and she turned to face him. Her left leg tucked underneath her on the bed, while her right foot held onto the ground. She was present with him and also ready to escape at any moment.

"You are frightened," Ivan said.

"You're sad," Sissy said.

They stared at each other for what felt to Sissy like an hour or more. She finally had to look away. When she did, he leaned forward.

"It's different," Ivan said.

Sissy nodded.

"Bad?" Ivan asked.

Sissy shook her head.

"Tell me," Ivan said.

"Forever, if I came in and you were upset, I'd just ignore it," Sissy said. "But now, I'm... And it never meant anything to me that you were... And now..."

"I see," Ivan said. "Yes. I feel the same way."

"You do?" Sissy asked.

"If you were my lover and not my beloved..." Ivan sighed, "I would have pulled you into bed with me for a cuddle or maybe more."

Sissy blushed.

"The door is open, and we are..." Ivan said.

"I don't want you to be sad," Sissy said. "I want to know... everything, but I don't know how..."

Ivan opened his mouth to speak.

"No," Sissy said. "I need to..."

Her palms came to her chest. As if she were pulling something out of her chest, she pulled her hands away and turned them over toward him. He gave her a "go ahead" nod.

"What has happened?" Sissy asked. "That's what Sandy says, but she also says, 'You'd better tell me now while I'm here and have time to listen, because I won't have time to listen later.'"

Ivan grinned, and Sissy smiled.

"So... I'm here," Sissy said. "I have time..."

"I went to see this magician you call Blane," Ivan said. "He told me that I had wrapped all of my horror into myself. Then he stuck in five — no, six — needles, and..."

Ivan imitated her gesture by putting his hands to his heart and folding them over in her direction.

"I broke wide open," Ivan said. "Your step-father, my friend Aden, stayed with me while all of my brokenness flowed out of me."

"You cried?" Sissy asked.

"I cried," Ivan said with a nod. "I vomited. I coughed up phlegm. I had terrible diarrhea. Aden got me to the toilet just in time. I. . ."

Ivan squinted his eyes and then looked back at her.

"Then your Blane comes meandering back in the room," Ivan said. "He gives me tea that smells like feces and told me to walk. At that point, I was like a torture victim. I would have done anything anyone said. I drank his foul tea and. . ."

Ivan shrugged.

"He put me on the table and did another round of needles," Ivan said. "There was some lighting of this incense which smelled like marijuana. Aden brought me here, and I have slept. I dreamt of my delight in meeting you. Now, I realized I have to go back to see this magician again."

"Blane's coming here for dinner," Sissy said. "He'll treat us here."

Ivan yawned and nodded at the same time.

"Was yours like that?" Ivan asked.

"No," Sissy said. "But I have had something like that happen. When I was sick with the eating disorder the last time. It feels horrible and amazing."

"Freeing," Ivan said.

Sissy nodded.

"Would you want a child?" Ivan asked.

"Someday," Sissy said. "Maybe. If I get better, if I can dance, I'd rather do that. Plus, I have the birth-control implant."

"You do?" Ivan's eyebrows shot up with surprise.

"Sandy made me and Noelle get them before we left for New York," Sissy said. "We thought it was stupid, but we'd do anything for Sandy."

Sissy nodded and turned over her arm to show where the implant was located.

"Why didn't I know?" Ivan asked.

"There was a lot going on," Sissy shrugged. "Do you want a child?"

"Yes," Ivan said. "But. . . I want. . ."

He sighed.

"Oh, Sissy — all I really want is you," Ivan said. "You want to dance. Okay. You want to have a child or five? Okay. I just don't know how to. . ."

"Get past this," Sissy said.

"Clumsiness," Ivan said.

They both fell silent. Sissy looked down at her hands. After a few moments, Ivan's hand appeared. He took her hand and pulled her to him while making sure she stayed on top of the sheet.

"Put your head right here." Ivan encouraged Sissy to rest her head on his shoulder. "You can turn this way. . ."

She rolled so that her non-injured side pressed against him. Her arm rested across him. They both lay like cardboard cut-outs for a few moments before the warmth of their familiarity and love caused them to relax. He stroked her hair.

"This is nice," Sissy said.

"Heaven," Ivan said.

~~~~~~~~~
Thursday night — 7:15 p.m.

"Hi!" Jeraine said. He peered into the screen at Tanesha. "You're blurry."

Tanesha pointed to her eyes. They were talking via video call over the Internet. He squinted at her before letting out a laugh.

"Of course," Jeraine said. "Just a second."

He set the computer tablet down and wandered away. Tanesha crawled into her new bed and lay down. She had settled in when he returned with his glasses.

"Where are you?" Jeraine asked.

"In my new bedroom," Tanesha said with a smile.

"Where is that?" Jeraine's voice rose with anxiety.

"The fairies — well, really, Jake — made me a bedroom under the basement stairs," Tanesha said.

"In the basement?" Jeraine asked. He shook his head. "I cannot imagine it."

"You want to see?" Tanesha scooted out from the bed. "The bed is tucked against the stairwell. See?"

She turned the tablet around so he could see. The stairs went up at an angle, creating a cubby where a bed was now located. Everything was a wash of bronze and rich cream color.

"That's very nice," Jeraine said.

"It's a queen bed," Tanesha said. "Perfect for two but not for three."

She kept walking to show a small closet filled with her clothes.

"There's a desk so I can study," Tanesha said. A small wooden desk with a lamp and hookups for her laptop sat under the basement window. "They moved the laundry to the area by the backdoor and made this... Here — I'll show you."

She went into her tiny bathroom.

"Is that a shower?" Jeraine asked.

"Yep," Tanesha said. "I can't use it for a couple days, until it dries."

"You can use the one in the studio," Jeraine said.

Tanesha nodded.

"It's wonderful," Jeraine said. "The fairies did all of this?"

"Jake and his team," Tanesha said. "Blane said they were here most of the day. The fairies helped, but most of it was Jill's design and Jake's hammer. He built a wall here between this area and your studio. He said he can take it out when you need him to, but it's actually really nice."

"That is nice," Jeraine said. "Perfect for one person or a person and a child."

"Akeem wants to move here when you get home," Tanesha said.

"Akeem?" Jeraine bristled with jealousy. Tanesha laughed at him. "Why would Akeem live with us?"

"Another one of my dad's mentees is getting out of Limon," Tanesha said. "It's time for Akeem to move on, but Jabari really likes him. Akeem's hoping he can be Jabari's nanny."

"Oh," Jeraine said.

"I've told you this," Tanesha said. "He doesn't want money. He just wants a safe, drug-free place to live."

"It sounds familiar," Jeraine scratched his head. "I've been kind of. . ."

"Immersed," Tanesha said.

"I'm going on in a bit," Jeraine said. "Nervous."

"Don't be," Tanesha said. "You'll do great."

"Do you miss me at all?" Jeraine asked.

"I do miss you," Tanesha said with a reassuring nod. One thing they'd learned at couple's therapy was that Tanesha needed to demonstrate how she felt toward him. "Jabari, too."

"He's having fun." Jeraine's face brightened.

"Talked to him and mom between classes," Tanesha said.

Jeraine nodded that he knew. Someone said something in the background, and he nodded again.

"Well, Miss T. . ." Jeraine's head continued to go up and down.

"Have fun," Tanesha said. "It doesn't do me any good for you to suffer. People have paid good money to see you. You may as well have fun."

"Love you," Jeraine said.

Tanesha smiled at him, and he clicked off the video call. She looked at the dark screen for a moment before setting it on the small desk.

The house was quiet because Blane had taken Tink and his sons to the Castle to meet up with Heather, who'd been helping Sandy get her business going again. Tanesha looked up the stairs. She could go up and eat the dinner Blane had left for her — chicken breast, small salad, fresh roll, chocolate cake for dessert. Instead, she climbed back into bed and pulled the covers over her head.

She was okay. In fact, she was pretty good. Without Jeraine and Jabari here, she could really focus on finishing the term. No man and no son meant she could sleep as much as she wanted. She could stay at school until late. She could get up in the middle of the night to study in the way she liked but drove Jeraine crazy. She smiled at herself. Her little apartment was absolutely perfect for her. Everything was really good.

She just wished she didn't miss him so much.

THAT'S A GOOD THING

Friday morning — 7:35 a.m.

"What do you mean?" Nash asked.

Everyone stopped talking at the sound of Nash's panicked voice.

"What's going on?" Sandy asked.

"He said. . ." Nash started and then stopped. "He said. . . and I. . ."

Nash jumped up from his seat and started toward the door. Sam caught the boy before he left the main dining room. He turned Nash around and gave him a slight push back to his seat. Since Sissy and Ivan were there, they were eating breakfast all together. Honey wheeled in with a platter of bacon.

"Come on, son," Sam said.

Sam herded Nash to his seat next to Ivan. Jill brought the twins to their matching high chairs. Katy skipped into the room beside Jacob.

"What did we miss?" Jill asked.

"Nash freaked out," Noelle said. "We don't know why?"

"Why in the world would Nash freak out?" Valerie asked as she came into the dining room.

"Can't everyone mind their own business?" Nash yelled.

"No." Laughing, Noelle shook her head.

"That's just not possible," Sissy said.

"Your business is our business, son," Aden said.

Aden set a platter of eggs down and went to sit next to Sandy. Nash sneered at them. Mike came in carrying Jackie. He set

Jackie next to Tanner and sat down beside her highchair. Valerie hugged her father and sat down next to Mike.

"Hey!" Sandy said to Valerie. "I didn't know you were back."

"We came in last night late for turn-the-garden-beds weekend," Valerie said.

"It's on our calendar," Sandy said. "We wouldn't miss it for the world. Charlie doesn't have to testify today or early next week, so he's moving home for a bit. He's not much use digging, but Dale said he was coming. Dale's pretty handy."

"And so cute," Valerie said.

Sandy smiled. Jill looked up and nodded.

"Why did you freak out?" Noelle asked Nash in her most annoying little-sister voice.

"Nothing," Nash said in his best teenager sullen.

"I told him that Nadia was coming tonight," Ivan said. "She called one hour ago. She has the weekend off and wants to visit. She said something about a new exhibit at the museum."

"There's an impressionist exhibit," Mike said. Gesturing to Noelle and himself, he added, "We're going tomorrow, early, before the crowds get there. You're welcome to join us."

"They are very slow," Valerie said.

"We go over every piece," Mike said. "We look at the lighting, the structure of the painting. . ."

"The subject," Noelle said. "How it was made."

"From brush strokes to vision," Mike nodded.

"It will take them most of the day," Valerie said with a nod.

"Jake and I are working on the first turn of the beds today," Mike said. "You could help us after school, Nash, or even go to the museum with Noelle and me. Either way."

Nash shook his head. He made an effort to stuff his breakfast into his mouth so that he could leave. The enormous bite left him choking. Sam pounded the boy's back until he sputtered. When Nash caught his breath, he looked up. Everyone at the table was staring at him. Maggie slipped off Honey's lap and toddled over to Nash. He pulled her up on his lap. Not quite speaking, Maggie leaned into Nash to show him that she loved him. Nash hugged the child to him. When no one said anything, Nash looked up again.

"What?" Nash asked.

Everyone laughed.

"Do not worry about this," Ivan said to Nash. "Nadia, she does what she does. She has always been this way. There's very little one can do about it."

Nash nodded.

"Plus, she wants to see you," Ivan said. "That's a good thing, no?"

"Maybe," Nash said. "I just wanted to be. . ."

"If you were, she might not like you as much," Mike said.

Nash looked across the table at him, and Mike nodded his head. Nash glanced toward where Delphie was sitting at the head of the table. She had been suspiciously silent through this entire event. Ivy said something to Delphie, and Delphie looked up at him. The Oracle read his face for a moment before giving him a sweet smile.

"You don't have anything to say?" Nash asked Delphie.

"We're going to have a great weekend," Delphie said.

Shaking his head, Nash had to smile. Maggie tugged on his thumb, and he gave her a piece of his bacon. When he looked up, everyone was talking and laughing. He glanced at Ivan and Sissy. They seemed genuinely happy. Sissy gave him an understanding smile, and he nodded. She knew exactly what he was going through. He let out a breath.

Maybe he could be happy like Sissy was now. He smiled and finished his breakfast.

~~~~~~~

Friday afternoon — 2:45 p.m.

"Hi," Dale said.

Heather looked up from where she and Mack were coloring on the steps of the Castle's deck off the main kitchen. She smiled at Dale and scooted Mack over so that Dale could get by.

"Uh," Dale said.

Heather looked up again. She put her hand on her brow to shade her eyes from the bright sun. Dale moved over so that his head blocked the sun, and Heather got a good look at the young man. He was five or six years younger than she. A thin layer of dirt clung to his sheen of sweat from working on the garden beds. With her look, Dale turned to glance over to where Charlie was sitting. Charlie gave him a "go on" gesture.

"Can I help you with something?" Heather asked.

Dale scowled.

"Ma-Ma." Mack tugged on her sleeve. He pointed to her mouth.

"Oh, sorry," Heather said in English. "Mack tells me I'm not speaking English. I apologize. I have to travel soon. I'm trying to learn a new language. Edie and I have been speaking it all day."

Heather gestured toward the kitchen. As if she'd heard Heather, Edie appeared carrying a tray with pitchers of lemonade and iced tea. Dale jogged up the steps to take the tray from her. He set the tray where Edie instructed him to, on the picnic table, and went back to where Heather was sitting. Heather was looking at Charlie. When Dale returned to the deck stairs, she glanced at him.

"How can I help?" Heather asked in English.

"Would you like me to pick up Tink?" Though clearly not his question, Dale asked it anyway.

"No," Heather said. "Wanda's dad is taking Tink, Wanda, and Sissy to the movies. They should be back for dinner."

Dale nodded. He looked like he was going to run off to the garden.

"Was that really your question?" Heather asked.

When Dale looked down, Mack and Heather were both looking up at him. Their open, honest faces reflected only their desire to help. His sorrow welled inside him, and he cleared his throat.

"Um," Dale said.

Dale tucked his dirty hands into his jeans pockets and looked down. He looked impossibly young and vulnerable. Mack reached up and tugged on his hand. Dale looked at the young boy.

"Mama helps," Mack said with a nod.

Dale glanced at Heather and then back at the child. Mack gave Dale one of his beautiful smiles. Dale couldn't help but grin at the child.

"How can I help?" Heather asked.

"Um," Dale said.

Mack tugged on his arm, and Dale sat down on the step next to them. Edie stepped by as she went to offer tea or lemonade to Jacob and Mike. They watched the interaction — Charlie making jokes, which made Jacob and Mike laugh, and Edie asking about lemonade before turning around and heading back toward them.

"Charlie told me about your mom and dad," Dale said.

"What about them?" Heather asked.

"Psyche and Eros," Dale said.

"Oh?" Heather's voice was mild, but Dale blushed.

"Charlie and me, man, we're really tight," Dale said in a flurry of words. "I can't really explain it, but we just hit it off. He's like my best friend, even though he's not eighteen yet. But I'm only twenty-three, so it's not that big of a difference."

Heather smiled at the young man.

"It's not a secret," Edie said as she passed. "Hedone has nothing to hide."

Dale looked at the fairy.

"She's not defensive," Edie said. "She is not her father. She actually wants to know how she can help."

"Really?" Dale asked.

Edie nodded and went to the deck. Dale looked at Heather, who nodded.

"I have to learn this language," Heather said. "My youngest son will be awake soon. Mack will go down for his nap in a half-hour. Blane's treating Ivan inside. He will need my help soon. I'm available now. Ask away. If I don't want to answer, I won't. If it's something you shouldn't know, I'll get Edie to alter your memory."

Heather shrugged.

"That's pretty straightforward," Dale said.

"Why complicate things?" Heather asked. She smiled at Dale. "You want to know about Beth."

Dale sucked in a breath. His green eyes locked on Heather's before he nodded.

"Were she and I. . . I mean. . ." Dale started.

Heather squinted at him for a moment. She reached over Mack and touched Dale's hand. Her smile dropped, and her face shifted to sorrow.

"Yes, I'm sorry," Heather said. "My father shot you and Beth with what are called 'Dark Arrows.' You could have love, experience it, but you were destined to tragically lose it."

Dale looked away from her and gave a sad nod.

"This kind of thing is an aberration, uh, a misuse of his gift," Heather said.

"Why would he do that?" Dale asked in words laced with strong emotion.

"He told me it was my fault," Heather said. "Aphrodite thinks it was some kind of mental illness caused by losing my mother. Hera thinks he's just a dick."

"And you?" Dale asked.

"I personally think that being male and a God was too much

power for a fairly broken being," Heather said. "But that's when I'm in a forgiving mood."

"And when you're not?" Dale asked.

"I spent a long, long time believing that all of this cruelty was my fault," Heather said. "I believed my father when he told me that I was the cause of all of this human pain. He was my father. He was a God. He had to know the truth. When I see my children and see how innocent they are, I think. . ."

Heather gave a quick shake of her head. Mack looked up at his mother. Seeing her pain, he put his head on her knee. She stroked Mack's curly black hair.

"He's not a very good being," Heather said.

"Charlie told me," Dale said.

"There's more, isn't there?" Heather asked.

Dale nodded.

"If I die, and I meet Beth in a next life, will we have to go through this again?"

"No," Heather said. "Hera, Aphrodite, and I are working to eliminate these dark arrows. We didn't get to you because. . ."

She turned her head to look at him, and he instinctively looked at her.

"Seth saved you," Heather said.

"Delphie, you mean," Dale said. "She told him to keep me at the house. She didn't tell him why."

"I doubt she knew why," Heather said. "It's a testament to you that you've survived this."

"I wasn't meant to?" Dale asked.

Heather nodded.

"I see Ivan or Nash," Dale said. He swallowed hard. "You know, I had Beth. The moment I met her, she was mine, and I was hers. We were one. But she was my age, Amelie's age. She wasn't a child or almost thirty years older than I am. I mean, we didn't. . . you know. . . nothing unsavory, but one look and. . ."

He fell silent. Heather let him think.

"I was very lucky," Dale said finally.

"Would you like to love like that again?" Heather asked.

"No," Dale said. "I'd rather wait for Beth."

Heather smiled.

"Will I. . .?" Dale asked. When he stopped talking, Heather looked at him. She read his face.

"You are capable of loving," Heather said. "That's all that matters. It will start in the most miniscule way — your love for Clara, the dog, or even your friendship with Charlie. Your heart will open a tiny bit. Then, over time, it will open a little bit more."

"Seth says not to rush it," Dale said.

Heather nodded.

"I see it," Dale said. "In him."

"See what?" Heather asked.

"He loves Amelie, you know, Ava?" Dale asked. "But he still loves Sandy's mom with all of his soul. Ava knows it. She doesn't mind. She's just like that. She thinks it's good that he can love, because so many people can't."

Heather smiled.

"What?" Dale asked.

Heather didn't say anything.

"Oh, Ava and Seth," Dale said. "Your doing?"

"Not me," Heather said. "Aphrodite."

Dale turned to look at Heather. He blinked a few times before nodding his head.

"You mean, some day, I could have what they have," Dale said.

Heather nodded.

"They really love each other," Dale said.

"They do," Heather said.

Dale fell quiet. They watched Jacob and Mike dig in the fertile earth for a while.

"I'm gonna. . ." Mack pointed to Jacob and Mike.

"When you get big," Heather said.

Mack nodded.

"'morrow, I get to help Katy," Mack nodded.

"With the planting?" Heather smiled at her kind little boy. "You sure do."

Mack beamed at the idea he would get to work in this garden tomorrow. Turn-the-beds-weekend started at the Castle, moved to Blane and Heather's house, and this year would finish at Tanesha and Jeraine's home. It was a full weekend of turning the earth, adding compost, and planting the early crops. By the end of the weekend, her little boy would be much less excited to help.

"Thanks," Dale said. He stood up. "I should get back to work."

Heather smiled at him. He turned to stand in front of her.

"It's going to take some time," Heather said.

"I can wait," Dale said. "I'm not really in any hurry."

He nodded.

"One thing about having Beth was that I missed out on a lot of stuff," Dale said.

"Stuff?" Heather asked.

"Having a guy for a best friend," Dale said. "Learning how to garden and fix things. There's a lot in my life now that I would never have had."

He tried to smile, but it came out as a grimace.

"Don't get me wrong," Dale said. "I would give it up in a heartbeat."

"Of course," Heather said.

Dale nodded. His heart felt a tiny little bit more at ease, and he walked away whistling.

"It's about time!" Jacob said. He picked up a long-handled, round digging shovel and walked it to Dale. "There's more work to do, son!"

"Son?" Dale laughed. "How did I get to be your son?"

"You talk about as little as his sons!" Mike said.

The men laughed. Heather smirked at the joke. Looking down, she saw that Mack was fading. She picked up her son and went inside to settle him down for a nap.

~~~~~~~~~

Friday evening — 5:50 p.m.

Nash looked down at his feet. He was wearing the new shoes he and Sandy had just purchased. In fact, everything he was wearing was new. Mrs. Anjelika had spent an entire afternoon going over men's clothing with Teddy and him. They'd chosen boxer briefs, like their father's. They'd picked similar shoes, although Teddy liked boots over actual dress shoes. Teddy liked a traditional western-wear look, while Nash had picked something more European.

Nash shifted. The boxer briefs were a little more constrictive than the boxers he'd worn as a child. That's how he thought of everything now.

At one time, he was a child.

And now he was not.

He swallowed hard. No one had laughed when he told them he was an adult now. Not a single adult had made fun of him. Not any of the girlfriends or his parents or anyone. Not even Noelle. They had just tried to help him and Teddy get what they wanted.

Noelle had said that Teddy looked "smashing" in his new clothes. Nash felt a pang of excitement race through him. He hoped that Nadia would think the same thing.

Nash knew he was hardly an adult. He didn't even have a driver's license yet.

He just knew that he felt really different. He felt serious and focused for the first time in his life. He knew where he was going and wanted to get there. He didn't have time for goofing around. Luckily, Teddy felt the same way. He nodded to himself.

There was a sound up the breezeway, and Nash looked up. His heart pounded in his chest. He stared down the passage for a few moments. Nadia did not appear. He let out a breath.

Scowling, he looked down at the flowers in his hand. His sweaty hands had mangled the paper around them. If she didn't come soon, he was going to have to put them down.

"Are those for me?"

He gasped. Nash's head jerked up, and Nadia was standing in front of him. When he looked up, her entire face transformed with radiant joy. He blushed, looked down, and pushed the flowers out to her. She took them from him.

"I wanted to. . ." Nash started.

He stopped talking when he saw her face. Like him, she didn't know what to do. They stood less than a foot apart with the bouquet of flowers between them.

"Ms. Kerminoff?" a man asked from behind Nadia.

They both looked up to see who it was. A man wearing a dark suit and dark glasses came up behind Nadia. He had an inch of stubble growing perfectly on his face and thick dark hair. He wasn't quite as tall as Nash, but his body was thick with well-groomed muscles. Everything about him whispered "Alpha Male."

"I've been informed that your friend has arranged adequate transportation," the man said. He set Nadia's luggage next to her. The man gave Nash a once-over. Raising an eyebrow, the man said, "Would you like me to escort you to the vehicle? Carry the bag?"

His tone indicated just what he thought. Nash was a little kid. Nash wasn't a big, hairy man with perfect facial hair. Nash couldn't carry Nadia's bag or keep her safe in the airport. Nash's eyes flicked to Nadia. She'd heard the man loud and clear. Her face was bright red, too.

"That won't be necessary." Mike's voice came from behind Nash.

The man looked past Nash to see Mike. This man might think

he was something, but you just had to get near Mike to know that Mike was the real deal. Mike radiated power and control. Nash felt like crying with relief. Mike got close to the man to pick up Nadia's bag. For a moment, the man was unwilling to give Mike an inch. Not one for subtle, Mike nudged the man out of the way. The man had to take a couple of steps back.

Mike gave the man an irritated smile and turned in place.

"Give her your elbow," Mike said to Nash under his breath.

Nash held out his elbow. Nadia latched on like a drowning victim. Mike made them go ahead of him.

"I. . ." Nash started to say.

Mike shook his head. Nash shut his mouth. They walked to where Mike had parked the small limousine. Mike helped Nadia and Nash into the back. He set Nadia's bag into the trunk before getting into the driver's seat.

"Who was that dick?" Mike asked.

"No one I know," Nadia said.

"You've never met him?" Mike asked.

"He's just someone from the charter company," Nadia said. "He was an attendant on my flight. Brought me sparkling water. Why?"

"Bruno called," Mike said. "Said I should get here fast."

"Is Nadia in danger?" Nash asked.

Mike didn't respond. He looked at Nash through the rearview mirror for a moment before his eyes flicked to Nadia.

"Did you take yourself off a dating list?" Mike asked.

"Matchmaker," Nadia said. "It was something my mom set up with her kooky Russian friends. I'm supposed to get married this year."

"You are?" Nash's voice cracked with panic.

Nadia grabbed his hand and held it to her chest.

"It's something my mother wanted," Nadia said. "She wanted to make sure I didn't invest in my career so much that I missed having kids. With the stuff with Sissy being in the newspapers, everyone knows that Ivan and I aren't a couple. But before, we let everyone think... plus, Ivan is Bratva. No one would dare bother me. But now everyone knows I'm single. This matchmaker has been calling non-stop."

"You need to get married?" Nash asked. "Now?"

"No," Nadia said. "I don't have to do anything. The Matchmaker had a couple of men she wants me to meet. She sent me their information, and they're..."

Nadia shrugged.

"After I met Nash, I called her," Nadia said. She turned in the seat to look at Nash. "I called at the nurse's station outside Sissy's room. Remember? I was on the phone when you left."

Nash nodded.

"I called her immediately," Nadia said. "She tried to talk me out of it, but..."

Nadia shook her head.

"She keeps calling," Nadia said. "But I don't have time for phone calls with services I've already cancelled."

"Bruno said that there are more than a few young men who wanted..." Mike said.

"My money," Nadia interrupted. "Of course, they do."

She slapped her free hand against the bench. Mike gave a curt nod and moved the car into traffic. After a moment, Mike put up the barrier between him and them. They both gave the barrier a panicked look.

Nash turned his body to look at her.

"I'm glad you came," Nash said. Nadia beamed at him. He put his arm around her, and they rode to Denver.

CHAPTER THREE HUNDRED AND SEVENTY-SEVEN
NOT THIS AGAIN

Saturday early morning — 3:11 a.m.

Bzz! Tweet, tweet, tweet! Bzz! Bzz! Tweet, tweet, tweet! Bzz! Bzz!

Tanesha groaned. Jabari loved to change her phone ring to what he called "tweetie birdie."

Tweet, tweet, tweet! Bzz! Bzz! Tweet, tweet, tweet! Bzz! Bzz!

She looked at the clock. Scowling, she answered the phone.

"It's three in the fucking morning," Tanesha said.

"Miss T! This is Shane D. . ."

Tanesha clicked off the call. She looked at the object in her hand. This phone was her private, non-registered cell phone. The only people who had this number were Jeraine, her mother, her father, Fin, and her girlfriends.

Bzz! Tweet, tweet, tweet! Bzz! Bzz!

She looked at the phone. It said "Undisclosed." She clicked ignore. She would just turn the phone off, but she wanted to be available in case Jeraine or Jabari needed her.

Bzz! Tweet, tweet, tweet! Bzz! Bzz!

It was someone with a Florida phone number. She clicked "Ignore."

Bzz! Tweet, tweet, tweet! Bzz! Bzz!

California number. She clicked "Ignore." There were soft footsteps of someone coming down from the bedroom upstairs.

"What is it?" Tink's sleep-filled voice came from above Tanesha's head.

Bzz! Tweet, tweet, tweet! Bzz! Bzz! Tanesha clicked "Ignore."

"Probably just Jeraine being an ass," Heather said in a low voice.

Tink chuckled and slipped across the hardwood floors toward the bathroom. The door to the basement opened, and the stairs creaked as Heather came down them.

Bzz! Tweet, tweet, tweet! Bzz! Bzz! Tanesha clicked ignore. She flicked on the light above her bed so that Heather could see her. Heather stopped at the end of the stairs and turned to look at Tanesha.

"What did he do?" Heather asked.

"No idea," Tanesha said.

Bzz! Tweet, tweet, tweet! Bzz! Bzz! Tanesha clicked "Ignore."

"Did they say anything?" Heather asked.

"I haven't let any of them talk," Tanesha said.

Heather nodded. She made a gesture with her hand, and Tanesha moved over. They sat in sleep-deprived silence while Tanesha's phone rang, and she clicked "Ignore." After a few moments, Tanesha turned the phone off.

"How'd they get your number?" Heather asked.

"How do they always get my number?" Tanesha asked. "From you."

"Not me," Heather said. "Jill — I'm always sure it's Jill."

They were silent for a few moments before they laughed.

"Ugh," Tanesha said and lay back on the bed.

"Don't you want to know what he did?" Heather asked.

"Does it matter?" Tanesha snorted a laugh. Heather chuckled.

"*He's a dick!*" Tink yelled from above their heads. Heather and Tanesha laughed.

Mack wailed from upstairs, and they looked up.

"Mama! Mama! Mama!" Mack screamed from upstairs. "T-iiiiinK! T-iiiiinK! T-iiiiinK!"

They heard Blane's deep mumble.

"Who's a dick?" Blane asked down the stairs.

"Jeraine!" Tink yelled back.

"We thought about naming the baby 'Jeraine' or maybe 'Jerry'," Heather said.

"Why?" Tanesha asked with a sneer.

"He's been really nice to us," Heather said. "But Tink said she'd call the baby only by his formal name, 'Richard.'"

Tanesha laughed. The door to the basement opened.

"I thought I'd make some pancakes," Blane said at the top of the stairs. "Is it enough to lure you from your basement lair?"

Tanesha made a grumbling noise, and Blane laughed. They sat staring at the wall for a few moments. They heard Blane set up the baby gate at the basement stairs. Mack stood at the gate saying, "Ma-ma" over and over again.

"What do you think he did?" Heather asked.

Tanesha shrugged.

"Use your senses," Heather said. "Pretend you were standing right next to him when he did it."

Tanesha closed her eyes and let out a breath. Her eyes popped open. She shrugged.

"And?" Heather asked.

"Nothing," Tanesha said. "I don't think he did a damned thing."

"Me, too," Heather said.

Tanesha shook her head. Heather scooted off the bed.

"Good thing they can't find the house," Heather said as she went up the stairs.

"Aunt Phy's spell gets them lost as soon as they turn onto the street," Tanesha said.

"Let's hope it holds," Heather said.

Heather nodded to Tanesha. She reached the top, and Mack squealed with delight at seeing her. Heather's laugh made Tanesha smile. She got out of bed to use the bathroom in the studio. Pulling a thick sweatshirt over her head, she went upstairs.

"Isn't that your mom?" Tink asked.

She held out her smartphone. Tanesha took the phone and looked at the image. Heather came to her side, and Blane looked over her shoulder.

"I think it's Yvonne," Tink said.

The picture was of Jeraine leaning forward, with his lips puckered as if to kiss the woman standing next to him. The woman's back was to the camera. The woman's hair was reddish-brown and straightened. The skin on the woman's neck looked white or maybe suntanned under flash. She was wearing a dress that was more suited for the Dick Van Dyke show than 2015.

"Looks like her," Tanesha said.

"Why would Jeraine kiss Yvonne?" Heather asked.

"Jabari's in her arms," Tanesha said. "I bet this is from before he went on stage. Kiss the kid; go on stage. Mom would have wanted to be there."

Tanesha looked at Tink.

"You're right," Tanesha said. "That's my mom."

"Doesn't mean he's not a lying, cheating *dick*," Tink said.

"Absolutely," Tanesha said, and they all laughed. Tink moved over on the day bed she'd been sleeping on. Tanesha sat next to her. Mack toddled by and wanted up. Tink pulled him up onto the bed between them.

"Who's up for waffles?" Blane asked from the kitchen. "I just found a waffle iron."

Heather's infant let out a hearty scream, and she went to get him. She returned to sit in an armchair nearby. The baby was wide awake and looking around at everything.

"Well?" Heather asked.

There was a screech of tires on the street outside. They looked toward the blinds. Another screech of tires, and a few motorcycles pulled up.

"I should probably call him," Tanesha said.

"Call Schmidty," Blane said. He appeared in the kitchen doorway. He was stirring some beige goo in a mixing bowl with a wooden spoon. "His job includes dealing with this."

"Good idea," Heather said. "My phone's in the kitchen."

"Use mine," Tink said. She held the phone out to Tanesha.

"You don't want to text your friends?" Tanesha asked.

"Friends don't text friends in the middle of the night," Tink said. "They'd kill me. Take it."

Tanesha took the phone and dialed Schmidty.

~~~~~~~~~

Saturday early morning — 4:17 a.m.

A blue light flashed in Katy's eyes, and she opened her eyes. She stared at the pictures of her family that Uncle Mike had painted on her wall for a while before closing her eyes again. The bright blue light appeared. When she opened her eyes, the light went out.

Katy closed her eyes again. The blue light appeared again, but, this time, Katy kept her eyes closed. The light lingered over her before moving across the room. Since Katy was no longer sleeping with Scooter, Jill had traded her queen bed for two twins. At Jill's insistence, Paddie was sound asleep in his own twin bed. The blue light hung over Paddie before moving toward Katy.

"Touch her, and I will slice you end to end!" Paddie screamed.

Katy opened her eyes to see an adult-sized blue fairy leaning over her bed. The fairy was wearing the blue tutu of the Fairy Corps, but she also had blue skin and hair. She had a funny wand and some weird hat on her head. She shone with an inner blue light. Katy heard Jill and Jacob jump out of bed and run toward Katy's room. The fairy looked terrified.

"Back up!" Paddie yelled.

The fairy backed up but didn't dare stand up.

"Paddie?" Jacob asked from the door of the room.

Jill pressed past him. She wedged herself between Katy and the fairy.

"What do you want?" Jill asked.

She held her hands in front of herself. The fairy looked at Jill's hands and gasped. The fairy looked so scared that Katy thought she might throw up.

"Mommy?" Katy asked.

Katy pulled Jill back just in time to avoid the fairy's vomit.

"What the hell?" Jacob asked.

"She got scared," Katy said.

Paddie deftly jumped from his twin bed onto Katy's bed. Jacob walked to the fairy. He tugged on her, and she collapsed. Jacob looked at Jill, and she shrugged.

"Oh, no," Edie gasped from the doorway. She came to the fairy's side. "Did she hurt you?"

Edie looked at Katy and Jill, who shook their heads.

"She was gonna *touc,* Katy!" Paddie said. His front teeth were missing so he lisped every word.

Edie looked at Paddie. Noticing his sword, she scowled.

"He has the Sword of Truth, Edith!" the fairy on the ground said.

"Yes, yes," Edie said. "Maughold gave it to him when they were putting the queendom back together."

"Maughold," the fairy gasped. "But the child. . . The child. . . he told me he would. . ."

"Slice you end to end," Edie said. "Yes, yes. Finegal has been working with him."

"And she. . . ." The fairy pointed to Jill. "She. . . she. . . ."

"She's a healer from the line out of Russ. Yes," Edie said. She looked at Jacob. "Can you help get her up?"

"Sure," Jacob said.

With Jacob's help, Edie was able to get the fairy on her feet. Once she was standing, she shone bright blue.

"Tone it down," Edie said. The light dimmed. "This is my

elder sister, Aife. She is second in line for the throne. She acts as the blue fairy."

The fairy curtsied.

"What do you want?" Jill asked with a scowl.

"I. . . well, I. . .," the blue fairy said. The fairy turned to look at Jacob. "You look just like my brother, Finegal."

"He looks like me," Jacob joked.

"No," the blue fairy said. "He is much, much older than you, and you are human — or mostly — and. . ."

"That was a joke," Edie said to the blue fairy.

"Oh." The blue fairy gave an awkward smile. Even her teeth were blue.

"She doesn't interact with a lot of people — well, anyone, really," Edie said. "Come on, Aife. Let's get you changed."

"No," Jill said with such power that Edie and Aife stopped walking. "No fairy comes to our world without wanting something. Does your mother wish to steal my daughter again?"

Edie gave Aife a hard look. Aife shook her head. Edie gave her a harder look.

"No," Aife said. "I came because. . ."

Aife nodded to Edie, and Edie looked surprised.

"You're sure?" Edie asked.

Aife nodded.

"Sure of what?" Jill asked.

"Abi's going to have her baby soon," Edie said. "Today or tomorrow."

"I'm just early," Aife said. "I thought I'd come to see the child — you know, the one Mom talks about. You were asleep, so. . ."

She looked at Katy and gave her a small smile.

"Sorry," Aife said. She looked at Paddie and gave him a terrified nod. "Really, I didn't mean for all of this to happen."

"I'm so sorry, Katy," Edie said.

"I'm okay," Katy said with a shrug. "Paddie?"

"I'm okay," Paddie said.

Edie gave the children a nod and started walking toward her room.

"Abi's having her baby?" Jacob asked. "What does that mean for us?"

"Abi will have to come here," Edie said. "It's the only secure place on this continent."

"And the Fairy Corps?" Jill asked.

"Oh, yeah. They're all coming," Edie said. "The moment Mari realizes that Aife is here, she will arrive. With great fanfare. Of course. And Keenan?"

Edie looked at Aife.

"Mom's keeping him home," Aife said. "The last time he was here, he got stuck in the Sea of Amber. *The Sea of Amber*, Edie. Is that going to happen to me?"

Edie sighed and shook her head.

"Now you know why she's here," Edie said to Jill and Jacob. "I'm sorry. I need to help my sister. She's not as weird when she changes out of blue and gets something to eat."

"Go ahead," Jacob said.

Edie put one arm under Aife's shoulder, and they walked toward her room.

"Can I see the twins?" Aife asked.

"No!" Jill yelled.

"Not just now, dear," Edie said.

She nodded to Jill, and they went into Edie's room. Jill took her first real breath when Edie's door closed.

"That was fun!" Paddie said. "What are we gonna do now?"

Jacob looked at Paddie and laughed.

"You saved the day again," Jacob said. "You get to choose. Would you like to go back to sleep or have something to eat or. . .?"

"Um," Paddie yawned.

"Come on, Paddie," Katy said.

Katy lifted the covers, and Paddie crawled in beside her. Tucked up against each other, they were fast asleep in seconds. Jill gave Jacob an irritated look. He smiled and shrugged. Jill turned off the light. She and Jacob went back to bed.

Of course, Jacob fell right to sleep while Jill stared at the ceiling for a while. Just when she was sure she would never get to sleep, the alarm was going off, and day two of turn-the-beds-weekend had already begun.

~~~~~~~~~

Saturday morning — 8:05 a.m.

"Oh, no," Nadia said. "No. No. No. No."

The sound of her voice launched Nash in her direction. From the main Castle kitchen, he ran through the living room. Passing Ivan on the way, he raced down the stairs to the suite where Nadia was staying. He tapped on the door. While he waited for an answer, Ivan caught up to him. Ivan gave him a nod.

"She is almost never naked," Ivan said. "You can go in."

Ivan pressed open the door. When Nash lingered in the hallway, Ivan grabbed the front of his shirt and dragged him into the room.

"*Chto proizoshlo*?" Ivan asked. Nash's pidgeon Russian translated to "What happened?"

Nadia held up her phone to him. Ivan took the phone. He scowled and gave the phone to Nash. There was a picture of Mike helping Nadia into the limousine. From that angle, it looked like Mike was Nadia's date. The headline read... something Nash couldn't translate. He held it out to Ivan, with a questioning look on his face.

"Valerie's greatest pain," Ivan said. "Implies Mike and Nadia..."

He waved his hand in Nadia's direction. Nash blinked at Ivan. Nash looked at Nadia for a moment.

"I'll take care of it," Nash said.

He sped out of the room. He jogged down the hallway and took the stairs two at a time. Valerie had been standing in the kitchen when he'd left. He sped through the living room and slid into the kitchen.

"Nadia," Nash said. He had to stop to pant. He bent over, his hands hitting his knees.

"Nash?" Valerie went to him. She put her hand on his back.

"There's a. . ." Nash panted.

"What's happened to Nadia?" Valerie asked.

"Picture," Nash panted. "Reason. . . paparazzi."

"We were just talking about how crazy they seem today," Valerie said with a shrug. "Are they after Nadia?"

Although a small woman, Valerie was a force to be reckoned with. She glared toward the front of the Castle.

"What did they do to Nadia?" Valerie asked. Her voice threatened rage.

"They took a photo of Mike helping Nadia into the limo," Nash said, swallowing hard. "It's in some Russian paper."

Valerie shrugged.

"They think Mike's with Nadia," Nash said. "It says 'Valerie's Heartbreak.'"

"Cheating on me with the beautiful heiress is my heartbreak?" Valerie laughed.

"I'm so sorry," Nadia said from the entrance to the kitchen. Ivan was standing just behind her.

Valerie put her head back and laughed. Nash, Nadia, and Ivan looked at Valerie as if she'd gone mad. Mike came in from the garden.

"What's so funny?" Mike asked.

"The papz are here to catch a photo of you with your new girlfriend," Valerie said.

"Noelle?" Mike asked. "Fucking pervs."

"Nadia," Valerie said. "It says, 'Valerie's greatest pain.'"

"The article says you can't get out of bed," Nadia said. "Your family is concerned you will kill yourself."

Valerie laughed.

"Why is that funny?" Nash asked.

"Because they think that some mix-up could possibly be worse than Mike going off to war or getting captured," Valerie said. "They have no idea what military families live with every single day."

Valerie gave them a nod.

"What do you want to do?" Nash asked.

"I think we take it to the papz," Valerie said. "We release a statement that says that Nadia is a dear family friend. And that my greatest pain was losing Mike as a casualty of war. Whatever happens, Mike and I will work it out. He's alive and breathing. We've proven that so far. But our military families deal with the greatest pain imaginable. To say this mix-up is my 'greatest pain' only serves to diminish their tremendous sacrifice."

Valerie gave Nash a nod. She smiled at Nadia.

"Sami will be here around noon," Valerie said. "Are we still on?"

"I. . . I. . ." Nadia nodded vigorously. "Are you sure you want to go. . . with me?"

"Of course," Valerie said. "Sami's already mapped out our afternoon — shopping, snack, spa. But first, we help Delphie with the fruit trees."

"I would love that," Nadia said.

"Great," Valerie said and went upstairs to Jill and Jacob's loft, where Jackie was playing.

"One good thing," Nadia said.

Mike lifted an eyebrow at her, and Nash turned to look at her.

"The matchmaker left a message saying that, since I was with a 'good Russian man' she would back off," Nadia said with a smile.

"Mike?" Nash asked.

Nadia nodded. Mike grunted.

"I'm ready," Noelle ran into the kitchen. She stopped short and said, "Did I miss something?"

"I'm having an affair with Nadia," Mike said with a glare.

"Oh?" Noelle asked. "Nash will kill you."

"Mmm," Mike said.

He nodded to Nash and turned in place. They grabbed their jackets at the door and went down into the tunnels.

"Are they angry?" Nadia asked in a quiet voice.

"Not at all," Delphie said as she came in from the backyard.

Nadia's eyes flicked to Nash, and he shook his head.

"Why not?" Nadia asked.

"It's happened before," Nash said. "They're always trying to make it seem like something's wrong between Mike and Valerie."

"Sells papers," Ivan said.

"I think they're jealous," Delphie said. She washed her dirty hands before turning on the electric kettle.

"What can I do to fix this?" Nadia asked.

"Did you make up the story?" Ivan asked.

"No, but. . ." Nadia said.

"Then there's nothing to do," Delphie said. "Valerie will call her people, and they will release a statement."

Nadia dropped down into a chair at the kitchen table.

"You seem upset," Delphie said.

"I'm just. . ." Nadia began to cry softly. Ivan pushed Nash forward to her. He knelt down beside her. He put his arm over her shoulder. "This is. . . And she. . ."

Nadia gestured up the stairs.

"I don't have. . . female friends," Nadia said. "And she. . . and Sami. . . They. . . and all of this. It's like a dream. Everyone is so dear. . ."

"You're welcome here," Delphie said. She put her arm around Nadia. In a low voice, she said, "Welcome home."

Nadia glanced at Nash, who nodded. She looked up at Delphie

before starting to weep in earnest.

CHAPTER THREE HUNDRED AND SEVENTY-EIGHT
FROG LEGS

Saturday morning — 8:35 a.m.

"Is this it?" Tanesha asked.

She peered at a rundown apartment complex in Glendale from the driver's side window of Jeraine's car. She glanced at Heather, who shrugged. There was a blonde brick path separating two sides of a sun-browned lawn. It was a warm day, and all of the windows were open. At least one infant was screaming at the top of his lungs.

"That's what the GPS says," Tink said.

Tink held out her cell phone from the back seat. Tanesha turned around to look at it.

"This is the place," Heather said.

"It's a dump," Tanesha said.

"Losing your nerve?" Heather asked.

"Oh, *hell*, no," Tanesha said. "This prick sells *my* phone number and address to the highest bidder. He's going to get a piece of my mind."

"We'd better get moving, then," Heather said. "They're expecting us at the Castle, and you need to study."

Nodding, Tanesha got out of the driver's seat. Heather met her on the sidewalk, and Tink followed close behind. By the time they were a few feet from the building, they could smell a mixture of grease, cigarette smoke, and food.

"Brings back memories," Heather said.

Tanesha nodded. She paused at the front door. At one time, there was a security system that kept the front door locked unless someone buzzed you in. Some time ago, someone had unloaded a handgun into the box and pried it from the wall. The metal plate dangled from the wall by electric wire. Heather pushed open the door, and they stepped onto a dirty, peeling linoleum floor. Tanesha pointed to the half-flight of stairs down.

They went down the threadbare, filthy carpeted stairs to a basement hallway. They continued along the dark hallway past the open doors where scantily clad women watching television were in full view.

"Looking for some fun?" A woman said from the doorway of the first apartment. She tugged on Tink's forearm to keep them from going anywhere.

"We're looking for Cody," Tanesha said.

The woman looked Tanesha up and down before pointing to the last door on the hallway.

"When you finished up, come back and see me," the woman said. "I'll give you an early bird discount."

"Gross," Tink said and pulled her arm away from the woman.

The woman gave her a creepy smile.

"No offense meant," the woman said. "Just trying to be friendly."

Tink gave Heather a disgusted look.

"Can't you do something?" Tink asked.

Heather raised an eyebrow. She clapped her hands together. One at a time, as they passed, the women closed their doors. They slowed at the last door on the hallway.

"What did you do?" Tink asked in a whisper.

"Boosted their self-respect," Heather said.

Tanesha touched Heather's arm in approval. Tink nodded. Tanesha pounded on Cody's door.

"Just a sec," a young man yelled from inside the apartment.

They waited a few minutes before the door opened a little bit. Cody was wearing baggy shorts over his full leg cast. His chest was bare and his hair wet as if he'd just stepped out of the shower.

He took one look at Tanesha and tried to slam the door closed. Tink held it open.

"Who do you think you are?" Tanesha asked.

"I. . . I. . ." Cody said.

"You *sold* my phone number and address to the paparazzi," Tanesha said.

Cody's eyes went wide, and his mouth hung open. He took a breath to respond.

"Don't deny it," Tanesha said. "I *know* you did it. What I don't know is: Why? Why do you hate me so much? What did I ever do to you?"

"I. . . uh. . ." Cody said.

"He's going to pass out," Heather said in a low tone to Tanesha. She nodded.

"I don't hate you," Cody said. "I don't. No. That's not it. I know you *think* that's it, but it's not."

"You call her the n-word!" Tink said.

Cody's panicked eyes flicked to Tink. Tanesha raised her eyebrows, and Cody swallowed hard.

"Well. . . I. . .." Cody started.

"So far, I haven't told the school that you *took* my phone number off the confidential class list and *sold* it to the vultures," Tanesha said with a sniff. "What do you think they're going to do?"

Cody shook his head.

"What do you think Fin's going to do when I tell him?" Tanesha asked.

"I. . ." Cody swallowed hard. "You don't have to. . ."

"Cody?" asked a male voice with the distinctive accent of someone with a mental challenge. "Who is it?"

"No one," Cody said.

"It sounds like somebody. Did they come to play video games with us?" the young man asked. A teenaged young man with

Down Syndrome appeared in the hallway. "That's Miss T. "

Cody glared at Tanesha.

"Hi, Miss T!" the young man said. "Hi, Miss T's friends. Are you famous, too?"

Heather glanced at Tink.

"Hey, dude," Tink said. She pushed by Cody. "I'll play video games with you."

"Great!" the young man said. "Hi! I'm Brian."

"Hi, Brian," Tink said with her usual giggle. "I'm Tink."

Tink followed Brian into the living-room area of the apartment. Tanesha watched as Brian gave Tink a video-game controller. She settled in, and they started to play.

"My parents died when I was in high school," Cody said. "Car accident. On the way to watch me play my last football game. The state wanted to put Brian in this home. I was. . ."

Cody nodded.

"You needed the money," Tanesha said with an understanding nod.

"I. . ." Cody swallowed hard. "You always seem like you've got it all together. Rich, famous husband, and Fin hanging on your every word."

Cody's resentment came forward with an angry glare.

"What do you care if anyone knows stuff about you?" Cody asked. "Just more fodder for your pathetic, ego-driven tragedy."

Locked in the laser beam of his rage, Tanesha took a step back. Heather touched Cody's arm. Surprised, he looked at her. After a moment, he let out a breath. Tink laughed at something Brian said, and they turned to look.

"That's my daughter," Heather said in a warm voice. "We call her Tink, but her name is Tiffanie. Before I knew her, she lived on the streets. But then, I did, too."

Cody looked up with surprise.

"Tanesha had to put her first year of medical school on hold because she had to work four jobs to save her Gran's house,"

Heather said. "Her Gran raised her."

"Why?" Cody asked.

"You can look it up online," Heather said. "I'm just trying to say that we understand your situation — just not your choices."

Cody nodded. He glanced at Tanesha.

"What's the deal with that guy Fin?" Cody asked. "Is he your boyfriend? He just reeks of sexuality. And that pseudo-not-quite-English accent. All the girls in our class want to get with him."

"He's family," Tanesha said. "And he can be a real prick."

"He acts like he's royalty or something," Cody said.

"Or something," Tanesha said with a laugh.

"I'm all Brian has," Cody said. "The social worker comes every month to see if they can take him away from me. We're barely scraping by, and then I broke my leg in lab that day. Your phone number and address will pay my rent for the next six months."

Heather glanced at Tanesha.

"So I'd like to say I'm sorry," Cody said. "But I'm not."

"You know, Jeraine lost everything," Heather said.

"IRS," Cody said. "I heard that. Serves him right."

Heather and Tanesha scowled at him.

"He's a lying, cheating asshole," Cody said. "He's treated you like garbage."

"Jeraine?" Tink yelled from inside the apartment.

"He has," Tanesha said with a nod. Heather nodded.

"What can you possibly see in that guy?" Cody asked.

"Why do you care?" Tanesha asked. "You going to sell the exclusive to some stupid magazine?"

"Fair enough," Cody said with a nod.

They stood in uncomfortable silence for a few moments before Cody cleared his throat.

"Listen, if you tell school, they'll kick me out."

"They sure will," Tanesha said.

Cody swallowed hard. For a moment, Tanesha and Cody just

looked at each other.

"I have another idea," Tanesha said. "Why don't we use you to sell the information we want people to know?"

"The dirt makes more money," Cody said.

"How would you know?" Tanesha asked.

Cody sucked his teeth for a second before he nodded.

"I'll give you an exclusive," Tanesha said. "You and only you will tell the world who Jeraine was kissing."

"Really?" Cody asked. "Why would you do that?"

"You need the money and have the contacts," Tanesha said. "It seems like a win-win to me."

"I'll think about it," Cody said.

"Think fast," Heather said. "We have to be somewhere."

"I have to go to school," Cody said.

"We can take Brian for the morning," Heather said. "You and Tanesha can go study."

"What would Brian do?" Cody said with a scowl.

"Hang out with Tink and her boyfriend," Heather said. "We're working on the garden this weekend. He can help if he wants to or play video games with them. They're nice kids. He'll like them."

"You'd do that?" Cody asked.

"Only if you stop calling me a n. . ." Tanesha started and then shook her head. "You know."

"One word versus a whole day of studying," Heather said. "Plus, Brian will have a blast."

"And a ride to school," Tanesha said.

"Done," Cody said.

He hopped away from the door. Tanesha and Heather waited for a few minutes before Cody arrived back at the door wearing a shirt and his backpack.

"Time to go, Brian," Cody said.

In what was clearly a daily ritual, Brian took his jacket from a hook by the door and picked up his backpack.

"Did you remember lunch?" Brian asked Cody.

"It's in your backpack," Cody said.

"Thank you, Cody," Brian said.

"They're going to take us," Cody said.

"Okay," Brian said with a smile.

He looked at Tanesha and gave her a bright smile.

"Shotgun," Brian said.

Tink squealed and laughed. They went down the hall and out of the apartment building.

"Someday, we're going to have a *real* house," Brian said.

Tanesha glanced at the young man. She remembered a time when she'd said those very same words over and over again. She had that house and that life now. She smiled to herself and got in the driver's seat. She could afford to be generous today.

"First stop, the biggest house you've ever seen in your entire life," Tanesha said.

"Goodie!" Brian said.

Smiling, Tanesha started toward the Castle.

~~~~~~~~~

Saturday morning — 11:35 a.m.

Warm and sleepy, Blane opened his eyes and stared at the sky. He'd been napping on a chaise lounge on the back deck of the Castle. Just one week ago, he'd been in his private hospital room. Today, he was napping in the warm sun while the turn-the-beds-weekend unfolded in the garden below him.

He leaned up to see what was going on. Nadia, ER doctor, friend of Ivan's, Nash's love, was hanging from one of the fruit trees. She was wielding a pair of loppers and was attacking the dry and dead limbs left by last year's early frost. At the base of the tree, Valerie and Delphie caught the limbs and offered encouragement.

In the garden bed nearest to him, Noelle and Sissy were leaning on garden rakes while Nash and Dale shoveled compost from the heavily laden wheelbarrow. Noelle and Sissy sprang into action once Nash and Dale had finished. While the girls spread the compost onto the bed, Dale raced the wheelbarrow back to the driveway, where Jacob was standing in the bed of a Lipson Construction truck filled with compost. Like every year, they had already used the compost they'd made from kitchen clippings and garden extras. They were finishing up with commercial compost.

If he'd been feeling better, he'd have been standing in the bed of the truck with Jacob as he'd done the last four or five years. But all of this week's activities had caught up with him. When he'd felt worn out, Delphie had pushed him to rest in the lounger.

He glanced to his right. A fairy was sound asleep in a chaise lounge next to him. The fairy was wearing a sweatshirt and sweatpants, and a hoodie over her head. She was wrapped in a thick blanket so that all of her skin was covered. Blane knew it was a female fairy because Delphie had said, "She was not feeling well." Otherwise, he knew nothing about her. He made a mental note to ask Edie if some acupuncture would help.

He looked at the garden bed near the driveway when Ivan laughed. He was currently managing a bed full of little children. Katy and Paddie were planting what Blane knew was lettuce. Katy poured the seed down a small trough in the row. Paddie followed close behind with a stick to spread the seed. They skipped back to cover the row. Honey sat on the grass, helping her daughter, Maggie, use her tiny fingers to make holes next to the pea trellis. One at a time, Mack stuffed the holes with peas. Mack put a pea in the hole and returned to Ivan for another. Ivan was laughing at Mack's insistence on planting one at a time. Blane grinned. Through no effort of his or Heather's, his son was meticulous.

"How are you feeling?" Heather asked.

Blane looked to see her coming from the Castle kitchen. As if his look had caused it, there was a great cheer from Tink, Charlie, Ivy, and their new friend Brian. He glanced at Heather, and she rolled her eyes.

"Wanda's coming over as soon as she can get away," Heather said. "She thinks Frankie can come, too."

"Wow," Blane said. "Is he out?"

"He goes for only half-days now," Heather said. "He's worked his butt off and is doing really well. His brother's testifying next week. They wanted to give Frankie some fun friend time in case next week is hard."

Heather nodded to where Sissy, Noelle, Nash, and Dale were working.

"They're wrapping it up for the morning," she said.

"The kids are amazing," Blane said with a yawn. "I wish we'd had them a few years ago."

Heather smiled.

"It's getting warm, so everyone's about to head inside," Heather said. "We'll finish up this evening when it cools off again."

"Aden will be home then," Blane said.

"Mike, too," Heather said. "Tanesha said that her dad was coming over after work."

"What's happening with our house and Jeraine's?" Blane asked.

"Dale, Mike, and Jake turned them over once," Heather said. "Delphie said the gardens are tiny compared to this one."

"You mean that Jake is heading there with the rest of the compost," Blane said.

"If you're feeling better, I know he'd love the company," Heather said with a smile.

Blane sent Jacob a wistful look. Jacob waved.

"Come on in!" Jacob yelled. "The compost's fine!"

Blane sat up. He paused for a moment before standing up.

"How do you feel?" Heather asked.

"Good," Blane said.

"Tired," Heather said.

"Tired," Blane said.

"You can always. . ." Heather started.

"I can sleep in the truck," Blane said. "I've done that often enough."

Heather smiled. She didn't want to discourage him from going with Jacob, but her eyes spoke her worry. Blane smiled and kissed her cheek. Blane gestured to the fairy sleeping in the chaise.

"No idea." Heather shook her head. "I made lunch — just sandwiches and stuff. Nothing fancy."

"Nice," Blane said. "Where is our second son?"

"With the babies upstairs," Heather said. "Jill and Edie are with them. They should be awake in a bit. Sandy's still at her salon."

"Sounds like I woke up at just the right time," Blane said.

Heather smiled. Blane looked out onto the garden again. Nash, Noelle, Sissy, and Dale were walking toward the shed with their tools. Valerie was helping Nadia down from the tree. Katy and Paddie were spinning in circles toward the deck. Ivan had Mack tucked under one arm and Maggie under the other. The children were squealing with laughter. Honey was rolling toward Delphie to return the extra seed. Blane glanced at Jacob. He had stowed the shovel and wheelbarrow and was closing the back of the bed.

"I'd better. . ." Blane gestured to Jacob.

Heather hugged him, and he kissed her cheek again.

"Try not to overdo it," she said.

He smiled and jogged toward the truck. Ivan was passing with Mack and Maggie. His eldest son held his hand out, and Blane slapped it.

"High five!" Mack said in more of a giggle than words.

"High five!" Blane slapped Jacob's hand.

He jogged around to the passenger side of the truck. Jacob slowed to let Samantha Hargreaves' Mercedes pass before they sped out of the driveway.

"Nice to see you," Jacob said.

"You have no idea how nice it is to see you," Blane said.

Laughing, they drove to Jeraine's house.

~~~~~~~~~

Saturday evening — 5:35 p.m.

"So. . ." Fin said to Tanesha as they walked to Jeraine's car.

"So?" Tanesha asked.

"Cody?" Fin asked.

"He's the guy who sold my phone number and address to the scumbag paparazzi," Tanesha said.

"Yeah," he said. He glanced at her out of the corner of his eye. "I thought you were going to kill him or at least maim him a little bit."

"I wanted to," Tanesha said with a grin.

"And?"

"I felt bad for the guy," Tanesha said. "He's taking care of his younger brother and. . . I don't know. I guess I felt like I had enough in my life that I could be generous."

Fin sniffed, and Tanesha looked at him.

"I expect you to behave yourself," Tanesha said.

"I assumed you expected me to give him frog legs," Fin said. The malice in his voice was palpable.

"No," Tanesha said. "That would be bad."

"Hmm," Fin said.

Tanesha hit the "Unlock" button on the car, and Fin got in on the passenger side.

"What will you do when he sells your secrets again?" Fin asked.

"Having frog legs isn't going to stop him from doing that," Tanesha said with a laugh.

Fin grinned at her. She started the car, and they drove back toward the library, where they were picking up Cody. He'd wanted to call Brian, so they'd left him there to get the car.

"I was thinking about using him," Tanesha said.

"For sex?" Fin asked.

"You're so predictable," Tanesha said with a laugh.

"I just can't imagine what you would need this creature for," Fin said.

"To pass information to the paparazzi," Tanesha said.

When Fin didn't respond, she turned to look at him.

"That's a good idea," Fin said.

"I know," Tanesha said.

She pulled over to the curb, and Cody got in the back. Tanesha waited for him to buckle his safety belt before starting toward the Castle.

"How's Brian?" Tanesha asked.

"Great," Cody said. "It sounds like he's had a really fun day. He said that he met a lady there who can tell fortunes?"

"Delphie," Tanesha said.

"She's an Oracle," Fin said.

"Wow, that's wild," Cody said. "He said to tell you, Fin, that your sister is sick."

"Edie?" Fin asked.

"A. . . something," Cody said.

"Aife," Fin said. He glanced at Tanesha before slipping into his own thoughts.

"That's probably it," Cody said. "I couldn't really figure out what he was saying."

"Fin has three younger sisters," Tanesha said. Fin looked at Tanesha. "You don't seem surprised that she's sick."

"She works a lot, so she gets sick when she stops," Fin said. "Know anyone like that?"

"Hey, that's why I never stop working," Tanesha said.

Fin smiled, and Cody laughed.

"I'm mostly surprised that she's here," Fin said. He glanced at Cody.

"What does it mean?" Tanesha asked.

"It could mean a lot of things," Fin said. "But my guess is that I'm going to be a dad soon."

"Is your wife pregnant?" Cody asked.

"Very," Tanesha said.

"That's exciting," Cody said. "I spent last summer in the maternity ward of Pres. St. Luke's. Where's she having the baby?"

"Since we are here, in Denver, we have only one option," Fin said.

"Where's that?" Cody asked.

"The house we're going to," Tanesha said. "Where Brian spent the day."

"I'd hoped we'd have the child at home," Fin said.

"Home?" Cody asked.

"Fin is from the Isle of Man," Tanesha said. "Hence the accent."

"Like the Bee Gees?" Cody asked.

Fin glanced at him in the rearview mirror before nodding. Cody smiled. They drove in silence for a while. Tanesha slowed at the light at Colfax Boulevard and Race Street. Cody saw the crowd of photographers surrounding the Castle.

"What is this place?" Cody asked.

"Home away from home," Fin said.

Tanesha turned right and pulled up to the gate.

CHAPTER THREE HUNDRED AND SEVENTY-NINE
FAMILY AFFAIR

Saturday evening — 5:35 p.m.

"Hello?" Abi asked as she came through the Castle's main living room.

"We're here!" Delphie called from the kitchen.

Abi gave Delphie a hug when she got to the kitchen.

"Where is everyone?" Abi asked.

"Backyard," Delphie said. "The teenagers are in the hot tub."

"What about Charlie's casts?" Abi asked.

"Sandy was wise enough to get fiberglass," Delphie said. "I wrapped it in a bag, just in case."

Abi smiled.

"Sam's running the barbeque," Delphie said. "Aden and Rodney aren't home from work yet. Tanesha and Fin are due here any minute. Sandy said she thought she wouldn't get home until seven. Edie and the babies have taken up the grassy area of the grass. Katy and Paddie are upstairs with Jill getting changed. I don't think Jake and Blane are back."

Delphie nodded.

"I think that's everyone." She gave Abi a vague smile. "Maybe."

Mike opened the door from the tunnels. An exhausted-looking Noelle followed him into the house.

"Is my mom here?" Noelle asked.

"Not yet, honey," Delphie said.

"I'm going to take a bath," Noelle said. "In her bathtub. You think she'll mind?"

"I doubt it," Delphie said. "Sounds like a good idea."

Noelle wandered toward the stairway to their apartment.

"How about a 'Thank you, Mike'?" Delphie asked.

"Thanks, Mike," Noelle said as she stumbled up the steps.

"Big day?" Abi asked.

"Long," Mike said. "But really great. We had a lot to look at. She was wired until we got to the car."

"I hear you're having a big day, Abi!" Valerie said as she came in from the back.

Mike grabbed her and held her tight. He kissed her neck.

"Oh, yeah — Val was bringing meat to Sam for the barbeque," Delphie said with a nod.

"Me?" Abi asked. She put her hand on her chest and shrugged. "Same old boring stuff. I just went to work."

"You're not having your baby today?" Valerie kissed Mike's lips.

Surprised, Abi shook her head.

"I love you guys, but, when I have a child, I want to be with my family — Fand, Liban, and Gil," Abi said. "Maybe Ne Ne."

"Not Fin?" Delphie asked.

"Huh — never occurred to me that he'd even want to be there," Abi said. "He wants us to be a modern Queendom. I guess he spends most of his time with Tanesha, and she would insist on it."

"Where was he when Ne Ne was born?" Valerie asked.

"Fighting the war," Abi said. She lifted a shoulder in a vague shrug. "He's a prince."

"If you're not having a baby, then why is. . .?" Valerie started.

Aife made a beeline from the back to Abi. She latched on to Abi before Abi could say a word. Abi held Aife tight. Having changed out of the blue, Aife's skin was milk-chocolate brown and her hair nearly blonde. Aife looked like a skeleton compared to Abi's full belly and vibrant health. Over Aife's head, Abi gave Valerie a sad smile.

"Aife, my dear," Abi said and helped her move back. "How are you?"

"I came like Mom told me to," Aife said. "Then I met the child and was threatened by the Sword of Truth, and then... How come you didn't get stuck in the Sea of Amber?"

Aife's blue, wide-set fairy eyes looked like saucepans in her nearly skeletal face. Abi hugged her again.

"I'm so sorry you were frightened," Abi said. "Paddie is very protective over Katy."

Aife sniffed and began to cry. Abi looked at Delphie and then at Valerie.

"Is there a place that we...?" Abi asked.

"Of course," Delphie said.

She led Abi to the room Charlie used for school. She was just pulling the sliding doors closed when Fin, Tanesha, and Cody came into the Castle. Fin took one look at Abi and Aife. He walked into the small room and closed the sliding doors in Delphie, Tanesha, and Cody's faces. Edie came up behind them.

"Excuse me," Edie said.

She went through the sliding doors and closed them behind her.

"What was that?" Cody asked.

Mari appeared in the Castle living room.

"Whoa," Cody said. Turning to Tanesha, he said, "Did you see that?"

Mari gave Cody an irritated look. She pointed to the closed doors.

"They're in there, dear," Delphie said.

"You'd better come," Mari said to Tanesha.

"Me?" Tanesha asked.

"It's a family affair, after all," Mari said. She gave Cody an evil look. "Are you keeping her here?"

Tanesha stepped in between them.

"No." Tanesha raised her index finger and pointed it to Mari, who shrugged.

The sliding doors opened, and Fin stuck his head out.

"Late, again," Fin said to Mari.

"You have to excuse my brother," Mari said. "He's an asshole."

She gave Cody a finger wave and swished her way into the room. She pointed to the doors, and they began to close. Fin's arm came out of the room. He grabbed the front of Tanesha's shirt and dragged her inside the room. The doors closed with a firm *Click!*

"Well, I guess that's that," Delphie said to Cody.

"What's what?" Cody asked.

"No idea." Delphie shrugged. She started walking toward the kitchen

"Your brother's in the hot tub with the kids," Delphie said. "Would you like to. . ."

"Where's Brian?" Cody asked.

Delphie turned to look at Cody. The young man's eyes were flicking back and forth while his eye lids were blinking. Clearly, one of the fairies had altered his memory.

"Cody?" Delphie put her hand on his arm. His eyes cleared and he looked at her.

"Do you have any idea where I am?" Cody asked.

"Welcome to my home," Delphie said with a twinkle in her eye. "Your brother's out back."

"I'm inside the Castle?" Cody asked. "Can I get a tour? I saw it this morning, and it's. . . wow."

"Of course," Delphie said. "But I promised Brian that I would take you to him as soon as you got here."

Cody grinned. He followed Delphie to the back.

"Do you know happen to know where Tanesha went?" Cody asked.

"She and Fin had to take care of something," Delphie said with a smile. "Family stuff."

"Jeez, at least she could have told me," Cody said.

"It was rude," Delphie said.

"Probably just Fin," Cody said. "He's kind of a dick."

"He is," Delphie said. "It's good to meet you, Cody. We've had such a nice day with Brian."

She patted his back, and they went out to the backyard.

~~~~~~~~~

Saturday evening — 6:55 p.m.

"I wondered if I might have a word," Ivan said as he approached Charlie.

Charlie was sitting in an orthopedic chair in the main Castle living room. Tink was sitting on the chair's leg rest, and Dale was standing next to him. Dale glanced at Charlie before putting his arm around Tink's shoulder.

"Come on, Tink," Dale said. "Let's find out what Sandy made for dessert."

Tink leaned over to kiss Charlie before getting up and leaving with Dale.

"Sorry, did I break up something?" Ivan asked.

"No," Charlie said with a smile. "We were making bets on what Sandy made for dessert. You just made them go check."

Charlie looked off for a moment. When he looked back, Ivan could see that he was in pain.

"I overdid it today," Charlie said.

"Can I get you something?" Ivan asked. "Ice, medications. . ."

Charlie waved his hands in front of his face, and Ivan stopped talking.

"I'm sick of all of that," Charlie said. "It's nice to be here. Awake."

"Yes," Ivan said.

"Plus, Honey will kill me if I get all drugged up again," Charlie said. "She's been helping me get moving again."

"You're coming with us on Sunday, right?" Ivan asked.

Charlie nodded. He looked off for a moment and then grinned.

"You're saying that, come tomorrow, you will be in charge," Charlie said with a laugh.

"Something like that." Ivan laughed.

"Is that why you wanted to talk to me?" Charlie asked. "Because I'm ready to get moving. Sissy, too."

"Actually, I wanted to speak with you about your sister," Ivan said.

Ivan flushed with color, and looked at Charlie. Charlie smiled. Ivan had known this boy almost the boy's entire life. He'd given Charlie money when Charlie had nowhere to turn. He'd lent an ear when Charlie was upset and bailed him out of jail. He'd even let the boy stay with him when Charlie had nowhere else to go. Looking at Charlie now, Ivan saw all of that history wrapped in Charlie's easy smile.

"There isn't anything you have to say," Charlie said.

"What do you mean?" Ivan asked.

"I guess, to me, you've always been my sister's... partner," Charlie said. "I mean, I know that..."

"Nothing has happened," Ivan said. "I can assure you that..."

Charlie raised his hands in submission. Ivan stopped talking.

"Sissy told me that you're still smarting from the spanking they gave you at her first eating-disorder treatment," Charlie said.

Ivan scowled and gave him a nod.

"I never thought you molested or groomed Sissy," Charlie said. "I always thought... well, I don't know what I thought. I guess I just saw you as family. Our family — Sissy's, mine, and Sandy's."

Ivan looked at Charlie out of the corner of his eye.

"I'm trying to say that I don't have a problem with you and Sissy," Charlie said with a nod. "I hope you're very happy. Sissy's over the moon. I've never seen her so happy — even with the injury. My Dad would have really wanted Sissy to be happy."

Ivan gave Charlie a curt nod.

"I've seen Sissy with you," Charlie said. "All of my life. You make Sissy really happy, even when you're being controlling and bossy. And Sissy... She's..."

Ivan turned to look into Charlie's face.

"Special," Ivan and Charlie said together.

"Yes," Ivan said.

"Hard," Charlie said. "Tink's easy. I can spend days with her. We laugh and just have fun. But Sissy? She wants to know the 'why' of everything. 'Why are you doing this?' 'What does this mean?' And she wants to do things the right way, or she won't do it. And I can tell you that she was like that even before you knew her."

Ivan nodded.

"Sandy tells this story about Sissy just learning to walk," Charlie said with a smile. "I was ready to move, get going, so I stumbled around until I could run. Sissy didn't want to take even one step if it wasn't done the best way."

"Correctly," Ivan said in agreement. "Yes."

"Plus," Charlie smiled, "I was there when Seth brought you from the Gulag. You didn't see me because I was playing with my cars on the floor. Sissy was on Dad's bed, telling him one of her nonsense stories. She still tells those, by the way."

"She does?" Ivan grinned.

Charlie gave a fast nod.

"So Seth opened the door, and Sissy stopped talking," Charlie said. "We all turned to see what was going on. And you walked into the room or crutched. I realize now that you must have been in tremendous pain. Your eyes were like *stuck* on the floor. And Sissy said..."

"There you are," Ivan said with a smile.

"'It's about time,'" Charlie said. "Or something like that. All of us were so surprised that we just stared at you. I don't think you realized because it was happening to you."

Charlie smiled.

"You were made for each other," Charlie said. "Who am I to disapprove of that?"

"So it won't bother you if your sister and I become more than teacher and student?" Ivan asked.

"I'm surprised you aren't already," Charlie said.

"And if we..." Embarrassed, Ivan looked away.

"You mean sex?" Charlie asked. He looked disgusted. "I'm still her older brother."

Ivan laughed.

"I don't want to hear about it or know about it," Charlie said.

Ivan smiled.

"I will return the favor," Charlie said.

Ivan laughed, and Charlie smiled. After a moment, Ivan squinted his eyes.

"You plan to find others?" Ivan gestured toward where Tink had gone.

"No," Charlie said. "That's never been my thing."

"You're not eighteen!" Ivan said. "Your thing may change."

"Nah," Charlie said. "I know myself. My Dad was too afraid to have what he truly wanted. That's not me. Plus, I like Tink too much to cheat on her, to hurt her in that way. She's been hurt enough."

Ivan nodded.

"You?" Charlie asked.

"No," Ivan said. "Your sister was all I have ever wanted."

"I'm certainly not going to get in the way," Charlie said.

Ivan smiled. He looked up to see Tink and Dale, watching to see if they were done talking. Ivan nodded to them, and they came up.

"Chocolate cake," Tink said with a smug smile. "Pay up, buddy!"

"Then why does he have coconut?" Charlie asked, pointing

toward Dale's plate.

"And cookies!" Dale said. "And brownies!"

"Sandy made all of that?" Charlie asked.

"Valerie and Blane," Tink said. "The chocolate cake is from Blane. I'd kill for this."

Despite what she had just said, she got a big bite of cake on her fork and gave it to Charlie. Ivan smiled at the sweet gesture.

"Wow," Charlie said. "But what did Sandy make?"

"Nothing," Tink said. "I was just kidding."

They laughed. Ivan smiled at them. He nodded his good-byes and went to find Sissy.

She was sitting on the edge of the deck watching the sprinklers water the new beds. The ugly dog, Buster, was resting, lying next to her with his head on her lap. When Ivan approached, the dog lifted his head to look at him. Ivan sat down next on the other side of Sissy, and the dog dropped his head.

"Where are your friends?" Ivan asked.

"Wanda left to take Freddie home," Sissy said. "They were taking Cody and Brian home, so Wanda and Freddie went with them. Freddie seems really good, don't you think?"

"Solid," Ivan said. "Stable. It's nice to see."

She turned to look at him.

"I like to watch the water hit the dirt," Sissy said. "It's like hope for what will come."

Ivan smiled.

"I can use some hope," Sissy said. "Did you talk with Charlie?'

"He said that he supports. . . us," Ivan said. He turned to look at her, and she smiled.

"It's still illegal for us to get married," Sissy said.

Ivan grinned. There were many easy ways around the law, but Sissy would never hear of it. She would only ever do what was legal and fair. Remembering what Charlie had said, he had to look away to keep from laughing.

"What?" Sissy asked.

"Oh, Charlie reminded me that you like to do things the correct way," Ivan said.

"I do," Sissy said. "That doesn't mean we can't date and stuff."

"And stuff," Ivan said. He looked at her for a long moment and then turned to look at the gardens. "Are you sure you want to leave all of this?"

"It's really hard to leave, but I have to," Sissy said. "Following my dream means I have to leave."

"We could easily get work here at the Denver Ballet," Ivan said.

Sissy looked at Ivan's face for a moment before turning to look at the garden again.

"What?" Ivan asked.

"I think we have to try to do it in New York," Sissy said. "You know, if I can make it there, I can make it anywhere."

Ivan smiled.

"Right?" Sissy asked.

"Sure," Ivan said.

He took her hand, and they watched the garden sprinklers for a while.

"Charlie tells me you still tell those great stories," Ivan said.

"The ones that don't make sense?" Sissy smiled. Ivan nodded.

"Will you?" Ivan asked.

"About the garden?" Sissy asked.

"Sprinklers," Ivan said as a challenge.

"Well. . ." Sissy launched into a goofy story.

~~~~~~~~~

Saturday evening — 7:00 p.m.

"What do you think is going on in there?" Jill asked as she brought a stack of dirty dishes into the kitchen.

Delphie looked up from where she was stacking dirty dishes on the counter. Jacob was washing dishes in the sink, and the dishwasher was chugging away.

"The fairies?" Delphie asked.

Jill nodded and set down the dishes.

"Anyone know anything about this Aife?" Jacob asked.

Delphie turned her head to look at him. Before she said anything, Jill took a breath to speak. Delphie's eyes flicked to Jill.

"I looked her up online," Jill said.

Delphie looked at Jill.

"It said that she was a great warrior," Jill said. "That some dude overcame her. But she's a fairy, right? How likely is it that he overcame anything? Anyway, dude got her pregnant and then left for Ireland. He told her to send her son when he was seven. The son should wear his ring. Of course, the dude kills the seven-year-old because the dude feels like a *seven-year-old* is a threat to him. Only then does he see the ring."

Delphie nodded and looked down at what she was doing.

"You're being weirdly silent," Jacob said.

"I just told you what I knew," Jill said.

"Delphie," Jacob said.

"Oh," Delphie said. She put a hand on her heart. "Me?"

Delphie remained silent. She looked at Jacob and then at Jill again.

"I guess I am a little quiet," Delphie said. She nodded as if she were thinking. "I think. . ."

Delphie lapsed into silence. Heather came into the kitchen with another stack of plates. Delphie gave Heather a wistful look, and Heather scowled.

"What are you talking about?" Heather asked.

"Aife," Jacob said from the sink.

His back was to Heather, so he couldn't see the silent exchange between Heather and Delphie. Heather scowled when Delphie gave her a sly look.

"Spit it out," Heather said in a hard voice that caused Jacob to turn to look at her.

He assessed Heather before turning to Delphie.

"What are you up to?" Jacob asked.

"Well. . ." Delphie said.

"Don't be angry with the oracle," Edie said as she came into the room. "I asked her not to say anything."

She put her hand on Heather's arm.

"And you're right to be suspicious, Heather," Edie said. "We concocted this plan when you received your father's gifts."

"Fairies," Jacob said, as if it were a curse, under his breath.

"I know," Edie said with a smile. "We do ask a lot."

"One thing is for certain," Heather said. "I'm not doing anything until we know what's going on."

"What's going on?" Sandy asked as she came into the kitchen from work. "What do the fairies want now?"

Heather raised her eyebrows at Edie, who nodded.

"I'll tell you everything," Edie said.

CHAPTER THREE HUNDRED AND EIGHTY
LYING FAIRIES

"No, you won't." Abi seemed to appear in the room.

"But. . ." Edie started.

"I will take care of this, Princess Edith," Abi said. "Your brother would like you to return."

"But. . ." Edie said.

"Princess Edith, you weren't born when these events took place," Abi said. "You weren't there. If we're going to ask Heather to help us. . ."

"Again," Heather said.

"Fair enough," Abi said with a nod. "Again, she deserves to hear what happened from someone who was there."

"You mean there's more to the story that I don't know?" Edie said.

Abi raised an eyebrow at her and pointed. When Abi didn't say anything, Jacob turned away from the kitchen sink to watch the interaction.

"Then I'm not going anywhere," Edie said.

"Fin. . ."

"He can handle it himself," Edie said. "Plus, Mari and Tanesha are there."

Abi scowled at Edie.

"I'm not afraid of you, Abi," Edie said.

Abi raised her eyebrows to Edie. Jill looked at Heather, who was scowling at Abi. Catching Jill's look and Heather's scowl, Edie smiled at them.

"You may or may not know this, but Abi is the most powerful fairy in our community," Edie said. "She and Gil are said to have stepped out of the earth's molten heat to cause the land to form."

Abi rolled her eyes at Edie.

"Stories," Jacob said. "There are always more stories. Why don't you just trust us?"

"Trust you?" Abi asked. "I thought we were."

"No, you don't trust us," Jacob said. "You tell us complicated tales that confound us."

"He wants you to ask for what you need," Heather said.

"Oh," Abi said. "We need Heather's help to correct something her father did."

"What's wrong with Aife?" Jill asked.

Abi raised an eyebrow to Edie, who gave her a defiant look.

"What is going on between you two?" Jacob asked. He looked at Delphie. "What are they doing?"

"That's the story," Delphie said. "Edie wants to tell what she knows because she believes it's the truth."

"It's not?" Edie asked.

Delphie shook her head.

"Abi wants Heather's help and knows that Jill will spot a lie," Delphie said. "She wants to tell the truth, but there are things that would be revealed that. . ."

"Might change our Edie," Abi said.

"My sister is dying!" Edie said. "Why would I give two craps about some history lesson in the face of the loss of my sister? Have you no heart?"

Abi and Edie looked at each other for a long moment before Abi nodded.

"I apologize, Edie," Abi said. "I forget sometimes how deep your bond is with your family."

Abi gave Edie a soft smile before looking at the others.

"It's not natural or normal for us fairies to care so deeply," Abi said. "Our Edie is truly one of a kind."

"You care," Edie said.

"Yes, but. . ." Abi started. She winced and then shrugged. "I'm me."

Edie held out her arms, and Abi hugged her tight. Jacob glanced at Jill, and she shrugged. He turned around and continued working on the dishes. Heather scowled at the fairies and went outside to get her boys. Delphie watched the fairies for a moment before heading out into the backyard.

Abi let go of Edie, stepped back, and looked around the room. Jacob was still working on the pile of dishes. Delphie came in with another stack of plates.

"I guess you guys are sick of us," Abi said.

"I think everyone is sick of being lied to and manipulated," Delphie said.

"Everyone?" Abi asked.

"Including me," Delphie said.

"Just tell us what you need," Jacob said from the sink, without turning around. "Ask for our help. We're glad to help, but the rest of this has to stop!"

Abi chewed her lip for a moment.

"So even though we helped with the construction site and helped Jabari and helped Yvonne and. . ." Abi scowled. "Heather! Fin and Tanesha saved her children and. . ."

"You helped at the construction site so that I would put the Queen back together and end the curse," Jacob said. Turning, he picked up a towel to dry his hands.

"And end the war," Delphie said.

"You helped Yvonne and Jabari because, let's face it, they're *your* family," Jacob said. "With us, you tricked us into the Sea of Amber."

"How many times do we have to tell you, Jacob?" Abi asked. "That was the serpents. It wasn't us."

"So you say," Jacob said. "What's more likely is that Fin tricked us into getting trapped in the Sea of Amber so that we would destroy the place. And clearly, you helped Heather and her children because you need to use her now for some unknown purpose."

"Wow," Abi said under her breath. "You believe this as well, Oracle?"

Delphie nodded.

"It's the deception, Abi," Delphie said.

"The tricks and lies and manipulations," Jacob said.

"Princess Edie cares for your children at no cost to you!" Abi said.

"Yeah, why is that?" Jacob asked. "What's your end game? Steal Katy? You've tried before. Take the boys? Teach them to be something you can use and manipulate to your end? Why are you helping us with the boys?"

"Because the Queen is interested in. . ." Edie started. "Oh, I see what you mean."

"And that's not to mention your interest in the Sword of Truth," Delphie said. "You think we didn't notice, but we all saw how upset you were when Perses secured the sword to Paddie and his children."

Abi squinted her eyes.

"I helped you put your wretched Queen together because you needed the help," Jacob said. "I asked for nothing in return."

"You wanted to break the curse!" Abi said.

"Jill self-heals," Jacob said. "She assures me that she would have survived. But everything with you fairies is some long game of manipulation and lies. That's no way to treat a friend or family or even an acquaintance."

"Hey, we're heading home," Heather said as she came into the kitchen.

She had their new son tucked into a sling. Blane came in carrying Mack. The child was sound asleep against him.

"But Hedone!" Abi said.

"You had all day to ask for what you wanted," Heather said

with a sniff. "In fact, you've had months and months to ask for help. Did you?"

She raised her eyes to Abi.

"Now, I need to get my children home," Heather said. "They've had a big day and will have another tomorrow. If you need help with your mysterious problem, you can stop by in an hour or so to *ask me* for help. Maybe I'll help you tomorrow."

"My sister won't survive the night," Edie said.

"What?" Heather asked. "Your sister's life is in danger, and you wait until the last minute to ask for my help?"

Heather looked at Abi. The fairy was looking down and chewing on her lip. Heather looked at Edie. Sorrow was etched on the princess's face.

"I'm sorry," Abi said in a soft voice.

"What?" Heather asked.

"I'm sorry," Abi said and looked up at Heather. "You're absolutely right. We have manipulated you. We have lied. And in this situation, we grossly miscalculated. I'm sorry. If you'd like, we'll leave and never return."

"So you're just going to pick up your toys and go home?" Jacob asked with a shake of his head. "What? Are you three? I thought you stepped out of the molten lava or some crap like that."

"What do you mean?" Abi asked.

"When there's a problem in a relationship, the brave work things out," Jacob said. "You say, 'I'm sorry,'..."

"I am," Abi said. "I really screwed up."

"And I say, 'Don't do it again,'" Jacob said.

"Oh," Abi said. "Really?"

"Jeez, you really are three," Heather said under her breath.

"Please," Delphie said. "Stop lying. Stop manipulating. Ask for what you want. We might not say 'yes,' but we'll help you find solutions."

"Your problems become our problems," Jacob said. "That's how we treat each other."

"Oh," Abi said.

"Will you help us?" Edie asked. She gave a little impatient hop. "We do need help."

Heather looked at Blane for a moment. He nodded.

"I'll help Blane get the kids home," Jacob said. "Edie, can you help Jill with the boys, Katy, and Paddie?"

"Of course," Edie said.

"And me?" Abi asked. "Am I forgiven, too?"

"You will sit down at that table right there and tell me what's going on," Heather said. "Leave nothing out. Delphie?"

Heather looked up at Delphie.

"I'll stay to make sure you're truthful," Delphie said.

Heather nodded.

"What if I show you?" Abi asked. "Nice bit of fairy magic."

"Parlor trick," Heather said. "Speak, and I will hear your truth."

Abi looked uncertain.

"What?" Heather asked.

"If I sit here, anyone can listen," Abi said.

"That's the point," Jacob said. "If you don't trust us, all of us, then why are you here at all?"

Abi bounced back and forth from one foot to another.

"Tanesha," Heather said in a low tone, and Tanesha appeared next to the table.

"Did you call me here?" Tanesha asked.

Heather nodded. Without saying another word, Tanesha pulled a chair out from the table and sat down. Heather sat next to her. Abi stood on the floor, biting her lip. Shrugging, Delphie went to the electric kettle. She filled it with water and turned it on.

"Come on, Blane," Jacob said. "Let's get these kids to bed."

Heather kissed her son and gave Jacob the sling. She touched Mack's back and kissed Blane. With a nod, Jacob and Blane left the room together.

"It's nice to see them together again," Delphie said.

Heather nodded.

"How is he feeling?" Delphie asked.

"Okay," Heather said. "He's a little worn out from working with Sissy and Ivan — Charlie, too. He's happy to do it, and, of course, he's happy to be home. It's just all new."

"He looks great," Tanesha said. "I saw his blood numbers. They're really good. He must feel like a new person."

"He does," Heather said.

Delphie nodded. Abi watched the women talk back and forth. After a few moments, the women looked up at Abi.

"What's it going to be?" Heather asked.

"Wait for us!" Jill jogged into the kitchen, with Sandy on her heels.

"I called you," Heather said in a low voice.

"I know, but we had to get the babies settled," Sandy said.

"How did you keep from coming?" Heather asked.

Sandy pointed to Jill.

"I knew you wouldn't mind," Jill said.

Sandy pulled out a chair at the kitchen table just as the electric pot clicked off. Jill went to make tea for everyone. Tanesha got up to get the cups. After a few moments, Jill set a pot of English tea on the table and gave Delphie a cup of green tea. She sat down on the end of the table between Delphie and Sandy.

"What's it going to be?" Heather asked.

"You don't know what you're asking!" Abi said.

"I know exactly what I'm asking," Heather said. "I'm asking a fellow being to sit at this table and speak her truth. I am allowed to have as many of my own counsel as I choose. I deserve a response, at the very least."

"But you're human!" Abi asked.

"Not any longer," Tanesha said.

Abi was visibly shaken. She blinked. Without saying another

word, she pulled out a chair and sat down next to Sandy.

"Hedone," Abi said.

"Really?" Heather asked. "You sat down only when you knew I wasn't human. Do you despise humans so much?"

Abi blushed. She shook her head.

"I. . ." Abi started. She let out a breath. "Uh. . ."

Giving Abi space to collect her thoughts, Sandy started pouring tea. The women doctored their tea and waited. By the time Sandy set down Abi's cup of tea, the fairy seemed clearer. Abi pressed her shoulders back and sat up straight.

"I want to apologize again," Abi said. "You're absolutely correct — all of you. I haven't trusted you or any human. I can give you reasons for that, but truth be told, my reasons don't matter very much."

She nodded.

"For a long, long time, Gil and I — and, eventually, Fand and Liban — danced across this Earth's surface without a care in the world," Abi said. "At some point, we knew that humans existed. But. . ."

Abi shrugged.

"It was Manannán who brought humans into our world, and we went from four fairy friends to an entire Queendom," Abi said. "Sometimes, it boggles my mind. And. . ."

She looked from face to face.

"I've never had a human friend," Abi said. She gave a partial smile. "When Fin proposed that we live here, I laughed in his face."

Abi gave a sad nod.

"So, I am sorry," Abi said. "I will try to be a better friend."

"And Olympia?" Heather asked.

"I've had plenty of trouble with Olympia," Abi said. "That's why I sat down, Hed. . . Heather. I know what happens when you cross Olympia. I was thinking while Sandy was pouring the tea. It would truly break something inside of me to not have you as my close friends. This is why I am so ashamed. I love you so much, and, yet, I still think of you as primitive little. . ."

Nodding, Abi opened her mouth.

"Don't say you're sorry again," Sandy said. She put her hand over Abi's. "We've all done plenty of thoughtless things in our lives. We understand."

Jill, Tanesha, and Heather nodded, and Delphie smiled.

"Please," Heather said. "Let's start with what you need."

"Since we are talking about truth," Abi said, "did you actually kill a breeding pair of serpents and all of their offspring?"

"I will take you to both locations," Tanesha said.

"Both locations?" Abi asked. "You killed them separately?"

The women nodded.

"Why?" Delphie asked.

"They are much more dangerous separately," Abi said.

"We had help from a dragon," Tanesha said. "At least, I *think* it was a dragon."

"For the female," Abi said.

"No, the male," Jill said with a shake of her head. "We killed the female on our own."

Abi's eyebrows went up with surprise. After a few moments, she nodded.

"Okay. Yes, I underestimated you," Abi said. "That was dumb."

"What do you need?" Heather asked.

"Aife's life force was perilously low when the Queen gave her the Blue Fairy role," Abi said. She shook her head and waved her hand. "The whole Blue Fairy thing is complicated and off point."

"Why does Aife spend so much time with Alex and John?" Sandy asked.

"Alex and Max are descendants of Aife's lover," Abi said. "Aife heard a whisper of Alex getting her tattoo — that's how it is for us. We can hear you when you think of us. Anyway, Aife met

John, and, well, she knew Brigid, John's mother, and..."

Abi shrugged.

"Why is Aife in such danger?" Tanesha asked.

"She was nearly dead when she became the Blue Fairy," Abi said. "The Blue Fairy is a mantle that is to be passed around. It's too much for one fairy. But Aife couldn't survive without it."

Abi looked into each woman's face and found understanding there.

"If the Blue Fairy is so important to Aife, why did Edie take it off?" Jill asked.

"Because it's killing her," Abi said. "And honestly, Aife will probably put the Blue Fairy back on when we're done."

"But she must be stronger to do it," Heather said. "To survive it."

"Exactly," Abi said. "Fin and Aife were born within a decade of each other. For fairies, that's like being twins. If she dies, which is likely, she will take a part of him with her."

"Oh, *that's* what he meant," Tanesha said.

Everyone looked at her.

"He said over and over again that he needed all of himself to lead their world into the modern era," Tanesha said.

"We need to transition to the modern era or wither and fade," Abi said. "That's just a fact."

"What do you believe Aife needs?" Jill asked. "Certainly, I can heal her."

Abi shook her head.

"She can heal herself," Abi said. "She must heal herself."

"Why doesn't she, then?" Tanesha asked.

"That's the question, isn't it?" Abi asked. "Fin and his sisters have staged this intervention to get her to see what must be done."

"She refuses," Tanesha said with a nod. "She wants to die to be with her lover."

"Oh," Heather said. "That's what you need."

"We need you to unveil her eyes to see the man for what he was," Abi said. "A monster. A rapist. The whole — *'Send my son to me'* thing — was merely a cruel joke. He always had intended to kill the child."

Abi's face twisted as she frowned with disgust.

"For the record, I relieved the man of his head with one blow," Abi said. "He was no warrior."

"You mean he's a great warrior only when he's fighting seven year olds?" Jill asked.

"Precisely," Abi nodded.

"Delphie?" Heather asked.

"There is something she's not saying," Delphie said. "Something about your father. She's afraid of offending you."

"What is it?" Heather asked.

"Unlike what his mother thinks, your father has always had a cruel streak," Abi said.

"You mean the dark arrows are not his first cruel love," Heather said.

Abi nodded.

"He did this?" Heather asked.

"With great intention," Abi said. "He ensnared Fin and would have trapped Edie and Mari had their father not concealed them from him."

"What did Manannán do?" Jill asked.

"Manannán made them seem human," Abi said. "Eros had no idea Fand had other children besides Fin and Abi. And Keenan — well, you know about the whole Patrick thing."

Abi's quick nod held the weight of Keenan's life as Maughold and the betrayal by Patrick of Ireland.

"Eros' hatred for Queen Fand is second only to his hatred of Liban, her twin," Abi said.

"Why?" Heather asked.

"She doesn't know," Delphie answered quickly.

"Do you?" Abi asked.

"It has to do with his father," Delphie said.

"Ares?" Jill asked.

"The God of War," Heather said under her breath.

"Eros has the urge to use love as war," Delphie said.

"How nice," Sandy said, shaking her head.

"Explains my awful relationships," Heather said with a smile. She looked off into the near distance for a moment before her eyes flicked to Abi. "I need to think and speak with my friends."

"Fair enough," Abi said. "I will wait with the Oracle until you return."

Heather nodded. Jill pointed upstairs, and the girlfriends nodded. They made their way to Jill and Jacob's loft.

CHAPTER THREE HUNDRED AND EIGHTY-ONE
SPARKLERS

"So, let me get this straight," Tanesha said as she, Sandy, Heather, and Jill entered Jill's loft.

They walked to the kitchen area and sat down in chairs at the bar counter. Jill went in to retrieve a tin of Sandy's chocolate crunch cookies.

"Tea?" Jill asked.

"I'd love some," Tanesha said.

"I bet you would," Heather said with a laugh. She nodded to Jill. "Before anything else, I want to hear about what happened when you were with the fairies."

"What a mess," Tanesha said. "It was like a drug intervention."

"Remember when we tried to do that with Sissy?" Sandy asked.

"Fucking horrible," Jill said. Unaccustomed to Jill swearing, the women looked up at her. "Well, it was!"

"It was like that," Tanesha said. "Aife was furious with Fin. They argued for what seemed like forever. Then Aife went after me. 'Why is this creature here?' Blah, blah. She's a little unhinged."

"A little?" Heather asked.

"What do you think is wrong with her?" Sandy asked.

"Remember how crazy Sissy was when she was sick?" Tanesha asked. "She was sure she was seeing reality, but. . ."

"Her reality was not actually based in fact," Sandy said with a nod.

"She didn't recognize that picture we took of her," Jill said.

"Accused me of doctoring it," Sandy said.

"Photoshop," Heather said. She looked at Tanesha. "It was like that?"

Tanesha nodded.

"She's addicted to feeling awful," Tanesha said. "Addicted to the pain and loss. She can't seem to let it go."

"What do you think I can do?" Heather asked. "She's been broken like this for a thousand years or more."

"You can teach her to love," Sandy said.

"How?" Heather asked. "If I cast love for her, she'll probably fall in love with a stone."

"Ain't that the truth," Tanesha said with a shake of her head.

"What if you taught her to love herself?" Jill asked.

The women fell silent.

"I want to know why Eros hates Fand," Tanesha said.

"She's pretty dislikeable," Sandy said.

"I think it's a good question," Jill said. "The fairy world has been brutalized. Fand ripped apart. This thing with Aife. Who has it in for them?"

"My father," Heather said. "I guess."

"Any idea why?" Jill asked.

Heather shook her head.

"Let's promise not to ask him," Tanesha said.

"After what happened with Sissy, I dare not," Heather said. "Did I tell you. . ."

She closed her mouth and shook her head. She fell silent before her rage came up.

"He made it so that Sissy and Ivan couldn't be together in one life," Heather said finally. "It was a hidden part of the arrow. If they got as close as they are now, they would die. They had to die."

"Is that what my father did?" Jill asked. "He never said."

"He forced Eros to tell me what he'd done," Heather said. "His mother fixed it for them and every other dark arrow."

"I wonder what special surprise Eros created for the fairies,"

Tanesha said.

"Exactly right," Heather said. "He controlled the most powerful force in the human world, and he wielded that power with..."

She shook her head. They fell into contemplative silence while they ate their cookies. When the electric pot finished heating the water, Jill made them individual cups of tea. They drank their tea and ate cookies in silence. After a few minutes, Heather sighed.

"Well?" Heather asked.

"You need to fix this," Sandy said. "For your own sake as well as Aife's."

Tanesha nodded. Heather looked at Jill. She was looking down, eating her cookie.

"What?" Heather asked.

"I guess I'm just wondering what will happen when Aife has her strength back," Jill said. "Should we run for cover? Will she destroy Alex and Max? She's obsessed with Alex's husband John, and he hates her."

"Lucky we know an Oracle," Heather said. "Let's go ask her."

The women set their cups in the sink and went downstairs. Abi and Delphie were sitting at the table in grim silence. They looked up when the girlfriends entered the room. Delphie scanned Heather for a moment before giving a nod.

"Aife will return to the mantle of the blue fairy," Delphie said with a nod. "We can't expect her to give up her obsession with Alex and Max. They are her heirs."

"I thought the jerk killed her son," Jill asked.

"She had a daughter first," Abi said. "No one mentions her because — let's face it — she's just a girl."

Abi rolled her eyes and shook her head.

"She was a beautiful girl," Abi said. "She was raised by Manannán's family after Aife lost her mind. She never had real promise as a fairy, but you have to admit that Alex and Max are magnificent even without specific magic powers."

Abi gave a sad smile.

"She had the most amazing smile," Abi said. "It lit up the world. She lived a hundred years or so and had many children."

Abi nodded.

"Will Aife exact revenge?" Heather asked. "Start a war with the humans?"

"Not if she doesn't remember," Delphie said. "But it would take a spectacular spell cast by a strong fairy to make it happen."

Abi gave Delphie a sideways look. Delphie grinned at the fairy. Shaking her head at Delphie, Abi nodded.

"We'll do it together," Heather said.

"As you wish," Abi said.

"Can you do this magic on someone so unwilling?" Tanesha asked. "Because when I was in there, that woman didn't give two craps about what any of her siblings had to say."

Abi sighed.

"Fand, Liban, Gil," Abi said in a low voice.

Queen Fand, her twin sister, Liban, and the gargoyle they knew as Gilfand appeared in the kitchen. Queen Fand's round belly was a match to Abi's.

"Hedone has agreed," Abi said.

"Thank you," Gilfand said.

Gilfand, Queen Fand, and Liban dropped to one knee in front of Heather. Abi smiled. When Gilfand gestured for her to drop, Abi did so immediately.

"We are in your debt," Abi said.

"So noted," Heather said. "If we can bring peace to your realm, we can begin to unite the realms in peace."

"We can only hope," Liban said in a sad voice.

"Ready?" Heather asked. The fairies got to their feet. "She's this way."

She nodded to her friends before leading the fairies toward the room off the living room. As if she'd forgotten something,

Heather returned to the kitchen in a second.

"Did you forget something?" Tanesha asked.

"It's done," Heather said.

"What?" Jill asked. As if it were impossible, Sandy gave a quick shake of her head.

"Aife took one look at her mother and caved," Heather said. "After that, she allowed me to touch her heart. I was able to heal the break and light a spark of self-love. Abi cleared her mind."

Heather shrugged.

"Pretty straightforward," Heather said.

"Well done!" Delphie cheered. "You are. . . amazing."

She held out her arms, and Heather let Delphie hug her. Abi appeared next to Delphie.

"I wanted to thank you personally," Abi said. "It means a great deal to me that you would choose to help us."

"Thank you for being honest," Heather said.

Abi smiled.

"Why does Eros hate Fand and Liban?" Tanesha asked.

"They are very beautiful," Abi said. "Alluring to an Olympian God, but completely unaffected by his charms."

Jill snorted a laugh.

"You mean the trouble they had with Olympia was about Eros lusting after Fand and Liban?" Jill asked.

"The word is 'rape,'" Abi said.

"Awful," Delphie said with a sad nod.

Abi gave the oracle a curt nod.

"Now, we are heading home," Abi said. "I will have my child. Fin should be back in time for his exams."

"We're excited to meet the child," Jill said.

"Me, too," Abi said.

With a nod, she disappeared. The girlfriends let out a breath.

"What's next?" Delphie asked.

"Getting everyone to bed," Sandy said. "We have a big day tomorrow, too."

With a nod, she left to get her children from the backyard. Jacob came in the side door and wandered into the kitchen.

"Did I miss everything?" he asked Jill.

"You did," Jill said.

"Thank God," Jacob said. "Where's Katy? Paddie?"

"Outside," Jill said. "Can you get the sparklers? I promised Katy that we could light some tonight before bed."

"Good idea," Jacob said. He jogged off downstairs to get the sparklers.

Delphie watched them go.

"You seem a little too happy," Tanesha said.

"I guess I am," Delphie said.

"Why?" Heather asked.

"I guess. . ." Delphie said and then gave a sigh. "When I was a child, I felt very hopeless. And when I looked at the greater world, everything seemed horrible. Fand in pieces. Eros raping and creating chaos. And. . . well, 'the realms,' as you called them, were in chaos. Little by little, everything is getting worked out. It's. . . more than I could have dreamed of."

Wiping a tear, Delphie gave them a smile.

"I do love sparklers," she said and went out into the backyard.

"I'm heading home," Heather said.

She hugged Jill and Tanesha before leaving for home. Jill waited for Jacob to return with sparklers. He kissed her, and they went out into the warm spring night.

~~~~~~~~~

Sunday afternoon — 3:12 p.m.

"This is my favorite party," Valerie said to no one in particular.

Seth's wife, Ava, turned to look at her. They were standing on the deck. The grass was filled with people holding beverages. The younger children were either watching a video inside or napping. Jacob and Blane were starting the barbeques. The teenagers were playing Frisbee along the back of the yard.

"It seems like there's a party here every time I'm here," Ava said.

"There's just a lot of people who live here," Valerie said. "The crowd makes it seem like a lot."

"I think it's great," Ava said. "No dragging yourself to work, shoving something in the microwave, and falling asleep in front of the television."

Valerie gave Ava a searching look, and Ava grinned.

"Not that I've ever done that," Ava chuckled.

"Oh, yes — me, neither," Valerie laughed. Shaking her head, she said, "Never."

Ava grinned.

"College?" Valerie asked.

"I worked at the FBI for a few months," Ava said. "It was forensics training, but you have to join the FBI to take it. And, college, I guess."

She shrugged and looked at Valerie.

"You?" Ava asked.

"College, certainly," Valerie said. "Oh. . ."

Valerie sighed.

"Probably every other time I'm away from here," Valerie said. "There's just something about being here that makes everything else seem so unimportant."

Ava nodded.

"How's New York?" Valerie asked.

"Okay," Ava said with a smile. "Weird."

"Weird?" Valerie asked.

"It was supposed to be our honeymoon," Ava said with a smile. "Of course, we *did* see the ballet put on the piece Seth wrote for me, and we *did* stay in a super-romantic swanky hotel."

"But?" Valerie asked.

"No, but," Ava said. "Just time with Seth is always a little weird. He's either exercising or visiting with old friends or looking for the next donut shop or playing the piano or dragging me into a dive restaurant for 'the best' whatever or leading sing-a-long. . ."

"Go, go, go?" Valerie asked.

"More like life on random," Ava said. "You know — like a record changer?"

Valerie nodded.

"I love it — and him. Every day is just a little. . ." Ava shrugged.

"Weird," Valerie said.

Ava nodded. She gestured to where Nadia and Nash were sitting.

"What's the story with them?" Ava asked.

"You've heard about the whole 'dark arrow' thing," Valerie said.

"From Alex," Ava said. "You know, Alex Hargreaves, Samantha's sister."

"They should be here soon," Valerie said with a nod.

"They seem so happy," Ava said. "In their own little world. I always look for Nash because he's such a great kid. He was really nice to me when everything went down with Seth. He kind of took care of me, you know? Since then he always hangs out with me at these events. That's why I was surprised to see him with Nadia together. I don't think Nash has moved all afternoon."

"All day," Valerie said. The women looked at Nash and Nadia. Nadia was talking, and Nash was intently watching her face. "I just met Nadia. I guess you met her when you went to see Sissy in the hospital."

Ava nodded.

"I was surprised to like her so much," Valerie said. "Sami, too. She's really wonderful. Funny, friendly, and incredibly smart. We went shopping yesterday and had a blast."

"It must be doubly weird to see her with a. . ." Ava shrugged.

"Kid?" Valerie asked. "Nash is so awesome. I wish I could say that I'm comfortable with it, but. . ."

Ava nodded.

"Sissy and Ivan, too," Valerie said. "Then, I see them together and. . . they look perfect together."

"Happy," Ava said with a nod. "In love."

Valerie lifted a shoulder in a shrug at her own Judgements.

"Wes was about as much older than me as Ivan is to Sissy," Valerie said. "So I'm a big hypocrite to say anything at all."

"The difference between Seth's and my age is more," Ava said.

Valerie squinted at Ava.

"I know," Ava said. "You and I were adults."

"I'm sure it's hell for Ivan and Nadia," Valerie said. "Can you imagine having a soulmate experience with someone who is fourteen?"

Ava nodded.

"The nice thing is that everything is out in the open," Valerie said. "Sandy and Aden talk about it with Nash and Sissy. Everyone is clear about what's going on."

"Very you-guys," Ava said.

"Kinda hard to hide things around here," Valerie said.

"I bet," Ava said. "Speaking of hiding things: What happened with *The Crucible*?"

"We started the film. Then there were those big snowstorms, and I had to go into hiding," Valerie said. "My part was recast."

"Sorry," Ava said.

"It happens," Valerie said. "So why aren't you going to New York?"

"Seth got this gig working on Sandy's mom's piece," Ava said. "It's in five or six movements. He's working them into film scores for a series."

Valerie nodded.

"Yeah, I have no idea what that means, either," Ava said with a laugh.

Valerie smiled.

"Move aside, ladies!" Mike said with good-natured enthusiasm.

He was on one side of a large aluminum pan filled with all manner of burgers, sausages, bison steaks, and other meaty things for the grill. Seth held the other side. He wiggled his eyebrows at Ava as they passed on their way to the barbeques.

"Never fear," Mike said. "There's another tray like this of veg."

"Maresol's cooking with Delphie, right?" Ava asked.

"Dionne's in there, too," Valerie said.

A burst of laughter came from the kitchen.

"They are hard at work," Seth said.

Mike laughed. Jacob cheered at the approach of the meat.

"Any idea who that is?" Ava gestured to a beautiful woman standing on the grass talking to Heather. She had long dark hair, large blue eyes, and a bright smile. Although short in stature, she looked fit and strong. "She looks like one of those fairies."

"Aife," Valerie said. "At least I think her name is Aife. She's been here about a day. Fin and Abi were here but they left to go home to have their baby."

Ava nodded.

"She's very beautiful," Ava said.

"I guess she's usually the blue fairy," Valerie said. "Tanesha said she'll go back to that after tonight."

Alex and Max Hargreaves came out onto the patio. They turned in unison, and John caught up with them. Aife, the fairy, gave them a sweet smile.

"She seems to like them," Ava said.

"They're related to her," Valerie said and shrugged.

Ava nodded. A few minutes later, Colin Hargreaves and his wife came out onto the deck. They stopped to say "hello" before getting a beer. Seeing Colin, Charlie whistled, and Teddy threw the Frisbee to him. Colin caught it and jogged to where the teenagers were playing.

"Like I said," Valerie said. "This is my favorite party."

Ava smiled.

<center>~~~~~~~~~</center>

Sunday afternoon — 8:20 p.m.

"You promise?" Noelle begged through her tears.

"I promise," Sissy said. Trying to be brave, Sissy sniffed to keep from crying. "We'll video chat every Sunday at the very least."

"Tuesdays and Thursdays after school, for sure," Noelle said at the same time that Sissy said, "Every day."

Afraid she'd start sobbing, Sissy nodded. She was four years older than Noelle, so she thought she should be strong.

"I wish I were coming with you," Noelle said.

"There's no reason for you to hide," Sissy said. "You can be *here*."

Her last word came out with such longing that Noelle began to cry harder.

"And if it's awful and... everything?" Noelle asked.

"I'll come home," Sissy said. "Ivan says we can get work at the Denver Ballet."

Noelle nodded.

"I will miss you, sister," Noelle said.

"I will miss you, too," Sissy said. "I'm sorry I'll miss you being on the stand."

"It's okay," Noelle said. "You can't come in with me anyway, and..."

Noelle sighed.

"I'll be okay," Noelle said.

"You'll take care of my dog?" Sissy asked.

"I'll take care of *my* dog," Noelle said with a snort. Sissy laughed. "It's really hard."

"What is?" Sissy asked.

"Growing up," Noelle said. "Becoming something."

Sissy nodded.

"I believe in you, Sissy," Noelle said.

"I believe in you, Noelle," Sissy said.

"I'm sorry. . ." Aden said from the doorway. "It's time to go."

Sissy stood up from her embrace with Noelle.

"Love you," Sissy said.

"Me, too," Noelle said.

Aden put his arm around Sissy and walked her toward the door of the apartment.

"You have your money?" Aden asked. "Your return ticket? And if things don't work out?"

"I'll come right home," Sissy said.

"And if things go south with Ivan?" Aden asked. "Don't let him pressure you or. . ."

"I'll come right home," Sissy said.

Aden stopped at the door.

"Thanks," Sissy said.

"For what?" Aden asked.

"For helping Sandy make a home for us," Sissy said.

She stretched up to kiss his cheek. She hugged him one last time and raced down the stairs to the main level of the Castle where Sandy was waiting. Sandy gave her a hug.

"You're coming to the airport, right?" Sissy asked.

"I wouldn't miss it," Sandy said.

Sissy took a long look around the Castle before heading out the door to the driveway where Ivan and Nadia were waiting.

Monday early morning — 1:30 a.m.

"Why are we stopping here?" Sissy asked as she looked out the window at the tall building before her. "Ms. Behur doesn't live *here*."

"Your rooms are completed," Ivan said with a smile.

"Plus, Ms. Behur is in Denver for the trial," Nadia said. "She said you could stay at her apartment, but we figured you'd like to come home with us."

Surprised, Sissy looked at Charlie. Her older brother gave her a confident nod.

"How did they do it so fast?" Sissy asked.

"Nadia owns a construction company," Ivan said.

"Sort of," Nadia said with a wave of her hands. "My father was an investor in this company. I sit on the board."

"Oh," Sissy said.

"I asked if they could look at our little project," Nadia said. "They called last night to tell me that it was completed."

"How...?" Sissy bit her lip to keep from asking the same question.

"I know, right?" Nadia said with a laugh.

Sissy looked up at the building. There was an almost tunnel-like awning that stretched from the entrance to the curb. The building rose up and seemed to scrape the sky. A man in a top hat and long coat walked toward the taxi.

"You live here?" Sissy asked.

"For a long time," Ivan said. "I purchased a floor when I moved to United States. No one cared about this area then."

The doorman opened the door to the cab.

"Shall we?" Ivan asked.

Sissy gave a quick, worried nod. The doorman extended his hand to Sissy. She glanced at Charlie, who shrugged.

"You give him your hand and let him help you from the taxi," Nadia said. "He should call you by name."

"How would he know it?" Sissy asked.

"I sent your photos ahead so that they would expect us," Nadia said. "And we could get in."

"Nadia owns the entire building," Ivan said. "Except our floor."

"Oh," Sissy said.

Sissy tentatively placed her hand in the doorman's. He helped her from the taxi and tucked her hand into his arm.

"I am Marcus, Ms. Delgado," he said as he escorted her toward the door. His accent was all New York. Yet, his mannerisms were strictly old world. "If you ever need anything, you can call me. It will be my pleasure to assist you with any task."

Sissy looked up at the man. He was about Sam Lipson's age and wore a big mustache. The hat gave him a severe look that was contrary to his kind eyes.

"Thank you," Sissy said. "My brother doesn't walk too well and. . ."

Sissy looked back to see a woman wearing Marcus's same outfit helping Charlie out of the car and into a wheelchair. Another woman, wearing all black, greeted Ivan with familiar charm. A thin, dark-haired man wearing a black suit, black shirt, and black tie stood to the side of the taxi, waiting to assist Nadia.

"So many people," Sissy said under her breath.

"We are here to help," Marcus said. "Now, I was told you might need oxygen."

"Only when I sleep now," Sissy said.

"That is wonderful news," Marcus said. "I have arranged for a fresh oxygen tank. It is waiting for you in your room."

"Have you seen it?" Sissy asked.

Marcus looked down at her anxious face.

"You will be pleased," Marcus said. His hand covered hers. "It's such a pleasure to meet you. I just know you'll be happy here."

Marcus turned at the door. They watched Charlie, Ivan, and Nadia get out of the taxi. The thin man spoke rapidly to Nadia in what Sissy thought must be a dialect of Russian. Nadia answered in the same language. Marcus leaned down.

"They are speaking Ukrainian," Marcus said in a low voice.

"Oh, thanks," Sissy said. "I wondered."

She was quiet for a moment.

"Is Nadia. . .?" Sissy started. She looked up at Marcus.

"Nadia inherited many responsibilities from her mother," Marcus said. He leaned over so only Sissy could hear. "Mostly debt. Her mother was beautiful, a true angel. But, she was no businesswoman. Nadia has turned things around. That is good for people like me."

"Why?" Sissy asked.

"I love my job," Marcus said. "Good pay, good people. Everyone who works for her says the same thing. We love her and would do anything for her."

"Like get up in the middle of the night to help us?" Sissy asked.

Marcus chuckled. He gave her hand a squeeze.

"I'm glad you have joined us," Marcus said.

When Charlie and his helper drew close, Marcus opened the door for them. Ivan said something to her as he passed. Nadia stopped midway to continue her conversation with the man in black. She looked at Ivan before nodding in agreement. She said something to the man in black, who said, "Of course." Ivan and his helper entered the building. When Nadia reached the door, she held out her hands to Marcus.

"Papa Bear," Nadia said.

Marcus took her hands and kissed her cheeks in warm greeting. Nadia beamed at the man.

"This is my mother's most favorite human being," Nadia said to Sissy.

"She would never marry me," Marcus said. "That's why I am 'Papa-Bear.'"

"He arranged all of this for us," Nadia said.

"Thank you," Sissy said to Marcus.

Marcus blushed. He gestured for Nadia to enter the building, which she did. As soon as she passed the threshold, she and the man in black fell into their conversation again.

"You and Nadia's mother?" Sissy asked.

"She was my angel, too," Marcus said.

He turned Sissy into the building, and they went to join the others at the elevators. Nadia and Ivan had left their helpers in the lobby, but Marcus stayed tight at Sissy's side.

The moment the elevator doors closed, Sissy's heart raced with panic. What if she didn't like Ivan's home? Her mind spun one awful scenario after another. She was so worried that she didn't notice how many floors they went up. The elevator stopped, and Charlie's helper rolled him out. At the back of the elevator, with Marcus's arm supporting her, Sissy couldn't see anything. She heard a door open.

"Whoa," Charlie said.

Nadia and Ivan exited the elevator, but Marcus stayed right at Sissy's side.

"Shall we?" Marcus asked.

"What if I don't like it?" Sissy asked.

"Then we will make it into something you love," Marcus said. He leaned down to speak in her ear. "You love Ivan as much as he loves you?"

Blushing, Sissy nodded.

"Then you will be the lady of this manor," Marcus said.

Sissy looked up at him with surprise. Marcus nodded. Sissy thought for a moment before pushing her shoulders back and standing tall.

"That's a girl," Marcus said.

With her hand on Marcus's arm, Sissy walked into Ivan's floor. Her first sight was of the buffed cement floors giving way to the ceiling-to-floor windows. The space was open and light. It was beautiful in its clean simplicity. There was an open sitting area on Sissy's left and a large dining table on her right. Most of the space was empty.

"Would you like to see where you will stay?" Ivan said to Sissy. He included Charlie to ease the tension.

"Sure!" Charlie said.

"I will take it from here," Ivan said to Charlie's helper.

She nodded and went back to the elevator.

"You don't have to go?" Sissy asked in a soft voice.

"My instructions were to stay with you until you were settled," Marcus said in a neutral voice. "Are you settled?"

Sissy shook her head.

"Let's take a look, then," Marcus said.

Near the middle of the floor was a modern kitchen. From the kitchen, Sissy could see the wood floors of a thousand-square-foot workout space in the corner. Sissy looked at Ivan.

"I stay here, next to our practice space," Ivan said.

He opened the door to a large, plain room. The walls were a kind of grey-white. There was a big bed, a built-in closet, and a door to what was probably a bathroom. Sissy imagined she would probably spend a lot of time there. The thought made her blush.

"Nice," Charlie said.

"Your rooms are smaller, of course," Nadia said. "My room is about this size, but it's along the other wall."

She gestured down the hallway to a door at the end.

"We put yours in between ours," Nadia said. She walked ahead to open the doors. "Charlie, this is kind of a guest room, so it's not too personal."

The room was painted a kind of sunny yellow. Two queen beds sat in the middle of the "smaller" space, which was about as large as Sandy and Aden's entire apartment in the Castle. There was also a built-in closet and a door to a bathroom along the walls. There were a few Swiss balls and stretch equipment situated on a swatch of rubber gym mats. Above them was a large painting of a sunflower.

"The equipment is to help you to stretch when you first get up and before bed," Ivan said.

"Cool," Charlie said.

"We put two beds in here because your friend Dale said he was coming," Nadia said.

"He did?" Charlie asked.

"He told me last night that he wanted to come," Nadia said with a smile. "So I invited him. O'Malley is here, and Maresol thought she could spare him. He should be here in a bit."

"Awesome," Charlie said. "That's really great."

He looked up from his wheelchair and smiled at Nadia.

"We can leave you to get ready for bed," Nadia said. "Giovanni is helping us around the house. He is here to help you get ready for bed."

On her words, a smiling young man appeared at the door. He raised a hand in "hello" to Charlie and said, "Hey." Charlie nodded in return.

"Can I see Sissy's space?" Charlie asked.

"Of course," Ivan said.

Without further comment, he turned in place. Sissy looked up at Marcus. He patted her hand that was still holding onto his arm. They went down the hallway between the bedrooms and the kitchen to the next wooden door. Ivan opened the door and walked inside.

This was it.

Sissy flushed with anxiety. She was about to step into the room where she would live for the next few months and possibly the rest of her life. She would heal here. She would start dancing here. She would sleep, by herself, here. *Everything* — her entire life! — depended on this room.

She might have run away, but Marcus nudged her forward. She gave Charlie a last glance before taking a breath.

She held her breath.

Marcus nudged her again. She glanced up at him. Still holding her breath, she stepped into the room.

Avoiding looking at the bed, Sissy focused on the walls. They were blush colored, like the color of the tulle on the pink tutu she never took off when she was three. There was a large painting on the wall that separated her room from Charlie's. Unable to see it from where she stood, she let go of Marcus's arm and slipped into the room. She stopped in front of the painting.

The painting was set in the Castle backyard. The large garden beds were deep brown, as if they had just been turned over. The trees were bare, and the vine that grew along the fence had only a few leaves. The grass was deep green. In one corner, a single-head sprinkler sent an arch of water across the yard. Sissy's fingers instinctively hovered over the stream as her ears filled with the memory of the "ptat, ptat, ptat" sound of the sprinklers moving across the Castle gardens.

"It's beautiful," Sissy said.

"Mikhail painted it for you," Ivan said. "He wanted you to have something from home."

She turned. Looking past the bed, she saw the opposite wall. At least forty picture frames hung on the opposite wall. There were pictures of her family — Sandy, Charlie, Noelle, Nash, and Aden; pictures of her friends; pictures of Jill and Jacob; Katy and Paddie; and a photo of the twins laughing. Valerie and Mike were holding Jackie between them. Delphie and Sam stood arm in arm in one picture next to an image of Nadia standing in the

ER. There was even a picture of Ivan dancing. Everyone she loved was on this wall. Her eyes welled with tears.

"What do you think?" Ivan asked.

Not wanting to cry, Sissy nodded and smiled. She noticed the oxygen tank next to the bed, the door to the bathroom, and a closet.

"It's perfect," Sissy said. "Thank you."

"Yay!" Nadia clapped. Ivan smiled, and even Charlie looked happy.

"I hope it's alright," Marcus said. "We've transferred your clothing from Ms. Behur's home to the closet. Shall I run you a bath?"

"No," Sissy said with a yawn. The excitement over, she suddenly felt very tired. "If it's okay, I'll go to bed."

"Of course," Marcus said. "Your luggage should be waiting for you at the elevator."

"Thank you," Ivan said.

He turned to escort Marcus out. At the door, Marcus looked back at Sissy. She smiled and nodded to him. He returned her smile.

"I know you will be very happy here," Marcus said.

"Me, too," Sissy said confidently.

He gave her one last smile and left the room. Ivan went with him to the door. Nadia hugged Sissy and left for her room. Charlie looked at Sissy. He opened his mouth to say something, and they heard: "Dude, this is amazing," coming from the front.

"Go," Sissy said.

She sat down on the bed and tried to take it all in. She flopped back to stare at the ceiling. On the ceiling, they had placed the star stickers that she and Noelle had on their ceiling. Sissy smiled.

"Oh, cool!" Charlie said from out in the apartment.

She heard a distinctive laugh. Sissy got up to go look. Dale was standing next to Honey's wheelchair. Honey waved to Sissy. Ivan came to her side.

"Last week, she and I worked in the gym together," Ivan said. "MJ is here for a while, so I invited her to come. She has Maggie with her. Do you mind?"

"Not at all," Sissy said. "She can stay with me."

"We have an actual guest room," Nadia said with a smile. "It's next to mine."

Nadia leaned in so that only Sissy could hear.

"There's a research group here that has a technique which uses stem cells to repair an injury like hers," Nadia said. "I sent them Honey's medical records, and they've accepted her into their project. Don't tell her. MJ wants to tell her himself."

The elevator rang, and MJ, carrying Maggie, stepped into their apartment.

"I must get to bed," Nadia said. "I have to be at work in three hours."

"Go," Ivan said. "I will make sure our guests are settled."

Ivan touched Sissy's arm and went to greet MJ and Honey. Charlie rolled back to where Sissy stood. She put her arm around him.

"It's really great," Charlie said.

"An adventure," Sissy said. "I'm glad you're here."

"Yeah," Charlie grinned. "Me, too."

He smiled at Sissy before he pointed to his bags.

"Dude, get mine too!" Charlie said to Dale.

"Get it yourself, lazy ass," Dale said with a laugh.

"I'll get yours, Sis," Charlie said before he rolled to get his bag.

Sissy stood where she was and watched everyone come in. Ivan walked MJ, Honey, and little Maggie to their room next to Nadia's. Charlie dropped Sissy's bag on the way to his room. With a smile, Sissy followed them to her room. She was unpacking her clothing when there was a light knock on her door.

"Yes?" Sissy asked.

Ivan came into the room.

"I wanted to say good night," he said.

She hugged him and he kissed her cheek.

"Are you happy?" he asked in a low tone.

"Very," Sissy said.

He gave her a tight squeeze. Before she could say anything else, he spun on his heel and walked to the door. Turning at the door, he looked at her.

"We will start at six tomorrow," Ivan said.

Sissy nodded. He smiled and left the room. She sat down on the bed.

It was the first time in a very long time that she'd been alone. Before this, she was at the people-packed Castle. Before that, she'd been at Bestat Behur's apartment. Before that, she had been in the hospital, surrounded by nurses and doctors and Sandy and Delphie and Abi. Before that, Noelle had been at her side every moment she wasn't in a people-packed school. And before that, she'd lived at the Castle and gone to East High in Denver and lived her regular life.

This was her first moment completely alone since. . . living with her mother.

A wave of desperate loneliness came over Sissy. She started to cry. Crying led to coughing. In less than a minute, she was gasping for breath. Sissy panicked. She heard Charlie scramble next door and then Ivan's firm, "I've got this." The world was a wash of red glow when Ivan entered the room. With two steps, he grabbed the oxygen tank and mask.

"Breathe," he ordered as he put the mask over her head.

Sissy gasped at the air.

"It's a lot," Ivan said.

Sissy nodded and focused on the slow healing breaths Ms. Behur's massage person had instructed her to take. Ivan got up and went into the bathroom. He returned with her big hairbrush. She gave him a questioning look.

"Focus on breathing," Ivan said in a tone that she would dare not disobey. Sissy nodded.

He pulled at the knot in her hair until it unwound. Her long hair fell down her back. He began gently brushing her hair.

"You may not know, but I am an expert at this," Ivan said. "My mother and father worked, so it was my job to get my sister ready for school."

Sissy felt more than saw movement. She looked up to see that Charlie and Dale were standing at the door. Dale put his hand on Charlie's arm. Charlie pulled the door closed, and they made their way back to their bedroom. In Ivan's hand, the brush stroked her long hair. Sissy focused on gasping for breath.

"I made a mess of it for a while," Ivan said. "I was too impatient. Too much of a boy."

Sissy heard his words, but couldn't quite make out what he was saying. Ivan's words felt warm and loving. Slowly, she began to feel the air moving in and out of her lungs.

"But I learned," Ivan said. She leaned into his warmth. "Truth be told, I have wanted to brush your beautiful hair for a long time. But what do you say? 'Hey baby, can I brush your hair?' Very creepy."

Despite herself, Sissy giggled. He stopped brushing.

"I know that it is a lot," Ivan said. "I know that you are giving a lot, being forced to trust beyond what is reasonable. You are ill and frightened. It is more than enough for any person, let alone a girl who almost died."

"I'm okay," Sissy said, but the mask made her words unintelligible.

One look at him, and she knew he understood what she was saying. He continued to stroke her hair with the brush. They sat in slow motion — Ivan stroking her hair with the brush and Sissy fighting for air — until long after her breath was easy and her hair was well brushed.

"Would you like me to stay with you?" Ivan asked.

For a long moment, they stared at each other. Despite her fear of what that might mean, she nodded. At this moment, she could not tolerate being away from him.

"As much or as little as you wish," he said, "*always* as you wish."

CHAPTER THREE HUNDRED AND EIGHTY-THREE
WARMING UP

Monday morning — 5:00 a.m.
New York City, New York

Sissy knew that she was alone before the alarm went off, before she opened her eyes. The warm, large hand that had lain across her belly all night was gone. When she touched her stomach, it was quite cool. She rolled onto her back and felt for the space that Ivan had lain in. It was also cool.

He'd been gone a while.

She wasn't sure how to feel. He'd stayed with her last night. He'd just held her tight. That's all. And it was probably the best night of her life.

Now he was gone.

She'd heard about the "walk of shame," but she thought that was when people "hooked up." She realized she wasn't really sure what "hooked up" meant. Did it mean sleep in the same bed, like she and Ivan had done? Did it mean something else? She made a mental note to ask Sandy when they had lunch on video today. Of course, Sandy would want to know how she felt.

How did Sissy feel? Good. Happy. Safe. She glanced at the clock. Late.

Sissy turned off the oxygen and set the nasal cannula on the register. She hopped out of bed and jogged to her bathroom. Her hair was ready because Ivan had perfectly braided it in a long braid down her back. She would leave it. She made quick use of the bathroom and went to find something to wear. All of her ballet clothing hung on one side of the closet. Sissy changed into a pair of footless tights that were now a little too short, a now too-tight sports bra, and a pink tank top with a white long sleeved T-shirt on top.

She went into the hall and banged on Charlie's door.

"What?" Charlie yelled.

"Workout in forty-five minutes," Sissy said as she leaned into the darkened room.

Charlie threw a pillow at her. Laughing, Sissy deftly tucked her head out of the room just in time. The pillow hit the door. Chuckling to herself, she went down the hallway toward the kitchen. She had just turned into the kitchen when the thought hit her.

Maybe Ivan was ashamed of sleeping next to the stupid little baby Sissy, who couldn't even stand being by herself for a minute.

She stopped dead in her tracks. Her entire body flushed with shame. She closed her eyes and wished that she would do everyone a favor and just disappear.

"Hello, my love." Ivan's voice came from behind her. He touched her arm and continued into the kitchen. "I checked last night. We have the ingredients for our delicious and nutritious green smoothie."

His voice became muffled as if he were in the refrigerator.

"Can you get down the immersion blender?" Ivan's muffled voice asked. "It's in the cabinet on your right. The other blender does a better job but it makes such a racket. After such a late night, I'd prefer peace over perfect texture. Wouldn't you?"

She hadn't moved. When she didn't respond, he turned to look at her.

"What is it?" Ivan asked.

She opened her eyes and took in the sight of him. He was bent over with his head in the refrigerator. His head was cranked in her direction and his hands were full of vegetables for their usual pre-workout drink. She noticed that his skin held a slight wet sheen. The hair on the back of his neck was slightly wet.

She groaned to herself.

Ivan had been instructed to take an infrared sauna when he got up in the morning. He needed the warmth to get moving, especially now. That's why he'd gotten up. He'd left her for the sauna. She had no idea there was one in the apartment.

"What has happened?" Ivan asked.

He stood up and set the vegetables on the counter.

"I thought. . ." Sissy said. "You. . ."

He smiled at her and put his arms around her.

"I had the best night's sleep I think I've ever had," Ivan said. "I had this amazing dream. You and I were swinging — yes, swinging! — in this amazing place of green grass as far as the eye can see and blue, blue clouds."

"White puffy clouds?" Sissy asked.

"Like a painting," Ivan said. "I kept trying to touch the perfect clouds. You were laughing and keeping up with me. I've never felt such peace and joy. Not at the same time. It was like being reborn."

"Sounds like Olympia," Sissy said.

"Olympia?" Ivan asked. He stepped back to look at her but didn't let go. "Like your dream?"

Sissy nodded.

"Olympia is a real place?" Ivan asked.

"I don't really know if it's a real place," Sissy said. "Maybe it's a spirit place or a place where only our souls can go."

"It felt so real," Ivan said. "Tangible. Alive."

He kissed her lips.

"Like this." His mouth hovered near hers. She reached out her lips and kissed his.

"Yes, like that," Sissy said.

Ivan raised his eyebrows in a "Wow" gesture.

"I am sorry to not be there when you awoke," Ivan said. "I took it on faith that you would remember that I need the sauna."

"Is there one here?" Sissy asked.

"In my bathroom; yours as well," Ivan said. "Was I wrong?"

"I forgot," Sissy said.

"I imagine that did not feel very good," Ivan said.

Sissy nodded.

"Can I make it up to you with a refreshing and delicious green smoothie?" he asked with a laugh.

She smiled. He grinned at her. Before she could say anything, he gave her a peck on the lips.

"Don't be sad, my love," Ivan said. "We have another chance today to move our bodies, to dance, to live, to love. I am so… excited for it all."

Ivan gave her a broad smile, and she realized he wasn't wearing his glasses. He was breathtakingly handsome. He reached into the cabinet to get the immersion blender.

"Me, too." Sissy said finally.

Ivan winked at her. Humming to himself, he put together their pre-dance smoothie while she watched.

"I wondered if you could run your brother and Dale through our warm-up Pilates routine," Ivan said. "That will give me a chance to get MJ and Honey started. Do you mind?"

Shaking her head, Sissy scowled.

"I don't know if I can," Sissy said.

"You will have to go very slow," Ivan said. "It will be very hard for them. It might be hard for you as well."

"Slow is better than injured," Sissy repeated what he usually said.

"I don't know what I can do as well," he said. "We are just days from being in the hospital. We need to start slowly and believe we will be dancing again."

"Time will tell," Sissy said.

"Time will tell," he said.

Sissy didn't have anything to say, so she didn't. She watched him get their drinks together. He was humming a noiseless tune. He glanced at her and then smiled.

"What?" Ivan asked.

"You seem really happy," Sissy said. "It makes me happy."

"Are you kidding?" Ivan asked. "I am not happy. I am over the moon. My life has just begun."

Grinning, he began mixing their drinks with the immersion blender. She stoically drank hers down only to discover that it was quite good. He smiled at her reaction and continued making smoothies. He'd just finished when Charlie and Dale came in. They drank the green concoction down without complaint. Ivan gave two drinks to MJ when he stopped by to check in. Charlie and Dale followed Sissy into the workout area.

She was just about to start their Pilates warm-up when she turned to look at Ivan. He was watching her. Noting her look, he gave her a broad, confident smile. She nodded.

Her life had just started, and she was over the moon, too.

~~~~~~~~~
Monday morning — 6:57 a.m.
Denver, Colorado

"Ready?" Cody asked.

He was sitting on Tanesha's couch. Tanesha was sitting in front of her laptop at the dining room table. She was connected to Jeraine and Jabari via a video chat. Tanesha turned to look at Cody. He raised his eyebrows conspiratorially, and she nodded. Rodney came out of the kitchen, where Blane was cooking up a storm. In the background, the shower was going.

"Here we go," Cody said.

He picked up his phone and dialed a number.

"It's Cody," he said.

The person on the line spoke for a while.

"Yeah," Cody said. "I found out who it was. I got a photo."

The person on the other end spoke for a while.

"Yeah, you won't believe it," Cody said.

The person said something.

"Gorgeous," Cody said. "Truly the most beautiful person I've ever seen."

Tanesha could hear the person on the other end laughing.

"Hey, you have no idea what I had to do to get this," Cody said while he looked at Tanesha. "They might kick me out of school."

The person on the other end had a lot to say to that.

"Same deal," Cody said. "I send half the image. You send the money."

The person on the phone must have agreed because Cody nodded. He clicked a few buttons on his phone and sent a partial image of Yvonne. The picture was one from her and Rodney's second wedding. Yvonne radiated beauty and joy. She was breathtaking. The person on the phone gave an appreciative whistle.

"I'll send the rest when I get the money," Cody said and hung up the phone.

He raised his eyebrows at Tanesha and then looked at her horrifying father.

"It's done," Cody said. "Now we wait."

Rodney snorted at Cody and went back into the kitchen. He came out a few minutes later with a cup of tea for Tanesha and a cup of coffee for Cody.

"This is a good idea," Rodney said to Tanesha. "We keep feeding the machine, and they don't know it's us."

"Exactly," Tanesha said. "Give the image a week to work its way through all the sites — then we respond."

"Schmidty's already holding our response," Jeraine said. "We never comment on. . ."

"Gossip," Tanesha said.

"Thank you," Rodney said to Cody. He put a hand on Cody's shoulder before heading to the kitchen. "Breakfast in five."

"You don't think someone's going to recognize your mom?" Cody asked. "You look like her."

"I can assure you," Tanesha said. "No one sees that in me."

"And Fin's not going to. . ." Cody grimaced.

"Fin's having a baby," Tanesha said. "By the time he gets back, we'll just have a story to tell."

"And enough money to pay for Brian's school for a year," Cody said with a smile.

"First, they have to pay," Tanesha said.

Cody nodded. He set his cell phone on the table in front of him. Tink came out of the downstairs bathroom in a bathrobe and headed to the basement to get dressed.

"I'm going to. . ." Cody pointed toward the bathroom.

Tanesha nodded. He got up and left.

"This is good work, Miss T," Jeraine said. "What made you. . . do this?"

"Heather," Tanesha said. "I saw this asshole who betrayed me. She saw a human being in trouble. She thought we could help, while we take control of this a little bit."

Tanesha shrugged.

"She was right," Tanesha said.

"You won't be disappointed if it doesn't work?" Jeraine asked.

"Sure," Tanesha said. "But that's life."

"You've got to try new things," Tanesha and Jeraine said in unison.

"How's the tour?" Tanesha asked.

"Very fun," Jeraine said. "I'm really glad we did this. Jabari's having a blast. Your mom's now best friends with the other mothers. It's pretty awesome."

Tanesha smiled.

"Yes, I'll be disappointed if it doesn't end well," Jeraine said with a shrug. "But that's life, you know?"

"Breakfast's ready," Rodney said.

"Got to go," Tanesha said. "Got to get the troops."

"Love you, girl," Jeraine said and clicked off the call.

"Love you, too," Tanesha said and closed her laptop.

She got up from her seat to get Heather and the babies. When she reached the stairs, she saw Heather and Cody deep in conversation at the top of the stairs. Tanesha undid the baby gate. She picked up Mack from the floor and brought him downstairs. A few minutes later, Cody and Heather, carrying their new son, came down after her.

"What was that?" Tanesha asked under her breath. She set Mack down so that he could wander around.

"He's trying to help name the baby," Heather said in a low tone. "He wants to be an obstetrician."

"Any suggestions?" Tanesha asked.

"I think they should name him 'Wyn,'" Cody said coming into the dining room. He took a seat at the table. "It means 'blessed' in Welsh."

Tanesha nodded.

"Seems like a kid who missed being killed by a paid assassin *and* had his mom survive," Cody nodded. "That kid is blessed."

"Wyn," Blane said. He set down a plate of warm biscuits. "I like it. Heather?"

Heather nodded. Rodney came in carrying a platter of eggs and sausage. Cody had just made a plate when his phone buzzed. He got up to see what happened.

"They sent the money," Cody said. "All of it."

Tanesha gave him a firm nod, and Cody sent the image of Yvonne. He set the phone down and came back to the table.

"Now we wait," Blane said, rubbing his hands together.

"For me?" Tink asked. She jogged up the stairs. "Did you eat everything?"

"I made you a plate," Heather said.

"Good," Tink said.

She picked up Mack and set him on her lap. Mack lifted a

sausage from her plate and started eating it.

"You don't reprimand that?" Cody asked.

"It's good that he's eating," Heather said.

"We have plenty of time to learn formal eating," Blane said. Cody smiled.

"This is a good morning," Cody said.

"I'll drink to that," Rodney said.

He picked up his coffee cup. They clicked cups around the table and settled into eating breakfast.

~~~~~~~~~

Monday morning — 10:10 a.m.
New York City, New York

The simple stretch and easy movement of Pilates had been too much for Sissy. Her healing bullet wounds had seized with pain. Without saying a word, she rolled onto the side away from the pain. Ivan came right to her side, but he was struggling himself. Dale was able to get her to her feet. Ivan took it from there.

Leaning heavily against Ivan, she made her way back to bed. Ivan stopped in to see her before he left. He was sore but ready to get back to ballet. He assured her that he wouldn't do more than he could. With a kiss, he disappeared from her bedside.

She'd agreed to meet with Charlie at 10:30 a.m. to go over where they were with schoolwork. They'd scheduled an appointment with Mrs. Anjelika every day from three to four. Sissy thought she might need the time today. But she would find out later.

She had lunch with Sandy at noon, and Mrs. Anjelika at three.

This morning, she could rest. For all of its light and openness, the apartment was remarkably quiet. She put on her oxygen mask and fell into a sound sleep.

"Madam?" an accented voice whispered.

Sissy woke with a gasp. She sat up in bed.

"I am so sorry," Giovanni, the house helper, said. "Your

brother said that you were sensitive when you wake."

Sissy nodded.

"You have a visitor," Giovanni said.

Sissy lifted the air mask to say, "I'm sleeping."

"He was quite urgent," Giovanni said.

Sissy shrugged. She knew she didn't have to do anything she didn't want to do. She was Sandy's little sister, after all.

"It's has to do with Master Ivan," Giovanni said. "Seems he has had some trouble this morning. They wish to speak with you."

Sissy pulled off the mask.

"Who is out there?" Sissy asked.

"He said his name was James Schmidt," Giovanni said. "He said he was your lawyer. I told him you were sleeping, but he said something about circling wagons and Indians. I apologize, but I didn't quite understand."

"Circle the wagons because the Indians are attacking?" Sissy asked.

"Why would South Asians attack hand carts?" Giovanni asked.

"It's a reference to covered wagons and the Plains Indian Wars," Sissy said.

"Don't you call them 'Native Americans'?" Giovanni asked.

"Not in archaic sayings," Sissy said.

Giovanni gave a vague nod.

"Can you help me?" Sissy asked.

"Of course," Giovanni said.

He came to the bed to help Sissy to her feet. She was surprised at how a few hours of sleep had restored her. Giovanni helped her to the bathroom and took his leave.

Her hair was still perfect, so she just tidied the ends. Her mind moved a little slowly from the pain medications while she tried to figure out what she needed to do next. One thought came to mind — get dressed. When she returned to her bedroom, she found that Giovanni had made her bed and left a cute, easy-to-put on outfit for her to wear. She got dressed and went out into the kitchen. Giovanni waited for her in the kitchen. He gave her a travel mug of black coffee and helped her into the apartment. Schmidty was sitting in an armchair by the window.

"This floor of Ivan's always blows me away," Schmidty said.

Schmidty turned to look at Sissy. She smiled.

"How are you?" Schmidty asked.

"Alive," Sissy said. "I tried some Pilates today, and it was too much for me. I..."

Sissy shook her head.

"I hate being sick," she said with finality.

"I do, too," Schmidty said to confirm that he understood. He turned away from her to look out the windows. "You know they can't see in, right?"

"Only at night when no one is there," Sissy said with a nod. "Ivan has these amazing blinds that allow us to look out, but no one can see in at night."

"Amazing," Schmidty said. "What gets me is that Nadia owns the entire building. The rest of the building is quite opulent, yet she chooses to live here, in the one place she does not own."

"Ivan says that she would live on the streets if she didn't live here," Sissy said.

As if Nadia were a mystery, Schmidty nodded and shrugged at the same time.

"What's happened?" Sissy asked.

"Ivan has run into some trouble," Schmidty said. "They wish to speak with you."

"What trouble?" Sissy asked.

"From their perspective, there were a lot of questions about you and Ivan, and then you disappeared," Schmidty said.

"You mean because Kate stabbed Ivan and I hemorrhaged?" Sissy asked.

"From their perspective, they had questions, and you disappeared," Schmidty said.

"They're still caught up in Kate's bullshit," Sissy said. "Did you tell them she almost killed Ivan?"

"Ivan argued that point to no avail," Schmidty said. In a softer, kinder voice, he said, "She almost killed you, as well."

"I don't want to think about that," Sissy said with a scowl. "Or stupid Kate."

Schmidty nodded that he understood.

"What do I have to do?" Sissy asked.

"I assured them that you are happy to answer their questions," Schmidty said.

"Why?" Sissy asked.

"Because you're hoping to re-join the company," Schmidty said with a shrug. "If you blow off this company, you'll have to deal with it at the next. Katia may be dead, but her innuendoes linger on."

"So, this is just the bullshit of life," Sissy said with a nod.

"I couldn't have said it better myself," Schmidty said.

"Sandy always says that," Sissy said.

"Sounds like her," Schmidty said with a broad smile.

"Am I dressed okay?" Sissy asked.

Schmidty looked her over and nodded. Without saying another word, Sissy went to the door to put on her shoes. Sitting down on the bench, she realized that Noelle had helped her put on her shoes. She couldn't wear these. Giovanni appeared to help, but Schmidty waved him away.

"I took the liberty to get the mistress some slip-on shoes," Giovanni said.

Giovanni held up a pair of Dansko clogs. Schmidty smiled his thanks and helped Sissy into her shoes. He sat down on the bench to put on his shoes.

"When shall I expect your return?" Giovanni asked.

Sissy looked at Schmidty.

"With any luck, this will take only an hour," Schmidty said.

"But it could easily take all day."

"Why?" Sissy asked.

"O'Malley and Otis insist on coming," Schmidty said.

"Oh," Sissy said. She looked at Giovanni. "Can you tell my brother?"

"I will tell him when he wakes," Giovanni said. With a straight face, he said, "I will prepare a remedy for arrow wounds."

Giovanni winked at Sissy, and Schmidty laughed. To Sissy's surprise, Giovanni clasped her shoulders.

"Have courage, little bird," Giovanni said. He kissed her cheeks in sequence. "Love always finds a way."

Not sure how to respond, Sissy nodded.

"You will take good care of her?" Giovanni asked Schmidty.

"I will," Schmidty said, suppressing a smile for the intense young man.

Giovanni gave him a curt nod and left to call the elevator.

"Shall we?" Schmidty asked.

Sissy nodded. Schmidty held out his elbow. Sissy picked up her traveling oxygen tank and latched onto his arm.

"Let's get this over with," Sissy said.

"That's my girl," Schmidty said.

The elevator bell rang, and they left the apartment.

CHAPTER THREE HUNDRED AND EIGHTY-FOUR
GHOSTS

Monday morning — 8:10 a.m.

"Will you come in with me, Mommy?" Katy asked. Sitting in the parking lot, Katy looked out at the enormous, and new-old building that was the recently opened Celia Marlowe School. "I can do it, but. . ."

Katy waved to the female ghost who was standing in a second-story window. The ghost smiled and waved to Katy.

"I thought you didn't like it when I went in," Jill said in a mild tone.

"It's so big," Katy said in a loud whisper.

"You remember when we went to orientation, right?" Jill asked.

"Uh, huh," Katy said.

"I guess it's different on your first real day at the new building," Jill said.

"Everybody's first day," Katy corrected.

"*Why* aren't you getting out?" Jill asked, before adding, "Look, there's Noelle and Nash."

Jill pointed to where Noelle and Nash were getting out of Aden's new "safest possible" luxury sedan, a present from Sandy.

"Nash looks so handsome in his uniform," Jill said.

"Noelle is beautiful," Katy said.

Noelle turned around and leaned into the backseat of the sedan. She grabbed a dark-green, paint-stained beret. In the silence of their car, they watched Noelle's mouth never stop moving. The girl jammed the beret on her long brown hair. Nash turned to yell at her, and she trotted to keep up.

"It's nice that he gets to come back to school here," Jill said.

"Hey!" They heard someone yell from the steps of the school. Jill and Katy's heads turned in unison to see Teddy standing on the top step. He greeted Nash and grabbed Noelle's hand. They went into the building.

"Teddy's here, too," Katy said.

"He's moving back in soon," Jill said.

"I like it when everybody's home," Katy said. Her voice was wistful.

"Are you missing Sissy?" Jill asked.

"Uh, huh," Katy said. "She would be here, too."

Jill turned around to look at Katy. Even though her daughter was five now, she still needed a booster seat. Jill touched Katy's hand.

"Are you okay?" Jill asked.

"Why, Mommy?" Katy asked.

"Because usually, you jump out of the car and run into school," Jill said.

"Oh," Katy said.

When Katy didn't move or say anything, Jill unbuckled her own safety belt and got out of the car. Katy still hadn't moved. Her daughter's eyes were fixed on the crowd of children moving into the building.

Katy looked up at her mom when Jill opened the door.

"Are you all right?" Jill asked.

She'd just put her hand on Katy's forehead, when Katy brightened. Jill turned around to look. Julie was driving into the parking lot, with Paddie in the back seat. Paddie had clearly seen them because his face was pressed against the glass. Katy waved at Paddie and then looked up at Jill.

"Paddie's afraid of ghosts," Katy said. "After being stuck in the dead place."

Jill held out her arms, and Katy climbed onto her mother.

They set off across the parking lot to where Julie had parked.

"Oh, thank God," Julie said. "Paddie's been in a state all morning."

Paddie jumped out of the car. He held his arms up and jumped up and down.

"Really, honey, I don't think Jill. . ." Julie started.

Jill bent her knees and picked up Paddie.

"Wow," Julie said.

"Waitressing has its privileges," Jill said with a smile.

"Actually, I'm glad you're here," Julie said. "I know you and Heather worked on the building. I wondered if you could give me a tour. We missed the official tour."

Jill opened her mouth to speak, but Julie gasped.

"How rude of me," Julie said. "Do you have time? I'm so sorry. I didn't even ask!"

Jill started to shake her head that she wasn't busy and opened her mouth to speak again.

"Oh, gosh," Julie said. "Really, we can set up something. . ."

"She has time," Heather said as she came up behind them.

"Where's Mack?" Jill asked.

"Inside," Heather said. "I saw you out here and thought I'd come say, 'Hi.'"

"I was going to say that I'm meeting Heather," Jill said. "We're going to check to see if there's anything else to fix before going over our next project."

Jill smiled at Julie.

"Julie would like a tour," Jill said. "Are you okay with that?"

"Sure," Heather said.

"First, we should get these monkeys inside," Jill said.

"Do I have to?" Paddie asked.

"Paddie!" Julie said.

"It's okay," Jill said. "I was afraid of ghosts before I met Jacob."

"You were?" Paddie asked. His voice held such awe that the

women smiled.

"I was," Jill said.

"What changed your mind?" Paddie asked.

"Daddy told her he'd get rid of any ghost that was mean," Katy said with a nod. "This ghost isn't mean."

Paddie gave the building a worried look.

"The white-eyed guy gave you the shiny sword!" Katy said. "That was when we were in the dead place."

Paddie nodded as if he'd heard this information before.

"Let's try it," Jill said. "If it doesn't work, then you can both come home with me."

Paddie gave another worried nod, and Katy nodded.

"You both love school," Julie said.

The children looked at her like they had no idea what she was talking about.

"Just last Friday, you didn't want to go home from school!" Julie said. "Two days ago."

"That was at the other building!" Paddie said in such a way that it was clear they'd been over this more than a few times.

"*Misneach*," Katy said.

"What's that?" Jill asked.

"'Courage,'" Julie said. "Paddie's Uncle Cian says that to him."

"All right, then," Jill said. "*Misneach*, it is."

She turned toward the school.

"School's about to start," Jill said. "Shall we try it?"

She looked down at Katy, who nodded. She looked at Paddie, who was looking at Katy.

"Paddie?" Jill asked.

He glanced at Jill and nodded. Jill walked across the parking lot and up to the building. She went up the short flight of stairs to the open main entrance.

"Wow," Paddie said under his breath.

"It's pretty 'wow,'" Jill said.

Katy squirmed, and Jill set her down. Once Katy's feet hit the floor, Paddie wanted down as well. Together, they walked Paddie to his classroom. Katy hugged the boy. Without even a word to his mother, Paddie went into the room. Katy reached up to Jill with puckered lips. Jill lowered her cheek. Katy kissed her mother's cheek.

"Have a good day," Jill said. "Daddy will pick you up."

Katy waved and ran into her classroom. The women stood in the hallway for a moment to see if either child came out. When all seemed to be well, Jill turned to Julie.

"Shall we start the tour?" Jill asked.

Julie nodded.

"This hallway is mostly classrooms," Jill said with a smile.

She led Heather and Julie down the hall and into the building.

~~~~~~~~~

Monday morning — 9:35 a.m.
Denver, Colorado

"Yes, ma'am, that's correct, " Frankie said. The District Attorney had changed the testimony schedule. Frankie was testifying before his brother this morning. "He's sitting right there."

"The defendant asked you to take videos of..." the Deputy District Attorney said.

"Uh, 'sexual adventure' — that's what he called it," Frankie said. "He asked if I minded if things were aggressive. I thought he meant like 'physical.' I didn't know what he meant."

Frankie swallowed hard. He took a drink of water from the plastic cup in front of him and looked up at the prosecutor.

"He said 'aggressive'?" the Deputy District Attorney asked.

"Uh, something like that," Frankie said. He lifted a shoulder in a shrug. "I wasn't feeling really great. He asked me to come and bring my video equipment. I was thinking about something else."

"What do you mean?" the Deputy District Attorney asked.

Frankie looked at the woman for a brief moment. His eyes flicked to Samantha Hargreaves, who nodded to him. He looked out into the audience, where his mother, Wanda, and her father were sitting.

"I. . ." Frankie let out a breath. "Listen, I don't have any excuses for what I did. This is the worst thing I could ever do, and. . ."

Unable to continue, Frankie nodded. The Judge covered the microphone with his hand and turned to Frankie.

"I think she's asking why you got involved," the Judge said. "Just tell her the story, son."

Frankie's eyes flicked to the Judge. He nodded.

"My life was kind of messed up," Frankie said. "My step-dad had a *thing* for me. Told me he'd kill my mom if I. . . Well, my mom worked all the time and came home to take care of my step-dad. She was exhausted, sick all the time. She didn't know he was *abusing* me, and I didn't know how to tell her. The only person who really *got* me was my friend, Wade. He was like my. . . soulmate, and his dad was like my dad. When Wade's dad found out about everything, you know?"

Frankie nodded.

"He beat the crap out of my step-dad and told my mom," Frankie said. "My mom grabbed me and ran away. My brother hid us from my step-dad, but. . . he tried to kill us a couple times. Then Wade got this sickness and went away to a hospital and almost died, and his mom and dad split up and. . . I was alone, all the time. I'm not making excuses but you asked and. . ."

Frankie looked at the Deputy District Attorney.

"I tried to kill myself," Frankie said. "I took all the pills in the house. My brother found me and took me to the hospital. He had my stomach pumped, and I was home before Mom got off work. I met this guy when I was walking home from school. I don't know really what he said. I don't know that I cared."

Feeling movement, Frankie looked up to see the District Attorney give something to the Bailiff.

"Let the record show that the defendant was informed of the witness's mental state," the Deputy District Attorney said.

"From the hacking of the school nurse's office?" the Judge asked. "The way he selected the other boys?"

He looked through the papers from the Deputy District Attorney.

"The Defense has already admitted to the hacking of the nurse's records," the lead Defense Attorney said.

Frankie caught Wanda's eye. Frankie raised his eyebrows, and Wanda nodded. They had suspected that this guy had preyed on boys who were struggling.

"Please continue," the Judge said. He set aside the document.

"The guy who had been doing it threw himself in front of a train," Frankie said. "So I shoulda figured it was bad, but, like I said, I wasn't really thinking straight."

Frankie shrugged.

"Then, after I went once, he told me he'd get me and my brother in trouble," Frankie said. "My mom was working at Walmart in the day and stocking the grocery at night because-a me. If my brother got into trouble. . ."

Frankie shook his head.

"And Wade? His father?" the Deputy District Attorney asked.

"Objection!" the lead Defense Attorney said. "Relevance."

"We're looking at the witness's state of mind," the Deputy District Attorney said. "He said that his friend and his friend's father were a big part of his life until suddenly they weren't."

"Overruled," the Judge said.

"My friend, Wade, well. . ." Frankie said. "Wade wanted to be a girl. No, that's not right. Wade used to say that he was a girl in a boy's body. And his dad thought it was just a phase. He tried to toughen Wade up. Wade *starved* himself and. . . was in this prison-like hospital. I was. . . stuck."

Frankie's eyes welled up. He glanced at the Judge and then at the jury.

"Wade is Wanda now," Frankie said. "He's... No. *She's* my *girl*friend. Her father got over it, and her parents are back together. But then? It was just me."

"How were you involved with the defendant?" the Deputy District Attorney asked.

"I videotaped the assault of the girls and a couple of boys," Frankie said. "They didn't want the video of the boys — not as valuable on the Internet."

"Did you join in?" the Deputy District Attorney asked.

"No," Frankie said.

"Not even with the boys?"

Frankie shook his head.

"Let the record show that there is no forensic evidence that this witness was an active participant in the sexual or physical nature of the assaults," the Deputy District Attorney said.

Frankie pointed to the defendant.

"He used to call me 'The Faggot,'" Frankie said with a shrug.

"So how did it work?" the Deputy District Attorney asked.

"He would tell me where to go," Frankie said.

"By 'he', you mean. . ." the Deputy District Attorney said.

Frankie pointed to the defendant.

"Please state his name for the record," the Judge said.

"I don't know it," Frankie said.

As if he were thinking, the Judge blinked at Frankie. He nodded to Frankie.

"Let the record show that the witness pointed at the defendant," the Judge said to the court reporter.

"What did you call the defendant?" the Deputy District Attorney asked.

"To his face?" Frankie asked.

The Deputy District Attorney shrugged.

"I called him 'The Boss,'" Frankie said. "That's what he told us to call him. Behind his back, I called him 'Herr Fuhrer,' you know, like Hitler."

"And if you didn't call him 'The Boss'?" the Deputy District Attorney asked.

"He would get everyone to beat on you for a while," Frankie said. "They wouldn't kill you. That woulda been great for me, but they'd just maim you a bit. Make an example outa you. We didn't have insurance so it would be really bad for my mom if I got beaten up."

"You were talking about how it worked," the Deputy District Attorney said.

"The Boss would tell me where to go," Frankie said. "I had to be there at a specific time. I would set up my cameras, and then everything went down."

"You didn't intervene," the Deputy District Attorney said in a mild tone.

The courtroom was silent. Frankie shook his head.

"No." Frankie's face flushed red, and his eyes welled with tears. "I... I don't have no excuse. I took videos. When they left, I'd call 9-1-1."

Frankie sneered at the defendant.

"Didn't know *that*, did you?" Frankie asked the defendant.

"We submit into evidence recordings of this witness's 9-1-1 calls," the Deputy District Attorney said. "His voice has been identified by forensic voice recognition."

"We acknowledge that those are recordings from the witness," the lead Defense Attorney said.

The Judge nodded.

"Why didn't you call them beforehand?" the Deputy District Attorney asked.

"My brother asked me the same thing when he found out I was there," Frankie said. He shrugged. "It sounds stupid but I didn't think about calling the cops beforehand. I usually tried to make sure this kid — I mean, now I know he's Charlie. I tried to make sure he knew where we were going to be."

"Why?" the Deputy District Attorney asked.

"Because he helped the. . . um. . . victims," Frankie said.

"So you took these video recordings," the Deputy District Attorney said. "What happened next?"

"I would compress them and give them to the Boss," Frankie said. "I don't know what happened to them after that."

"Did the defendant ever pay you for the recordings?" the Deputy District Attorney asked.

"No," Frankie said.

"Did the defendant ever give you things?" the Deputy District Attorney asked.

"Things?" Frankie asked.

"Computers, games, drugs. . ."

"No," Frankie said. "He only gave me shit. All the time. And, me? I was either trying to kill myself, in school, or getting crap from the Boss. I would cry for days after it happened. I tried to stop, you know, videotaping that. . . stuff, but the Boss was clear. The only way out was death. I tried to kill myself, but I was too much of a failure to even be able to kill myself right."

Frankie shrugged. The courtroom went silent.

"How did you get out of it?" the Deputy District Attorney asked.

"They tried to beat up Wanda," Frankie said. "She called me and. . . I hadn't talked to her. . . I mean the last time I'd talked to her, she was Wade! Then she screamed my name and. . . I went to help. Of course. Her dad showed up and took care of the guys trying to hurt Wanda. Then we followed them and got into the big rumble later."

"Thank you, Frankie," the Deputy District Attorney said. She looked at the Judge. "No further questions at this time. We reserve the right to recall the witness."

The Judge banged the gavel. Frankie braced himself for the defense. Without being asked, the lead Defense Attorney hopped to his feet.

"Just to be clear," the lead Defense Attorney said. "You got a deal from the DA. Would you care to share what they gave you?"

"You mean sentence?" Frankie asked.

"Yes," the lead Defense Attorney said.

"I spent some time in Juvie, and now I'm at Denver Children's Home," Frankie said. "I get evaluated every month. If I'm not participating, I go back to Juvie. Depending on how I am when I get done, then I either go to Juvie or I get out. If I screw up, anything in the next five years, I go to prison. Period."

"So you got some therapy," the lead Defense Attorney said with a sneer. "After what you've done? That's pretty easy."

"If you think it's easy, you haven't been there," Frankie said. "And anyway, it wasn't the DA. It was Doc Bumpy helped me. He had records about everything that happened and all my suicides and even the stuff with my step-dad."

"Why are you testifying then?" the lead Defense Attorney asked.

"It's the least I can do," Frankie said. "That guy's a monster, a true monster. Not just for what he does to girls and guys — victims — but what he does to get the guys to do all this violence."

The lead Defense Attorney opened his mouth to say something, but Frankie interrupted.

"I've been to every family to apologize and ask if there's something I can do," Frankie said. "Wanda's dad takes me and stays with me. They all say they feel better when I leave."

"But you ruined your brother's career," the lead Defense Attorney said.

"Is there a point here?" the Judge asked.

"Your honor," the lead Defense Attorney said. "Some large portion of this crime revolves around the videotapes and income made from these tapes. *This* young man set up these violent situations so that he could take videos. He states that he gave the videos to my client, but the truth is that *he sold the videos for profit.*"

Frankie was so floored that his mouth fell open.

"He is the only person who stood to profit from these acts," the lead Defense Attorney said. "You are looking at the ringleader, the only person who stood to profit from these horrific crimes."

Frankie shook his head.

"Where's the money?" Frankie asked.

"How should we know?" the lead Defense Attorney asked in a mock bewildered tone.

"Objection," the District Attorney said. "The defense is making wild innuendo. Are we making up stories here or interviewing a witness?"

"Do you have any evidence to back your claims, Counselor?" the Judge said.

"His brother is a police detective," the lead Defense Attorney said. "Any evidence was destroyed by his brother."

"Do you have evidence that backs up your assertion?" the Judge asked.

"It's not my place to do the Prosecution's work for them," the lead Defense Attorney said.

The Judge looked at the lead Defense Attorney for a moment and banged his gavel.

"Next witness," the Judge said.

Samantha Hargreaves jumped to her feet. She helped Frankie down from the witness stand. They followed Frankie's mother, Wanda, and her father out of the courtroom. Frankie waited for the door to close before turning to Samantha.

"What was that?" Frankie asked.

"All he has to do is create a reasonable doubt that his client didn't do what he's charged with," Samantha said. "Saying you did it can create doubt in the jury's mind."

"Did it?" Frankie asked.

Samantha shook her head. Imitating her movement, Frankie shook his head too.

"If you're all right, I should go back," Samantha said.

Frankie nodded. He watched two uniformed police officers walk toward the courtroom with his brother. Frankie's older brother raised a hand in hello. Frankie ran to his brother, and the brothers hugged each other until the police officers dragged Frankie away.

"Don't talk about the trial," Samantha said to Frankie and his brother.

His brother nodded to Samantha.

"We won't," Wanda said. She gave Frankie a confident smile, and he nodded. They watched Frankie's brother head into the courtroom.

"How 'bout brunch?" Erik, Wanda's father, asked. "My treat."

Frankie nodded. He put his arm around Wanda, and they walked out of the courthouse. Standing in front of the courthouse, Frankie looked up at the deep blue sky. For better or worse, the thing he'd dreaded most was over. He smiled at his mother.

"Can we get burgers?" Frankie asked with a smile.

"Cheeseburgers," Wanda said.

"Oh, that sounds good," Frankie's mother said.

"And fries," Frankie said.

"A man after my own heart," Erik said. "Come on, I parked over here."

Frankie took Wanda's hand and followed her father to lunch.

CHAPTER THREE HUNDRED AND EIGHTY-FIVE
ENOUGH IS ENOUGH

Monday mid-morning — 11:35 a.m.
New York City, New York

"Here we go," Schmidty said.

Sissy glanced at Schmidty before stepping through the door he was holding open. Schmidty was maybe ten or eleven years older — she wasn't sure which — than she was. In those years, he'd made a happy life for himself. In this single glance, Sissy felt the distance between where she was now and what she wanted for her life.

Right now, her life was a mess. All of her hopes and dreams had come crashing down onto the sidewalk in front of Bestat Behur's apartment. Every dream had ended the moment the bullets had barreled through her rib cage. Sissy felt the yawning empty space where her certainty about the future had once lived. The space wasn't filled with panic or despair or even worry. It was unnervingly empty, silent, and dark as if her plans for her life had simply evaporated without a trace.

Sissy hadn't counted on the bullets. She hadn't counted on Ivan, either.

And now, the ballet company wanted a chance to "speak to" Sissy.

Stepping into the building was like stepping in to that empty space. She wondered where her foot — and her life — would land.

"This way," Schmidty said. "We're meeting in the administration office."

"How do you know?" Sissy asked.

"I was here this morning," Schmidty said. He took her elbow and leaned near her ear, "You didn't think that I would let Ivan come here by himself, did you?"

Surprised, Sissy looked up at Schmidty. He gave her a confident wink. They went into the administration office. Schmidty announced that he had arrived with "Ms. Delgado," and the woman behind the desk disappeared into the back.

"Your party is waiting in here," the receptionist said when she returned.

Sissy looked at Schmidty. He kept her close to him as they followed the woman through what felt like a maze of hallways. Down the hallway, Sissy could see into a small room ahead of them. She saw the side of Otis's face through the door. He was standing next to a small woman standing with her back to the door. The woman had her hair in a tight blond bun, wearing an expensive suit, and high heels. Facing the door, Seth saw Sissy first. Seth gave Sissy a big smile and touched the arm of blond-bun woman. Ivan sat nearest to the door with his head in his hands. A complete opposite of this morning, he looked exhausted and in pain.

Ivan must have felt her nearby, because he looked down the hallway at her. His face shifted from ashen exhaustion to sheer joy. He hopped to his feet and seemed to immediately regret it. He folded for the briefest second before moving to her. They stood in front of each other for a moment before she put her arms out. He held her tight.

"I'm so sorry," he said in her ear.

"To every life a little bullshit must fall," Sissy said.

Ivan laughed and pulled away. When he stepped back, Sissy saw that everyone was looking at her. Blond-bun had turned to look. In this light, she looked so much like Seth that Sissy wasn't sure who this blond-bun could be. Then the woman smiled.

"Sandy!" Sissy said.

She skipped forward to hug her sister.

"What are you doing here?" Sissy asked.

"After you left, Delphie told me that I should come," Sandy said. "I flew in with MJ, Honey, and Dale."

"But. . ." Sissy waved her hand in front of Sandy to indicate her expensive clothing.

Sandy leaned forward.

"Bestat," Sandy said. "She left the outfit for me. Pretty amazing, huh?"

"Grown up!" Sissy said with a smile and a nod.

Sissy turned to greet Otis and his girlfriend, Mari. Seth gave her a hug.

"Wow," Sissy said. "You're all here."

Ivan put his arm around Sissy's waist. Everyone smiled at Sissy.

"*Why* are you all here?" Sissy asked.

Everyone opened their mouths to speak, but Otis beat them to the punch.

"Is time to end this, once and for all," Otis said with a nod.

The other adults nodded.

"You either stay here, or we take you back on the market," Schmidty said.

"What does that mean?" Sissy asked. Her eyes flitted from one face to the next before settling on Seth's.

"If this ballet company wishes to keep you, that's great," Seth said. "They just need to decide. Today. Because this has gone on too long."

"But what if they don't?" Sissy asked.

She turned to face Ivan. He gave her a soft smile and nodded to Schmidty.

"Then we go to one of the seven ballet companies that have already contacted me," Schmidty said. "Including Denver Ballet Company. Everyone has heard about the little ballerina who was shot by some very bad men. You are in demand."

"And Ivan?" Sissy asked.

"Ivan is always in demand," Schmidty said.

"But no one wanted me before," Sissy said.

"Things change," Seth said with a shrug.

Sissy knew there was more to it than that, but she knew better than to press the topic in public. Her eyes flicked to Sandy, who nodded that she would tell Sissy everything later. Sissy smiled.

"Ms. Delgado?" the woman from the front asked from front of the room. "Would you follow me?"

Sissy started out the door. Schmidty appeared at her side.

"I'm sorry, Mr. Schmidty," the woman said. "We only wish to speak with Ms. Delgado."

"As Ms. Delgado's representative, you cannot. . ." Schmidty started.

"I'm afraid they only wish to speak with Ms. Delgado," the woman said. "Of course, if Ms. Delgado's parents were. . ."

Sandy moved to Sissy's side. Seth stepped behind her.

"We are Sissy's guardians," Sandy said.

Surprised, the woman looked from Sandy to Seth. Schmidty took a sheet from the inside pocket of his suit jacket and gave it to the woman. She read the paper.

"You're Sandra Delgado?" the woman asked.

"I am," Sandy said with a smile.

The woman paused for a moment before giving a tiny shrug. She spun in place and started down the hallway. Seth held onto Sissy's shoulder for a moment.

"No need to rush," Seth said in a low tone.

"But she's. . ." Sissy whispered.

"Don't let them set the tone," Schmidty said. He patted Seth on the back. "If you're not out in an hour, I'll come to get you."

Seth nodded to Schmidty, and they went to follow the woman. By this time, she had stopped to wait for them a few feet ahead. They reached the room a few minutes later.

"Here we go," Sissy said under her breath.

They entered the room.

~~~~~~~~~

Monday morning — 10:02 a.m.
Denver, Colorado

"My name?" Noelle blinked at the Deputy District Attorney. "Why, I'm Noelle Norsen. Most people call me, 'Noelle.' I go by my last name, 'Norsen,' for my art."

Noelle scowled at the Deputy District Attorney.

"Didn't that guy just say my name to call me up here?" Noelle asked.

"It's just procedure," the Judge said, as he suppressed a grin.

"Oh," Noelle said. She gave a curt nod. "That's who I am."

"Do you know why you're here?" the Deputy District Attorney asked.

"You called my school and told me I had to be here?" Noelle asked. She gestured to her uniform. "This is my new school uniform. Today was my first day at the new school building. It's not a new school or anything. And it's not a new building. It's a really, really old building that got fixed up, and now my school is there."

The Deputy District Attorney turned away from the jury to suppress a grin.

"I don't mean to be sassy," Noelle said. "Am I being sassy?"

"You're fine," the Judge said to Noelle before turning to the Deputy District Attorney. "Can we get on with this so that 'Norsen' here can get back to school?"

"Yes, Judge," the Deputy District Attorney said. "I wondered if you could tell us about what happened in the park the day you went to paint your boyfriend's step-mother."

"Oh," Noelle said.

Her happy face dropped. She looked at the Deputy District Attorney before looking out into the audience to see her father,

Aden, and Delphie.

"I guess I have to," Noelle said. She scowled and nodded to the Deputy District Attorney. "Go ahead. Ask your questions. I'll behave."

"First, can you tell us about your painting?" the Deputy District Attorney asked.

"I paint things," Noelle said. "I used to just draw stuff. I mean, my dad raised me and my brother. We spent a lot of time at daycare and stuff. I drew pictures there to pass the time. Turns out, I'm pretty good. Then, a couple years ago, we moved into the Castle, um, a big house, where Mike Roper lives. He's a master painter, really amazing, and famous, too. Most people don't know that he's a famous artist, more famous even than his wife, Valerie Lipson. And she's an actress! Anyway, he took me under his wing, and I've been learning about painting."

The Deputy District Attorney turned away.

"Oh, and I went to an art school in New York for a month or so," Noelle said. "Until someone tried to *kill* me and Sissy. Um. . . Sandy is my Mom — she's not my birth mom, she's my step-mom, but I call her 'Mom' because my mom is in prison. Anyway, Sissy is my Mom's little sister. Her mom's in prison, too. Sissy's an amazing ballerina. She's a couple years, well four years, older than me. We're like sisters. She got *shot. Twice. Boom. Boom.* Right on the sidewalk!"

Noelle nodded and licked her lips. Thinking Noelle was taking a break from talking, the Deputy District Attorney opened her mouth.

"And *died*! Like dead. Right on the sidewalk in front of me," Noelle said. "And she would have died if MJ hadn't saved her. He does medicine in the military. And I would have died, too! Except MJ picked me up, and the bullets went into his clothes. He has bulletproof clothes. I didn't even know they existed — bulletproof clothes, you know — until he used them to keep me from being shot and maybe dying on the sidewalk like Sissy did."

The Deputy District Attorney gave a quick shake of her head to clear her ears. She glanced at the Judge and he nodded for her to continue.

"Why would someone try to kill you?" the Deputy District Attorney asked.

"Oh, that's easy," Noelle said. "That guy over there and the creepy jerk who financed the websites and stuff — they wanted to kill me so I couldn't testify in *this very trial*! Like I am *today*! But. . ."

Noelle looked at the defendant and smiled.

"I guess that didn't work out very well for you, did it?" Noelle asked as she smoothed out the pleats in her skirt.

~~~~~~~~~~

Monday midday — 12:02 p.m.
New York City, New York

"Uh," Sissy said. She licked her lips and fidgeted with the tube to the nasal cannula that blew oxygen into her nose. At this moment, she was glad Sandy had insisted on hooking her to the portable oxygen tank before coming into this room. "Do you want the medical diagnosis? Or what happened? Or. . .?"

"You are in possession of Sissy's medical records," Sandy said in a firm voice.

The ten adults around the table started shuffling through the papers in front of them. After a minute, the man in the center pushed the papers aside.

"If I may speak for everyone," the man said.

The man looked around the table at the five women and four other men. Sissy noticed that one of the men was the man that Nadia had talked to on the way into the building last night. Noticing her look, the man gave her a slight nod. The man running the show looked at Seth last. Sissy had the distinct impression that the man knew Seth.

"I believe the heart of the issue is very simply this," the man said. "Ms. Delgado is an apprentice in our program. We take our responsibility for our apprentices very seriously. We want them to flourish as dancers without the pernicious influence of lascivious teachers preying on our young people."

Sissy blinked at him.

"'Pernicious' means..." Sissy's morning warm up teacher started to say.

"I understand what he's saying," Sissy said in an irritated voice. "I'm not an idiot."

The woman grinned. The man in the center's lips flicked up in a fast smile before settling to more neutral.

"I just find the question irritating," Sissy said. "You know Ivan! Many of you have known him *intimately*. How can you even think..."

"We have a tremendous responsibility," the man in the center said.

"That you take seriously — yes, I heard you," Sissy said. "I'm sorry. I'm very tired, and my side has started to hurt. What is it that you wish to know?"

"We'd like to know about your relationship with Ivan," the woman sitting to Sissy's right asked.

"You know about my relationship with Ivan!" Sissy said.

The adults looked up from the papers in front of them to focus on Sissy.

"This woman," Sissy gestured to the woman who'd just spoken, "the one next to you, the one over there, and I've seen a photo of Ivan with the one sitting there — they've all dated Ivan."

The man in the center raised his eyebrows with surprise.

"Why don't you tell the room what my relationship with Ivan was like when you were dating him, Janet?" Sissy asked the woman on her right.

"Uh," Janet said. She blushed bright red.

"Go ahead," Seth said.

Janet looked at the man in the center, and he nodded.

"She was his student," Janet said. "She was a child. He was quite fond of her. He worked with her every afternoon after school for an hour or so. I believe Mr. O'Malley paid him. Um. . ."

Under the table, Sandy gave Sissy's hand a squeeze. The woman on Sissy's left gave Sissy an ironic smile.

"I dated Ivan for a while when he was here in New York," the woman said. "I'm Eva, Sissy. He had just returned after working with Sissy in Denver."

Eva shrugged.

"He told me about Sissy," Eva said. "Sissy had a terrible eating disorder. He was worried that she might die. He also told me about Katia."

Eva's voice hardened.

"Frankly, I was more worried that Katia would murder me in my sleep than the insane idea that Ivan had molested Sissy," Eva said. "The woman was completely mad. I cannot believe that we are even entertaining the idea that. . ."

The man in the center cleared his throat, and Eva shut her mouth. The man gestured to another one of the women. She raised her eyebrows, but he gave her an insistent nod.

"I have seen the video." The woman's voice had a thick German accent. "Isadora, Sissy dear. I saw my dear friend Ivan trying to save his student's life. That is what I saw."

"And your relationship with Ivan?" the man in the center asked.

"He was a dear friend to me," Isadora said with a soft smile. "He still is a dear friend to me. As for his relationship with Sissy, I can only tell you what I saw when they were here, as I had Sissy in class. She has an incredible talent, the best I've seen in a long, long time. Ivan treated her with the utmost professionalism. If that is no longer the case, then something has changed. They both faced death. I imagine a lot of things have changed."

"I had Sissy for morning warm-up," another woman said. "Sissy, you might not remember, but I'm..."

"Melinda," Sissy said. "I remember you from Denver."

Melinda smiled at Sissy.

"I dated Ivan when I was in Esprit de Corps in Denver," Melinda said. "I met him because I wanted to improve my chances of moving to a New York ballet. I found him... captivating."

Melinda smiled.

"I can tell you that he loved Sissy, very much, in fact," Melinda said. "I have been around the... what did you say? 'Pernicious influence of lascivious teachers'?"

A beautiful woman in her prime as a soloist ballerina, Melinda's smile lit up the room.

"I grew up with such a pernicious influence," Melinda said. "I know what it is to be groomed by a pedophile. That is not what was going on between Ivan and Sissy. Ivan loved her. Her father saved him from the gulag specifically so he could work with Sissy, for God's sake. She's extraordinarily talented. How could he not love her?"

Melinda sniffed at the man in the center.

"Are you married to Ivan?" a man on Sissy's left asked.

"No," Sissy said.

"Are you dating?" the man asked.

"I've never been on a date with Ivan," Sissy said.

"But you're involved?" the man in the center asked as a way to regain control of the room.

"Involved?" Sissy asked. "What does *that* mean?"

"I think they want to assess what's going on with you and Ivan," Seth said.

"Just tell them about Ivan," Sandy said. "I can fill in what you don't remember."

Sandy looked up at the adults in the room.

"I've known Ivan most of my life," Sandy said. "I can assure you that he has not been anything but appropriate and professional with Sissy — and every other child he's been around, for that matter."

"Did something change?" the woman sitting on Sandy's right asked.

Sandy nodded to Sissy.

"I died," Sissy said. "I think that's what happened. I died on the sidewalk and then again when I was saving Ivan from Katia. He died on the surgery table after Katia tried to kill him."

Sissy sighed. She felt the weight of everything that had happened catching up with her.

"I think death has a way of clarifying things," Sissy said. "Don't get me wrong. I have *always* loved Ivan, and he has *always* loved me. Don't most teachers love their students? I can tell you that most students love their teachers."

"That is why it's so important to ensure that our students are not vulnerable to their teachers!" an elderly man said with a distinctive lilt.

Sissy gave him an exhausted sigh.

"I know you've spoken with Ivan," Sissy said. "And. . . I. . ."

"Just answer for yourself, Sis," Seth said.

"Um. . ." Sissy licked her lips and took a breath. "Well. . ."

~~~~~~~~~~

Monday midday — 11:02 a.m.
Denver, Colorado

Noelle waited while the lawyers argued over this tiny, stupid stuff. She thought the jury was going to scream in bored frustration. The Judge certainly seemed angry. Noelle was pretty sick of it herself. She'd hoped to get back to school. As the clock ticked, she knew they were going to break for lunch soon. She was going to be stuck here all afternoon.

The Deputy District Attorney turned to Noelle, and Noelle gave her a hopeful smile.

"Looking at the time, why don't we take a break?" the Judge asked. "Ms. Norsen, remember you are still under oath during lunch."

"We don't talk about the trial," Noelle said. "None of us. It's important to take out the garbage."

Noelle sneered at the defendant ,and the jury chuckled. The defending attorney jumped to his feet and started yelling. The Deputy District Attorney shook her head.

Noelle leaned back in her chair.

She was definitely going to be here all afternoon.

CHAPTER THREE HUNDRED AND EIGHTY-SIX
FINISHING UP

Monday midday — 12:42 p.m.
New York City, New York

Sissy paused to catch her breath. Remembering Seth's encouragement to not let them set the tone, she let the pause linger. She focused on calming her breath as she looked around the room. She took the time to look into the face of each of the people in the room. When her breath was easy, she gave a slight smile before nodding.

"I get it," Sissy said. "I really do. You see me — a young woman, a ballerina, from Denver — and you think 'These people from nowhere-ville Denver, they're all inbred and stupid. They are not as sophisticated as we are here in New York City. They can't possibly know what was going on.'"

Isabelle cleared her throat and raised an eyebrow to the man across from her. Sissy nodded at her acknowledgment.

"You couldn't be more wrong," Sissy said. "Someone I love very much was involved in child pornography for most of her upbringing. Her situation was a topic of conversation in my household growing up. I knew as a young child that children could be preyed upon. I knew how to catch it before things got out of hand and what to do if it happened. Moving to New York, my sister and her husband both worked with me so that I knew strategies to keep myself safe. I spent an hour with my patron, Otis, while he warned me of the dangers of ballet companies. None of this was about Ivan. This thing with Ivan... It's new."

Sissy gave a firm nod before continuing. "We have no secrets in our family. We also don't pretend that life is easy and the world is safe. I knew there was a risk moving to New York. More than that, I knew exactly what to do if something awful happened to me.

"Before that, myself and my brothers and sister had to go through dating school. We learned how everything worked. I wasn't thrust out into the world. I was informed of what happens between men and women. I was also given real skills how to know what was right for me and how to deal with things if they weren't. That's not to mention that many of my closest friends and my brother are now embroiled in a big rape case in Denver.

"*That's* how I ended up getting shot. *That's* where I was last week — to testify in a huge, violent *rape* case. So you see, these issues are ones that even unsophisticated Denverites have to deal with."

Sissy stopped to take her breath.

"That doesn't mean..." the man across from Isabella said at the same time the man in the middle said, "We have every right..."

"I haven't finished," Sissy said cutting them off.

Seth leaned toward Sissy in support.

"You're asking me if Ivan groomed me to be his lover," Sissy said. "Let's get down to what you're really asking. Did Ivan ask me to touch his penis? No. Did he encourage me to kiss him in a sexual way? No. Did he take naked pictures of me? No. Did he reward me for being seductive? No. Did he subtly encourage me to meet his sexual or other needs? No. Did he touch me, stroke me, or bend me in positions that were sexual in nature? No. Did he give me presents when I was seductive? No. Did he touch my genitals? No."

Sissy asked and answered each question in quick succession.

"What Ivan did was love me," Sissy said.

One of the men opened his mouth to speak.

"I haven't finished," Sissy said. "You *made* me come here and answer *your* questions. You cannot then cut me off when I'm doing just that."

"Go ahead, Sissy," the man in the middle said.

"When I say that Ivan loved me, I mean that he held me on his lap while I bawled my eyes out at my father's funeral," Sissy said. "He talked to me like I mattered. He treated me like a human being, not a stupid child. He bullied me until I believed that I could possibly be more than I was. He believed in my dreams, sometimes more than I did. He showed up, was present, listened to me and responded thoughtfully — every single day for years."

"Was his love sexual in nature? No," Sissy said. "Did I know that he was a sexual being? Yes. He had lots of girlfriends, a few of them you've heard from. Did I believe that he wanted me to be one of them? No. Did I ever feel pressure to be his girlfriend? No. He treated me like his precious 'Sissy.' I only ever wanted to be just that."

Sissy nodded.

"That's what I have to say," Sissy said.

"Has something changed in your relationship?" the man in the center asked.

"I have answered this question, more than once," Sissy said. "For the record — death changes things. The rest is none of your business."

"We need to. . ." the man in the center said.

"No," the man who'd met Nadia at the limo last night spoke up. Sissy was surprised that he had an Australian accent. "We have heard what we were concerned about. We do not need to know the intimate details of Ivan and Sissy's relationship."

He looked up at Sissy and smiled.

"I'm Ian Beckenshire, Ms. Delgado," the man said with a nod. "Ms. Delgado told us that her relationship has changed since she and Ivan battled back from the very brink of death. I can tell you that she is not lying or exaggerating. They nearly died. It's a miracle that we are not mourning the loss of our student and teacher instead of badgering her with provincial questions from paranoid busybodies."

Sissy raised her eyebrows in surprise. She felt more than saw Sandy do the exact same expression. She glanced at Seth. He seemed amused.

"You cannot. . ." the man in the middle said.

"Yes, in fact, I can," Ian said. "It has only been a week or possibly two. How does this young woman have any idea what her relationship with Ivan is or will be? She is young and injured. He is still recovering. She's just returned to New York after testifying to her attempted murder at a horrific trial and, now, has testify to us about the very nature of love. I, for one, have heard enough. The rest is, indeed, none of our business."

He nodded in Seth's direction.

"Out of sheer, human decency, I move that we let this matter drop," Ian said. "Who agrees with me?"

All of the women and some of the men raised their hands.

"That is the majority," Ian said. "You must now drop this!"

The man in the center shook his head.

"If you're truly unwilling to stop this witch hunt," Sandy said, "I am exercising my right to cancel Sissy from her contract. I will also be fighting Ivan's contract. They have both received offers from ballet companies all over the world. There is no reason they should stay here and have to put up with this inquisition."

The adults looked at Sandy with surprise.

"Ivan's contract is binding," the man in the center said.

"I'm so glad you're clear on that point," Seth said. "If Ivan is not relieved of his contract, I will remove all levels of my support of this ballet company. I can assure you that Otis and his family will no longer financially support this ballet. Katia's husband will remove his support. Further, I will speak with all of your remaining benefactors. I think you'll be surprised at how persuasive I can be."

"I can assure you that Kerminoff Industries will retire their support of the ballet company as soon as possible," Ian said.

"You will lose most, if not all, of your charitable support," Sandy said with a raise of her eyebrows.

Sandy got up from her seat. She held her hand out to Sissy.

"Come on, Sis," Sandy said. "We'll let the lawyers work out the rest."

Sissy gave Sandy a confused look but didn't dare not to do what Sandy asked. With Sandy's help, she got to her feet, and they left the meeting. Seth followed behind.

"Your turn," Sandy said to Schmidty, who was waiting by the door to the room.

Schmidty gave a quick nod with his head and went into the room. Sissy leaned on Sandy as they threaded their way through the hallways to get back to where Ivan and the others were waiting. Ivan held her for a long moment before letting it go.

"How did it go?" Ivan asked.

"Awful," Sissy said.

"Sissy was fantastic!" Seth said.

Otis gave Sissy a pat on the back while Mari hugged her tight.

"What now?" Sissy asked.

"You should take her to expensive hotel for good food and rest," Otis said.

"I'd rather just go home, if that's okay," Sissy said.

Otis gave her a big smile and brief hug.

"Are we done?" Ivan asked.

"For now," Seth said. "Schmidty is in there, finishing up the details."

Ivan nodded.

"I would love to go home, as well," Ivan said. "Please, you are all welcome. I will call ahead and have Giovanni get lunch together."

Mari looked at Otis, and he smiled.

"I'd love to see the apartment," Sandy said. "To meet Giovanni."

"You know Giovanni?" Sissy asked.

"I helped him with your room," Sandy said with a smile. "I wanted to take Sissy shopping after lunch if she's up for it. Then I need to rush off to get back to Denver. Noelle is testifying today, and I have marriage class tonight."

"We should keep moving," Seth said.

"I can't go shopping," Sissy said. "I have to meet with school."

Sandy smiled, and Ivan chuckled.

"What?" Sissy asked.

"You just went through the fire," Seth said. "You can rest this afternoon."

"Take on next fight tomorrow," Otis said.

Sissy shrugged, and Ivan laughed out loud.

"What?" Mari asked Ivan.

"She will still meet with school," Ivan said. He kissed her forehead. "My Sissy."

She blushed.

"Let's get the hell out of here," Seth said.

Grinning at Seth, Sissy took Ivan's hand, and they walked out of the office. They were whisked into a waiting limousine and home in a few minutes.

"This is really nice!" Sandy said at the entrance to the apartment.

"*Sandy!*" Charlie yelled.

For this brief moment, Sissy knew that everything was perfect. For now.

Never again would she assume that her life could unfold only in response to her dreams and wishes. Two bullets had ended that childish dream. Real life — with its ups and downs, awful and amazing times — was so much more than that dream.

Sissy hoped to never forget the overwhelming gratitude she felt right this moment. She was grateful for her life, for Ivan, for all those who rallied around her, for love, and most importantly for the chance to live one more day.

"What is it?" Ivan whispered to Sissy.

"Just happy, I guess," Sissy said in the same tone.

He laughed.

~~~~~~~~~

Monday afternoon — 2:02 p.m.
Denver, Colorado

When they'd returned to the courtroom, the Judge had warned the attorneys not to argue so much. Or at least that's what Noelle thought he'd said. Over the last two hours or so, she'd testified to what had happened the day she was supposed to get beaten up in the park.

Of course, she left out the parts about Bestat being a dragon and Jacob stopping time, and all the weird stuff. No one needed to know those things. Knowing all of that would just confuse the issue. At least that's what Sandy had said. Noelle's job today was to help convict this awful man.

The Deputy District Attorney made a big deal of the pictures Noelle had taken on her phone. Before she'd started painting Bestat, Noelle had taken a series of pictures of the area and of Bestat. The police had collected the phone from her before she went to the hospital. The defendant could be seen in a corner of every picture. The police department had blown up the pictures so he was the center of the pictures.

The grainy images showed the defendant standing alone among the trees. The date stamp showed that he had been there for a while before the boys showed up. In the first image, the young man was staring at Noelle through the trees. The look on his face was one of... well, she didn't know what: Lust, maybe? Rage? Hatred? Some mixture of all of that. She hadn't noticed him that day. When the Deputy District Attorney showed her the photo, Noelle's entire body had shaken. The look on his face terrified her. Had he planned to do to her what he'd done to Ivy? Hurt her and then carve his name on her most private place?

The next photo showed him with a cell phone to his head, as if he were calling someone on his phone. The photo after that showed him taking pictures of her with his phone. He was messing with his phone in the next photo. The Deputy District Attorney said that his phone records showed that he was sending the pictures of Noelle to the boys so they would know who to attack and where.

Noelle shivered at the thought.

After all of the questions and arguments and boring moments, the Deputy District Attorney said she didn't have any more questions. Now, it was time for Noelle to deal with the Defense. Noelle knew from Samantha Hargreaves that the defense had made it a policy to harass the "kids" in the trial. As the Deputy District Attorney sat down, Noelle felt the mood of the courtroom shift. Everyone sat up as if they were on guard for whatever horrible thing the Defense did next.

Noelle leaned back in her chair. By leaning back, her legs came off the ground. She unconsciously swung her legs because she could. The Defense Attorney noticed right away.

"Stop that," the Defense Attorney said.

The Judge's head jerked up to look at the Defense Attorney.

"What am I doing?" Noelle asked.

"Your honor, I would like to submit that this witness has been coached," the Defense Attorney said.

"What does that mean?" Noelle asked.

"Good question," the Judge said. "What exactly are you referring to, counselor?"

"This witness is trying to convince this courtroom that she's an innocent girl," the Defense Attorney said. "Rather than a conniving, manipulating, scam artist who would like. . ."

Noelle didn't hear the rest because Samantha Hargreaves popped to her feet and started throwing out "Objections" and "Warnings" and whatever else. It took a few moments for the courtroom to settle down.

"In the first place," Noelle said, "I *am* an innocent girl. Nobody had to teach me that. That's what I am! And in the second place, I not a scam artist. What would I be scamming? I went to the part to paint my boyfriend's step-mother. Why is that so weird?"

The courtroom fell very silent. The Defense Attorney sniffed as if he was laughing. Noelle scowled and shook her head.

"I don't have any skin in this game," Noelle repeated what Nash always said in these situations. "If anything, I wanted to spend my first day at the new school building *at school*!"

The Defense Attorney gave one of his sick smiles.

"Why did you take photos of my client?" the Defense Attorney asked.

"I didn't," Noelle said. "I was taking photos of the entire area. Your client happened to be there."

"Why did you take his picture?" the Defense Attorney asked.

"I didn't," Noelle said.

"Are you saying that you did not take these photos?" the Defense Attorney asked. He shook his head in exaggerated confusion.

"I took these photos," Noelle said. "I didn't take them of him. He just happened to be there."

"We all know that this witness took photos for her painting and that your client was in the scene," the Judge said. "Ask a different question, or I'm releasing this witness,"

"Where is this painting?" the Defense Attorney asked. "The one you supposedly were painting."

"My Dad has it," Noelle said. She looked at the Judge. "Can I get it?"

"If you do, we'll have to admit it into evidence," the Judge said.

"But I'd get it back — right?" Noelle asked.

"Eventually," the Judge said.

Noelle thought for a moment before shrugging.

"I can always paint another," Noelle said.

"Bailiff?" the Judge asked.

The bailiff went out into the audience to take the canvas from Aden. He held the painted side against him so that no one could see it. He gave it to Noelle. There was a subtle gasp around the room when Noelle held the painting up.

The painting was a lovely mix of trees and grass. In the center, sat Bestat Behur on a mustard colored blanket. Bestat's face was placid and she had a soft loving smile. Her hair was braided down her back. Noelle turned it so the Judge could see.

"That's quite lovely," the Judge said. "You have quite a talent, Norsen."

"Thanks," Noelle said.

"You expect me to believe that you painted this?" the Defense Attorney asked.

"I don't know what you believe or don't believe," Noelle said. "You asked me if I had made the painting and I'm showing you the painting I made."

Noelle shrugged.

"Is there anything else, counselor?" the Judge asked.

The Defense Attorney looked at the table where his co-counsel were sitting. They shook their heads.

"It would appear not," the Defense Attorney said.

"Looks like you can head back to school, Norsen," the Judge said.

"No, sir," Noelle said. "They're done for the day. But I'll get to spend some time with my dad, which will be great. Daddy? Can we go for ice cream?"

Embarrassed, Aden just waved at her from the aisle.

"I want to see all of the attorneys in my chambers," the Judge said with a bang of his gavel.

Noelle popped out of the witness box and ran to him. They hugged. Samantha Hargreaves got up to walk them out.

"That was awful," Noelle said.

"You were amazing," Samantha said.

"Do I have to come back?" Noelle asked.

"Maybe," Samantha said. "We'll see. Remember. . ."

"I won't talk to anyone about it," Noelle said. "Well, maybe Buster. He's an expert on creepy people. He knows them when he sees them. Can I tell Buster?"

"Buster?" Samantha asked.

"Our dog," Aden said.

Samantha was so charmed by Noelle that she hugged the girl.

"I have to go in to see what's going on," Samantha said. "Can you walk yourselves out?"

"Of course," Aden said.

"I'll stop by tonight," Samantha said.

"Thanks," Aden said.

Aden and Noelle watched as Samantha went back into the courtroom.

"Ice cream?" Aden asked Noelle.

Noelle nodded, and they walked toward the front of the courthouse.

"When does Mom get home?" Noelle asked.

"This evening," Aden said. "She wants to make sure she has a chance to see you."

"And go to marriage class," Noelle said with a grin.

"That, too," Aden said with a smile. "That's pretty nice, huh?"

"Very nice," Noelle said.

They walked out of the courtroom.

CHAPTER THREE HUNDRED AND EIGHTY-SEVEN
THE TRUTH

Monday evening — 6:32 p.m.
New York City, New York

"Thank you," Honey said to the maître d' when he gave her a napkin.

She and MJ were sitting in one of New York City's nicest restaurants. Usually closed on Mondays, the restaurant was hosting a special meal for the Fey Team, paid for by a grateful patron. Honey was the only life-partner there. The rest of the team was sitting around the restaurant floor in tables of three and four. She and MJ had been seated at a two-person table overlooking the Hudson.

Honey leaned forward in her wheelchair. A tall, lanky man, MJ leaned all the way across the table to kiss her lips.

"I hope this makes up for missing marriage classes," MJ said.

Honey smiled. She looked up when MJ's superior officer, Alex Hargreaves, and her work-partner Raz came by the table to say "Hello." After a few minutes of happy chatter, they wandered off to check in with other tables. She smiled at MJ.

"I know that smile," MJ said. "What's going on?"

"I wondered when you're going to tell *me* what's going on," Honey said.

"What do you mean?" MJ made a considerable effort to look indignant. He wasn't fooling Honey, and he knew it. That didn't keep him from laying it on thicker. "The team is getting this nice meal as a thank-you. I thought you'd like to come!"

Honey grinned at his efforts.

"Don't you want to be here?" MJ continued. "Look around. No other Fey wife or husband is here. Only you. That alone should *mean* something to you."

He threw his hands up in mock exasperation.

"Sometimes, I just don't know what you want," MJ said.

Honey kept grinning. The waiter came up to offer them wine. MJ ordered a glass of red wine for himself. He and the waiter settled on some raspberry-infused water for Honey. She was on such a thick regimen of muscle relaxants and pain meds for her injured spine that alcohol was out of the question, and carbonated drinks caused her Crohn's Disease to flare up.

When the waiter disappeared, MJ shook his head. He opened his mouth to continue his odd rant.

"Stop," Honey said.

"But. . ." MJ said.

He was never one to let anyone have the last word. She held her index finger to her lips. He closed his mouth, and she leaned forward again. He leaned across the table toward her.

"How 'bout the truth?" Honey said. She raised her eyebrows in amusement.

"What are you talking about?" MJ started.

"Okay, okay," Honey said with a chuckle. "I get it. You and the team are here for a special thank-you dinner. I'm here because I happen to be in town. And yes, I plan to take photos to brag to the rest of the Fey wives and husbands. They will wish they were here with us. I feel very lucky."

Honey gave him a curt nod that caused her shoulder-length white-blond hair to bounce. Her hair was so fine that it flew up in a static halo around her head. He stroked the back of her head to smooth it down. Sure that he'd dodged her question, he leaned back in his chair.

The waiter brought their drinks and explained their dinner. The menu was a *Prix Fixe*, which meant that there was only one menu, no choices. He explained that one of the reasons this restaurant was so popular was that the Chef prepared the menus based on whichever customer had the most extreme dietary needs. Because Honey had Crohn's Disease, the Chef had prepared a feast of food based on her restrictions.

"Are you sure?" Honey asked. "I usually just eat around. . ."

"It's our pleasure," the waiter said. "The Chef finds it to be an interesting challenge. And. . ."

The waiter knelt down to Honey's wheelchair height.

"The staff eats dinner before we serve so that everyone knows the menu," the waiter said. "I will tell you that this is the best menu I've tried, so far. Trust me. You're going to love tonight's dinner."

Honey smiled.

"In honor of your service as a military wife," the waiter continued, "the Chef has offered to provide you with the recipes, in case you'd like to make this yourself."

MJ beamed at Honey, and she smiled.

"Now sit back and relax," the waiter said. "Let us do the rest."

"Pretty nice, huh?" MJ said.

"Very nice," Honey said.

MJ smiled and took a drink of his wine.

"Why am I in New York?" Honey tried a different question to see if he'd actually answer.

He squinted at her while he tried to come up with an answer.

"Why don't we try the truth?" Honey asked.

She raised her eyebrows in expectation. MJ turned to look at the water. The lights of the city made the Hudson sparkle like tiny diamonds. MJ was silent so long that Honey began to worry. She touched his hand. When he turned, his eyes were filled with tears.

"I don't know how to tell you," MJ said.

"Are you sick? Cancer? You caught some deadly flesh-eating, antibiotic-resistant Ebola-like bacteria? Virus?" Honey said with a gasp. "Is it your leg?"

"Oh." MJ gave her a slight smile. "No. I'm fine."

"Then what is going on?" Honey asked.

He opened his mouth.

"Just tell me the truth," Honey said. "We'll deal with whatever it is."

He closed his mouth and nodded. Honey made every effort to wait patiently. But as the minutes dragged, she wanted to kick him. If she'd had working legs, she would have, in fact, kicked him.

The waiter came by to drop off some warm bread. He set a small cup of butter for MJ and another cup for Honey. He explained that the Chef had found a recipe for a butter substitute that tasted good and shouldn't cause a flare-up.

"I'll try it!" Honey said with a smile.

"Let us know if anything bothers you," the waiter said.

Honey smiled and watched him leave to serve another table. When she looked back, MJ was watching her intently.

"Just tell me," Honey said.

"You know how Blane used one of Jill's twin's umbilical blood to reseed his bone marrow?" MJ asked.

"Blane's doing really well," Honey said. "His AIDS is gone. I mean, no one's sure if it's forever, but, for now, he's virus free. He's done the HepC treatment, and his liver has healed. He says he feels better than he has since he was a small child."

"Jill had twins, right?" MJ asked.

"Right – Tanner and Bladen," Honey said. "Maggie and I spend Thursday afternoons with the twins and Jackie. They're hilarious."

"Well. . ." MJ nodded.

"Well?" Honey asked.

MJ blew out the breath that Honey hadn't realized he had been holding. Her eyebrows lowered with concern. MJ took a breath and began talking at a rapid pace.

"There's a new technique that's shown a lot of promise for people who are paralyzed. They use stem cells by injecting them into the injury sites. I've been following the studies in case maybe we have another child. If we did, we could use their umbilical blood or whatever. But Nadia, you remember Nadia?"

He looked up expectantly.

"The woman whose guest bedroom we're staying in?" Honey asked. "Yes, in fact, I do remember Nadia. I expect we'll see her after dinner."

MJ chuckled. He took a breath and started talking again.

"She learned about you from Nash. I didn't ask her or anything, but she called me last week. She asked for your medical records. I was busy with an action, so I just sent them to her. I knew she was a close family friend and a doctor. I figured she would just look at them or review them or whatever. I didn't know she was super-duper rich, you know?"

"What did she do?" Honey threw into his stream of words.

"She sent your records to this team of people. I never... I mean, how likely is it that we could ever afford it, or even, who knows when we'll be able to have another child? I mean, this team, of scientists, you know, they're doing it for free with two disabled veterans a year. And it's working, but it's really expensive. Really expensive. And then, Jill talked to Nadia last weekend, and you know how Jill is."

As if he's expressed an entire thought, MJ stopped talking and looked at Honey.

"And that means?" Honey asked.

"I brought the other umbilical cord with me. I mean, Tanner's or Bladen's or...," MJ said. "You have an appointment tomorrow."

"I have an appointment?" Honey asked with a shrug.

"They're able to restore people to full functioning," MJ said.

"But I function really well," Honey said. "Maybe we should

donate the blood to someone who really needs it."

"People can walk again," MJ said. "It's not perfect, so they don't call it a cure. But they looked at your records. Because you're so young and weren't injured that long ago, and something about your blood that I don't remember, you're a candidate. A good candidate."

He looked up at her face and stopped talking. Tears streamed down Honey's face.

"There's a risk," MJ said at a slower pace. "Stem cells aren't always stable. It's possible they'll cause cancer or whatever, but. . ."

MJ leaned forward across the table again.

"It's possible that you could walk again," MJ said. "I mean, not tomorrow. Tomorrow's just a visit with the doctors. They want to examine you and talk to you. They'll explain everything a lot better. Then, you get to decide."

"I get to decide?" Honey asked. "How will we pay for it?"

"Oh, I didn't say that?" MJ asked.

Honey shook her head.

"Nadia has offered to pay for everything the insurance doesn't cover," MJ said. "Sandy offered to pay for your recovery — hospital visits, hotels, stuff like that so you can stay at home to recuperate between treatments. You know, she got that money from her mom's music."

Honey started crying in earnest. MJ fell to his knees and knee-crawled to her side. He held her tight.

"You get to say 'yes' or 'no,'" MJ said in her ear. "And I promised the LC that I would respect your decision and never bug you about it again. And a promise to the LC is unbreakable because she'll kick my ass if I don't do it."

He held Honey for what felt like a long time to his impatient self.

"So what do you say?" MJ asked.

He pulled away from the hug to look at her. She nodded, and

the room erupted into applause. She looked up to see that the entire Fey Team had been following their conversation. The restaurant staff clapped in support. Blushing at their attention, she waved. MJ hugged her again.

"And you know," MJ said in her ear. "Jill has that healing thing. Her grandfather said that the cells could easily cure your Crohn's."

Honey gasped and looked at him. He nodded.

"Nothing's sure," MJ said. "But maybe it could be better."

Honey hugged him tight.

"I hate to interrupt, but your first course is ready," the waiter said.

"This might be your last meal for a while," MJ said.

"And it's going to be a good one," the waiter said. He gave Honey a tissue box. "Shall I bring it?'

Wiping her face, Honey nodded. The waiter touched her shoulder.

"I'm very happy for you," the waiter said before turning away to get the meal.

"How many people did you tell?" Honey asked.

"Just the owner," MJ said.

"Then how does...?" Honey asked. "You mean that's the owner?"

"He started as a waiter and says he's planning on being a waiter until the day he dies," MJ said.

Honey smiled. She looked up as the waiter returned.

"Your first course..." the waiter said.

He explained everything in the first course but Honey was too caught up in this happy moment to understand what he was saying. She let out a breath and smiled. MJ grinned at her.

"Happy you married me?" MJ said. "It is all worth it now?"

Honey laughed.

~~~~~~~~~~

Monday evening — 6:47 p.m.
New York City, New York

Sissy woke up in her room on Ivan's floor. All of her pain, sadness, and indignation had caught up with her after lunch. Sandy had helped her to bed, set up her oxygen, and sat with her until she was asleep. She'd even unplugged Sissy's clock. Sandy had promised to call when she knew about Noelle.

Sissy had a sense that she'd missed Sandy's call. She'd most certainly missed her appointment with school. At this moment, she couldn't care less. She rolled onto her back, and her side erupted in agony. She tried to take a breath to deal with the pain, but the increased movement of her rib cage only caused more pain.

"Help," Sissy croaked. "Charlie? Giovanni? Ivan? I need help!"

She tried to roll back onto her side, but the movement only brought more pain.

"Please," Sissy said, but her voice only came out as a whisper.

Sissy felt so helpless that she started to cry. The door opened in the dark room. In her pain, she felt more than saw the person enter the room. A small, cool, hand touched her forehead. Sissy opened her eyes to see Nadia.

"You're burning up," Nadia said. "Oh, Sis."

Nadia's face showed so much concern that Sissy started to cry harder. Nadia returned from the bathroom with a thermometer.

"What is it?" Giovanni asked from the door.

"She's spiked a fever," Nadia said. "And is in terrible pain."

Giovanni ran out of the room. Mumbling to herself, Nadia stuck a thermometer in Sissy's mouth.

"Stupid fucking. . ." was all Sissy could make out until Nadia said, "God damn it!"

Sissy touched Nadia's arm.

"No, no, it's not you," Nadia said. "It's that stupid ballet. I told Ian that you were too sick to go. He said you were fantastic, by the way. 'Like a movie star of old.' Those were his exact words. You have a fan in Ian, that's for sure."

"He's very cute," Sissy said around the thermometer.

"He is gorgeous," Nadia said. "And very gay."

Sissy shrugged as if it didn't matter. Nadia laughed. Her laugh brought Giovanni. He jogged to the bed. Nadia took the thermometer from Sissy's mouth at the same time that she took something from Giovanni. She fiddled with the oxygen hose before turning back to Sissy.

"Okay, Sissy," Nadia said. "Take a deep breath when I tell you. We practiced this in the hospital. I'm going to give you some morphine."

"Can't breathe," Sissy said.

Silent tears ran down her face as she shook her head. Sissy yelped with pain. Nadia gave her a soft smile. Sissy gave a slow nod, and Nadia connected the morphine to her air mask.

"Deep breath," Nadia said.

Sissy did as she was told.

"Another," Nadia said.

Sissy's eyes floated to half-open.

"That's enough for now," Nadia said.

"Fever?" Sissy asked.

"Your temperature is about 100," Nadia said. "High, but likely due to the pain. Did you take all your meds today?"

"Everything but pain meds," Sissy said. "I needed to be clear headed."

Nadia sat down on the bed and rubbed Sissy's arm. Giovanni appeared with a cup of water and a straw, which he set on the table. He disappeared for a moment and reappeared with a hot-water bottle.

"For comfort," Giovanni said.

He tucked the hot water bottle above Sissy's knees. Sissy wrapped her arms around the warm rubber and focused on breathing. The morphine and albuterol worked on her lungs. After a few minutes, she felt better — high on morphine, but definitely better.

"School?" Sissy pulled off her air mask to ask. Nadia put the mask back on her.

"Charlie took the call," Giovanni said. "The work that he has done this year has put you both at the same level at school."

Sissy smiled.

"This is good news?" Giovanni asked. Sissy nodded. "I was afraid you would be disappointed."

Sissy shook her head.

"Then this is good," Giovanni said. "You and Charlie will take summer school to get ahead. They see no problem with you both graduating on time or possibly a little early."

Sissy smiled.

"You can go faster," Giovanni said. "But until you are both well, this is the best plan."

Sissy closed her eyes for a moment to rest. Her eyes popped open. She pulled off the mask.

"Sandy? Noelle?" Sissy asked.

"Your sister testified this afternoon," Giovanni said. "According to her father, she did very well. Noelle was disappointed not to speak with you but glad you were resting. She hopes to talk to you tomorrow afternoon."

Sissy smiled. For a moment, she let herself drift. She pulled off the mask again.

"Ballet?" Sissy said in a stronger voice.

"Schmidty? This is what you call him, yes?" Giovanni said. Nadia nodded. "He worked something out. He spoke with Ivan. It is all arranged. Ivan gave a tentative agreement that is not permanent until he speaks with you."

"Where?" Sissy asked.

"He's in bed, Sissy," Nadia said. "He is also still very ill. Charlie, too. You have all been doing so well that I'm afraid you pushed it. The trip here, these stressful days."

"Charlie and Ivan took to bed right after you," Giovanni said.

"Ballet?" Sissy asked again.

"The ballet company is allowing Ivan to take whatever time he needs to heal. Your contract remains if you'd like it. Everyone will meet at the end of the summer to see where you are. If you're already dancing by then, great. If not, they have agreed to wait. They've also agreed to let your personal life be your personal life."

Nadia leaned in.

"But don't worry, Sissy," Nadia said. "Everyone has agreed to wait."

"Everyone?" Sissy asked.

"All of the ballet companies interested in you," Nadia said. "All you have to do right now is rest."

"And school," Sissy said.

"And some school," Nadia said. "Charlie arranged for you to start a week from today."

"And speak with your sister tomorrow," Giovanni said.

Sissy gave a slow nod as unconsciousness caught up with her.

"You don't have to leave this bed for a week," Nadia said in a low voice. "If then."

"I will care for you, Sissy," Giovanni said. "Sleep. Life will wait for you."

Sissy opened her eyes to look at him and then closed them again. For the first time in a very long time, everything felt taken care of. Sissy fell into a drugged sleep.

~~~~~~~~~

Tuesday morning — 9:30 a.m.
Denver, Colorado

Bestat Behur casually walked up to the witness stand. As usual, she left a trail of dazed people in her wake. She stepped onto the stand and was sworn in by the bailiff.

"Thank you for being here, Ms. Behur," the District Attorney said. "For the record, Ms. Behur is a diplomat for the Egyptian government."

"I won't say that being here is my pleasure," Bestat said with a smile.

The District Attorney blushed. The Judge looked at Bestat and then at the District Attorney.

"Do you have questions for this witness?" the District Attorney asked.

Bestat looked at the Judge. He seemed immune to her draw. The Judge knew exactly what she was, which made her smile. He nodded.

"Yes," the District Attorney said. "Can you tell us in your own words what happened in the park the day your step-son's girlfriend..."

"Noelle," Bestat said.

"Noelle Norsen, yes," the District Attorney said. "The day Noelle Norsen went to paint your image."

"The tiny creature sitting at the other table decided he was going to attack my dear Noelle," Bestat said with a wave of her hand.

"And you know this because...?" the District Attorney asked.

"I heard him on the telephone, of course," Bestat said.

The court became very still.

"What did you hear?" the District Attorney said.

"I heard that tiny creature..." Bestat started.

"By 'tiny creature,' you mean...?" the Judge asked.

"The defendant," Bestat said. She sent an unnerving smile to the defendant.

"What did you hear?" the District Attorney asked.

"The tiny creature saw us sitting by ourselves," Bestat said. "He called someone and told them to bring video equipment. He then started calling people, telling them to come to our location."

"Why didn't you leave?" the District Attorney asked.

"That's a good question," Bestat said. "I don't have a great answer for that."

She looked up and to the right for a moment.

"I was pregnant at the time," Bestat said. "My mind was not clear, plus..."

"And what happened to the baby?" the District Attorney asked.

"I lost the pregnancy," Bestat's voice dropped to a whisper.

Her sorrow was palpable. The District Attorney turned away from her to give her a moment to collect herself.

"Did your doctor tell you why?" the District Attorney asked.

"My doctor said it was from the..." Bestat's eyes welled with tears. "...violence and..."

Bestat waved her hand.

"All of this," Bestat said. "I'm not as young as I once was, and this whole thing... I lost my child."

Bestat gave a stiff nod. The mood of the court became serious and sad.

"At the time — that time with Noelle — I didn't take him seriously," Bestat said. "I mean, this is the United States. Little Denver, no less. We were not in some uncivilized corner of the world where roving bands of unemployed men look for women to destroy. We were not in the Sudan or Darfur or India or even Malaysia. This was a nice-looking young man. We were sitting under the trees in Denver's City Park. I... uh... underestimated, I guess is the word, the vile nature of this tiny creature."

Bestat turned her eyes to the District Attorney.

"I was wrong," Bestat said. "If I had understood what he wanted or even what he was capable of, I would have insisted that we left. But as I said, I was pregnant, and..."

She lifted a shoulder and shook her head.

"As it was, it was only luck and good fortune that allowed us to escape with our lives," Bestat said. "I believe this young man would have raped and murdered myself and Noelle. I know he wanted to do just that."

"You know this how?" the District Attorney asked.

"He told me," Bestat said with a smile.

"He told you," the District Attorney said. "You can imagine that many would find that a little unbelievable."

"Sure," Bestat said. "But they weren't there. They didn't see the droves of young, angry, drugged out men rushing into the park. You didn't see him leading the charge by telling us exactly what he was going to do to us. You weren't there."

Bestat nodded.

"You simply cannot imagine the horror of the entire event," Bestat said.

Denver Cereal continues...

Aaron Alvin:
Father of Ava; also called "The spider" by Yvonne Smith.

Abi the Fairy:
General in Fairy Corps; great-grandmother of Tanesha; Fin's partner

Aden Norsen:
CEO at Lipson construction; single father of Nash and Noelle; husband of Sandy.

Alma Fontaine:
Mother of Heather Lipson; Psyche.

Alexandra Hargreaves:
Identical twin to Max Hargreaves; 'The Fey;' the leader of the Fey Team; wife of Dr. John Drayson; sister to Colin and Samantha Hargreaves.

Anjelika:
Megan, Mike, Steve, Candy and Jill's mother; grandmother to Katy; wife of Perses.

Andrea Menendez or Andy Mendy:
Mother of Sandy; Seth's love & lover from the time he was 14 until he lost her when he was 30.

Annette:
Reality television star; mother to Jabari; Jeraine Wilson's ex.

Arthur "Raz" Rasmussen:
Member of the Fey team; boyfriend of Samantha Hargreaves.

Ava — Amelie Vivian Alvin:
Denver Police Crime Lab Technician; fiancé of Seth O'Malley; daughter of Aaron Alvin.

Ben Red Bear, Detective:
Denver Police Detective in charge of investigation of rapes; possibly involved in the distribution chain.

Bestat Behur:
Partner to Zack Jakkman; stepmother to Teddy; dragon.

Beth Baker:
Ava's best friend; Child Psychologist; murdered by Saint Jude.

Blane Lipson:
Jacob's 'cousin;' assistant to Jacob Marlowe at Lipson Construction; Chinese Medicine doctor; husband of Heather; father of Mack; getting bone marrow transplant for HIV infection.

Bob aka 'Blood spatter Bob': Former expert forensics instructor with the FBI; currently a laboratory technician in Ava's Denver Police Department lab.

Bumpy Wilson:
Good friend of Seth's; medical doctor; father of Jeraine Wilson, husband of Dionne, born Leroy Wilson.

Candace or Candy Roper:
Daughter of Anjelika; sister to Jill.

Charlie Delgado:
Stepbrother of Sandy; street kid; drug addict; moved in with Sandy in *Cimarron*.

Chesterfield or Mr. Chesterfield:
Rodney Smith's large black dog, which he was given in prison from the Puppies for Prisoners program; best friend of Jabari.

Celia Marlowe:
Wife of Sam Lipson; mother of Valerie Lipson and Jacob Marlowe; Delphie's best friend; died of cancer nine years before Denver Cereal begins.

Cleo:
Black and white cat belonging to Sandy.

Colin Hargreaves:
Brother of Alex, Max and Samantha Hargreaves; Homeland Security Agent; Fey Team member; father of Paddie Hargreaves.

Dale:
Boyfriend of Beth Baker, Amelie's best friend; housemate of Amelie; Handyman who lives with Seth O'Malley, best friend to Charlie.

Delphinium or Delphie:
Psychic; beekeeper; master gardener; best friend of Celia Marlowe; girlfriend to Sam Lipson.

DeShawn Jones:
Ex-drug dealer; current site manager at Lipson Construction

Dionne Wilson:
Wife of Bumpy Wilson; mother of Jeraine and LaTonya; medical nurse; singer.

Erik Le Monde:
Father of Wanda; plumber; works for Lipson Construction.

Edie the Fairy:
Second daughter of Queen Fand & Manannán; younger sister to the Blue Fairy and elder sister to Mari; nanny to Jill and Jacob's twins.

Edith Stiefel:
Mother of Wanda. Ex-wife of Erik Le Monde.

Evette:
Secretary of Jacob's for one week; claims romantic relationship between them.

Fand, usually Queen Fand:
Queen of the Fairies; wife of Manannán; ancestor of Jacob Lipson.

Fin, Finegal, sometimes Prince Finegal:
Eldest son of Queen Fand and Manannán; heir to throne; great-grandfather to Tanesha; partner to Abi; medical student.

Fran: A laboratory tech in Ava's Denver Police Department lab.

Frankie Aziz:
Boyfriend of Wanda Le Monde; videographer of group of rapists; brother of DPD Sergeant Aziz.

Giovani:
Live in helper to Ivan and Nadia. Lives in New York. From small village in Italy.

Gilfand:
Loyal male servant of Queen Fand; one of the oldest fairies; appears as a gargoyle.

Heather Lipson:
One of Jillian Roper's group of best friends; mother to Mack and Wyn; wife to Blane Lipson; mother of Tink; Hedone, child of Psyche and Eros; current acting Eros/Cupid.

Honey Lipson:
Paralyzed; stepdaughter of Sam Lipson; wife of Sergeant MJ Scully; mother of Maggie; Lives at the Castle and works at Lipson Construction.

Jabari Wilson: Young son of Jeraine Wilson and Annette; biological child of Tanesha Smith and Jeraine Wilson

Jacob Marlowe:
Son of Sam Lipson and Celia Marlowe; husband of Jillian Roper; brother of Valerie Lipson; president of Lipson Construction; owns his own rehabilitation business; carpenter; hockey player, teller of Denver Cereal.

Jeraine Wilson:
R&B sensation; husband of Tanesha Smith; son of Bumpy; drug and sex addict.

Jeraine Wilson, Junior: Young son of Jeraine Wilson.

Jillian or Jill Roper:
Daughter of Anjelika and Perses; mother of Katy Roper; wife of Jacob Marlowe; ex-wife of Trevor Mc Guinsey; pregnant with twin boys.

John Drayson, MD:
Vascular surgeons; husband of Alex Hargreaves.

Julie Hargreaves:
Mother of Paddie Hargreaves; wife of Colin Hargreaves.

"Ivy" Anna Marie McDonald:
Street child; friend of Tink and Charlie's; youngest assaulted in rape case with worst injuries; Delphie's niece.

Katy or Katherine Anjelika Roper Marlowe:
Daughter of Jillian Roper and Jacob Marlowe.

Leslie: A laboratory tech in Ava's Denver Police Department lab.

Leslie Roper:
Wife of Steve Roper; mother of infant Elisa Roper.

Levi Johansen:
Won Delphie in a card game when she was 5-6; held her as a slave/The Oracle Tabor; attempted to kill Delphie; deceased.

Liban:
Queen Fand's twin sister; looks like Cleopatra.

Lizzie O'Malley:
Daughter of Seth O'Malley; Biological mother to Conner Hargreaves. Girlfriend of James Schmidt.

Mack Lipson: Infant son of Heather and Blane Lipson.

Margaret Peaches or Sergeant Margaret Peaches:
Fey team member; partner of Sergeant MJ Scully.

Manannán:
A Celtic sea deity; possibly first ruler of the Isle of Man; husband of Queen Fand, ancestor of Jacob Lipson

Maresol Tafoya:
Seth O'Malley's housekeeper; mother of Bonita's Seth's second wife; friend of Delphie.

Max Hargreaves:
Identical twin to Alex Hargreaves; brother to Colin and Samantha Hargreaves.

Megan Roper:
Daughter of Anjelika and Perses; partner of Tim; mother to Ryan and two other boys.

Mike Roper:
Son of Anjelika and Perses; husband of Valerie Lipson; art mentor to Noelle Norsen; hockey goalie; painter.

Michael Bladen Roper Marlowe:
Infant son of Jill and Jacob Roper-Marlowe; identical twin of Tanner.

Mitch Delgado:
Sandy's stepfather who she called 'Dad'; father of Charlie and Sissy; Seth O'Malley's best friend; died of lung cancer 8 or 9 years ago.

MJ or Sergeant Michael Scully Jr.:
Fey team member; partner of Sergeant Margaret Peaches; husband of Honey Lipson.

Molly:
Bookkeeper for Jacob Marlowe's rehabilitation business; wife of Pete.

Nadia Kerminoff, MD
ER doctor, ex-lover of Ivan, Russian mother, wealthy American father; "dark arrow" soulmate of Nash Norsen.

Nash Norsen:
Son of Aden and Nuala Norsen; brother of Noelle Norsen; "dark arrow" soulmate of Nadia Kerminoff.

Nelson: A lab technician in Ava's Denver Police Department lab; potential love interest of Blane Lipson.

Noelle Norsen:
Daughter of Aden and Nuala Norsen; sister of Nash Norsen; artist.

Nuala Norsen:
Ex-wife of Aden Norsen; biological mother of Nash and Noelle Norsen.

Paddie Hargreaves:
Best friend of Katy Roper; nephew of Alex and Max Hargreaves; son of Colin Hargreaves.

Patty Delgado:
Mother of Sissy and Charlie; mother to Sandy; wife of Mitch Delgado.

Pete:
Husband of Molly; father of her children; friend of Aden Norsen.

Perses:
Paid assassin; rescuer, Titan, and biological father of Jillian Roper.

Rodney Smith:
Father of Tanesha; imprisoned for 26 years for a murder he didn't commit; husband of Yvonne Smith; site manager at Lipson Construction.

Ryan:
Oldest son of Megan Roper and Tim.

Sam Lipson:
Husband to Celia Marlowe; married to Tiffanie Lipson; boyfriend of Delphie; father to Valerie and Jacob Marlowe-Lipson; step-father to Brianna, Becky, Honey and the 'step-whore.'

Samantha Hargreaves:
Sister to Alex, Max and Colin Hargreaves; girlfriend of Art Rasmussen; best friend of Valerie Lipson; criminal defense attorney.

Sandy Delgado Norsen:
Best friend of Jillian Roper; one of Jill's group of best friends; wife of Aden Norsen; hairdresser.

Sarah:
Yellow Labrador belonging to Jacob Marlowe.

Scooter:
Gift from Celia and Delphie to Jillian on her marriage to Trevor McGuinsey; taken care of for last 4 years by Delphie after Trevor put him up for adoption; Katy's constant companion.

Sergeant Aziz:
Denver Police detective assigned to investigate rapes; does nothing to protect his brother, Frankie.

Seth O'Malley:
Godfather and biological father of Sandy; best friend of Sandy's step father; Denver Police Detective; gifted composer and prodigy pianist

Stepsister or Stepwhore:
Eldest daughter of Tiffanie Lipson; sister to Honey, Briana, and Becky Lipson; step-daughter of Sam Lipson; second wife of Trevor McGuinsey.

Steve or Stephen Roper:
Son of Anjelika; middle child of Roper family; medical nurse to Honey Lipson; husband of Leslie.

Sissy Delgado:
Stepsister of Sandy; anorexic; talented ballet dancer; lives with Sandy and Aden.

Tanesha Smith:
One of Jillian Roper's best friends; wife of Jeraine Wilson; medical student.

Tanner Handy Roper Marlowe:
Infant son of Jill and Jacob Roper Marlowe; identical twin of Michael.

Teddy Jakkman
Son of Fey Team member Captain Zack 'the Jakker' Jakkman; best friend of Nash Norsen; dates Noelle Norsen.

Tink or Tiffanie:
Street kid; friend of Charlie Delgado's; attacked and beaten by gang of rapists, Heather and Blane Lipson's adopted daughter.

Tim:
Partner to Megan Roper; father of Ryan and two other children.

Trevor Mc Guinsey:
Ex-husband of Jillian Roper; assumed father of Katy Roper; fiancé to the step-whore.

Valerie Lipson:
Daughter of Sam and Celia Marlowe; wife to Mike Roper; soap opera and movie actress.

Wanda (Wade) Le Monde:
Met Sissy at Eating Disorder Inpatient Treatment; transgender child; daughter/son of Erik and Edith; girlfriend of Frankie Aziz.

Wes or Wesley Kapanski:
Hollywood producer; Was engaged to Valerie Lipson at the beginning of Denver Cereal.

Yvonne Smith:
Mother of Tanesha Smith; forced into prostitution after her husband was imprisoned.

Zack 'The Jakker' Jakkman
Father of Teddy, Britanie, and Samuel Jakkman; 'The pilot' to Sissy & Charlie; Sandy's childhood pen pal; friend of Sandy's.

THE STORY CONTINUES AT

DENVER CEREAL.COM

FIND US ON FACEBOOK:

FACEBOOK.COM/DENVERCEREAL

If you like *Denver Cereal*,
please take a moment and leave a review.
Your review helps *Denver Cereal* continue.

MORE ABOUT CLAUDIA AT:

CLAUDIAHALLCHRISTIAN.COM

www.ingramcontent.com/pod-product-compliance
Lightning Source LLC
Chambersburg PA
CBHW031428240626
47154CB00001B/242